The Forrests

THE FORRESTS

EMILY PERKINS

BLOOMSBURY CIRCUS
LONDON · BERLIN · NEW YORK · SYDNEY

First published in Great Britain 2012

Copyright © 2012 by Emily Perkins

Extract from 'State of Grace' on page vii, by Clarice Lispector, translated by Giovanni Ponteiro:
British Commonwealth excluding Canada – taken from *Discovering the World* (1992),
reproduced by kind permission of Carcanet Press Limited; rest of the world – taken from
Selected Cronicas (1984), reproduced by kind permission of New Directions
Publishing Corp. Translation copyright © 1992 by Giovanni Ponteiro.

The moral right of the author has been asserted

Bloomsbury Publishing, London, Berlin, New York and Sydney
50 Bedford Square, London WC1B 3DP

A CIP catalogue record for this book is available from the British Library

ISBN 978 1 4088 0923 5
10 9 8 7 6 5 4 3 2 1

Typeset by Hewer Text UK Ltd, Edinburgh
Printed in Great Britain by Clays Ltd, St Ives plc

www.bloomsbury.com/emilyperkins

For Karl, Veronica, Cass and Mary

And there is a physical bliss which cannot be compared to anything. The body is transformed into a gift. And one feels it is a gift because one is experiencing at source the unmistakable good fortune of material existence.

Clarice Lispector, 'State of Grace'

Begin anywhere

John Cage

1. HOME

THEIR FATHER BALANCED behind the movie camera, shouting directions as he walked backwards and forwards in front of them. He handled the Kodak, their most valuable possession, as though it were an undulating live animal, a ferret or a snake, and it was leading him. The children took turns hunching under a cardboard box in the back garden for a sequence he told them would be funny later. When it was Dorothy's turn she crouched like a turtle on the grass, forehead pressed into her bony knees, arms tucked down by her sides, and breathed hotly into her own skin while Michael lifted the box and placed it over her, a warm shadow, a rare private space. She inhaled it.

Clover flowers bumbled her cheeks and the cardboard smelled sandy and soft and the noises outside – a trickling bird, Michael, her sisters, their father's voice, Daniel – were faint. A thick purple scab was escaping from one knee and the fresh skin beneath was suddenly there as the box lifted off and Evelyn said that it was her turn now and Dot tipped sideways and rolled onto her back, the sky exploding with light, Daniel leaning in to block the sun, his face dark in silhouette. 'I am the dribble king.'

She grabbed him by the ankles, fingers around the bones and the tight band of his Achilles tendon, and toppled him so that he fell knees first to the grass. They scrambled up and he chased her round the garden, his shins and palms grazed with dirt and grass stains, and her father shouted, 'Not there, you're crossing the shot,' and everyone else joined in the game and the sister under the box called mutedly, 'What's happening?' and knelt up, the box over her head and shoulders, and their father said, 'Not yet, Eve,' but she lifted the box from her head, dropped it and said, 'I'm thirsty,' and trudged back past the clothesline and into the house, bending down to stroke the heavily pregnant family cat, who was climbing up the back step in the sun. Their father kicked the box.

By the lemon tree, laden with dimpled yellow blimps of fruit, Dorothy fake-dodged Daniel and wheeled round, squaring off to chase him back, and he sprinted up the side of the house, leaping in his bare feet over the shelled front yard as though it was hot coals, up the footpath that bulged and splintered with tree roots, past the houses of their neighbours and the home beautician's where Dot's mother got her legs waxed, around the spilled rubbish bag on the corner, past that kid on her bike with the ribbed pink handles, and the newsagent's and the man leaning on the wall outside the half-way house, and across the empty street past the Chinese takeaway and the baker's whose white bread went pasty over your teeth and the butcher with the smouldering fumes out the back from the smoking system. Suddenly Daniel was nowhere to be seen. The

sour smell of potassium nitrate bloomed and the afternoon brack-
eted out in front of her; the street may as well have been empty.
Dorothy turned and ran from the wide open space, the disappearing road behind.

When she burst through the front door, panting, and jogged
towards the kitchen for a drink, Daniel was already there. He
sat opposite Eve, tipped back on the chair legs. Fingers lightly
anchored him to the edge of the table. Eve poured the clattering
Scrabble letters out of their velvet drawstring bag, and pushed them
round into a rough circle. 'Michael!' she called, her head tilted in
the direction of the stairs. 'Come on!'

Dorothy drained the glass of water and wiped her mouth with
the back of her hand. 'How did you get home so fast?'

'Just generally supersonic.' Daniel pulled the tea towel from the
rung on the oven door, took the glass from her, shook it free of
drops and wiped it dry. 'We need this,' he said, and plonked it upside
down in the centre of the table.

A thick shaft of sunlight angled into the room, illuminating the
fine dust over its surface like the near-invisible hairs on the children's skin. Dorothy sat and felt something nudge against her knees.
Her younger sister was hiding beneath the table. 'Ruthie.'

'Shh, I was going to tap,' her sister said.

Eve pulled her out and onto her lap. 'Are you scared?'

'No.' But she buried her face into Evelyn's neck.

'Go and get Michael.'

Ruth snuggled further into Eve, her arms clinging. Eve held the
glass up to the light, squinting at the print that was still there from
Dorothy's lip. She rubbed it on her T-shirt. At the creaking of the

back door, Ruth yelped, but it was just her brother. 'Budge up,' said Michael, pulling a chair in. They made a circle around the table, each of them touching the upside-down glass with their fingertips. The cream Scrabble tiles spread in the round, like fragments of an ancient mosaic sun. Afternoon breath. Stillness. In the waiting silence, a mewling came from upstairs.

The bottom drawer of the girls' dresser protuded as it always did, the runners too stiff for the girls to jam back. On top of their clumsily folded sweaters lay the cat, licking goo off two newborn kittens, so tiny, their tails abrupt.

'Shall we get Mom?' asked Ruth, and the others said, 'No, she's out.' The children crowded round, the Ouija board forgotten. This was what they had been waiting for. The cat convulsed and another kitten emerged, blind and squeaking with a tiny rasp, its mouth hingeing a yawn, the body shaky, the paws and face so complete. The mother cat craned towards it with her rough tongue and began to clean its fur.

The Forrests had moved, when Evelyn was eight, Dorothy seven and their youngest sister Ruth not yet at school, from oh my god the hub of the world, New York City, to Westmere, Auckland, New Zealand. Dot thought her father said, 'At last we live in a cloudless society.' Reasons to do, she later figured, with lack of success back home, a paucity of funds, an excess of entitlement. Frank was a second son and despite the Forrest trust fund he claimed to have been 'cut *loose* without a net'. Even after emigration he couldn't get a break into professional theatre. He took on Westmere's amateur dramatics society where over time he would dwindle the membership on a diet of Brecht and Ionesco. Each month their mother, Lee to the older kids, Mommy to Ruth, would go to the bank and withdraw the allowance that they lived on. It was never quite enough to travel home, which was probably no accident, though, 'They just don't understand the price of *plane fares*,' she would cry.

They arrived in late summer, drowsing from the slow flight via Honolulu, the last of the high living in a hotel pool although the beach was *right there*, into the weird openness of southern sky that came with its colours all the way down to the deserted streets, filled in the space between houses. In the first weeks they knew no one, saw no one but each other, walked only to that shop called the dairy, the fish-eyed stares of those leaning kids under the soft warmth of its awning making each Forrest child want to turn and run away.

When school finally started, Evelyn was recovering from croup and the doctor with his comb-over and dark suit ordered her to stay home. Their mother dressed Dot in the frock she'd worn to a cousin's wedding, because she hadn't known where to source the uniform and it was important to look well put together. Persil white, with broderie anglaise around the hem, and a satin sash. It turned out there was no uniform. The sash Dot managed to retrieve from the cistern in the girls' toilets, and the mud rinsed out of the broderie anglaise eyelets, but nothing, not even vinegar, not even turpentine, would shift the chewing gum from where it stuck all through her long blonde new-girl American hair, and so Lee had to cut it off with the fingernail scissors, the other utensils being in a container ship in transit somewhere along the swelling blue sea.

Lee sobbed as the hair came away and Dot stood perfectly still, breath deep in her belly, and reassured her mother with a phrase she'd learned that afternoon. Michael's new friend, Daniel, had punched her in the shoulder and said, 'Shit happens.' At that she'd stopped crying, brought back into herself. The chewing gum was nothing. She had spent her first day at school without Eve. Nobody even knew she had an older sister. She had been alone and had survived it.

Cartwheeling along the planked row of school benches. Pale green institutional paint, bubbled, thick and waxy. Tiny pock-marks left by the asphalt on the heels of palms. The whirl of blue sky and black ground. The hot-metal smell from the pole on the adventure playground, the taste of metal on her fingers. She pressed her palm down on the basin's shining button, the distorted spray of water splitting the air.

On the walk home, Michael had told her that Daniel's father lived in the halfway house down the road. This hadn't occurred to Dorothy, that the neighbourhood men they held their breath about would have families. She'd rubbed her shoulder, still feeling Daniel's touch. A clump of gum in her bangs batted her forehead with each step.

Their mother slowly sobered as the haircut progressed. In the small bathroom, Evelyn, still wheezing, watched with solemn inter-est. When it was done Dot looked like a windblown pixie, and without stopping to study the effect Lee gathered the clippings in a sheet of newspaper and went to make dinner. Eve picked up the scissors from the windowsill, turning their flashing points in the afternoon sun. She bumped Dorothy out of the way of the mirror, lifted a strand of her own hair and began to snip, pausing every now and then to cough. When she'd gone round the front she handed the scissors to Dorothy. 'Do the back?' The amount of hair felt alarming in Dot's hands, but she did it. Eve covered her smile with her palm, and looked at Dot in the mirror, her eyes glazed with croup and anarchy. The room orbited slowly around the scissors. When Eve was well they would go to school together, and then *look out*.

Dot and Eve agreed that they hated their father. 'There's truth in jokes,' he said. 'That's why they're funny,' and Dot would spend days willing herself not to laugh, even when Michael burped at the table, or their father used that phrase '. . . and it's a rather large but', or their mother said, 'I don't have a sense of humour. My family never laughed. Ours was a house without laughter.' Or, 'Frank, you're brilliant. They'll regret this.' Somebody else always wanted to keep their father *down*, or *out*, or to suppress his critical *view*. Lee was his cheerleader. She did star-jumps around him, high-kicked down the alopecic hallway carpet, give me an F!

Why did they hate their father? For more than his views on comedy, for more than the way he viewed other people as a series of hostile gatekeepers, keeping him from the gold of life. Because their mother loved him more than she loved the kids? Write it in the sky. OK, another question. Why, for decades, would he still appear in Dorothy's dreams? And why wouldn't he speak! In life he'd say things like, 'Ninety per cent of success is showing up,' and that's what he did long after his death, a bad joke.

★ ★ ★

1970, the year Dorothy was ten, their mother managed to save up and at last Frank went, in his large navy winter coat and carrying a briefcase full of black-and-whites from *The Good Person of Szechuan* and *Ubu Roi*, his blond hair combed down carefully with water, which Dot knew would dry before he got there. This worried her greatly, that her father would walk the streets of Manhattan with boofy hair completely unaware of the whispers and laughs, and in his absence she forgot to hate him, and maybe knew on some core level that all this rage was love that had nowhere to go. What did Manhattan mean? She could only remember living here, now, though she and Eve at night in bed told stories of that alternative family, the ones who never left, living out their days in a sparkle of fairy lights and pine boughs, glittering ice powder spraying from their skates as they twirled and twirled around that legendary rink.

The first morning Frank was gone, their mother woke early to hear someone in the house, moving around downstairs. She tied her thin floral robe around her and followed the noises, floating on the helium of fear. The kitchen door was open. That boy, Daniel, sat at the table with his back to her. She took in his slim shoulders, the newspaper in front of him, steam rising from the kettle. He was writing on the paper and when she said, 'Good morning,' and walked around the side of the table he smiled and said, 'Hi, Lee. Hope you don't mind me doing the crossword.' He twiddled the ballpoint between his fingers and thumb so it became a plastic blur.

'Did you stay the night in Michael's room?'

'Yeah.' His smile was relaxed, as though everything was normal, as though in fact he lived here.

'Good.'

Daniel took his cereal bowl to the sink. More than half of the crossword had been filled in. When he rinsed the bowl and wiped it and put it away he also wiped the bench. She watched his familiarity with where things belonged. He said, 'I have to go to work now.'

'Where do you work?'

'At the taxi company. I clean the cars. Just on the weekends.'

'OK.'

'See you later. Hey this plum tree up the road has got heaps of plums, do you need any?'

Lee stared into the fruit bowl, where two apples lay next to a giraffe-skinned banana. Her brain was fuzzy.

'It's not a private tree or anything. It's on the verge. I'll bring them later.'

'Thanks,' she said, and he wiped the air with his palm in a low wave as he left the kitchen. She heard the front door being carefully closed. Daniel was thirteen.

Lee walked quickly back up the stairs to check Michael and he was there, still, oval mouth open, in his single bed, the candlewick bedcover half slid to the floor, his body nearly filling the whole mattress now, weighty with sleep. There was a neatly rolled sleeping bag placed on a pillow in front of the wardrobe door.

She took the children up north, to the wimmin's commune, Hungry Creek, while Frank was gone, waking them from their beds one midnight and hurrying them out to where a strange van idled, packed already with their stuff. Daniel, who hadn't stopped sleeping over, came with. He jiggled with excitement behind Evelyn and Dot, turning his head from one to the other and pretending

9

to double take. 'Don't you ever get confused,' he said, 'wake up one day thinking you're the other one?'

'We're not twins.' Dorothy wanted to sink down and close her eyes, but the night pressed against the windows and she knew anything might happen.

'You're practically identical.'

'We're not even fraternal.'

'That would mean you're brothers,' Daniel said. 'Fratricide is when you kill your brother.'

'Really?' said Dorothy. 'What is it when you kill your brother's friend?'

The van smelled of sandalwood, and dust burst slowly from the velvet-and-corduroy patchwork cushions whenever they were bumped. They drove under randomly spaced streetlights. In synch, Dorothy and Evelyn sucked back a puff of Ventolin from their inhalers.

Michael said, 'Are there snakes in the creek?'

'Eels,' said the woman driving, a woman they didn't really know called Rena, who was a new friend of Lee's and wore a headscarf over an incredible bush of copper hair.

Rena washed herself under the outside shower, where the water collected above the nozzle in a black polythene bag and was slightly warmed by the sun, and she crossed the path to her cabin still naked, wearing her towel around her neck like the changing-room athletes Dorothy had seen in magazine advertisements for deodorant, only they wore aerobics leotards or tennis whites. Rena, with her springy hair and strong body, did not use deodorant.

It was strange being in this place without television or a flushing toilet. Dot lay in the children's cabin on a bunk bed, on top of the thin red sleeping bag, sloughed like a cocoon over the foam mattress, yellow and bitten, that covered the plywood bunk base, and she wept over *The Little Mermaid* and for all her selfishness. When her father returned she would love him with an open heart. In the bunk opposite, Daniel stretched out on his stomach, reading a tattered comic. He gave off the tangy smell of hay.

'Daniel,' she said, wiping her face on the flannel sleeping-bag lining, 'how come you're not living with your family?'

For a moment she wasn't sure whether he'd heard. His knees were bent, dirty-soled feet in the air. Eyes still on the comic, he told her that his dad was in between lodgings and his mother had a new boyfriend. 'Didn't Lee say?' He turned a page.

'No. She might have.' Where was Eve? It had been a long time with no Eve. Dorothy stretched as her sister came through the doorway. 'I was looking for you,' they both said at the same time, and Evelyn added, 'Do you want to play go home stay home?'

Dot held the book up. Eve came and lay beside her on the bunk, her body warm, and she put her cheek against her neck and held her bare arm and walked her fingers up from her wrist to the crook of her elbow. They whispered to each other. Daniel farted, and the potato-ish smell drifted over to the girls and they giggled and paddled the air as though drowning. He ignored them.

The sunflower stalks were thick and bristly, and the faces of the flowers too large to be beautiful, collared with pointed amber petals. Dorothy helped shake the seeds from the carpety black flower heads onto a white canvas sheet that had been spread in the light outside the cookhouse. She and Evelyn worked together, alongside an older girl who had changed her name by deed poll to Name. Name had got her face tattooed. She had a heart-shaped face and the tattoo was a love-heart outline framing all her features, tapering to a point at her chin, making it clear that the phrase 'heart-shaped face' was inexact.

Name worked for hours in the vegetable plot, hoeing and raking and digging, muscled shoulders moving up and down from the bow of her collarbone. Always a marmalade cat followed her, padding around as though inspecting the work. The sisters weeded along the rows, dirt packed beneath Evelyn's nails, ingrained in Dorothy's knees, everyone humming to 'Cheryl Moana Marie'. They chewed peppery nasturtium leaves and Name rubbed the clinging earth off two radishes with her big square thumb and passed them to the girls. She told them the story of Rapunzel as though it had really happened, or was an anecdote they might never have heard. Name smoked a lot of weed and from the way she talked it seemed she believed that the story was true. Later, in the privacy of their cabin, the Forrest girls agreed that they feared for her.

Days passed free of lessons and duties. Time belonged to the sunlight, and the Forrests' stay might have been a week or several months. The kids played rounders into the twilight, and hung around the scarred wooden table in the cookhouse, playing gin rummy and trying to be invisible while the wimmin passed a joint between them and bitched about the patriarchy. In the afternoons the best place to dodge the working bees was in the stand of native trees surrounding the stream. The children waded through sticky long grass to get there, biddy-bids catching on their shorts, the small diamonds of grass-flower scales in their hair.

There were glow-worms in the bushes that edged the compound and in the darkness their clusters mirrored the sky above so that Michael wondered if he was standing the right way up. A giggle floated from him, answered by the low hoot of a night bird. His neck still felt hot and bruised where Rena had kissed him and he rubbed at it as though the fact of the event might go away. It was confusing to be repulsed by her, her old mouth, her tongue pushing into his mouth, the possum smell of her hair, but also to be pleased she liked him, even though he had that coughing fit from the marijuana smoke, eyes leaking and nose running, his chest on fire before the weed dooshed off in his brain like a slow-motion water bomb. The candle in Rena's cabin had hardly lit the place and they'd sat side by side on the bed. After a few more puffs, the wetness of the cigarette paper where her lips had been, he'd dropped the joint and the fear of burning the cabin down flared in his mind but she kicked it aside uncaringly and kissed him.

Now he felt a sticky shame that an uncertain amount of time had passed before he jerked away – that his hand had risen to her breast because man he wanted to know what a woman's breast felt like, it was one of his main life goals so far. Her throaty moan when he touched her was awful. He'd snatched his hand away and she put it back there, moved her fingers up between his legs, grabbed him and he wanted to stay there holy shit a woman was touching his dick but then her hand was on the back of his neck pushing his face towards her lap, she let go her grip a bit to pull her shorts down and he got to his feet and knocked over the enamel nursery-rhyme candle holder, the light source suddenly out. The door wasn't where he'd thought and for a long few seconds he hit against the rough battened wall, feeling for a way out, Rena laughing huskily from the bed. And here he was in the darkness, mosquitoes at his ankles and knees, hungry.

He didn't know how long he was there looking at the glow-worms or the stars. Time breathed around him, his feet bare in the juicy grass, until the savoury smell of cooking made him realise he was cold and hungry. A small light led him to the cookhouse, which he arrived at more quickly than he expected, surprised that home was so close to the wilderness. Through the doorway he could see his mother at the coal range stirring a pan, the frying onions maybe the best thing he had ever smelled, and he wanted to put his arms around her gentle body.

'Lee,' he said, his voice breaking, but then Rena appeared beside Lee, a hand on her shoulder. 'Come in, Mike,' she said. 'You must be starving. You can help me set the table.'

Inside, the battery-powered overhead light made him blink. Rena poured him a drink of water, cold and sweet. He had another, and another, facing the sink so as not to have to look at her. His bladder was bursting but he didn't know how to leave. A plate of onions and cheese was a hundred miles away on the table. Rena was staring at him so intensely she may as well have been shouting 'aaaaahhhh' in his face. Slowly he raised his head looking for his mother. Where was she? And Daniel bounded in, shook off the night air like a dog, snapped the room back into one piece and low-fived him. 'Hey man, there you are. Lee, can we take dinner to our cabin? We're in the middle of a card game.'

'OK,' she said, ladling stir-fry into two wonky pottery bowls. 'Remember you can't put these down or they'll fall over. Hold them in your lap.'

Michael watched them talking, beings from another planet. His eyelids itched.

'Cool,' said Daniel, 'I'll send the girls in for some too.'

'Bring the bowls back and wash them.' Lee no longer came at bedtime to make sure the candles were extinguished and the children tucked in. She scraped vegetable peelings into the compost bucket and said, 'Night, boys.'

'Goodnight,' said Rena from the doorway. She brushed her hand along Mike's leg as he squeezed past. He hurried to catch up with Daniel, help him carry the food.

Between two pine trees, Eve watched Daniel, not far away, looking at something in his hands. The ground beneath the pines was white and sandy, and the pine needles smelled sweet, and the bark beneath Evelyn's palm was thick, spongy. She peeled off a crust. Daniel held his hands towards her and Evelyn saw the rabbit, not much bigger than a tennis ball, its ears laid flat against its shoulders, the bark-grey fur soft even to look at, like a layer of mist. The rabbit was very still, eyes black and wet, small river stones, and the space between the trees was full of its quick heart beating. Daniel held the creature lightly, one hand cupped over its hindquarters. Evelyn reached out a finger and stroked its back.

'Do you want a hold?' he said.

'OK.' She thought it would be claws and scrabbling but the animal plopped unresistingly into her hands, and Daniel drew his away and she felt vaguely stuck, feet rooted to the earth and the small warm body nestled against hers. It was very light, belonging only to itself.

'Don't tell your mum,' Daniel said. 'They've got a shotgun. Rena keeps talking about rabbit stew.'

'Do you want it back?' Once he took it, Evelyn was free to move. She followed him out of the pines to the long grass, the feathery tips brushing their knees, and he squatted down and opened his hands just enough and the rabbit disappeared, but Daniel kept the steadiness it seemed to have given him. He rose and looked calmly at the field, and smiled at the distance, and together they walked down the dip and over the rise towards the mudflats, where the other kids were playing.

Dressed in a singlet, shorts and work boots, braless, Rena squatted in the catcher position behind Michael, who was at bat. If you walked past her you could see down her top, her melony breasts. Michael swung the bat and missed the ball and Rena lobbed it over his head to Evelyn, the pitcher. 'Foul ball,' she called.

'But he tried to hit it.'

'Yeah, well he shouldn't have.'

Michael called, 'Just pitch again.'

'Yeah but strike one, OK?' and Evelyn pitched and he thwacked the ball and flung the bat aside as he launched into a sprint that made it to Dorothy at second base. He grinned crookedly, as though his face was doing something against his will.

When Rena hit the ball – miles out, low-bouncing into the tawny edges of the field – she ran like hell, her breasts joggling side to side, and made it to home base while Daniel still mooched through the bunny-tailed grass, hunting for it. Michael, who was catcher now, tackled her to the ground and they rolled around in the pale dust, legs flailing, laughter hooting from Rena, Michael's face shiny and determined, the top lip downy. He was ready to start shaving but there was no man here to teach him how. Dorothy saw his body against Rena's, the way his shoulders had broadened, his strong leg jammed between that woman's, breath coming from her in a regular panting sound, a sound that made Dot grind the nubby end of the baseball bat into the dirt as though she could drill a hole through the earth.

The humidity of the day gathered at last into rain, and the ball game was abandoned. 'We're going to play cards in my cabin,' Rena said, an arm slung over Michael's shoulder. 'Anyone else?'

'No.' Daniel lifted Rena's rusty bicycle from the grass and rode it over the ground towards the children's cabin like he was Butch and Sundance both at once, wheeling in the rain. Dot and Evelyn looked at their brother, who flicked his head to get the wet hair out of his eyes, a short, proud gesture. 'No,' the girls said in unison. They passed the vegetable patch on the way back to their cabin, where Name was jogging along the rows of seedlings with her arms above her head in a rain dance, watched by the cat, who shivered under the tool-shed eaves, droplets scattered over the ends of its puffed fur like a net of crystals, and a trail dragging through the dirt behind them from the end of the baseball bat, showing where they'd been.

Daniel stood by the weir in the braided stream, poking its bank with a long stick, the water halfway up his shins. Stepping through the trees Dorothy saw him, and stopped under a gap in the branches, where white sunlight pooled onto her shoulder and ran down one arm. 'Have you got anything?'

'Got an eel. Had an eel.'

'We could put it in Mike's pillow.'

'Mike says we're too old for this place.'

'True.' But she liked it here. Their bare feet and strange clothes were like everyone else's, and the food was good. At school people looked oddly at their American T-shirts emblazoned with brand slogans for a petrol company or bank or some other giveaway, Lee's old clothes baggy on the girls, Michael in some handed-down shorts held up by Frank's belt with extra holes punched along the leather. Ruth hated it the most, and had made friends with an older girl who passed on clothes made for an actual seven-year-old. She looked close to normal.

The water ran green-gold over the rocks, spangled where light came through the trees, and in places the current formed a pattern that was like the dévoré-velvet dress Lee wore. Dot's heels skidded as she picked her way down the muddy bank, leaving soft grooves, and she stumbled into the water, bone-cold under the arches of her feet and between the toes, where silty mud oozed. Moss and waterweeds streamed in the current, as though they grew out of rocks. 'Where's the eel?'

'His name's Gordon.'

'Where's Gordon?'

'Gone in there.' A silky shadow brushed through the water and Daniel jabbed it with the forked end of his stick. Dot sploshed down on the stream bed, sitting up to her waist in water that soaked quickly through her shorts, T-shirt, over her skin, and she lay back so that it inched and breathed right over her hair, into her ears, and sound belonged to the submerged world. She stopped trying to fight the cold and it became bearable. The trees were dark in the periphery and the sky very faded and far away, and there was the splash of Daniel marching upstream, past the channel bend, towards the rocks where they had hidden the chocolate money.

Water pushed her hair around and from below the surface her cold ears heard a holler and Dot sat up and twisted to see. Down the stream floated a large, thick leaf, dark green with, now, as it bobbed closer, brown mould spots and a larger spot, a gold foil coin, resting in the scoop along its spine. With a shout of delight, she reached for it.

Michael and Daniel sat on the side of the bunk reading a floppy, faded comic, their heads close together. Daniel scratched. 'You got cooties?' Michael asked, but he didn't move away.

In the comic an advertisement offered them the chance to earn money by selling another magazine, 'Sunshine', to their local community. Daniel already had a paper round. 'I could sell Sunshine too,' he said.

'Sunshine's for little kids,' Michael said. 'Babies.'

'What do you know, you're only fourteen.'

Michael didn't say anything.

'What?' asked Daniel. He turned the page. Michael said, 'Hey I haven't finished.' He turned the page back. The air in the cabin smelled like hot dust, but here in the shade of the bunk it was cool. A blowfly stuttered at the rust-clogged window screen. Michael said, 'Which superhero do you want to be?'

'Hey.' Daniel closed the comic. 'Let's go frog hunting. It's always good after rain.'

'Nah.'

'We should make our own Sunshine and sell it.'

'OK.' Michael leaned over to check the praying mantis that was in a jar on the bedside fruit box, its matt apple green different from the blades of grass they had provided it with to climb on. The mantis waggled front legs at the cling film covering the jar top, as though to poke more holes in it.

'That campground shop's got paper. Come on. Let's get some now.' Daniel stood and stretched, his stripy T-shirt pulling up over his lower abdomen, the stomach muscles that pointed in a wide V down into the waistband of his shorts.

'We've got no money,' said Michael.

'So?'

He thought a moment. 'Rena's got loads of money,' he said. 'In her room.'

'Have you been in her room?'

Michael shrugged and gathered the collar of his polo shirt – *Firestone Tyres* – and bunched it around his neck. 'No.'

Daniel reached up to pull the collar aside. Michael swatted him away. 'Fuck off,' he said. 'Are we going to the shops or aren't we?'

'Hang on,' said Daniel. He moved the praying mantis jar out of the sunspot on the bedside cabinet and into the shadows, the glass warm beneath his fingers.

Lee was somewhere in the bush, helping dig the new long drop, when a strange station wagon drove up. It parked by the cattle stop, on the other side of the chain-link gate that marked the commune's boundary. The back doors of the car opened and Daniel and Michael got out. Without a backward glance Daniel trotted over to the cattle stop, leapt the chain and disappeared behind the cook-house. Michael stayed by the car, staring a hole into the ground, and Frank emerged from the driver's seat. A baseball cap shaded his eyes from the afternoon glare. He called for his wife.

'I found these boys two miles down the *road*,' he shouted. 'The camp owner wants them for *shoplifting*. What kind of operation *is* this?' Leaning into the car, he honked the horn. The purple spiral on the commune entrance sign sent out a force field, keeping him from crossing the gate.

Dorothy and Evelyn ran up and stopped shy of the chain, waving. 'Hi Daddy,' they called. He looked American again, he looked bigger and different and so much more like a man than anyone they'd seen for a long time. The boys were young, Dorothy realised: the boys knew nothing.

Frank took off the cap and waved it. His hair was plastered to his head with sweat. 'Girls! Go and get your mother!'

They stepped closer together and Dot reached for Eve's hand. 'What happened to New York?' she asked.

An emergency meeting gathered outside the cookhouse to decide whether to let him onto the property. Wimmin stood on the sunflower-seed sheet in their dirty, cracked bare feet. Everyone went silent, and Dot turned to see that Rena had emerged from the tool shed. She lifted her arm to reveal the communal shotgun. From the distant estuary came the sharp whine of a speedboat. The shotgun was thin and dark, catching the light as she shook off a hovering fly.

'What do you want?' she called.

Their father had raised his palms in surrender and now lowered them again, as though he'd realised what he was doing. 'Rena, put that down. I just want my family.'

'You sure about that? You're a family man?'

Frank's words fired from him separately, crimson. 'I caught these boys in the camp store. Shoplifting. The owner saw them.'

The gun waved in Michael's direction as Rena turned towards him. 'Is this true?'

'Fuck you,' he said, quietly, but enough so it carried. Dorothy felt it tight in her chest.

'You ladies should expect a visit from the cops.' Frank was breathing heavily, craning his neck. 'So check your patch, Rena, check your fucking patch.'

'Frank!' Lee burst out of the tangled trees, her face wild and smeary. Daniel followed, carrying Ruth on his hip. He must have run and got them, Dorothy realised, with a swell of gratitude. It was Daniel after all who knew what to do; he was the only one who did.

Their father's shining face, his grim mouth were terrible to see but impossible to look away from as he advanced on the group of wimmin and his children. Dorothy felt Eve's face buried in her neck, her fingers painful in their grip. Rena stepped forwards with the gun.

'For god's sake Rena,' Lee said, 'he's my husband.'

Just before the chain fence Frank's body halted with a jolt, unable to go further: the cattle stop had trapped his foot. Deflated, he shrugged, a one-man pantomime. 'Everything's gone,' he said.

Lee shouted at the kids to get their clothes out of the cabins, they were going *home*.

Rena leaned the gun against the feathered, worn planks of the cookhouse and said, 'Just making sure.'

'Why didn't you call me? Why didn't you write?' Lee said to Frank. He was meant to bring back some gold dust, some kind of *mojo* to carry him through the rest of their lives.

'Jesus Christ hell.'

Dorothy was afraid that he would cry. Lee crossed the fence and hugged him. He melted into her.

'Everything's gone,' he said again. 'Everything.'

'Oh darling,' she said. 'You know, I actually feel relieved.' She held his face. 'Don't leave again,' she said. 'I need you here.'

She helped his body find the angle it needed to slide the foot up and out of the grid, though at first he shook off her help. It was like when they fed turnips to the feral horses, Dorothy thought, feeling acutely the limply socked foot emerging from the trench beneath the bars, his sneaker trapped still. He bent and wrenched it out and stood there with one shoe on his foot and the other in his hand, and his cheeks were flushed and sweat blistered his forehead. Ruth ran now, scissor-legged the fence and wrapped herself around his waist. From the cookhouse came the toasty smell of burned rice. One of the wimmin said, 'Oh no,' and disappeared inside.

In the cabin Dorothy and Evelyn collected their and Ruth's things in silence. There wasn't much to carry.

Their mother said, 'Sorry, Rena,' and, 'Thanks,' and kissed her on the temple and gathered the unrolled sleeping bags up from the girls and threw them onto the bonnet of the car, where they slid off into the dust.

Rena said, 'Ah, what are you going to do,' in a tone that meant she didn't expect an answer. She pulled Evelyn to her in a pungent hug and reached next for Michael but he ducked out, raising his forearm in defence, and said, 'Piss off.'

'Michael,' Lee said.

He turned and walked to the car and Dorothy saw his face, clouded with fury.

'What's up?' she asked.

'Nothing. I want to go home.'

Dot was jammed in the back seat of the car next to Evelyn, who was next to Daniel, who checked the time on a grown-up's large watch, the new digital kind.

'Where'd you get that?' Dorothy asked.

He smiled and pressed a button and made the display light pulse. Michael was in the back, Ruth hefty on their mother's knee, and their father slammed shut the boot and Name came running down the gravel road, waving her arm above her head, Dot's paperback of folktales in her hand.

A fresh start.

After the New York trip Frank was obsessed with Leadership. This, he maintained, was what had failed his family, the Forrest seniors whose money had vanished, poof, in tanking investments: no unity, no vision. Every book he read was on this subject, as were the status games he introduced over dinner, where there was always one fewer chair than person, and whoever was last to the table had to stand and serve everyone else. 'Lead,' he roared at the rest of the kids, the ones sitting down, but all of them resisted. Instead they worked on different ways to revel in the lowliness and make the others laugh, which made him angrier, which made them laugh more. Evelyn passing the tomato sauce around on her knees, Ruth bowing so low after handing out each plate that her fringe scraped the floor.

A new rule: whoever reached the table first won the role of leader, got the juiciest chop, the largest helpings. They stopped bringing friends home; even Daniel spent some time at his mother's instead. Nobody wanted to be first at the table. The kids all hovered at the backs of their chairs while Lee cried that the food was getting *cold* and their father glowered, until one of them whooped for distraction and pushed a brother or sister into their seat, or until everyone stuck their thumbs to their foreheads and the last one had to reluctantly sit down and direct the rest. They developed a technique of doing nothing without being given precise instructions. 'Hold this plate for a minute' meant that after sixty seconds the plate was dropped to the floor. Frank thought this was progress.

A dramaturge position came up at the Mercury Theatre where 'you know they are doing *Peer Gynt*' but he lost out to a man who also came from New York City, armed with a long CV and letters of recommendation that had Frank ranting as he emptied the rubbish bin.

'What does nepotism mean?' Dorothy asked, and her father roared 'Argh' at a soggy patch on the side of the brown-paper Kleensak tearing, the shoulder of an empty cereal box poking through.

'What's that?' Lee asked Daniel, who'd just put an envelope on the kitchen bench, secured beneath the notepad that advertised the minicab company.

'My rent,' he said. 'And they're looking for someone to answer the phones. At work.'

'I could do that,' said Dorothy.

'Don't be stupid, you're ten. And Danny, you're not paying rent, don't be silly. I'll talk to your mother.'

'It's OK,' he said.

'I'm eleven,' Dorothy said.

Lee took the envelope off the bench and pressed it against Daniel's chest. She kissed him on the side of the head. It was the first time Dot had seen her mother kiss him and it struck her that it was different from watching her kiss Michael, or Evelyn, or Ruth. It was a parental kiss, but more as if she meant it, hard enough to make Daniel's neck sway under the pressure. 'You don't have to,' Lee said, her voice a bit hoarse. 'Frank, I'm begging you.'

'What?' The rubbish sack in his arms, the back door open. He gave a laugh, incredulous. 'Take a job at a cab company?'

'OK, kids, go outside.'

'It's night-time.'

'All right then. Go to bed.'

As he left the room, Daniel placed the envelope on the bench, and nobody said anything about it.

For once Michael was home instead of hanging out, as he'd been doing since their return from the commune, with that bunch of older boys outside the zoo or at the Transport Museum tram station. When they walked past, arms interlinked, on their way back from school, Eve and Dot could see behind his dangled hand the lit cigarette, and they saw him drinking red cans of beer. Now the children gathered in the girls' room and sat on the two single beds side by side, trying to read and listening through the quiet of the house for the sound of raised voices, or slamming doors. The silence expanded. Ruth snuggled up beneath the crocheted blanket at the foot of Dorothy's bed and fell asleep, or pretended to be asleep so that nobody would move her. Outside, the plane tree leaves scraped the window and a car drove past. After a while the front door did slam, and there was the hyphenated splutter of their car's attempt to start in the cold night. Michael looked up from his *Mad Magazine*. Eve met his pink-rimmed gaze. As she was about to reach for her brother – felt it in her muscles, the movement anticipating the touch of his skin – he wiped a brusque forearm over his face and looked down again at the page. The bed creaked when Daniel stood. Without saying anything he went down to see if Lee was all right. A few minutes later he came back and said, 'She's OK,' and one by one the children all fell asleep on the beds, top and tailing, spooning, still in their clothes.

2. BLOOM

WHEN RUTH FINALLY opened the front door because the knocking and the bell ringing just would not stop, the couple standing in the doorway cast a long shadow down the length of the hall.

'We're here to see Mr Forrest.'

Frank had left without breakfast, taken the bus into town, and Lee was on dawn shift at the delicatessen. Ruth stood, breathing hard from trombone practice, and shouted at the stairs behind her, 'Dorothy! Evelyn!'

Michael paused in the hallway, muddy football boots swinging from their laces by his side. 'What do they want?'

'You're so rude. Dad or Mum.'

'They're out.' He slammed the kitchen door.

Ruth gave her public smile to the man and the lady, and bellowed again. 'Dorothy! Eve!'

The lady spoke. 'Or anyone in the family over eighteen?'

'Michael,' Ruth shouted. 'Come back!'

The kitchen door pulsed with his disdain. Last week Michael had bounced back home after another attempt to leave. His flat-mates always stole from him, you could never trust people, and he was like a lodger from a foreign country now, someone who appeared at mealtimes but didn't talk and who gazed at you, if you addressed him, with implacable confusion.

'Sorry,' said Ruth. Over the rooftop across the road the sky was charged with light, shining through an invisible skin about to burst open.

From the bedroom upstairs Evelyn peered through the window, past the branches of the plane tree, but could see only the unfa-miliar white Datsun parked outside, a sparrow on the bonnet. She returned to the mirror and finished spraying her hair, flipped it in a backcombed tangle over her shoulders. Daniel, rumpled in his dressing gown, ambled in, a thin joint lit between his fingers. 'They're calling for you,' he drawled.

'You should get dressed.'

'I'm not well.'

'Go back to bed then.'

'I'm bored.'

Ruth cried, '*Dorothy!*' then, less convinced, 'or Eve!' The sound reverberated.

Evelyn pulled her bottom eyelid down to draw kohl along the inside. 'It's far too early for this kerfuffle.'

'There are two of them. It must be serious.'

He stopped outside the bathroom and knocked on the door. 'There's someone downstairs for you,' he said, his mouth up close against the surface. The words travelled through the grains and particles of wood and into the steamy air of the bathroom where they disintegrated and Dot, drying herself with a sharp-smelling, slightly damp towel, heard a murmur. She put her bathrobe on and opened the door. Steam escaped. Daniel jerked his head in the direction of the stairs. 'Someone there for you.'

'For me?'

'Think so.' He pinched out the joint and left it on the basin ledge. 'Warm in here.' His gaze combed the room, took in the leavings of the female body, cotton-wool discs hardening with old nail-polish remover, the hairbrush bristles puffed with a cobweb of fine blonde hair, a cardboard tampon wrapper unfurling in the toilet bowl.

'Have my bath. Haven't you got a lecture?'

'Lectures are a colossal waste of time.'

'I know, but you've got to go.'

'I actually think I'm going to rebel.' He undid the cord on his dressing gown. 'Go away now.'

Ruth appeared at the top of the stairs, her face red. 'What are you doing? One of you get down here.'

As Dorothy passed the bedroom Evelyn swung out, braced in the door frame, her almond eyes through the sludgy make-up doing their trick of radiating heat. 'Thanks,' she whispered.

The trombone started up again. '*God,*' cried Eve. Dorothy walked down the stairs, hair wet, air from the open front door coming up chilly beneath the bathrobe, the towel smelling not very nice in her hand. The man and the woman were in the hallway now, and the man gently shut the front door behind him and the woman turned from examining the family portrait that hung next to the hallway mirror. In the portrait, for which the Forrests had sat some years ago, the painter – a goateed friend of Frank's with white bristles on the backs of his hands – had given the children rosy cheeks and shiny eyes, as though they had that minute run in from playing outdoors, and made Frank look dignified with his collar unbuttoned and their mother wear a pale-blue sweater and a string of fake pearls, her smile soft. *I have become a wife again.* The children, created from short little dabs and longer streaks of paint, clustered around their parents, eyelashes thick and dark and spiky, Michael's nose straight and fine, a white gleam brush-stroked down the centre. Daniel should have been in the picture. Sometimes at night Dorothy thought she could make out his shape behind her shoulder, hidden beneath a layer of paint. The woman sighed as her gaze left the painting and fell on Dot. 'Miss Forrest?'

A hand on the bottom newel post of the banister. 'Yes.'

'May we talk with your parents?'

'They're not here.'

There were teenagers somewhere, behind doorways, breathing. From upstairs, the glug of draining bath water.

'May we talk to you?'

'Yes. Of course.'

Dot opened the door to the front room. The loose rosette jiggled on the protruding screws so that she put a hand to it to stop the sound. It was dark; the couple stood tentative in the space before she drew back the heavy tasselled curtains and the room came into view. Nestled in a wooden bowl, dried petals of potpourri sweetened the air.

'That smells nice,' said the woman.

'My sister's got a stall at Cook Street Market.' Dot gestured for the man and woman to sit on the grey corduroy sofa, and moved the ashtray with the acrid remnants of her father's *one luxury* cigarettes onto the bookshelves on the other side of the room.

The front door slammed. Michael passed the window in his work overalls. Dorothy tucked the bathrobe in around her legs and sat on the cracked maroon leather of her father's chair. The woman wore an olive-green skirt suit; the man was in a double-breasted pinstriped jacket and trousers, with a brown tie. His hair had been stuck down with some sort of cream but tufts of it pushed upwards, giving him the look of a boxer on his day off. He gripped his briefcase between his calves.

'What's it about?' Dorothy asked.

'We're from the collection agency.' There was a pause in which he might have extended a hand for shaking, but didn't. 'May I confirm your age, Miss Forrest?'

'I'm eighteen. Sorry, I'm not sure what you want?'

The woman gave a small shake of the head. 'We're here to take possession of your father's car. Where is he?'

'He's out.' Sun glinted across Dot's line of vision and she straightened her back to look over it. 'Why do you need his car?'

'Does he have it with him?'

'Probably.' Her mother had driven it to work. She'd be home before long. Dot imagined running to the street corner, intercepting her – 'Hide the vehicle!'

The man spoke. 'All right. Miss Forrest, we need you to sign a walking possession agreement.'

The woman nodded at the dead green screen of the television in the corner. 'Is there a second TV in the house?'

33

'Debt has been incurred,' said the man, 'and we are here to remove property as payment.'

Parts of Dot lifted and floated around the room. 'Debt.' A moment went by. She blinked. 'Can you do that?'

'There is a series of complaints. Court costs arising from various unpaid fines dating back several years, water bills, hire purchase payments. Consolidated' – this nasal recitation – 'and to be dealt with by us.'

'Court costs.'

She leaned forward with the powerful, irrational urge to explain the joy of driving hard out with no headlights while Daniel sat in the passenger seat singing, the music as loud as the 8-track would go. The way the intense, furious guitar calmed the air, released what pressure was inside him, or inside her. The blinding joy of it, even when dread trickled down like an egg cracked over her scalp that first time she realised the flashing lights and the siren of the cop car were actually directed at her.

The man was checking the file. 'Yes, we have the car registered in your father's name and the fines are addressed to him.'

Now the broken bits of Dot reassembled, stuck back together like guilty tar. When eventually the envelopes had come with Frank's name on them, the Crown insignia in the top left corner, *Ministry of Justice*, she knew. Opened the first one and intercepted all the rest. They were her secret, even from Daniel. It would spoil everything to tell him: what they had was freedom, possibility; not another Forrest mess, this, reminders. Multiplying fines. Court summonses. She'd been vigilant, torn them up and thrown the shreds in the bin, shoved the day's newspaper or the cornered toast crusts on top. Now, on the sofa, in the dust and potpourri and stuffy heat, smelling the nasty stink of panic from under her arms, Dorothy wanted to punch herself. What had she thought was going to happen? This was the world.

The man popped open the clasp of his briefcase. 'Here are the papers.' He rose and deposited a form and a pen in Dorothy's lap – a whiff of minty cologne – explaining that today they would take her signature. He pointing out the agreed daily charge. The rate of interest. The debt had to be resolved or they would come back to remove – he gestured – 'this television, any non-essential furniture, books, your family car, the paintings, any other goods that fall within our rights'.

'I won't sign it.' She wrapped the bathrobe sash around her hand until the fingers went purple. The shoulders of the robe were cold with the water from her hair. 'Why have you come now when my father's out? It's not his fault. You can't take our things.'

'Dorothy.' The woman spoke softly. 'I'm afraid that we can.'

'Do you have a brother or sister also eighteen or over? We just need the one signature.'

'What happens if I don't sign it?'

'We come back until payments are made.' The same adenoidal tone. 'You won't like that.'

There was a tap on the door. She darted to it, held herself between Evelyn and the room. 'What's going on?' Eve asked between her teeth. She was wearing Dorothy's fake-leopardskin coat. She never asked.

'Real estate agents. I'm about to get rid of them.'

Her sister raised an eyebrow. 'Good job. See you then.'

Daniel pulled Dorothy into the hallway, his eyes locking hers. 'Hang on.' It was obvious he was stoned. It would be so good to bring him into the room. She held on to his lapel. 'Are you sure you're OK? Who are they?'

'Estate agents. I told Eve.'

'Shall I take them on a tour?' He tugged her dressing-gown sash. Had forgotten Eve was right there.

'No.' She moved away. 'No it's fine.'

So Evelyn and Daniel nodded, and she watched them patter down the path, arms hugged across their bodies, hair flung as though by static in the wind, before she went back into the room to sign the paper.

After the man and woman were gone and Ruth had left for school, Dorothy washed again in cold water and got dressed. Soon their mother would be home with bags of stale pastries, faintly smelling of that fancy imported cheese, Camembert and Gruyère, boiling from another outrage pulled by the posh woman she worked for, a coiffed bitch in a fob-watch chain necklace and raised shirt collar who patronised Lee because despite her genteel bearing she badly needed the job which for a woman like her was only just on the acceptable side of retail, the European vocab dressed it up but really she was a salad hand, a till monkey, because they were broke, broke, and it was the imminent return of this fury that finally propelled Dot out towards the bus stop.

The morning street was alive with disco from a portable radio, a couple of men in super-tight jeans peering over a car engine, a woman holding her toddler's hands as he slowly put one foot in front of the other along a low brick wall. The mother lifted the boy down and wiggled her hips in time to the music and the sound of dance floors carried on the wind over the whole street, even reaching inside the wooden shelter. A Falcon full of young men drove past and whistled.

Except for the usher, a young man in a blue jacket doing something unseen with ticket rolls or sweet packets behind the desk, the cinema foyer was empty, the day's first screening a few minutes away. Dorothy sat on a chair upholstered in grey tartan, a splodge of stain showing up on one of the paler checks. The sport section of yesterday's newspaper was folded on the next chair: half a headline and a photo of half a man running towards the camera, a ball tucked under his visible arm. The cameraman probably had one of those telephoto lenses, the ones that trumpeted out of the camera's cubed rectangle, too long, disproportionate, exposing what the human eye couldn't see.

At the sound of hydraulic doors Dorothy looked up. Her father came into the foyer eating a chocolate-coated ice cream in a cone. There was a moment, alone with his pleasure, where he didn't register Dot, and she was struck mute, longing to leave him in peace, this happy cloud. *Don't look over.* Then he did, and finished his mouthful. 'Dottie. What are you doing here?'

Her palms buzzed as she showed him the copy of the form they had given her, a thin ghost paper, the collection company's logo in a faint banner across the top, and at the bottom the tracing of her name. Aside from Dot's Post Office bank account this was her first time signing an official document and the curves and loops looked like someone's idea of a signature, not a proper adult one.

Frank scanned the paper and took bites of ice cream. She waited. 'Driving fines? Goddamn it, Michael,' her father said.

'No,' she said. 'Michael didn't take the car. It was me.'

Again that feeling, the way he looked at her, as though she'd only just materialised in front of him. At last Frank sat down. She put the newspaper on the floor between them; her fingers felt dirty with a sense of whoever had touched it before. For a while, she told her father, a couple of years ago, when she was fifteen, she used to take the car at night. She didn't mention Daniel. Now her face burned and the clog in her throat was hard to talk over as she apologised.

'Is Evelyn in on all this too?'

An elderly couple entered the foyer, one stick between them, and crossed the perilous carpet to the ticket desk.

'She never came. She doesn't know about it. Dad –'

'Look, I'm just catching up.'

'I'll leave teachers' college. I'll work full-time and pay you back.'

'Right,' he said. His voice was dry, a bit splintery. 'You'd better leave this with me.' He spoke to the sheet of paper. 'Never mind,' he said, 'I'll take care of this now.'

'I'm so sorry.' The more she apologised, the worse she felt.

'Don't worry. It's more than those fines,' he said. 'There's been – we haven't been as careful as we could.' He rubbed a flat hand over his mouth. *Don't cry.* 'It's more than that.'

'Are we going to be OK?' Would their things be taken? Could they pay the rent? Where would they go? Not possible to ask out loud.

'Dottie,' her father said. 'We're going to be great. Things are great. Sure we have some obligations but everyone –' In the middle of his sentence the tannoy bonged and the usher announced that the feature would begin in one minute. As though summoned in a dream he stood and wiped his ice-cream hand on his suit jacket. 'I'll sort them out. Don't worry about it.'

'Thanks, Dad,' she said. 'Thank you.' She kissed the side of his head, the sun-spotted skin over his temple where the hair was receding. She felt the need for more words from him but he was already moving through the foyer, towards the doors opened onto the dark screening room. He waved her away with the back of a hand and nodded graciously – not a care in the world – to the usher who now stood at the cinema entrance, his patient blue arm held out for Frank's ticket.

In a stationery shop down the road she leafed through the women's magazines, searching out advice columns. There was an advertisement for bedding that used the word *Manchester*. Daniel would like that. Creepy language was their joke after visiting his mother in her unit: *doily, shunt, fecund*. She could slide a shuddery sort of word into every exchange. *Martin's recovering from surgery but he's going to need a bag. Gina's youngest has phlegm on the lung. Cut a section from his bowel. Ganglia. Aorta. My gout.* Dorothy had sat on the flat couch next to Daniel, ignoring the needling claws of the cat that had colonised her lap, wanting so much for his mother to like her.

None of the agony aunts mentioned money, the lack of it, the plunging of one's family into the poorhouse, what to do if your mother was enraged and your father was a wastrel, how to leave home without breaking your older sister's heart, how to stop your sister from stealing everything, how not to tell her about you and

Daniel even though it was probably perfectly bloody obvious to everyone, if they were looking, which they maybe were not because their own lives were full too of the one foot in front of the other, the confusion about how best to proceed. Nothing about brothers, mental health of, or younger sisters, possible alien host factor, or why Marc Bolan had to die or why there were so many born-again Christians at Teachers' College or whether she would go to jail or what to do next. If she changed the names there would likely be an opinion on whether [Daniel] truly loved [her], but it would depend on the magazine, whether he was her soulmate or just using her for sex.

They were all at dinner for the first time in weeks. Dorothy waited for what her father might do. The grilled-cheese roll was making her feel sick; she passed it to Daniel, who nodded thanks, and poured herself another red wine from the cask. Frank must have told Lee. It would come out about the night drives, the fines, everything. Eve took her plate to the sink, lit a cigarette and stood by the open back door, blowing smoke out into the night air. The fact that Lee wouldn't meet Dot's eye wasn't necessarily unusual but she wished, just wished, someone would speak. Get it over with.

'So those people who came this morning,' she found herself beginning.

'I had a letter today,' Lee cut across her. 'From an old schoolfriend. She's got a fine life now, done very well for herself. Nice neighbourhood, three beautiful children, architect husband on the town council and she's on the school board, though she doesn't have to work.'

Frank snorted.

'And you know what just happened? Just last year, when she's forty-five years old? He shows up. The baby she had at seventeen and adopted out and never told anyone about. Her husband doesn't even know. The baby's father, whoever he is, doesn't know. And the boy, in his late twenties now, comes back.'

As Lee was talking, Dorothy saw it, only the hallway was their hallway, the street outside their own. A few days before Christmas she walked down the hall and saw the wobbly shape of a strange man through the bubbled-glass front door. She slung the bolt on. Opened the door. Through the safety of the gap, she asked if he was lost. She could see now he was no threat, a slight man, narrow shoulders, wearing a coat that didn't look enough for the weather. ' "Are you lost, honey?" and he said to her, "You don't know me. But I think I am your son." '

'She had a baby when she was seventeen?' Ruth asked.

'Seventeen.'

Dot felt it like an electric jolt, that lost baby transformed into a young man wearing a suit especially for the visit, a man who had brushed his hair and shaved and cleaned his teeth that morning knowing what he was about to do.

A friend of Frank's tooted from the street, his car idling. Their father pushed his chair back and took his plate to the sink and stepped into the hallway and stumbled over the box that waited for the antique dealer's assessment. It contained a fox-fur shrug, three crystal decanters, a couple of picture frames with the family photos removed, a blue vase made of Danish glass, Georgian candelabras, several round and rectangular silver trays, an incomplete set of silver cutlery with mother-of-pearl handles, a tangled rhine-stone necklace, the thick lacquered folder that housed an ancestor's coin collection and the Kodak Instamatic camera, the device on which Frank had recorded their childhoods, its black nose sticking out between the twisty stalks of the candlesticks as though it was coming up for air.

3. YEAH, EVERYTHING

FRANK WAS WAITING at the bottom of the escalator with his thinning hair, and Eve hugged the familiar leanness of his body underneath the woollen jumper, the angled plates of his shoulders. 'I thought Dorothy was coming?' he said.

'She said to send her love. She's got a classroom placement.'

'Yes, yes. She must be very busy.'

'She said to say sorry. She sends her love.'

'You've got thin, Evie.'

'Have I?'

They waited for her suitcase at the conveyor belt together. The other travellers were middle-aged suits. Sales reps maybe, or farmers. Evelyn lurched towards the wrong suitcase twice before hers passed, the same bright blue as the others, the colour that reminded her of the hospice where she often delivered flowers.

'Your mother ties a ribbon around the handle.'

'I should do that.'

The airport was tiny, and a station wagon was just outside. Not his; the car belonged to the person whose house he was minding. The dog panted in the boot, a handsome dog, black and tan and watching intently as they approached. Her father opened the boot and pushed a hand towards the dog, holding it back when it rose as though to get out.

'Hey. Boy,' Evelyn said, unable to remember this latest dog's name though her father might have mentioned it in one of his recent late-night calls. It circled itself and sniffed at the suitcase, growling slightly. She buckled herself into the passenger seat and Frank drove them away from the signs directing traffic towards the city. The car smelled doggy. Evelyn pulled the inhaler from her bag, unwound the Walkman cord from around it, shook fluff out of the mouthpiece and blew into the top to dislodge any random scraps.

'Are you still smoking?' her father asked.

'No. A little bit. I just went through a break-up.'

He patted her knee. 'You'll live.'

'Woo hoo,' she hooted at a truck full of live sheep as they over-took it.

They were quickly on a country road, muzzy hills in the distance the only relief from the flatness of the floodplain. Frank drove down the middle of the narrow road, getting faster and faster. He took a bend at speed and she grabbed the handle above the window and braced her other hand above the glove box. She turned to check on the dog, who was whining, and the car swung again. 'Dad. You're driving too fast.'

The road crossed a river, tumbling silvery grey beneath them. A man in waders was planted downstream to the left and she put a palm to the car window, wanted to stop, talk to him, pass time there with the sand flies and the river stones, the khaki box with compartments, coloured feathers, hooks. The road rushed on, lined with poplars feathering the sky, and the world was pale, grey and white and green. The speed on this stretch dizzied her eyes.

Evelyn's body lifted from the seat as they bounced along the unsealed drive, and when the car reeled into its spot outside an old building she took a second of stillness to catch up with herself. The dog leaped from the car and disappeared round the side of the house, a flash of black.

'So this is it.'

The house was made of wooden weatherboards and the corrugated-iron roof bowed in the middle. The no-colour paint on the windowsills and door frame was crackled, and as soon as she stepped inside there was a grapey, rotten smell that got stronger as she followed her father to the kitchen.

'Have you had lunch?' He boiled the scuffed white plastic kettle. She told him about Kimiko and the florist shop, about the volley-ball team. The tea was strong with a rainbow film floating on the surface. The phone rang and Frank went to another room to answer.

Everything in the bathroom, next to the kitchen, was freezing: the toilet seat, the tap that left a rusting smudge on her hands, the clean-tasting water. When she returned to the kitchen her father was still not back. Evelyn looked in the cupboard for biscuits and a smudgy grey meal moth flew out, into her face. There were three opened packets of biscuits, one of them mouldy and the other two soft. She had a bowel-deep urge to get into the borrowed car and drive away, but instead did what was needed: in the bottom of the cupboard she found a large brown rubbish bag, propped it open and shook the weevil-infested flour and the clumpy bran flakes into it, and dropped two half-empty jars of crusted peanut butter and one of crystallised honey on top of the pile.

Eve turned the radio on but the battery was dead. She pulled out the kitchen drawer to look for new ones, pushing aside the battens of string and pricking a finger on a drawing pin. Her father's name registered before she really read it – yes – his full name, Frank Michael Forrest – and she pulled the envelope from the drawer. Two more lay beneath it, and all were addressed to her father at Lee's house, bearing the Ministry of Justice insignia in the top left corner. They had been redirected in her mother's handwriting, and remained unopened. Evelyn rifled through the rest of the drawer. Nothing else. She stood there holding the envelopes, then shoved them deep in the drawer, covering them with an old phone bill and a couple of Christmas cards decorated with glued glitter that was sandpapery to the touch.

'You need batteries,' Evelyn said when her father came back. 'We're going to the supermarket.'

'I've just been.' He opened the fridge and gestured at flat card-board boxes of pizza, a string bag of green apples and new bottles of milk, the silver-foil tops not yet opened.

'You've got meal moths.'

'Oh.' He looked perplexed. 'What are they?'

She would clear out the cupboards and vacuum in the corners and wipe down all the boxes. She would find enough fresh food to make something hearty for dinner, and light the fire and pick flowers for the table and in the morning would sand down the windowsills and paint them and clean the windows and re-roof the house and mow the lawns and burn this house down and build a better one and bring her father back from the dead. She stood on the kitchen doorstep and punched one hand into the corner of the pocket of her ex-boyfriend's leather jacket, and with the other smoked a cigarette.

Most people were jammed in the front half of the pub, near the low stage. The band had been due to start an hour ago but the only action was the occasional puff of dry ice being sent from the wings to mingle with all the cigarette smoke and thicken the air, to make it visible so that the musicians wouldn't have to emerge into transparency. Dorothy balanced the beers. Someone jostled her and liquid sloshed over her hands. She passed one to Daniel, restrained herself from kissing him even though she just wanted to kiss him all the, all the time.

'Bears are thrust upon me,' said Daniel, and he growled like he always did with that joke while he stared at the stage. He drank, and leaned away from his hip bone to rummage in the front pocket of his jeans for his lighter. Dot slanted her cigarette into the flame. She loved to watch his body, the way he managed pockets, jackets, basketballs, the things he touched. A couple of Dot's friends waved from over near the bar but there was no way of getting through the crush. Dan's flatmate was talking about that incredible sound system. He said something else and it was lost because the drummer walked on and then the rest of the band, and there was a surge of people who had been waiting outside in the smoking section to do this push when the band appeared and with bodies pressing into every side Dot's feet lifted from the ground as the music began. It hit her in the breastbone – punched through the honeycombed tissue and split out from there, and she dispersed into the other bodies, radiating with the vibrating sound, lost in it and him.

A fierce orange light from the three-bar heater blazed by the pantry door; the soles of Evelyn's sneakers smelled melty where her legs were stretched towards it. Frank came into the kitchen and washed white paint out of a thick wide brush into the sink, water running opaque beneath the spiky black bristles.

She put down her reading. 'When are the owners coming back?'

'Oh, another couple of months yet.'

'Do you know where you're going to go then?'

'Your mother and I have been talking again.'

'Really? Oh, that's great.' She half rose to hug her father but he knocked the brush on the side of the sink and laid it on the stainless-steel bench, where a small white puddle formed around it.

'Come and see the orchard,' he said. 'Before it gets dark.'

Through the kitchen window was a steeliness to the sky she hadn't noticed happening.

Frank led the way out the front of the house and past an empty flowerbed, a large oval of rich brown soil, to a wooden stile. He was a dark figure ahead, halfway into the new field. On the other side of the fence the dog trotted up and bumped into Evelyn, wagging his tail. She patted his flank. He clambered the stile after her. The wind picked up now they were away from the shelter of the house. Her father's path was a bit like a sidewinder's as he walked. She wondered when he'd last eaten; what he'd had to drink. The light was dropping quickly and she called out, 'How far is it?'

Frank tottered backwards as though her voice was a lasso. 'Not far.'

They walked along the side of a saggy wire fence and he gestured behind them. 'Deer over there. And they're outside the irrigation scheme. But there's talk of a drought.' He spoke airily, as though the problems of nature were not his.

'I'd like to see a deer.'

'Who'd you break up with?' he asked.

'Just a guy. It's OK.'

'Has Dorothy got a boyfriend yet?'

'No. She says she's too busy.'

'Your mother and I were married at your age. You can't muck around.'

'The florist's moving. I'm going to look for a new flat, closer. With a couple of friends.'

'How's your brother, how's Michael?'

'All right. Don't know. He's all like, hangs out with his friends. Do the others know about you and Mum?' Talking about it gave her a false-hope feeling, one she wanted to back off from, as though she was repeating somebody else's lie.

'No rush,' he said. 'Best to wait.' He started singing an American folk song, his voice old-fashioned in the growing dark.

'Hey, did you bring a torch? Should we be heading back?'

'No, this is it.'

There were some old trees dotted around but without the leaves to go on Evelyn couldn't tell if they were fruit trees. She touched one. The bark was scalloped with flakes of silvery green lichen. 'Is this an apple tree?'

Frank was just behind her. He held her elbow with gripping fingers and shifted his weight from foot to foot. 'An apple tree? Let's see.' She extracted her arm and walked on. There was not much sound. The thick wing-flaps of roosting birds, the breathing of the dog. Venus appeared above the distant hills, a speck of light in the blue dusk.

He stumbled, and half fell onto Evelyn, heavy against her arm. She pushed him upright. 'Come on Dad, let's go back to the house. You need to eat something.'

'No, I haven't shown you the orchard yet.'

'No. No Dad, let's go back to the house.'

'No.' His hand was around her wrist, dragging it downwards. 'I want to show you the orchard.' His eyes were juicy, young, he was grinning like a schoolboy, he was somewhere inside his own head and the trees were pressing in.

She twisted her hand around to pull at his arm. 'We're going back to the house. Come on.'

The only light on in the house shone small through the evening and they crossed the field towards it, Evelyn leading as though she knew what she was doing, her father following somewhere in the back. Distance grew and shrank and soon they were at the stile. Evelyn hopped over and ran the last metres to the house, the flowerbed giving softly beneath her shoes, round the side of the building and into the back door and the kitchen. She put all the lights on, and the oven, and washed her hands and was drying them on the holey, starchy linen tea towel when the planked back door opened and her father came in. He sat at the table.

She pulled a soft plastic bag of bread from the enamel bread bin and spread little scoopings of cold butter on it, the knife going through the bread in places, her hands trembling. She pushed a plate and a glass of water across the table towards him. 'Eat up.'

'I'm not hungry.'

'Eat it.' She turned her back and busied herself with the pizza and an oven tray and didn't look at him again until she was sure he was eating. She cut the mould off the end of a block of cheese and added it to the plate. 'This can't happen any more.'

He rolled a chunk of cheese in a slice of bread and shoved it right in his mouth like his hand belonged to somebody else. He chewed and said gluggily, 'Is there any peanut butter?'

'You can't keep doing this. The not eating, all of it. We can't keep worrying about you.'

'Yes, sorry.' He wiped his fingers on the paper napkin she had torn off for him, and dropped it on the floor.

She laughed, feeling helpless. 'You're going to stop?'

From under the table, balancing on his fingertips, patting the floor with the other hand to pick up the paper towel, a slow, uncertain, 'Yes.'

The stainless-steel sink bench was cold against Evelyn's back and she tugged down the hem of her jumper. 'You're going to look after yourself?'

'I'm fine.'

She stared at the loaf of bread, its doughy satisfactions, but instead took the cigarettes and lighter from the pocket of her ex-boyfriend's jacket and lit one. 'Good. Me too.'

★　★　★

At the bottom of the stairs she opened the door off the hallway onto her father's study. The oak table filled most of the room and was spread with a range of open-faced, hardback journals for his History of Theatre project. She flicked through the pile of carbon-copied typewritten pages near by and saw the coloured edge of a magazine, the flat pink of bare flesh. Hastily she covered the papers again. Evelyn looked into space and didn't move. She listened. It had been a photo of a man. She didn't want to lift the papers back to check. Maybe it had been a photo of a woman. Maybe it had been a theatre programme, one of those shows her father liked to talk about from the sixties, a kind of performance art. She sneezed in the dust, the shock of that the impetus needed to get out of the room and shut the door.

The guest bedroom was large, with a high ceiling and a view of shorn fields, lumpy in the moonlight. The curtains, sprigged with the sort of daisy pattern Evelyn had longed for as a child, didn't quite reach the bottom of the window. She held the window wide open and stuck her head out and inhaled the piny air. Stars swarmed overhead. She shut the window latch and shook out the duvet, dust motes floating in the air, the satin fabric smelling coldly of naphthalene. The bedside light was broken so she read with the main light on, moths tapping against the window glass, a couple fizzing on the light bulb. Her father's room was across the landing and there was the unpausing sound of his footsteps up the stairs and going into his own room and shutting the door. She unhooked her bra and pulled it out the side of her sleeve and curled up with the asthma inhaler gripped in her hand, wearing the leather jacket, her T-shirt, jeans, and socks.

★ ★ ★

After the gig, in his bedroom, Daniel pulled the sheets up over Dorothy's bare back and all the way over her head so that they were in a tent and she moved herself down his body, her ears still ringing.

The dog woke Evelyn with his barking. It was still dark, although the sky was tinged yellow right along the edge of the horizon. She kicked her feet into their trainers and opened the door carefully, the round metal handle stiff and creaky on the angled shaft. There was no noise now and it was possible the dog's barking happened in a dream. She made her way down the stairs, through the kitchen and its smell of cold pizza, and out the unlocked back door, breathing in the watery clean air as she crossed the yard to the kennel. Pinkish-grey clouds floated on the felt-like sky. The dog was standing awake, a chain running from the kennel to his collar. The moon cast light and shadows over the links. His shaggy smell rose up as she unhooked the collar clip. He passed Evelyn and turned back to look at her, and she followed him round to the front of the house and up the long rutted drive towards the main road. Old pine trees stood at intervals like giants either side, the ground beneath them scattered with needles and cones, darker shapes on the dark earth. The house was dark at their backs, and she tripped once or twice on the large pits in the unsealed drive, but the dog trotted alongside, nimble and even. She ran the last stretch to the road and followed the dog in the direction he took, forward in the half-light.

A few hundred metres down the road a gravelled lay-by housed some crumpled DB cans and she dragged the dog away from sniffing at a spent condom. Bird calls spiralled in the dense trees. The breeze was almost warm, holding a suggestion of rain. Eve began to make a little shrine of stones. Against their tiny scale she felt like the Incredible Hulk, bursting to escape her body, her father's house, the countryside. Her stomach burned with envy of Dorothy's ability to be not *here* with the loneliest man in the Western world but back in her own life, her studies and her teaching and her sunny flat and her *thing*, the secret she held onto. Fucking Daniel. Eve refused to be the one to bring it up. To ask the question would only make real the ice field between them, the blank that she was left standing in, alone. This was the worst of it — this plunging sense that everyone else had got something she had not. The dog nosed around in the weeds between the gravel and the trees, wagging its stiff rope of tail.

The hum of an engine broke the night. The dog and Evelyn looked up at the bend in the road, anticipating, and it was several seconds before light beamed round the corner then a car emerged and cruised past. It slowed and she stood up. The car reversed back. A growl came from deep in the dog's throat.

'You all right?' The driver was a lady in her thirties or forties, wearing a woolly hat and a checked shirt, open over what might be a petticoat. The engine cut out and a baby cried. The woman reached an arm towards the back seat where a child of a few months old lay in a safety cradle. She started the car again and the baby stopped crying, and after yanking the handbrake on she walked around to Evelyn. The dog barked once and stepped up to the woman and stood looking at her. She scruffled him behind the ears. 'Is this your dog?'

'No,' Evelyn said.

The woman leaned down to examine his collar. 'Where did you find him?'

'He's my dad's.' She pointed down the road in the direction the woman came from. 'I don't know his name.'

'Blackie?' The woman was speaking to the dog. 'Blackie?'

The dog barked again, loud over the running car engine.

'It's acting like it can talk,' Evelyn said. 'Like you're having a conversation.'

The woman laughed.

'Is he yours?' Evelyn asked. 'Blackie?'

'Yes. He's grown a bit.'

Exhaust fumes coloured the air. The light of early morning had found its way onto everything now, on the dog's conker-coloured eyes and the woman's sleep-deprived face, in the spaces beneath the tree trunks and over the pile of grey stones Evelyn had gathered.

Evelyn dug at the stones with her foot, sending one skittering over to the woman. 'Sorry,' she said. 'My dad's really going to miss him.'

The woman frowned. 'Can you help me bring him home? I don't want him disturbing the baby.'

Blackie sat panting in the passenger seat and Evelyn sat in the back behind him, next to the sleeping infant, one hand reached forwards to hold the dog by the soft leather collar. The woman drove slowly, with the windows halfway down, back past the turn-off to Eve's father's house and on.

'Do you have deer?' Evelyn asked.

'Yes,' the woman said.

The baby woke and squalled. Blackie began to lunge around and Evelyn pulled him back into place. 'What should I do?'

'It's all right. We're nearly there.'

The car grated to a halt on the gravel drive outside a one-storey, red-brick farmhouse. The front door was white, with concrete pillars either side. 'Can you wait in the car with Blackie?' the woman said. 'I want to surprise the kids.'

She unpicked the baby from the car seat and it stopped crying as she held it to her, its round little head nodding hungrily into the mother's clavicle. The dog and Evelyn waited in the car. Blackie huffed. Evelyn hugged her knees up to her chest and pulled her ex's leather jacket tighter around her. In the last few minutes the temperature seemed to have dropped; the lawns were dusted in patches with frost; her breath puffed, visible, into the air. Sometimes Daniel called in at the florist's, and Kimiko teased her after he'd gone. The woman came out the front door, still holding the baby, and a man in a thick tartan flannel shirt, jeans and boots steered two children wearing pyjamas towards the car, his hands resting lightly on their shoulders, their little hands covering their eyes. The girl's pyjamas were blue with a pink-pig pattern and the boy's were covered with pictures of yellow trucks.

The woman crunched over the gravel back towards her car and Eve. Her children had clamoured over Blackie and hugged their parents tightly before chasing him inside. 'Thank you,' she said. 'Now would you like to see the deer?'

Dorothy woke around dawn short of breath, and Daniel wasn't there. It was the carpet dust. The insides of her ears were hot and itchy.

Between her shoulder blades was a raspy blockedness, weak and immovable at the same time. Leaning out over the edge of the bed, hair falling around her face, Dot scrabbled in the bottom of her bag, grit collecting under her fingernails, retrieved the inhaler and took a puff. Then there was a kind of glottal stop and she couldn't breathe any more. She coughed but no air came out, there was just a retching sound. Something was blocking her windpipe. Launching around the dimly lit room naked she banged herself on the back as hard as she could, her body getting tighter and tighter with the lack of air. In the darkness came a sensation of the edges closing in. Another convulsion shook her and the thing in her throat entered her mouth wetly and she gasped, eyes streaming water, and the tiny scrap of fabric could be picked off her tongue and flicked aside.

She pulled Dan's sweatshirt on and found some knickers in the ruched sheet at the bottom of the bed. The bedroom door was stiff. She yanked it open, her arm shaking, and pitched down the hallway towards the kitchen. The door of his new flatmate's room was ajar. They were cross-legged on the bed, smoking a bong, and when they became aware of her they leaned back on the pillows. It was a boy's room, the floor strewn with unlaced Doc Martens and Army-surplus jumpers and record covers. Daniel looked flushed and gorgeous, and his friend started laughing and said, 'Sorry, sorry, it's just nerves. I thought you were the cops. It's not funny, sorry.'

The Red Squad burst in and hauled him crucifixion-style from the room, feet dragging, a clatter of shields and batons dividing the air.

'Daniel? What's the story?'

He reached an arm out towards her but didn't move from the

bed. 'Dot – there's no story. Bryce, this is my sister, Dorothy.' His voice was fantastically slow.

'I'm not really his sister.'

Bryce said, 'Sorry, I just, I'll stop in a minute.' But before he'd finished saying it he had stopped laughing.

'I'm not your fucking sister, Daniel.'

Daniel leaned forward over the sheets as though he might be going to get out of bed or reach for Dot but then he sank down again flat on the bed like a mannequin and said in a long almost sung note, '*Aahhhh.*'

In the communal living room that guy Andrew, the house scapegoat, was practising karate, slow-motion punching the air, his legs in a lunge position on his purple mat.

'Can't you do that in your own room?' Dorothy said. 'Your breathing is so loud.'

The scapegoat closed his eyes. 'You don't even live here,' he said. 'And by the way is your brother smoking drugs? Tell him my stepmother's a cop.'

In the communal kitchen the scapegoat's frozen yoghurt was defrosting on the bench.

'It's just the same as ice cream,' Dorothy shouted through the wall. She tipped his Fresh Up down the sink, put her face right under the tap and drank, and coughed until she could breathe freely. One of Daniel's sweatshirt sleeves rode up and she licked a finger and rubbed at the stamp mark still there on the inside of her wrist.

4. INSTINCT

ANDREW HAD BEEN surprised the first time he saw Dorothy pluck her eyebrows or floss her teeth, but the cheese toasties and wine on the couch while they listened to albums together was the right kind of intimacy, and maybe a few clipped toenails on the bathroom floor was the price you had to pay. He had never before lived with anyone he was sleeping with. The fact of her being there, lesson plans spread over the table when he came back from work, the ponytail swing as she rose to hug him, was astounding.

They lay in bed in the middle of a Sunday afternoon. It was an old apartment building, the bed covered in sunlight, the sheets a buttery yellow. And finally, after he asked and asked again, she told him a lot of juicy detail about her sex life with the man before him, which included, in a roundabout and quite tortured rendition, so that it took Andrew ages to work out what she was saying, she and this *bean*, this *joke*, this *guy whose name she wouldn't say*, trying out tying each other up.

'Not at the same time,' she said. 'Obviously.' The sound of traffic rushed through the rooms like wind through leaves. Andrew sat up, thought for a minute and announced that he wanted to fuck her.

'You did just fuck me.'

'With something else.'

She lay there breathing, her eyes on his, and it was apparent that after what she'd just told him she had to go along with it. He banged in and out of the bathroom and the kitchen, everything he looked at, plates and bowls and her bunches of dried flowers, uselessly shaped. That was the part he remembered later, the bouncing panic, returning to the room terrified she would be laughing at him, unprepared for the erotic charge of her body lying there on the bed in the goldy heat being fucked with some implement or another. And he remembered his cheeks hot with the sense of expansion, of these are the ways we can be with each other, there are not any limits.

There was no food in the apartment. While a record spun on the stereo, Dorothy and Andrew sat on the floor with their bank statements spread in front of them, covering her yoga mat.

Coffee, lunch and bus money lived in a ceramic mug Dorothy had made at high school, and they shook all the coins onto the bench and counted them, and jogged down the three flights of stairs, Andrew's coat pockets clanking, and walked the long road of car dealerships and square concrete churches to the nearest grocery shop, which was closed. Dorothy began to weep. The fucking, the disclosures and the hunger overwhelmed her. 'I'm sorry I told you about that guy,' she sobbed. 'I thought that's what you were meant to do when you got engaged. Tell each other everything.' In truth she was afraid that she had talked about Daniel simply for herself, to bring him closer, never mind that it hurt.

He sat down next to her on the red wooden bench outside the grocer's and put his arm around her shoulders, stroking her head. Her hair ran like water through his fingers. 'Don't worry,' he said. A square-bodied woman in a coatdress crossed the chipped bark in front of them carrying a paper bag with pointy green leeks sprouting from the top and he called out to ask her where she had got her shopping from.

They walked in silence.

'I know,' he said when the Sunday market appeared just around the corner, 'we'll plant a garden on the windowsill.'

Dorothy waved as Andrew drove off. They'd have to get a new car; he'd ripped out the back seat for his canvases. He tooted from the traffic lights and she blew him a kiss. The interior of Evelyn's flower shop was clouded and cool from the mist spray, and the scents of tuberose and potting mix made time heavy, dream-like. Surely smells weren't usually this intense. She toured the displays of roses, geraniums, the hyacinths with their obscenely bulging soil.

'Your friend isn't joining you today?' asked Kimiko.

'Andrew? He's gone back to work.' She was dying to say it: you mean my fiancé.

Evelyn wiped flakes of green florist foam off her hands onto her legs and swizzled the apron off and flung it on the stalk-stained cutting board. 'She means Daniel. He's been popping in.'

Oh Daniel. Dorothy hadn't seen him since he'd got back from

Melbourne. 'This smells amazing,' she said, inhaling the air above a small potted lavender, waving it under Eve's nose.

She veered away. 'Sends me to sleep. I was at the flower markets at dawn.'

The sisters took paper-bag sandwiches down to the harbour and sat on the jetty with their legs over the edge. Six feet below swelled the choppy bottle-green sea, chunks of water buffeting the splintered pylons, the salt smell deep as petroleum, filthy, alive. Evelyn unpeeled her sandwich and tweezed out the alfalfa sprouts with her fingertips and dropped them in the sea. Birds swooped. Dorothy told her the news that she was pregnant. Eve's face fell open and she placed the sandwich into her lap and wiped her fingers on the fabric of her coat. 'And you're happy about it?' she asked, picking at a couple of pilled spots on the sleeve.

'Yes,' said Dorothy, amazed that she could ask, slightly frightened at the gap between them that the question exposed. 'Of course. We're going to get married.'

'Will you keep teaching?'

'Don't know.'

'Can I come to the scan with you?' Eve hugged her sister fiercely, water rising in the side of Dot's vision so that she felt she might fall in. They sat close together, foreheads touching. A cormorant plunged into the dark sea. 'I can't believe it,' Eve said. Eye make-up had run on her cheek, and when she exhaled one laughing breath translucent snot bubbled out of her nose. 'Why do I always get dumped? Sorry, sorry.'

Dorothy passed her the inadequate, one-ply paper napkin from her sandwich bag.

'How's Andrew?'

'He's excited.'

'Have you told Frank and Lee?'

'Not yet.'

Evelyn quizzed her more, about where she would live, they couldn't stay in Andrew's flat, and how would they live, would she go on the benefit, and what names she liked and what would the baby look like, questions Dorothy had no answer to. The wind died down and the sisters leaned forward to look at their reflections in the smoothly undulating, repetitive water, giant feet and small blurred heads. Evelyn held Dorothy by the shoulder and fake-shoved her as if to push her in, and they squealed and giggled and crab-crawled back away from the sea to the relative safety of the middle of the timbered jetty.

Daniel refused to be drawn on how long he would stay before leaving again, working his way, woofing or whatever. It was not enough that he had to be off-hand about his Melbourne ex-girl-friend, *Tammy*, a fucking *performance* artist, which probably meant stripper, or that he had to be so cool about the record shop he had worked in and the squat he'd lived in with this and that band and the frequent use of the adjectives *underground* and *independent* before anyone's job title so that she had already decided to refer to his closest friend, some heroin-addicted PhD candidate, as Underground Pat. Now he made allusions to a job on a cargo ship leaving for South America, but for all that he clearly liked saying the place names he hadn't decided. Paranaguá. Montevideo. Zárate.

'I don't know the date.'

'You'll be the date. All those sailors. They'd love you.'

They sat on the wall outside the library. Daniel's satchel strap cut a thick diagonal across his body. He dug a ready-rolled cigarette from the pocket of his jacket. Tiny brown curls of tobacco dangled from the end of the cigarette paper and when touched by the flame from his match they illuminated bright orange and disappeared. He inhaled, and exhaled. She held her fingers out for a puff.

'You shouldn't be smoking,' he said.

'Just one.'

'Why'd you do it, Dottie?' The darkness in his eyes really did seem to flicker – coal, jet, a hot shiny chestnut.

Dorothy passed the cigarette back to him and their hands touched momentarily. 'Which part?'

He looked at passers-by from under his brows. 'Karate boy.'

'Shut up.'

'Sorry. He's a good guy.'

'Yeah, he is. Anyway, what were you doing? You just ... went away.' The memory of those months after he'd gone made her pity her former self, a twenty-one-year-old girl who was small in Dot's mind as though she'd been photocopied on a reduction setting, when really it was the same body she inhabited now, four years on, no different in size. The bricks were damp. She slid off, the edge of the wall scraping against her thighs, and picked at the mossy bits with a thumbnail. The sun shone through stacked, strangely cornered dark clouds, and down the street an empty parking space glittered with window glass, like shattered mentholated sweets.

'It was horrible,' she said. 'When you left.'

'Dottie.' He shook his head. 'I couldn't really handle it.'

'No.'

Their knees were touching. She felt the air between them densely electric. It sent her moral compass on the spin, tocking lazily, directionlessly around as though she would do anything, he only had to say.

Daniel waved at someone down the road and the young man ambled towards them, curly hair and stone-washed jeans, and they raised chins at each other and started talking about the support act for the gig that was on that night. It was a skill she had noted since Daniel's return, that he could pick up with people right where he left off. Dorothy bit into the apple that thank god was in her bag because she was constantly hungry and accidentally dribbled a little bit of juice on her T-shirt, and the boys kept talking and the guilty burn of the cigarette still tingled in her mouth.

Her parents kept laughing, like they just couldn't believe it. Frank would shake his head and say how proud he was and then he'd set himself off again.

'But you're a baby.'

'I'm twenty-five.'

She blamed Michael. Home still at nearly thirty, he had warped their expectations. Dorothy sat between him and their mother on the reunited family sofa, Andrew across the room on a kitchen chair. The doorbell rang and Ruth let Andrew's parents in, each of them with new partners, awkwardly joking from their collision on the doorstep. Dot greeted them and went to sit with Andrew because it was hard for him, everyone in the same room, his defensive father and the sullen policewoman stepmother, his mother overcompensating, her second husband oblivious, his mind on a hiking track somewhere, filled with tussock. 'Lovely,' said Andrew's mother. 'So what time is our booking at Chang's?'

'It's not Japanese, is it? I don't like Japanese food,' said the step-mother, staring at the peace-sign badge on Dorothy's cardigan. 'What is that?'

'She's allergic to fish.'

'It's Chinese. Andrew,' said his mother, 'are you still vegetarian?'

'Yes.'

'A vegetarian!' said the stepmother. 'Whatever happened to a good steak?'

'Arrest me,' Andrew whispered in Dot's ear, and she whispered back, 'Fifteen to life.'

His mother shrugged and laughed around the room. 'And yet he's so tall!'

'Listen, darling,' Lee said to Dot as the Lazy Susan spun clockwise, moving the bowls of pak choi and flecky chilli sauce and pale, glis-tening chicken around, 'let's invite some of the Americans.' Frank was negotiating a possible return to the States. Someone remote had 'passed' and there was more 'moolah rolling about'. Dorothy wished she wouldn't talk like that, as though money wasn't real. Ruth wanted to move with their parents; she had always longed for that place she could not remember. 'They won't come,' Lee said, 'but you've got to invite them.'

'Can I think about it?' She wanted to be a good daughter. But no thanks, none of this I pay, I say. She and Andrew would front the wedding themselves. He'd taken a job in the caretaking division at the polytechnic, since no one was interested in showing or buying his paintings. Everyone had their own definition of survival.

They were interrupted by the ting of Frank's chopstick against his glass. Wine lurched close to the lip as he raised the glass and made a toast to the engaged couple and welcomed Andrew's parents into their family, although he called Andrew's mother by the step-mother's name. She hooted gaily. 'Wrong wife, dear, wrong wife!' Evelyn hid her face behind Dot's shoulder and snorted. Dorothy, the zip of her dress tight up her side, held back the laugh that threatened to rip out.

Andrew lifted his drink. 'Thank you,' he said, cutting Dot's father off from a relaunch. 'Thanks, everyone!' One arm in the air, the other around his fiancée's thickening middle, his lean face lifted, shadowed by the twisty red tassels that hung down.

At some point someone mentioned the new anti-nuclear policy and Andrew's stepmother said loudly, 'Totally ridiculous,' and Frank, who hated any talk of politics, began to sing a tune from *My Fair Lady*. Other diners looked over. 'My family,' Dorothy said to Andrew's father and stepmother, who were acting as though nothing was happening except the urgent need to get a pork bun split between them, the stepmother's chopsticks sawing at the white fleshy dough. On the other side of the round table Michael sat next to the outdoor-enthusiast stepfather, and they were deep in conversation, ignoring the musical interlude too. Andrew's stepfather was a gesticulator, and he flung a hand back into the approaching waiter's white shirt so that the waiter dropped a tray of bowls and everyone startled at the crash apart from Frank, who continued singing without pause. Dorothy and Evelyn helped pick up the broken pieces. The zip on her dress did bust a little bit, she felt it split and straightened up carefully, hands full of china. Andrew's mother bobbed her head along to the song. When it finished she clapped, solitarily. More crispy spring rolls arrived, the wrappers like stiff brown paper spiralled at the ends, and there was the judder of the tinted glass door to the street opening and a wave of cold night air and Daniel was making his way to the table, hands thrust into the pockets of his denim jacket, hair hacked short in a home-made job, scruffy and uneven.

Evelyn flushed. Dorothy saw it. 'Hi,' she said, through a smile that couldn't be controlled.

Lee rose from her seat and embraced Daniel warmly, ruffling his new hair. He sat down next to the stepmother, thrust a hand towards her and said, 'You must be the cop.'

She scowled. 'And you are?'

'I instruct Andrew in the ancient art of karate.' He gave a little bow.

'Shut up, Daniel,' Dorothy said, and made the proper introductions.

'*Oh*,' he said, staring at her waist as though it was finally dawning on him. 'You're *pregnant*.' He nodded at Andrew and half stood from his chair, roughly aiming a congratulatory hand-slap that missed.

Dorothy wondered if he was high. She said to Evelyn, fixed on her sister's pinkness, the way she ran her fingers along her collar-bone while she looked at Daniel as though nobody could see, 'We had the scan today. Andrew wanted it to be just us.' And then Evelyn's sweet smile melted and Dot said, 'I'm sorry. I should have told you. I'm sorry.'

'What are you eating?' Daniel asked. Without thinking Dorothy leaned across the table towards him and held her chopsticks forward, the piece of gingery chicken wedged between them. Her arm outstretched. It was just for a second but she knew the table froze. Family members poised motionless, watching. Daniel held Dorothy's gaze, his eyes dark and steady as he ate the mouthful from her chopsticks.

'Did anyone go to the Queen concert?' Andrew's mother asked.

Quickly Dot sank back into her chair, stared down at her bowl. 'I did,' said Michael.

Daniel went to the bathroom and after half a minute Dorothy followed, but the hand-stained white sliding door to the men's toilet was locked. She thought about knocking. Out of control, she felt *out of control* and wanted to shout those three words through the door. She ducked her head round the corner to see if they were visible, and realised Andrew had a clear sightline to where she stood.

When Dot came out of the women's bathroom Daniel was back in his seat, eating rice with a ceramic spoon. She shifted her mother along and sat next to Andrew, who looked intently at her, then away, with a sharp turn of his head.

'What?' she said.

A chair fell on its side. Andrew's stepmother stood and retched into the potted palm behind the table. She rounded on them, eyes wide, her lips hugely swollen. Hives bloomed from her neck up her cheeks. A terrible noise came from the back of her throat, a hiss like a feral cat, and she pushed the table with the heels of her palms, retching again. 'Fhihh.'

'Oh my god,' said Andrew's father, scrabbling through his wife's handbag. 'Where's your EpiPen?' He tipped the bag upside down and spilled the contents over the table – a lipstick rolled off the edge and onto the floor, a receipt floated onto a plate and absorbed the dark liquid of a beef sauce – then he snatched the pen about the size of a vivid marker and popped the lid and yanked up his wife's skirt and jammed it through the black tights into her leg. A long look at the control-top pants. All of them held still while he counted to ten in one-thousands. The stepmother's breathing came fast and shallow, but the internal war was calming as the epinephrine moved through her blood. Andrew's mother offered her a glass of water and she held it with both trembling hands and drank.

The stepmother and Andrew's father left for the ER and the remaining parents fake-argued about the bill and drove off, stale mints from the duck-egg blue bowl at the till dissolving to granules in their mouths. The restaurant staff stood in their wake holding foil-covered plastic boxes of leftovers, concerned in white jackets.

'Are you OK?' Dorothy asked Andrew. 'I think we better go.'

He slid away from the hand she'd put on his forearm.

Daniel passed the leftovers to Ruth. 'You should take these home,' he said.

'Thanks. Eve? Can you give me a lift?'

Evelyn was the only one with a car. She focused on Daniel's chest as she asked whether anyone else needed a ride home, a hand twisting the rope of her long blonde plait.

'No thanks,' he said. 'I'm into walking after that.'

Dorothy hugged her sisters goodbye and watched them walk away towards the parking building, their matching light sashay, Eve's arm suddenly around Ruth's slim waist and Ruth doing the same thing back, the two of them holding onto each other as they rounded the corner, heads close. *This is what happens*, Dot told herself. *You end up with men. It's normal.*

Michael crossed the road for a soft drink from the all-night service station and the strange girls passing had bare arms and legs and riding-up dresses in the chilly night. Dorothy was saying something, commenting on the short tight dresses, the bare thighs, when without warning Andrew pushed Daniel hard in the chest right there on the street outside the Chinese restaurant. Daniel pushed back. Andrew recovered his balance, lunged and wrapped an ankle around Daniel's. They went down together and for a moment the two of them lay on the pavement violently hugging. But Andrew extricated himself fast, then cursed and kicked their old friend, this waif and stray, in the side as he began to rise from all fours on the ground.

'Stop it,' Dorothy yelled. 'Just stop,' and Daniel scrambled up against the wall outside the restaurant, tiled slippery white below spray-blasted concrete.

Michael jogged across the road between oncoming cars and yelled, 'What the fuck.'

'What are you doing?' Dorothy cried, and Andrew said, 'I know, I fucking saw you,' and he was shaking and strung out. 'I saw you, I know,' and she shouted, 'Saw what, there's nothing to see.'

Daniel examined his palm where it was grazed from the rough concrete wall, and licked it.

Michael pushed Andrew's shoulder and he staggered backwards. A couple of bouncers from the club on the corner approached. Dorothy remembered the time Andrew had sent a random car tyre hurtling down the road; that was how they walked, unexpectedly heavy, not quite in control of their velocity.

'We're good,' Michael said, 'we're OK, thanks.'

'You all right, miss?' one of the big men directed at Dorothy, and when she said, 'Yes. Thanks. Sorry,' they moseyed back to their spots either side of the Irish tavern doors, where bass thumped beneath people shouting to be heard.

Daniel was still, watching them, a couple of fingers now up to his gums as though holding onto something. 'Ha,' he said, and wheezed. A finger came away bloody and he wiped it on his jeans. He shook his head at Dorothy. She moved towards him but his face made her stop. She held out the blue-and-grey plastic inhaler from her bag and said, 'Do you need this?'

'No.'

'Why the fuck,' she said to Andrew.

'Sorry,' he said. He kicked the wall and his foot skidded on the tiles. A gritted-teeth roar came from him and he walked off down the street saying, 'All right, I get it. All right.'

'Anger management,' said Daniel, and Dorothy said, 'Don't,' and after she had half run, half walked down the road after Andrew, Daniel raised his arms priestlike to Michael and said, 'That guy is a master of the fucking obvious.'

Outside her family house, in the passenger seat of Andrew's spray-painted car, Dorothy sat with an arm over her head like a bird's wing, ducked down under the dash. That hard rolling sound was Michael wheeling the rubbish bin back to its spot by the front door. He hadn't seen them. It had to be in and out, get the last of her old stuff and leave. When Lee heard about the fight she rang up to say she was 'very disappointed in Andrew'. It was too late. Dot had chosen. They'd walked all the way home together after the Chinese restaurant and he'd asked her please don't see that guy any more. She peered out, slowly straightening up as her brother double-checked that the front door was locked and headed down the street, away from the car, past the bus stop, to disappear round the corner.

'He's gone,' said Andrew, and he opened his car door and stepped one leg onto the pavement. He held his palm out and Dorothy put her small silver house key in his hand. He entered the house. She exhaled, as nervous as if he were breaking in. Fluffy yellow pollen floated thickly from the plane tree. Dorothy got out and leaned against the car. Sunlight flared off the windowpane of her bedroom upstairs then vanished as Andrew lifted the sash and threw a bundle of her old clothes onto the pavement. Half of them would be too small now that her body was changing. She gathered the things and threw them across the back seat. A bra stuck in the hedge; Dorothy tore out a small branch as she yanked it free. Andrew was the one up there helping her get out and the baby was inside her and Daniel wouldn't be in the house anyway, he didn't live there any more, nor did Evelyn, nor did she. The owner, Osborne, was selling it. The estate agent's sign showed a fish-eye photograph of the front room that made it look larger than it was, and a shot of the house from across the road at night-time, every light behind the plane tree blazing with comfort.

Instinct made her duck as a dark shape fell from the window – a box that bounced and shed its contents over the small front yard – old schoolbooks and childhood stuff – Daniel's exercise books, the kid's microscope Michael had saved up for – 'No,' Dorothy called, but now Michael's guitar landed on the end of its neck, the body thwanging on the ground. 'No,' she shouted. She threw herself into the driver's seat and leaned on the horn. In the silence that followed, the upstairs window closed. Papers and parts of toys had scattered everywhere and Dorothy collected them, hugged them to her, dropped them in the squashed cardboard box, pushed it onto her pile of clothes inside the car. In the driver's seat she pulled the seat belt across and stepped on the clutch and turned the key, shaking.

Andrew appeared by the car window. A moment passed in which the two of them watched each other through the glass. She was afraid of him. And then he was the one who looked frightened. Slowly she released the gearstick into neutral and unwound the window.

'Oh my god,' he said. 'I don't know why I did that.' He knelt on the ground by the car, his eyes red, his voice solid. 'I'll buy a new guitar. Please. Help me take those things back inside. Please, Dorothy. Help me.'

On the other side of the road a neighbour emerged from her front door, pulling her dressing gown tight around her, a telephone receiver in her hand. She walked a step towards them, as far as the cord would allow. Dorothy got out of the car and waved to the woman and called that she was Frank and Lee's daughter, the Forrests' daughter, everything was all right.

5. OUT THERE

THERE WAS NO queue yet for the second chairlift, and Evelyn had the bench seat to herself; it rocked under her shifting weight when she yanked the gloves and hat on and rubbed her ears through the wool. The ski-hut roof was icing white and smooth with snow. Up in the mountains, crumbs of rock faced outwards through the snowfall, dark and bumpy. The last of the pine trees passed beneath her feet. The boots hung heavy with the skis. Behind the sunglasses, her eyes stung and watered.

The chair reached the top and she lifted the bar and skied away before it arced the half-circle for its slow return journey. She kept climbing the slope, cutting the skis horizontally into the gradient, heading for a ridge that snaked upwards to a peak. At the ridge she faced up-mountain and was able to walk directly forwards. Her arms and legs worked hard; inside the ski suit was effort and heat. Her vision filled with the whiteness of snow. She panted heavily, thirstily, and lactic acid seared her muscles, and the slim Vs of her steps in the skis inched closer together until she was shuffling. She pushed on with the poles.

At the top of the ridge, where the ground fell away into a valley that led to another hill, Evelyn rotated the skis like irregular hands of a clock, the ticking spread and smashed in the snow in a five-point manoeuvre until she was positioned to head downhill. She took off the hat and listened to the whistling. Her hot head quickly cooled, the air like fingers through her hair. Velvety blue shadows ran down the side of the ridge's spine. There were the dotted pines below, gathering further down into a white and black forest. And the car park, and the roads out, and very far away the muzzy village, some farmland, a greenness that was probably trees, and a shining fingernail of silver that might have been the edge of a lake, or a stretch of highway hit by the sun, or the tubing of an industrial greenhouse. Above, nothing but the pressure of the sky. For a moment it thudded closely onto her head, onto the speck that she was. She whooped – a ringing shout bounced back off the slopes – pulled the beanie back on, took a breath and launched forwards.

In the late afternoon, Daniel and the boy from the new family stood on the elevated deck of the hut. Daniel's wrists hung over the railing and he held a cigarette between his fingers, the acrid smell drifting on a channel of air, and he and the boy looked out across the snowfields towards the pines. The boy was talking; Daniel smoked and listened, and at something the boy said he barked a short laugh. Evelyn waved up and pushed at her ski buckle with the pole to unclick it. A blast of wind scoured her face. As she entered the hut, Daniel and the boy retreated from the deck. In the shade of the cork-floored entranceway, the drying room and the utility room to either side, their overhead footsteps echoed. A cosy smell of wet wool rose as soon as she levered off the snow boots. The outer socks were thick and tongue-shaped, with a tweed-like pattern, dark around the edges with dissolved snow.

Evelyn stepped around the crusts of ice left by her boot prints on her way into the drying room, where she unzipped the ski jacket and emerged from the waterproof overalls and hung them up next to Daniel's giant orange ski suit, a discarded lobster shell. She ran a hand down the leg of his overalls, the polyurethane coating slightly stiff. Her fingers found something hard halfway down the leg and she slid her hand into the slit of the trouser pocket. She felt a leathery flatness and drew out the small, dried body of Daniel's lucky frog, long dead and tanned by long-gone air. How many years had he kept this?

There was other stuff in the pocket and although Evelyn held the entire frog between her fingers, could see its squashed diamond completeness, a dread passed through her that there would be half a frog left behind. But there was just a scrunkled lift-pass sticker and two barley sugars. Daniel wore his lift pass around his neck; he was so known here that his whole face was a lift pass, and the date on this one was from last year, and the last mountain, before she had caught up with him.

Evelyn had never touched the frog before and this was the first time she'd taken a close look. It had no smell; all she could detect on her fingers was the wet-fleece scent from the inside of the ski gloves. There was the sound of boots being scraped and stamped on the grill outside. The new family came in the door and they smiled, and exchanged hellos in each other's languages. The father pulled his dark blue beanie off and batted snow from it, his fine blond hair sticking out crazily from his head. Evelyn finished pulling the sheepskin boots on and nodded at the family once more before climbing the pine stairs to the body of the chalet. The frog was in her pocket now.

She called a greeting to Daniel and he called back from somewhere in the hut. Evelyn tightened her ponytail and washed her hands under the kitchen tap. While she waited to feel his warmth behind her, to be enveloped in his arms, Evelyn tried to focus on the food. The onions in the wicker basket were firm, golden orbs, crunchy green beneath the skin where the knife sliced in and left pungent milky droplets on the chopping board. At the industrial-sized oven she turned on the dials, stiff with trapped food crumbs, and kept chopping. The chopped onions were soft and translucent in the frying pan. The kitchen smelled of their cooking and of melted cheese. There was a tumbling sound as she tipped dried macaroni into the boiling water, which fizzed up and almost over the rim of the saucepan in a rush of white froth. The salt shaker clogged in the steam. She put the macaroni cheese in the oven and started on the birthday cake. She cut adze-shaped chunks of butter and wiped them off the knife with a finger into a large bowl with a chip out of its rim the size of a fingernail. The fine white sugar poured into a peak on top of the butter, a mountain in the bowl. She sniffed the wooden spoon, which smelled of onions, and scrubbed it under hot water then used it to beat the butter and sugar together hard. The eggs were thick-shelled, hard to crack, with a taut matt skin between each shell and the contents. In

the bowl they created a separated viscous swirl with the creamed-
butter mixture, the yolk trailing through the pale butter, the transparent whites floating jellyishly around the surface. The fragments
of shell were tacky and sharp when Evelyn carried them in cupped
palms to the rubbish bin. She sifted flour and baking powder over
the wet mixture and a fine dust sprayed over the bench, down her
apron and onto the floor. The vanilla essence bottle was empty; she
shook it over the bowl but only that sweet, oozy smell wafted out,
and she threw the bottle over to the bin, and it bounced off the rim
and skittered along the floor.

Daniel was not in the bedroom. Evelyn held the banister and swung
off the top stair to look down into the entranceway: his boots had
gone from the neat row of pairs. In the kitchen she looked at the clustered red heart-shaped strawberries in the plastic punnet the family
had brought with them. In winter! She was over the shock of it now.
    The family was settled in the lounge, the father on a couch
reading to the girl of about eight by his side, the mother and
older girl playing a game at the table. There was the hard rattle of
blocks inside a plastic shell, and the girl flipped a timer. She said,
'OK, Mama, go.' Yellow salt crystals slipped through the timer and
the girl scribbled on her paper, an arm crooked over it so nobody
could see what she wrote.
    'Dinner is ready in half an hour,' Evelyn said, aware as she finished
the sentence that she was speaking English as if it were her second
language, not theirs. She poured the mother a glass of the red wine
she liked and tilted the gin bottle towards the father, who shook his
head. 'Daniel and . . .' the son, the thirteen-year-old. She gestured to

the window, where there was still sun on half of the field of snow, a grey shadow from one of the rises bisecting it.

The father nodded. 'One last run,' he said.

'Thank you,' said the mother, taking a gulp of wine. 'Gut, du fängst an.'

The daughter recited the words she had found, her voice like stiff springs.

Although Evelyn had washed her hands she still felt the frog's body on them, the desiccated skin between the pads of her fingers, the light ridge of bones beneath the skin. It sat in her pocket like a piece of gold. She washed the cooking dishes. Outside the small window, the snow was blue.

In the living room she turned on the lamp, and its warm glow made outside seem darker. 'Thank you,' said the father.

There was some exchange between the children and their parents, and she understood the words *video* and *film*. The girl left the room and the older sister shut her book and followed her. Eve hadn't seen the third daughter; perhaps she was asleep in her bunk. Their mother was holding the edges of the rust-coloured raw linen curtains. She pulled them across a little bit then left them open. 'Die Scheibe ist kalt,' she said.

'Close the curtains,' said her husband.

'Nein, not yet.'

Evelyn levered open the door of the wood burner and added another log. A splinter caught in the pad of her index finger. She pressed at the buried end, faintly visible through the layer of skin like a drawing viewed through tracing paper. In the small bathroom off her and Daniel's bedroom, she took a pair of tweezers from the cabinet and tried to pincer it out, but her left hand didn't have the necessary deftness and the splinter buried further beneath the skin.

In the living room she held out her finger, palm upwards, and the tweezers, to the mother, and said slowly, 'I have a splinter. Splinter? Could you, please?'

The woman nodded and took Evelyn's finger in her own. Her nails were short, without varnish. She pushed at the sides of the finger pad and a micrometre more of the black wood emerged, emphatic as a speck of dirt. The pointed ends of the tweezers delicately gripped the splinter and the woman drew it towards her, and out of Evelyn's body, and held it up into the light. A dot of blood emerged from the skin where the splinter had been. The mother passed the tweezers back, the splinter still stuck to one arm. Evelyn took the finger out of her mouth and said, 'Thanks,' her tongue tasting a little of the blood and the resiny firewood. In the bathroom she wiped the splinter off onto a tissue and put the tissue in the rubbish bag that hung on a hook on the bathroom door, its contents – wilted tissues like flowers, flattened cardboard toilet rolls – visible innards through the transparent plastic. Far off in the mountains behind the hut there was a crack. The sound registered through the back of her head like the soft pop of a neighbour's firework; a long second later she understood what it was.

Evelyn reached behind the gathered curtains, opened the ranch sliders as narrowly as possible and squeezed through into the limpid evening air. Light from the living room cut across the balcony. She thrust her hands into her pockets and felt the frog. The white lights on top of the chairlift pylons glistened with a small bright radius. Rope tow poles on a shallow run could have been skiers crouching in tableau. Down the slope, at the base of the first chair, the ski café lights were still on, an octagonal constellation. She thought of electric fish in the deep. Wind shook over the surface of the ski field like a sheet being thrown on a bed and there was a high, glassy ringing that might have been lift wires or the wind running over the snow.

The door behind her opened and the father said, 'Excuse me, the alarm in the kitchen is tooting.'

In the living room the parents looked expectant. 'Well,' Evelyn said. 'I think we should call the mountain patrol.'

'OK,' the man said, and translated for his wife.

She said, 'Really? No. They're OK.'

'I don't know,' Evelyn said. 'It's getting dark. It's Thursday. There's no night skiing. No lights.' Her voice was growing louder, a function of the language barrier. She tried to moderate it. 'How good a skier is your son?'

The man nodded. 'He's very good. Very accomplished.'

'Right. I shouldn't have said anything. I'm making us all worry for no reason.'

'You are worried.'

'Yes. But Daniel is a good skier too and so. Would you like to eat now, or to wait?'

The man and woman consulted each other. 'Let's feed the children,' he said.

Evelyn was on the phone to the ski patrol when there was a knocking sound from downstairs and Daniel and the boy were down there, in the cold entranceway, the door to the drying room open, ski jackets half off, laughing, stamping feet, the smell of snow on them. 'Where have you been?' Evelyn cried. 'I've been freaking out.'

'Sorry,' Daniel said. 'It was incredible, we had the sweetest run.'

'Fuck that,' Evelyn said, and the boy looked up sharply. 'You can't just do that.'

'I said I was sorry!' He said something to the boy in German and the boy ducked his head as if he wanted to laugh but knew it would be a bad idea. He kept his head low as he followed Daniel up the wooden stairs and past Evelyn, still with the phone in her hand although the patrol coordinator had said, 'All good? My other line's going,' and hung up.

Eve marched to the fire and opened the door and threw the frog in. There. She shut the door, an extra lick of bright flame flaring through the soot-stained glass. The mother beamed at her son and said, 'Wasche deine Hände.'

The boy tucked into his macaroni and cheese and Eve placed the salad lightly in front of him, the vinegary dressing buzzing in the small atmosphere above the bowl. The boy's family watched him eat. He told a story, in German, while he was chewing, spearing creamy blond pasta onto his fork, holding it high while he swallowed. He broke a crusty roll in half and wiped it through the pale green traces of olive oil that pooled on the plate.

Evelyn sieved icing sugar over the birthday cake and poked spiralled candles, miniature barley twists, in a circle around the top and lit them, the first couple of matches snapping at the waist, the smell of phosphorous lingering until the cake was safely ablaze. Daniel turned out the living-room lights and the family breathed in as one and sang the English happy birthday song to their boy. Everyone clapped at the blazing cake. Its candles flickered while the mother and father cleared space in the middle of the table and the father found a woven tablemat in the cabinet drawer.

'Sorry.' Evelyn shook a strand of hair out of her eyes. 'I should have done that.'

The boy leaned forward and blew out the candles and everyone cheered quietly, a hushed happy sound that warmed the whole chalet as though it was crammed full of well-wishers, people standing in every room, giving soft applause for this boy's life.

As they ate, the family's conversation became louder, the children talking over each other, the mother laughing when she had to intervene. The father followed Daniel into the kitchen, where Evelyn was washing the dinner plates.

'Could you take him for another lesson the day after tomorrow? Tomorrow we go to the village. We will spend the day together.'

'Sure. Kein Problem.' Daniel stretched out the red rubber band that held the plastic wrap over the punnet of strawberries. He reached under the wrap and drew one out as though it were a large jewel. The father and Evelyn watched as he opened his mouth and put the strawberry in, twisting the green cap and stalk off with his fingers, while the rest of it was chewed and swallowed.

'Good?' said the father.

'Sehr gut,' said Daniel.

Oh fuck up, Evelyn said, to the sink.

In bed there was the sound of wind shearing the ice, and the noises from the bathroom of Daniel brushing his teeth. He didn't use much water; the brushing was loud and healthy-sounding, like someone eating an apple in your face. The light went out; the room was dark except for a bright line of orange beneath the door.

'Can you turn out the hall light?'

Daniel did, and the room disappeared. The mattress shifted with his weight. He began walking his thumbs between Evelyn's shoulders.

'You can't just be so late when you've got a child with you,' she said.

'He's not a child.'

'He's thirteen. Don't you think they wanted to be with him on his birthday?'

'Sorry.'

'You don't sound sorry.'

He flopped over onto his side, away from her. 'Jesus, I said sorry.'

'You don't sound it. You don't mean it. You make it worse with your fake sorry, how defensive you get.'

'What am I meant to say?'

'You're meant to mean it.'

'OK, I'm sorry I worried you.'

Evelyn stuck her face into the pillow and growled.

Daniel laughed. 'I'm not sorry we had the last run.'

She got out of bed. 'It's not funny.' The air through her T-shirt was sharply cold; her feet froze; she climbed back into bed and under the blankets again.

He cupped a handful of her hair and rubbed a thumb over her hip bone. 'Do you want to have angry sex?'

'No.' It was too long since they'd done it, and always weird when there were people staying. She curled up, facing away, and smoodged her body back into him, his arm slung over her ribcage.

Eve woke in the night to see him sitting on the end of the bed, something in his hand – no, flicking through a pile of something – money. He was counting money. She sat up, pulling the blankets up and her long hair down over her neck to keep warm. 'What are you doing?'

'Just seeing how much I've got left. It's payday tomorrow from the ski school.'

'Looks like you've got loads.' She was pretty sure that wasn't all of it.

'I want to . . .' He folded the bills back into an envelope and put it in his knapsack, the zip loud as he closed it. 'I really want to go to New York. Next. I want to stay there. Get some work, bar work or whatever, go and see your folks upstate, spend some time. I mean, Canada's fine, but.' His gaze went through the knotted pine wall and out into the lightless snow. 'Enough mountains, I want to go and live in a city. I just, I'm not sure how I'm going to do it, that's all.'

'What about –' Later, she wasn't sure where she had got the courage to say it. Daylight would dissolve her: after any more than a moment's thought, Dorothy would have entered her mind, clapped a hand over her mouth, said no. Daniel's face was barely visible. 'I've got citizenship,' Eve said. 'A green card. We could get married.' She felt the silence burn.

'Eve, shh.' He put a hand on her knee. Over the blanket. 'Shh, it's the middle of the night. Let's not make things complicated. You don't mean it.'

She did. 'Goodnight,' she said, and curled up again and was amazed and grateful to succumb quickly to the iron pull of sleep.

In the morning neither of them spoke of it. She got the family ready for their day and Daniel left in his ski gear straight after breakfast. He called up from the snow if she had seen his frog and she stood on the deck and said she couldn't hear him. He turned and skied away, knees bent, legs in close, expert parallel. The family raised their arms in a faceless goodbye salute as they skied down towards the car park with packs on their backs, shouting and laughing amongst themselves, and Evelyn closed the ranch slider against the white sky. The vacuum cleaner was in the cupboard in the utility room and she dragged its dwarfish body around on the end of the snaky hose, sucking at the channels of crumbs and dust all over the cabin until the floor was clear.

In the children's room a tubular bundle of duvet on a top bunk made her heart stop. It looked like a sleeping body. But she had seen the family ski off, all six of them. 'Hello?' she said, and took a quick breath and yanked the duvet aside to make sure. Nothing but a rippled sheet.

She adjusted the bunk mattresses and pulled up the bedding and shook out the pillows, which smelled of scalps. There was a dog-eared paperback on the floor, in German, its pages oxidised yellow, the cover dotted with brown like a liver-spotted hand. In the top drawer were neatly piled thermals and socks sausaged into pairs. Some cash tucked down the side, a small torch. Evelyn turned the head of the torch so it glowed, and waved the dot of white over the ceiling, the walls, the floor, light streaking past the mirror, and blew on it when she turned it off as though blowing out a candle.

Downstairs, she took the washing from the tumble dryer and folded it, picking out clotted dust and peeling away the occasional long single hair. She carried the clothes up the stairs in the latticed plastic basket and distributed T-shirts and knickers and jeans where they belonged. Outside, the snow closed in. The automated service said the chairlifts would stop running at noon. The family might have to stay at a hotel in the village, but in case they made it back Evelyn prepared lasagne. She took her diary out from the bottom drawer in the bedroom and wrote in it.

At noon the lifts creaked to a halt. Eve poured a large neat whisky, the taste abrasive and leathery. The ski-school phone number went straight to the answer service. She called Daniel's mobile, and heard it ringing down the hall and in the bedroom. 'Well that was stupid,' she said.

As soon as she hung up the chalet phone it rang, and she answered expecting a dial tone or the bleeping of a fault, but it was the family's father, his voice warm and close. 'We're stuck down the mountain,' he said.

Through the whiteout the blurry shape of a chair swung high on its cable. 'Do you have somewhere to stay?'

'Yes, we've found a hotel with a hot pool, the children are happy.'

'Good.' Evelyn tightened the screw cap of the whisky bottle and wiped it all over with the apron for stray drops. 'Nice treat.'

'Yes,' he said.

She opened the door of the wood burner onto the smell of

cooled embers, the inside shardy with charcoal. Using the poker she jabbed around in the squeaking ash, but the frog had gone.

'Sorry we won't be back tonight,' he said.

'That's fine. I hope it's good for skiing tomorrow. The fresh fall.' Evelyn found that she was holding her breath to try and hear his breathing. 'Keep in touch,' she said after a moment. 'Let me know when you're going to be back.'

'OK. For sure. Are you going to be all right up there?'

'Oh yes. Fine.'

'Daniel is with you.'

'. . . yes.'

In the living room she swept out the wood burner and took the ashes to the bin in the kitchen. Soot dropped on the floor; she spread it around with a foot so that some disappeared into the sole of her slipper and some dispersed into particles too small to see. She crumpled newspaper and laid kindling on top and lit the fire, crouching before it, watching the pale sticks catch along the edges. The whiteout was complete. Evelyn added a chafed, cylindrical log to the fire. In the kitchen she tore a bread roll in half and stuffed it into her mouth.

Nobody picked up at mountain patrol. She left a message about Daniel, disconnected, then pressed redial and got the answer phone again. Looking out at the wall of white she pressed redial. She opened the door onto the snowstorm and pressed redial again. She shut the door and hung up the phone and went to the bedroom to check Daniel's phone, which registered two missed calls, one from the number here at the hut and an earlier call from a withheld number. The messages inbox stored 340 messages. The hut shook in the wind. Evelyn covered the unbaked lasagne with cling film and put it in the fridge, then washed her hands. She ate another hunk of bread. The oven fan whirred.

The phone rang; the mountain patrol. They asked what time Daniel had left that morning and where he had been going.

'I'm not sure. I was in the kitchen, I guess about seven thirty, eight?'

'Did he say where he was headed?'

'No, I thought he had a class, ski school. Did he show up?'

'We'll check and get back to you. Have you got everything you need?'

The DVDs were kids' cartoons, their covers yellow, orange and purple. The wind howled. Evelyn stood in front of the whisky bottle and looked at it. From the mantelpiece she took Daniel's soft blue bag of tobacco, the slice of apple in the bottom tinged orangey brown, and rolled an amateur cigarette.

Overnight, the storm calmed. Morning came with the sound of graders, a pale blue sky over the curving dunes of snow. Cloud wisps hung below the peaks across the valley, as though the mountains were steaming. The patrol leader stood by his snowmobile and shouted up that they'd found no sign of anyone, not in the back country, not on the black runs or in the valleys.

'A chopper's been out since light. Nothing. But Liam at the school reckons he was headed down the mountain, into town.'

'Yeah. Thanks . . . Daniel left his phone here, so.'

'Maybe he was hitting the casinos, didn't want you checking up on him.'

'No doubt. Thanks, Bernie.'

'We'll send him home soon as anyone lays eyes on him. Might have been an all-nighter.'

'Ha ha.'

There was a clunk and grind and the patroller turned to watch the chairlift swing into action. Red- and yellow-coloured figures, riding on the air, skis pointing upwards. 'Incoming,' he said.

Evelyn left a note for the family with heating instructions and a promise to be back after lunch. She placed it under the whisky bottle, which she turned on an angle as though that might make a difference to how much was left. In the bathroom she took a couple of painkillers, the tablets' smooth coating momentarily sweet, and washed her face with warm water. She checked Daniel's phone again but there was nothing new and she tossed it back on the pillowy white duvet. Evelyn went downstairs to put her overalls and parka and hat and ski boots on and finally the gloves. About two inches of new snow was piled outside the front door. She lifted her feet in a small march through the powder to the rack, and her skis. A thick length of melting snow slid through the slats in the deck.

6. MOJO

WHAT SHE THOUGHT of as her *situation*, a sleeping bag on her boss's couch, no utility bills in her name, still living out of the knapsack that had accompanied her travels, Evelyn felt most keenly when visiting Dot. It was all very well being penniless and heartbroken and back in her job at the florist's as though the past months had never happened, but the romance faded at her sister's rented house miles from anywhere, ages on the bus to a neighbourhood of charity shops and the TAB, here in the constant turn of the washing-machine drum, the bottles forever sterilising on the stovetop. In this family home she was an alien, the night's adventures clinging like foreign gas. Dorothy welcomed her, happy to have adult company that came without judgement, but Evelyn wished she would for once finish a sentence. Half the times Dot went to Grace there wasn't anything the matter, and if she was being fed, or changed, or entertained, the conversation inevitably dwindled, funnelled into the baby's endless need. It was a surprise of the mildly unpleasant kind, how time-consuming this small creature was, and Evelyn couldn't help but suspect, punnishly, that Dottie milked it, let every spill and leakage require maximum clean-up, burped the baby at length, hand-scrubbed a square of muslin and pegged it out after a single use, because it was a way of occupying time. What else was she going to do, home all day long in the new-mum smock costume she had taken to wearing?

Andrew would come back from work each night and kiss his wife and cuddle the baby then disappear into the garage where his painting was set up.

'Is it me?' Eve wondered, and Dottie said, 'No, it's not you. He needs to do some painting every day. It keeps his head together.'

'Like the karate.'

'Yes.'

'Whatever it takes.'

'Yes.'

Sometimes they met in a café and just as Dorothy's pot of tea or heated-up pie was served Grace would squall until Dot, refusing Eve's help, took her outside. Mostly Evelyn wound up eating and drinking alone, reading the newspaper or watching her sister pace the footpath as she joggled the baby, and then Dot would flurry in all apologies and close to tears, slurp her tea, have a mouthful of cake and announce she had to go.

Despite being a colonised baby domain, some weeks Dorothy's house was the only really human place Eve found herself. She had to admit that her social life was out of control. She also had to admit that social life was a euphemism. Her random fucking was out of control. They lived in a small place. Sooner or later she was going to fuck her way into a corner and would have to leave town. This was what she said to her sister one afternoon in the tiny back garden, Grace fatly in her nappy on a blanket, eating pieces of cut-up peach with her fingers, crawling to swipe at the Disney ball and watch it roll.

'A corner,' Eve said. 'I can see it. There will be no one left.'

'Well why are you doing it? I worry about you.'

'It's not that bad. I'm exaggerating. One day I'll meet someone lovely.'

'Not in a bar.'

'Dorothy, nice men go to bars too. Anyway, I met this guy last night who was really sweet and so funny –'

'And that's another thing, you always go to their place. What if some psycho? It's completely self-destructive.'

'Do you want to hear the story or not?'

Of course Dorothy did. At least one of them was having a life. Andrew worked until six every night and early in the morning he went to the gym. More than anything in the world she hated that gym. No, perhaps she hated karate more than the gym, because that was what he did there. If Andrew didn't do karate, if he didn't go to the gym, he got strung out, so she tried to love karate, but mostly she tried not to drink alone. 'Go on,' she said. 'Nothing too grisly.' More than once Eve had recounted some sexual disaster explicitly as she held the baby in her arms, which made Dot wince although Grace was too young to understand.

'I might be off intimate detail for life.' Evelyn went on to tell Dot how this man had talked non-stop, how he constantly described what he was doing to her or worse, what she was doing to him – 'You're squeezing my balls' – until it had stopped being amusing and gone way past turning her on. He kept going even when she asked him point blank to stop. Finally, after 'I'm reaching for the condom' she'd jumped out of bed and yelled 'LA LA LA' in his face.

'What did he do then?'

'He asked me to leave. So I did – "I'm pulling my knickers on now, I'm getting into my jeans, you're lying on the bed staring, I'm looking for my shoes, I'm not giving you my phone number, you're storming out of the room, you're slamming the bathroom door, I'm picking up my bag, I'm LEAVING YOUR HOUSE." '

'Shh.' Dot gestured at the fence, the closeness of the neighbours. 'And what does Kimiko think? When you come home at three in the morning?'

'I'm very quiet. I'm a good girl, Dot. She doesn't mind as long as I'm at work on time.'

'Fresh as a daisy.'

'Ha.'

'Seriously, you should be careful.' An aeroplane inched across the sky. Dot looked at her sister, the tawny hair, the energy rising off her like tendrils of smoke, her undeniable fuckability, and said, 'Do you regret coming back?'

'Not yet. Sometimes. Yes. It's only been a few months but it's been like forever.'

'You know Daniel's in South America. Guatemala or something. Or is that Central? He sent a postcard, don't tell Andrew. Wait, I'll get it.'

The mention of his name made Eve want to rip a hunk of grass from the earth. This could not be done, and nothing could be said to her sister. Better to bury Daniel because face it, she'd had no right to him and she'd wanted him for so long and followed him across the world and by anyone's standards she probably deserved to have him leave her but she could never, never tell Dot. How to know whether the secrecy – really the *lying* – came from love, or shame, or the sheer envy of having been the one left out by those two for all that time? They'd never talked about it but she *knew*, like she knew about Michael being a pot fiend when their parents insisted it was just that he was shy. Could she judge whether or not Daniel had been worth it? She was frightened that, if she looked in her heart, she would discover that he was, and would have to face up to what that meant, now he was gone. 'Actually, I should get home. I'm on dinner. What should I make?'

'Pasta? I don't know, you're the cook.'

'Yeah. Daniel doesn't send me postcards.' Partly it was what Dorothy would expect to hear, if she were to maintain the pretence, and partly it was true, and it hurt, and it felt good to say it.

'He probably doesn't know where you live. How would he know where you are?'

Dot's voice had risen the way it did when she felt defensive. Huh. Eve lifted Grace high in the air and drew her in, giggling, for kisses and cuddles. 'Bye bye, lovely one,' she said.

Grace stopped laughing. She gazed over Eve's shoulder and said, 'Bye bye.'

Dorothy's hand flew to her mouth.

'Oh my god,' said Eve.

'Did you hear that? Say it again.'

'Bye bye,' Evelyn said, and Grace said, 'Bye bye, Evie.'

'She's talking!'

The baby girl looked from her mother to her aunt and back again with a wide crescent smile, amazing connections firing in her brain. 'Bye bye.'

7. DANDELION CLOCK

ON THE DRIVE to the cabin the sky began to set and darken, the colour of wet concrete. Rain prickled the windscreen. 'Great,' said Andrew. 'Stuck inside with the perfect robot child for a week.'

Dorothy squeezed his leg, the hard muscle above his knee, and moved her hand up his thigh a bit. 'I like these jeans.'

'Hello,' he said.

'Hi.' She kissed his shoulder. In the back seat Amy, the baby, started to cry. 'I'm thirsty,' said Grace, and Dorothy swivelled around to pass her the king-size Schweppes bottle filled with water. Grace dropped it and Dot unbuckled her seat belt and said to Andrew, 'Don't crash,' and squeezed through the gap between the front seats to the back and sat with one hand stroking the side of the baby's breathtakingly soft face and the other hand propping up the bottom of the heavy bottle so that Grace could drink from it. 'Lou's only little,' she said to Andrew. 'Give her a chance. She'll turn weird and difficult soon enough.'

'You're probably right,' said Andrew. 'Look at the parents.'

'Do you mean Aunty Eve and Uncle Nathan?' said Grace.

'No,' said Dorothy, hitting Andrew in the arm. 'We're talking about someone else.'

'Lou means toilet,' said Grace.

'It's a pretty name,' Dorothy said. 'Be nice.'

Things had changed for Grace with the baby's arrival. Maybe it was the week Dot spent away from her, with bird-like, premature Amy in the NICU. Maybe it was simply the fact of another child. The parenting books had a lot to say about introducing new siblings. The word *sibling* was deceptively bloodless. Grace threw stuff and she wouldn't take a daytime sleep. She railed against the wind or the sun or the straps on her pushchair and she let food fall half chewed from her mouth and always removed her clothes and shoes once she'd been dressed. She liked being read to, and attempting skew-whiff jigsaw puzzles and perching on the kitchen bench while Dorothy baked, and she liked sitting up against her mother's side while she breastfed the baby and hitting her lightly in the face.

An electronic jazz riff on the radio announced a traffic report and Andrew turned it up and the newsreader said that a tropical storm was heading east and could develop into a hurricane. Residents were advised to prepare hurricane kits and a flash-flood warning was issued. 'Motherfucker,' said Andrew.

'What do we do?'

'Everyone's still driving.' It was true; the traffic out of town had slowed but all three lanes were moving, the red and yellow car lights glistening through the grey rain.

The car shook in the wind as it edged forward and the windscreen was a blur, carved by the metronome of the wipers, the shifting of water from side to side. The traffic slowed to a crawl and Dot said to Andrew, 'OK really don't crash,' and undid the clasp over Amy's belly and lifted her into her arms and rucked up her T-shirt and clicked the plastic toggle to release the cup of her bra.

'This is my one fucking week off, man,' Andrew shouted at the traffic.

'Hold my hand, Mummy,' said Grace, and once the baby was plugged into that rhythmic sucking and the milk was drawing from all the way under Dot's arm, through the breast and into Amy's mouth, the fine hair at the nape of her neck damp with sweat, she could free a hand and find Grace's palm.

Nathan's newspaper said that the storm might move further east and pass them, that there might not even be lightning and thunder, no need for the canned food, torches, extra nappies and colouring-in books they'd picked up on the way. He showed them a satellite image of the storm, a startling spiral with a tiny hole at its centre through which you could imagine seeing the surface of the earth, the whorl around the eye terrifying to look at, a pocket-size image of force, magnetic suction, and Andrew said, 'Come on, how is that not a hurricane.'

'Maybe we're just out of its path,' Nathan said. 'No radio range so we just got to wait and see.'

'Nathan,' Dot said, touching his upper arm, 'I'm so sorry about your father.'

He nodded. 'Thanks. Yeah, it's been rough on my mum.'

Evelyn came out of the bedroom, closing the door quietly behind her, and crossed the room on tiptoe towards them, streaky blonde hair tumbled over her shoulders, smudged eyeliner, bare feet and a long cotton sundress. Beside her, Dorothy could feel Andrew tense up, and she was conscious of her nursing bra, coffee-stained T-shirt, the roll of flesh over her waistband. Eve whispered, 'Louisa's asleep,' and opened her arms wide to embrace Dot and the baby on her hip in slow motion, her touch like feathers.

The pool was a natural crater in some rocks, sealed roughly in patches with concrete, filled with rainwater and sterilised with salt. The rocks were mossy. Even for an adult it was hard to clamber out, pulling up on the slippery round edges that sloped too gradually for hands and feet to get any real purchase. Rain pocked the irre-sistible surface. The water was the temperature of blood, warmer than the air above. After the first dip Dorothy emerged on all fours, knees bright red from the effort of gripping the rock.

'Primordial slime,' Nathan said. 'You're like the first stage of mammalisation.'

'Is mammalisation a word?'

'Mammalial.'

'That might be something to do with breasts.'

'Oh yes.'

Dot wrapped herself in a towel and sat on the covered porch watching the rain come down, and Grace came and sat on her knee, the child's head fitting perfectly underneath her mother's chin.

They were on hyper-alert about the kids: Grace, Louisa and even Amy, although she could not yet crawl. The fence had to be locked at all times. At least one adult per child. No running on the wet rocks. Don't give them water wings, a polystyrene flutter board, they won't ever learn to float. Everyone knew someone who had let the child run ahead to the water, who had gone back to answer the phone, whose pool gate had swollen in the rain and wouldn't shut properly, who had been helping another child with a grazed elbow that needed sterilising when – And the images were there and you couldn't erase them and it was then that you wondered why have the children in the first place, loss was too possible, you can't be a parent, surely this can't be what a parent is?

The men cooked, raggedy T-shirts beside the barbecue, smoke gathering under the awning, a current of air drawing it out and dispersing it over the pool. The storm had passed and the atmosphere felt rich, charged with negative ions as though just breathing it could get you high. After a few wines Evelyn said to Dot, 'I thought Andrew was a vegetarian?'

'Used to be.'

'That was a cool thing for him to do. Brave. I mean anyone can be a vegetarian now. Except Nathan.' She drained her glass and poured another one, started in on that.

'How are things?'

'Great! How's Andrew's work?'

'The caretaking, or the painting?'

'. . . Both.'

'He's doing abstracts now.'

'It's great that he keeps with it.'

Dorothy bit her thumbnail. 'What are you thinking about any

more kids?' she asked. 'Louisa's so gorgeous. She's being lovely with Amy.'

'To be honest,' Evelyn said, 'I'm not sure. Nate would like to have another but I don't get why he's so keen.'

'Maybe, since his dad . . . ?'

'I don't know.' Her vague voice, the habitual hand over her mouth. 'Sometimes I wonder if it's better to just have one kid and try to do that right.'

'Bit late for me now,' Dot said. Her breasts hardened and ached; she pressed down on them before milk could spot her new sundress. Was the baby alive? Ah her brain.

Through the shambles of early parenthood Eve had retained her knack of making things lovely, wild flowers pluming from a milk jug, herbs scattered over the salad. Their mother's floating-skirts phase was in here somewhere, but Eve's grace was her own. Yet even though she and Nathan touched each other, kissed in passing with an ease and enthusiasm Dorothy envied, and even though they had Louisa, a seamless child, Evelyn carried this twisting, claret undercurrent, the thing that set her finger tapping on the table when her husband told a story.

Standing now, Eve supported herself with a palm on the table before, Dorothy knew, she would walk unevenly to the fridge for another bottle.

'Did I ever tell you about that guy I caught trying on my knickers?'

Dorothy laughed so suddenly she spat some wine. 'No.'

'Yeah, well he had erection issues which he said were my fault, demoralising et cetera, and we started using sex toys and then he tried using his Sega Light Phaser on me. You don't recover from that. As a couple, I mean. But he wasn't the worst, there was one, ohohoho no. No no no no no. But at least he could have straight sex, not like those ones that will only –'

'Come on, girls, it's ready,' Nathan called.

Evelyn leaned into Dot. 'He doesn't like me to talk about the past,' she said. 'He likes to think I was a virgin, like him.'

Dorothy couldn't wait to get alone with Andrew.

'His Sega?'

'Mark III.'

'You're shitting me.'

'Mate, I shit you not.'

Sometimes they talked like people they were not. Language just came out their mouths, it didn't belong to them.

'Where are my war stories, man,' Dot complained. 'You never fuck me in your karate gear. What's the name of that move? Crushing the demon?'

He stopped laughing. 'That's different.'

'I was joking.'

'OK. I get it. But.'

'Seriously.' She turned away from him in the bed and spoke it to the darkness. 'We're running out of kindness. If we don't have sex soon we're going to be fucked.'

'Yeah I want to, I do.' That tone in his voice, like he was trying to convince himself.

'Are you really going hunting tomorrow?'

'Have to. Otherwise Nathan will think I'm some kind of pansy who can't bonk his wife or shoot a boar.' Sleepily, he murmured,

'At least he doesn't make me feel like I've got the most boring job in the world.' Nathan was an accountant. Dorothy reached an arm back to pat Andrew's hip. Yes, he was the one in her life.

Rain truckled outside, heavier drops collecting and falling from the guttering. It was time to go and check whether the baby had a pulse and whether the blanket was too close to her mouth.

The mothers took the children for a walk over some fields, Louisa staggering ahead beside the hedgerows, Grace issuing orders from her pushchair, the baby strapped against Dorothy's chest. Around dawn the rain had stopped and the green world glistened. Water hung in the cow parsley, the same colour as the thin circle of moon Louisa was calling to. Mud tugged at their feet. On a hill a clutch of crows burst from a tree like black stones. Dot pulled at the corduroy baby sling to make sure Amy's maroon lips were parted, put a finger in front of them to feel the short hot exhale of her breath.

'Keep pushing,' Grace shouted in her cracking voice. Everything around them was part of the same feeling but Dot could only see one element at a time – the moon, the high bird, the nodding flowers – and tried to take them in all together, sense how the parts melded into this hot noticing, this sweating under the weight of the babies, the sun bearing down.

'Keep pushing, stupid lady.'

'Grace,' said Evelyn, 'don't talk to your mother like that.'

'It's OK,' Dot said. She stepped back from the buggy, fingers red and puffy from gripping the handle, and sat on the damp earth, lay down on her back so that the baby was balanced on her chest, the straps of the sling falling loose. The grass bore her weight until the world turned and she could feel herself hanging upside down in space, glued to the underside of the earth. 'I don't care, she can say what she likes.'

'Yes but you should care.'

'Yes but I plainly don't.' Dorothy plucked the soft transparent sunburst of a dandelion head. 'This place reminds me of the commune.'

Evelyn was silent for a moment, then she said, 'Have you heard from Mum lately?'

'No. Grace's birthday.'

'Sometimes it amazes me that everything I'm going through with Lou, the intensity, the attachment, the way they take over your life, the sort of *total love*, she had with all of us. It's so odd when you can't remember it. Ever sitting with her the way you sit with Grace. We must have seen her pregnant with Ruth, and feeding her, and bathing us and all that, but I don't remember it. Do you?'

'No. We were too young to have memories.'

'But even later.' Eve removed her fingers from her lips and gave a little smile, a conscious effort to brighten. 'She was good at helping us with our homework and stuff.'

'I think she was different with Daniel. Close, or whatever.'

'Oh my god what a gorgeous day.' The words erupted from Evelyn with bizarre energy, and she flung her arms to the sky as if to jump forward in time.

Dot sat up and made a cushion for the baby out of the padded sling, unclipped her bra and began to feed her. Thank god.

Eve laughed. 'You look like a gypsy.' She drew a camera from her overstuffed daypack and snapped a picture of Dorothy as she squinted up at her, mouth open, nose wrinkled, before understanding that her sister wasn't going to photograph the view.

The baby wouldn't sleep; there were mosquitoes in the room and Dot held her under a square of muslin while Eve grated carrots for the salad. The men came in from shooting wild goat and sat on the grass untying their muddy boots. Later, back in Auckland, an envelope would arrive from Nathan containing photos of them both on quad bikes with brown hairy carcasses, hides intact but split and hollowed dark in the middle, roped on board. For now the meat hung in the local farmer's cool store; the cabin did not have enough refrigeration. Dorothy kissed Andrew.

'Why are you looking at me like that?' he said.

'I'm studying your face for signs of blood lust.'

He smiled sheepishly and shrugged. 'Yeah?'

'Yeah.' She kissed him again. 'We should – you know. Later. I'm going to go and check on Grace.' After all the day's anger the girl lay stonelike in bed, immobile as her mother leaned closer and closer, as she reached a finger to stroke her cheek – was it cold? too cold? Could that pillow fall on her?

Dot leaned in the doorway by the pool, the baby hot against her neck, Amy's long body so sweet in the rabbit suit, her legs dangling bare and warm from the dry, light nappy.

'. . . like what,' Andrew was saying, 'like that's because you're just looking for an end, for an end to your single life. I don't know, married, it's one way of living.'

Nathan laughed.

'I mean, as soon as you have a wife and a kid this whole world opens up. Sexy airhead mothers. Pre-school teachers, nurses.' The evening light was going, the pool spread darkly in front of him. Soon Dot would light the outdoor candles, but not yet. 'The midwife that delivered Amy gave me her number. How sick is that!'

Dorothy laid the sleeping baby down in her travel cot and went to join the others playing drunk touch-rugby by the pool. Andrew tackled her to the ground and Nathan leapt on the grass next to them both and wrestled the ball out of her arms, banging her breast with his elbow. It burned. She kicked out at him and he ducked away and Dot charged up and went in low and pushed Andrew into the pool, roaring. He crashed into the water and came up coughing, laughing, and called out, 'Watch it or I'll root you with my Joy Pad.' The greeny dark night spread flat, a sheet held taut by two people. Andrew disappeared under the surface again in an ostentatious, teenage-boy plunge. Bubbles rose. Dot turned around, taking a few moments to get her balance and see Evelyn in the night, where she was, she and Nathan hanging in space, their feet just touching the ground.

'That's great,' Evelyn said to Dot, or Nathan said to Evelyn. Dot was confused. Soon after that Eve and Nathan went inside. Dot looked down at the oily surface of the pool, the mossy rocks, and imagined engineering a moment with her sister as she rinsed the dishes, finding the right words to say to brush away the indiscretion. But when she followed them inside the cabin was empty and all the doors off the living room were closed. Andrew came to bed smelling of beer and waterweeds, leaving the sheets damp wherever he turned over.

★ ★ ★

Early in the morning Dorothy sat with her legs in the pool, kicking slowly, her body the same temperature as the water, walking in space. The cabin was quiet and glowed in the lemony light that the sun cast over the garden, the outdoor tables and chairs, the slippery rocks. Over towards the edge of the property, silhouetted eucalypts stretched dark explosions of leaves into the sky. She'd pumped off the milk that might have gotten laced with wine, though if Amy had drunk it maybe she would have slept better. Thinking of the baby made her afraid of everything that could go wrong. She knew in her heart it must have been her fault Amy was so ill when she was born. They were still only inches away from that having happened. She let the fear in, sweating, and then it passed.

Dot was going to make coffee when Grace came out of the bedroom, pulling at the sticky tabs on the sides of her nappy. 'Morning, darling,' she said.

Grace dropped the nappy on the floor and walked on, naked. Dot picked it up and found a plastic shopping bag for it and tied a knot in the top and shoved it to the bottom of the kitchen bin, past the scrapings of last night's salad and spaghetti. She went back to the veranda and saw Grace walking straight towards the pool. 'Grace,' she called. The child sat down on the edge and tipped herself forward and disappeared.

Under the water Grace sat cross-legged on the bottom of the pool, her face a surprised O, her body shimmering and pink. She was all Dot saw, just sitting there, chubby and wavering, as she lunged through the heavy water to reach her. Grace was easy to grip onto and they emerged together. Dot sat her on the edge and scraped herself out to sit next to her. Grace's chest moved up and down. She was breathing. Dot clambered to her feet, her body very heavy, and lifted her daughter and held her upside down. She was breathing normally. There was nothing else to do. A towel was draped over a deckchair and she swaddled Grace in it and carried her to the veranda where they sat on the painted wooden floorboards, breathing. Dot's eyes stung from the salt water. She wiped away the blood that ran from her calves, mixing with the pool water and threading down over her veined feet. Behind them the house was quiet.

'The thing is,' Evelyn said later from the pool, where she was breast-stroking lazy, sensual laps, 'if you don't get Grace's behaviour under control she's going to take it into kindy and school, and she's going to have a real problem making friends.'

'But she's only like that with me.'

'And you're OK with that.'

'No, but I am too tired to do anything about it.' Jesus damn it. The baby was fine now, she wasn't meant to play that card. Dorothy called over to the veranda, where Andrew had the baby on his hip. 'Does she need a feed?'

'How are you two going?' Evelyn was giving her The Gaze, and Dot wondered how they had come this far. The urge to tell her sister about Daniel's latest postcard was physical in her mouth, as though the words themselves were made of pebbles or candy, but she restrained it, knowing Eve didn't like to hear news of him from her. His postcards, from Paris now, arrived like bullets in the post. Randomly, sometimes not for two or three months, then one a week, even two in a day, short notes, funny, pissed off, a simple update. Often the messages were so cryptic she doubted her ability to decipher the handwriting: *Dozen oranges hurled at me today. Frank would approve.* What mattered was not so much the message as the sending. From the other side of the world, speaking and dreaming in a different language, he still thought of her.

'What about teaching?' Evelyn asked.

'Maybe. One day, yes. I mean, we need the money, but then we'd have to pay childcare and it basically costs as much as I would earn.' She had a gut feeling that Amy wouldn't be her last baby; babies were what she wanted, and Andrew too, but paying for them was the trick. He had vowed to get out of the polytech's caretaking division and find an art gallery by the end of the year. Even if he sold a painting. Just one. 'Evie,' Dot said. 'It's hard, isn't it?'

Her sister leaned her chin on her arms, which were folded over the edge of the pool, ghostly legs kicking slowly far beneath her. Water slicked her hair back from her face and you could see she was older, lines at the corners of her eyes and mouth. Evelyn and Nathan lived in the eastern suburbs, with a sea view, in a bigger house. It was the way things were. 'Mmm,' she said. 'Nathan's been so *angry* since his father died.'

'Really? I haven't seen it.'

'Well, I know Andrew's got his mood issues.'

Dorothy lay on her stomach, propped up on an elbow, close, and reached the other hand into the water, fanning the weighty liquid with her fingers. 'Hey,' she said, 'I'm sorry about the whole Joy Pad thing.'

'That's OK.' Evelyn crinkled a smile, water in her eyelashes. 'We're all grown-ups here.'

She pushed off and then there were the soft sounds of her

moving through the water, Andrew talking nonsense to the baby, Nathan and Louisa playing a game passing leaves back and forth like money. Maybe Eve was right about Nathan's anger. Everybody knew someone who'd been in the room you never wanted to go into. Whether it was cancer or what, there was a room, and it was bad enough but it was nowhere near as bad as the room you didn't come out of. The room they took the families into, to tell them the news. There was an actual door, she'd seen it. Painted grey, with the words *FAMILY ROOM* in metal letters by the handle.

Something heavy landed on Dorothy's back, pressing her breasts painfully into the ground. Her daughter. Grace's knees were in her shoulders, her forearms around Dot's throat, choking her mother's windpipe. Dot rolled to the side but the girl clung on tight. 'Mummy, Mummy,' she rasped in her kitten voice.

Pulling back onto her haunches, scraping her already-scraped knees, Dot swung Grace round into her arms and held her there. 'Baby,' she said, and Grace smiled up at her, gaps between her square little teeth, her face so open, needing nothing but love. 'You're my mummy,' Grace said.

Together on the ground beside the pool they rocked back and forth. Grace's arms were short and squeezy in Dorothy's brown, bevelled grown-up's arms. From the other side of the pool Louisa and Nathan waved, and though Dot couldn't focus that far, in her mind there were the blue eyes of her sister's child, bluer than the sky, or the pool, or the Mexican drinking glasses on the mosaic table, just watching them calmly.

'Baby girl, baby girl.' Dorothy held Grace and caressed her hot cheek, her damp hair.

8 . STORIES

THE TEXT ON the questionnaire swam and blurred as Evelyn looked at it, or at the air that hovered above it. She'd thought the run-through with the press officer's secretary, the woman who would be her immediate boss, had covered everything. It wasn't much of a job, for god's sake. Obediently she'd sat by the desk waiting for the interview and watched the door handle turning, the door opening a crack. In the corridor the secretary conducted a loud, careless conversation with a colleague – 'I'm recruiting the phoners, you wouldn't believe how many people want to do it, such an exciting job, *not.*' Evelyn thought, then, of the photocopied paper notices that had begun to appear nailed to trees and lamp posts in her neighbourhood advertising jobs for housewives, work from home, earn \$30 per hour, surely a figure of complete bullshit. Who rang those numbers? Data entry, cold calling, persuading people to be surveyed. Her sister would do it, but Dorothy was out of her gourd on oestrogen, progesterone, always with the baby at her breast or another one on the way.

The secretary had come in sipping coffee from a polystyrene cup, then biffed it in the wastepaper basket, the rim stained with her lipstick, the bitter smell drifting over, making Evelyn's mouth water. She'd folded her hands in her lap and smiled at the woman, jumped through the hoops.

And then this arrived in the mail a week later and required her signature before the job could be formally offered. The document ran to seven pages. There was new stuff here.

'How're your taxes?' the secretary had asked, and Evelyn laughed. Nathan was an accountant. He did TV producers, musicians, people who paid at the last possible minute, and he was not grand enough that he could fiddle things. For all his bad Hawaiian shirts he wouldn't dream of filing a late return or failing to include every taxable penny paid to his assistant.

'And this gap in your employment history?'

Explained of course by Louisa, now at school, enabling this model mother, this parent helper, yes, the secretary could see the list of relevant although unpaid volunteer experience, to return, usefully, to the workforce. 'I used to be a florist.'

'And what is it about the candidate that makes you want to serve him?'

Evelyn had prepared for this. She wanted to live in a world – no, world was too loose, too New Age – she wanted to live in a society where the small had as much weight as the big. As much importance. Maybe the candidate stood for the same values? She wanted to play a role. Besides, her friend Tania already worked for him and had told Evelyn this would be an in.

'Have you ever been hospitalised? If so, for what condition?' Tonsils, at thirteen. Done less and less these days, isn't it? The secretary had a daughter who suffered, rounds of antibiotics every winter, but the doctors refused to whip them out. *Penicillin aller-gies, me too.* They both knew the words Erythromycin, quinsy. Eve remembered her mother in the chair by her hospital bed, the bliss-ful rarity of having Lee all to herself.

'And have you ever been treated by a psychiatrist or psycholo-gist? If so, for what condition?'

No, she had not been treated for drug addiction or alcohol-ism. No, there was no health-related reason she might not be able to perform the job of telephoning people for donations. Driving violations, only parking. Violations were not going to be a problem. Minor violations.

And the credit report was fine, and she had never been arrested. Evelyn fought the shameful urge to reveal her father's subterranean credit rating, those Ministry of Justice envelopes, the embossed crest against her fingers. In some unspoken way his failure was the children's fault. Proof: now that Frank, Lee and Ruth lived in the States, they were fine. Survivors, no longer pulled under by the thrashing octopus of family.

Yes definitely, the interview had gone well. Her stockings hadn't laddered, she had pitched the political details right, and that evening she'd sat with Nate on the back steps, distant clouds under-lit a brilliant peach by the low sun, and believed she was entering the world again, coming back into her own skin after five years of being nothing but a mother. A mother, *a mother*, she scolded herself, not *nothing but*. Soon there'd be a phone call – 'Come in, get started, you're just who we need!' – but instead here was the final-stage questionnaire, letter-headed, watermarked paper, beneath her hands on the kitchen table, a thick black line at the bottom of the seventh page waiting for a verifying signature. Please return along with all relevant documentation. She slid it back into the white A4 envelope, also bearing the insignia of the candidate's office, and folded the lip of the envelope down. But since the flap had been opened, the glue had dried up and left chewy little traces and it would not stick.

On Sunday they went with friends to Mission Bay, the water warm enough to paddle in, shelly orange sand sticking in tide-marks along the edges of their bare feet. Nathan and Louisa threw pebbles into the sea. A bird strutted up to Evelyn, all sinew, and thrust its face towards her. It batted huge wings and hopped at the sandwich in her hand. She lifted it above her head but the bird kept coming, ruffling and jumping at her, and Eve shrieked and threw the sandwich away and the bird followed it, every-one laughing. Later, when the others had run back to the play-ground, Nathan asked what stage the application was at. Evelyn's hair striped about her face. 'Still waiting,' she said, pulling a strand from her mouth, 'for them to send that final questionnaire.'

If you keep or have ever kept a diary that contains anything that could suggest a conflict of interest or be a possible source of embarrassment to you, your family or the candidate if it were made public, please describe.

That night they made love. Drifting into the relaxed, soft-limbed sleep that followed, Evelyn knew, from friends and their problems, that their married sex life was a kind of luck. If Nathan cared about his male pattern baldness and his bad posture, she didn't. Like Dorothy, she had married a provider, no accident. Of course Andrew was permanently pissed off about that role. A small, sharp feeling turned over in Eve's gut. She had to admit life was easier now that she was more happily married than Dot, who kept having babies to plug that gap, the love gap. The unworthiness of that feeling burned for a moment before she willed her mind away.

Then as though her subconscious was playing a joke, getting her back for the smugness about her marriage, she dreamed about Daniel on the mountain, and she stood on the snow and he leaned forward from the gently rocking chairlift and kissed her, in that way that Nathan never could.

Evelyn was walking from the bathroom to the kitchen behind Louisa, brushing her daughter's hair as she tried to pull away, when Nathan called out, 'Is this about the job?'

He had the questionnaire in one hand and a piece of toast in the other. The top kitchen drawer, a no-go zone full of Sellotape and miniature wooden pegs and zoo passes on lanyards and mosquito spray and emergency candles and vivid markers and sunglasses and gift ribbon and keys, where she had hidden the questionnaire, was open. 'I thought they hadn't sent it yet?'

The radio news presenter was talking about him, the candidate Evelyn wanted to work for, and she said, 'Shh,' hoping to hear something to use in the final final interview, assuming there would be one, assuming they would get over this questionnaire issue. But it was just an item about polls. The job had nothing to do with polls; it was entry-level donation hunting, removed from the candidate by six or seven layers, depending on whether or not you counted the press secretary's secretary as a superior. But there was still this process. She had to be legitimate. Nobody wanted a diversion.

Nathan handed the questionnaire over. 'We should do this tonight. You've got to get back to them sharpish.'

After a late-morning bike ride along the waterfront, *just because she could*, Evelyn went upstairs, drew down the rope ladder from the ceiling and climbed up it, swinging from side to side until she found her balance, through the hatch into the attic. On one side of the wide, low-roofed space was an old mattress and wire-wove base, and Nathan's teenage skis and poles that he fantasised Louisa might one day use, and the last VHS player and boxes of the photo albums and records of wedding and funeral services and the bone mahjongg set that he had inherited when his father died and his mother moved into the home. The rest of the attic was full of cardboard boxes, reconstituted fruit boxes and wine boxes and appliance boxes and shoeboxes, containing all of their lifetime-accumulated shit. To walk across the space Evelyn had to bend nearly double. She was reminded of the old house in Westmere. The dress-up box, the ancient comics, the warm feathery smell, the black cartridge-paper pages in the album of that coin collection, the shapes of the coins, decagons, wavy circles, tiny silver coins with holes in the centre, the layers of cracked yellow sticky tape over the spine. One day, Eve told herself, her chest would no longer squeeze at the thought of her parents. When she had properly adjusted her expectations.

Near the back of the stacks, under a heavy, collapsing box of folded hippy bedcovers, soft and quilted with Indian paisley prints and hand-stitched stars, was the box that held her diaries from the years before she met Nathan. Here was a journal with a dark-red cover and no dates. A photo fell out and she drew her breath sharply. Daniel had taken it and although the sight of herself, the nakedness, her body, made her stomach pitch there was at the same time as this sick feeling a pang of amazement that he had loved her like that once. But this picture, and the diary it came from. They would never be connected to the questionnaire, come on, they so didn't matter. She was unrecognisable! Why not pretend it was Dorothy, although then she would have to explain why such a photo of her sister might be here in her belongings. Explain to whom? Nobody was ever going to go looking in her attic, this was a symptom of narcissism, bored-housewife syndrome, she was paranoid. *Nobody cares! You're an invisible person!* But still she rifled through the diary pages knowing that the negative would not be there, that she didn't have it. Her mouth felt muffled and silenced, like it remembered, and she stretched it open and moved her tongue around in the air because she could, making a long *aahhh* sound with the breath that rose over the vocal cords. But the silence had gone inside, where it was meant to be. It was the secrets that made you all alone. Eve remembered blankness, bliss.

On the patio she took the domed hatch off the gas barbecue, removed the slightly greasy grill, lit it and fed the diaries into it, pages at a time, without stopping to read the entries. They frightened her, these words in her handwriting that may as well have been written by someone else, a woman who was capable of having those thoughts and doing those things.

Smoke curled up like long planed wood shavings; the air became sweet and particulate. She sprinkled the little bits of torn photograph onto the fire and they burned a cold greeny blue. While everything disappeared she swept the early autumn leaves into a pile. Please list any membership you have had with any political, social, fraternal or religious organisation or private club including any type of tax-exempt organisation over the past ten years. Please include dates of membership and any positions you may have held with the organisation. What would Daniel look like now, nearly ten years on, how much had he changed? Would the decade that had made her a woman have made him a man? On the other side of the high, vine-covered fence two of her neighbours stopped and talked invisibly about the cost of keeping their dogs.

'Is that you, Evelyn?' one of them called. 'Having an early bonfire?'

'Just making my spells.'

'Should we be worried?'

'Should Nathan be worried?'

'Ha ha,' she called back. 'Watch out.'

Another neighbour, after years off the cigarettes, had lately started smoking again, standing on his front step after dinner because he wasn't meant to do it in the house. Eve got it now. A need could resurface. Cinders rose from the small fire in a cloud, catching in the rough, unsanded wood-grain of the fence. While the handwriting burned Evelyn went into the house to find the questionnaire. A gust of wind blew ash across the patio in front of her. She came back and added the questionnaire to the flames, watching it scroll and brown at the edges, its thick-paged whiteness threatening to smother the fire altogether. She imagined time reversing, smoke sucked down from where it clung to the vine leaves into the burning photograph. *Nathan*, she thought. *Nathan cares.*

Tell us about your political philosophy. There are different groups of Liberals, for example, Progressive Liberal, Socialist Liberal, Free Market Liberal. Evelyn made Louisa's supper, the stir-fried rice dish that was fun to do because it was so occupying, chopping the onion and garlic and celery and mushrooms and peppers, and because of the challenge of getting Louisa to eat it. Evelyn was picking grains of rice out from between the floorboards beneath the table all night but she didn't mind. She bathed Lou and combed her hair, checking for head lice because so many of the school parents couldn't be bothered, or were too busy working, to do it. At first she had felt horror on seeing the clinging white eggs in the fine web of Louisa's hair, the black shadows crawling along her scalp. And now head lice were normal, part of life.

When Lou was in her pyjamas Evelyn read her a story, supervised brushing her teeth and took her to bed, where she listened to what her daughter had to say, finally, about the day, able to reveal her fights and victories now that she was cosily tucked up and it was all nearly over. In this way the hours between five and seven disappeared magically into the child's existence, and Evelyn was able to lose herself, just as in those preschool years of newsprint and glue for papier mâché and rolling sheets of beeswax into candles and cutting out strings of paper dolls, which were meant to be identical but the ones at the back of the folded paper, where the scissor blades had further to reach, were always a little bit fuzzy around the edges. These years in the house had erased something, too, holes worn through the paper with all that rubbing. She emerged into the hallway and blinked in the hollow light.

Small groups of parents huddled in conversation across the quad. A woman Eve had fought with at the quiz-night fundraiser a week earlier was holding Tania hostage. Grown-ups, hunched over the papers just like students, had scribbled furiously on the answer sheets in the school hall, and for a minute the scene could have been an examination room, all of them fifteen again, sitting their School C. 'Name four famous Belgians,' said the quizmaster, a local radio host with a voice that loved itself. After that there were gaps in her memory of the evening, leading up to the moment when the trestle tables were being folded away and the woman – Brenda – came over and started trying to be friendly. Everyone knew Brenda and one of the school dads, the one who OK had great abs but did he really need to be so ready to go shirtless at the end-of-year picnics, were getting it on.

'Have you seen *Three Sisters*, at the Mercury?' Brenda asked. 'It's the most wonderful production.'

'Yes. I know.' Evelyn had gripped the ridged handle of the Stanley knife for popping balloons hard in her fist. 'It made me want to have an affair too.'

Now Brenda's eyes flicked across the playground to Evelyn's and away, and she pushed her hair back with one hand and kept on talking, and Tania shifted awkwardly on her feet. She should go over and apologise. She should lie and blame the drink, or invent some marital strife or a sick parent, an entity from outside that had taken over her body and opened the mouth and made it say rude hurtful things that she could not help. Why was she such a bitch? The bell rang, releasing her, and she looked amongst the running children for her daughter's shining head, her windmill arms. God damn it, the asphalt was vertiginous, there was that hole again, she wanted to fill up with pastries, buns, the sort of stodge she used to cram in her mouth when she was younger and it didn't matter. Distractions, distractions. Food, then sex, then endless preschool craft then school help, remedial reading, and now she had to do something else or she was going to turn into one of those uber-fit freaks you saw at aerobics, the women who did two classes back to back, anything to fill the hours between mothering and lunch. Or – she felt the whisper slide across her mind – she would find someone, a man, a way to lose control.

That night she sat next to Nathan while he watched *Newsnight*. In the ad break he said, 'Have you heard anything about the job?'

Evelyn said, 'No.'

'It's really slack of them. You should call.'

'I had a lover,' Evelyn imagined saying, 'that I've never told anyone about.' Nathan would turn to her, then back to the TV, then press mute and swivel sideways on the sofa. 'Tell me about it.' Oh it would be good if he already knew. Would she say the next bit? Could she talk about that, the way things were with her and Daniel, the things they did to each other, the person she was before she became this respectable (narcissistic, bored, paranoid) housewife? How would it go? He'd shrink back a bit. Be embarrassed. Ask if she had ever been abused. Or want to try it, and get it wrong.

Nathan wouldn't let it drop about the job. Evelyn told him again she had sent the questionnaire off and was waiting to hear, but perhaps should start looking for other work anyway. Kimiko needed help in the old flower shop.

'But you wanted to be involved? I don't get it, you were so set on doing something that counts.'

Evelyn shrugged. 'Maybe making people nice bouquets for their birthdays is important. Wedding flowers, funeral wreaths, doing something beautiful, better than a windowless room with your ear getting sore from the phone the whole day.'

'You could do that and then I'd bring you flowers.' He pressed the remote and the screen fizzed to black and her husband stood over her, smiling down, and said, 'Maybe it's a good thing you don't work for that guy. You're too cute to be in politics. Some dork will just try and get you into bed.'

After he left for his card game Evelyn turned the stereo up full bore and lay on the floor and let the vibrations run through her until Louisa came and shook her wrist and said, 'Turn it down, Mum, I'm trying to get to sleep.' She poured a glass of wine and reached for the phone to call her sister, then remembered that Dorothy, pregnant again, was in bed at the same time as her kids these days.

She looked for Daniel in the phone directory. Seven *D. Hills* in Auckland. She could try the numbers one by one, though Daniel would surely not be here, wouldn't have a listed number, maybe not even a phone. He was probably somewhere like Prague, being revolutionary with a Czech hottie he'd met at clown school. Or he would answer. And then what? He wouldn't know it was her, couldn't tell from her breathing. 'This is Evelyn, obsessing about you.' Obsessing was too strong a word. What this was, was trying to integrate. Either integration or a burn-off. You made a decision and everything followed from that, and the older you got the more impossible it was to see through the Vaseline lens of time back into the past, your alternative lives, the ones you never now would lead.

Nathan had won at cards. He pulled the bedcovers over his shoulder and turned on his side, wuffling through his mouth. At about three in the morning Louisa stood in their doorway and said, 'I've wet the bed,' and Evelyn listened in the darkness as Nathan got out of bed, took Louisa to the bathroom, cleaned her up, dressed her in fresh pyjama pants, brought her in to sleep between them, crossed the landing, stripped her bed, took the sheets down to the laundry and came back up the stairs to land heavily in bed again. Evelyn fell asleep to the soft rumble and slosh below them of the washing machine spinning round.

The secretary rang to find out why she hadn't sent in the questionnaire.

'But I did. Days ago. Oh, damn. It must have got lost in the post. That seems crazy.'

'Oh.' The woman exhaled sharply. 'What a pain. We're trying to file all these positions now, we want to finalise it today, it's a waste of time for HR to do them individually.'

'Yes. I understand, of course, I'm so sorry to muck you around. Look, I don't want to mess up your systems, perhaps the best thing is just to forget about it.'

'Forget about it?'

'Yes, perhaps it's best if I just withdraw my application, just scratch me off the list.'

'Well do you want the job or not?'

'Yes, well I do, I think he's brilliant, it's a great cause, I'm sure you'll have every success, it would be a wonderful thing to be involved in but I don't want to hold you up, not on my account, maybe you should just – just don't consider me.'

'Are you withdrawing your application?'

'The thing is my mother-in-law isn't well.'

A pause.

'Actually, she's dead.'

'Right. Goodbye.'

Evelyn put the phone down, liberated and ashamed. Then she pulled the White Pages towards her, opened it at the folded-over triangle marking *Hicks* to *Hills*, found the first number and began to press the buttons.

9. FAMILY ROOM

DOROTHY AND ANDREW were in Cornwall Park with the kids when the call came through. The toddler, Donald, clutched at a length of banana with his fists, and squelches of creamy fruit bulged through his fingers. Shadows from the latticed leaves flitted over the tartan rug. The big roll of kitchen towel unravelled when Dorothy tried to tear off a sheet, not enough perforation, and Donald dropped the banana to grab at the soft white cone of a flower. She took him by the wrists and wiped his hands back and forth over the grass. At the sharp ringing of the cell phone, a wedding party posing for photos looked over from the ginkgo trees. Dorothy called out, 'Sorry!' Andrew liked to keep up with technology; it was a guy thing. One day that groom would understand.

Finally Andrew found the persistent phone and answered the call, taking it away from the rest of them, by the russet-winged paradise ducks. Those birds, stalking the paths, gawkily big. Reggae music started from a boom box at someone else's picnic and Amy jumped along off the beat, around and under the picnic table, and Grace read a book on her stomach on the grass, her hair so long and falling into the clover.

Dorothy watched Andrew nod and listen. There was, in the air around his head, a sort of pulsing that she could feel too. Amy yelped sharply and emerged from under the table. She stood in front of her mother, face pruned-up with pain, tears in her eyes, rubbing her forehead. At last Dorothy saw the child, she came into focus, and she drew Amy into her arms and kissed her hair. The phone call ended – Andrew reached the handset out towards Dot across the metres of grass, as though he was showing her something on the screen or wanted her to take this contaminated object from him, and he gestured clumsily for her to come, past the children, through the bright afternoon, his nose wrinkled, his face helpless. One duck charged another, chests up, wings pointed to the ground, and a small terrier barked at them, straining at the leash.

10. MASCULINITY STUDIES

THE HIGH DEPENDENCY Unit smelled like an old folks' home, which smelled like stale flower water, which smelled stagnant, like unmoving curtains onto a double-glazed aluminium-framed window through which there was a manicured rock garden, koi carp drifting in a pool. Dorothy stood at the reception desk waiting for the nurse to get off the phone. This was the next stage, after the long waiting while Eve was in surgery, and it was good to have a place to be. The flowers she had bought from the shop downstairs had to stay outside the ward's double doors, in the nothing space by the lifts, stems set in an old ice-cream container on the floor, the flowers balancing tenuously against the wall. It was inevitable that a small human movement would make the flowers slide down, the bases of their stems emerging dripping from the water, so that who knew what state they would be in later. She had already decided to take them to Nathan and Eve's, where she was going to stay, Andrew holding the fort at home with the kids. The flowers would make a good payment in kind for one of the casseroles Nathan would be brought that night. There hadn't been time to make casseroles at home, or do anything but get here.

The nurse got off the phone and pointed Dot in the direction of Evelyn's room. 'You're her sister?' Usually this wouldn't have to be asked. Usually there would be the resemblance. 'Hubby's in the family room. Think he's having a wee rest. Long day.'

Evelyn was asleep, her head encased in a giant white turban of bandages so that she looked like she had encephalitis, which she did not, or like her head was an enormous cartoon thumb. 'What's the worst that could happen,' she'd said once when Dorothy felt guilty over the children watching *Tom & Jerry*, 'they grow up with a sense of comic timing?' Her face was swollen, streaked with purplish and yellow bruises. Between the lacerations her skin shone greasily in the light that came from the window. Dorothy took a tissue from the bedside table – it came out of the box with a long, pulling hoosh – and gently, hardly touching at all, patted her sister's nose and the grazed cheekbones and chin. A heavier breath escaped Evelyn but she didn't wake. Dorothy sat down and took the newspaper out of her bag and dug her fingernails into her palms when an image rose up of *sitting in the hospital* beside Amy's incubator, the tubes and lines going into her baby.

Before long a little clutch of people crowded towards Evelyn's bed, the surgeon's walk-through, and Dorothy rose from the chair to greet them and to make space. 'I'll get her husband,' she said, but was rooted to the spot; she wanted to see her sister conscious. Someone shook Evelyn awake and Dot tried to poke her head in between the shoulders of the doctors and interns so that Eve would know she

was there. Evelyn's gaze rolled over Dot the way it rolled over everyone else surrounding her, and her eyes clammed shut again. A brief
exchange agreed that this drowsiness was fine.

'Been breathing on her own, good girl. So there's head injury
here,' the surgeon said to a – what, a student? – using the sort
of elegant hand gestures people made when selling jewellery on
late-night infomercials. 'Broke the left arm here and here, and the
shoulder here.' He examined his folder. 'There was another frac-
ture here, the ulna, but that's old, probably a childhood break.' He
looked at Dorothy.

'Yes,' she said. 'When she was nine. Or ten.' She couldn't remember how Eve had done it, only that their parents had brushed off
her complaints of a sore arm and it wasn't till a fortnight later when
she got bumped at school, rebroke it, that the secretary had called
Lee and said, *Your daughter needs an X-ray*.

'It doesn't matter.'

'I think she was ten.'

A girl in a white coat said, 'The hip?'

'No, she was lucky. Internal bleeding, ribs. She was on a bicycle?'
A question, to Dorothy.

'Yes, she, the driver just opened the car door, it threw her off.
She hit the road.' Unnecessary to add *no helmet*. Enough people had
remarked on that.

'Thank you.' He addressed the others, again, telling them the
serious issue was brain swelling, 'but we've gone in here – and here
– to relieve pressure.'

Perhaps these were the hand movements of a weather presenter,
or an air hostess in a safety demonstration, the hand that mimes

pulling down the oxygen mask and gripping the life-jacket whistle although there's nothing there. It was hard to concentrate. She was panicking.

'I'll just go and get Nathan,' Dot said, 'can you please, please wait.' Standing up had brought her body back to her; the muscles that were stiff and creaky, Play-Doh left out overnight. As she left to find the family room she heard, 'Another scan.'

The family room was smaller than she'd imagined, with an aluminium window frame and a pile of pamphlets on the table. Brain injury, a child's guide to bereavement. No thanks. Nathan lay on his side on the pink velour couch, his face stuffed into a cushion. She shook him. He followed her back into the HDU, his entire self folds of hanging grey fabric.

The curtains were pulled around Evelyn's bed and a smiling nurse emerged. 'Just changing the drip,' she said. Evelyn lay there alone, still asleep, the space around her bed empty. The surgeon and his entourage had moved on to the next patient, the next case.

Nathan sat and took Evelyn's pliant hand in his. 'Come on,' he said. 'Come on.' Her chest rose and fell. He stroked the side of her damaged face. Another nurse came in and noted saturation levels from the oximeter.

'I'm going for a walk,' Nathan said. 'I need the air.'

The nurse directed Dorothy to a mini-kitchen down the hall. 'Cereal, toast. Wee coffee maker. You may as well have a little walk too. We'll find you if anything happens, but I think she's going to rest a weeny bit longer.'

'I might get something,' said Dorothy. She had eaten a yellow pie from the hospital café at some stage, but had lost track of time. Maybe low blood sugar was why the nurse's little wee talk of weeny wee things, probably designed to shrink the fear, instead made her want to scream. 'I won't be long.'

The wall in the hospital corridor was just clean enough to lean against while she waited for the toast to pop. If Evelyn's head resembled a throbbing hammered thumb, the head on the guy waiting with her looked like a sliced-off finger.

'I've had fourteen operations,' he said, yes, to her, she must have been staring. That he could talk was astounding, that he had any brain function with that steep slope of his forehead, the near non-existence of his skull.

'Really?'

'This will be my fifteenth.'

An older woman stood pulling at her hands, possibly his mother. Dot wanted to stare at her too. She wanted to laugh at the impossibility of the man's head and tell him how totally incredible he was. She left the toast and walked to the stairwell and rang Tania, the friend of Eve's who'd come round to look after Lou. In the background was the sound of a television cartoon.

'Lou won't go to bed. She doesn't want to go to school tomorrow either.' How could you know what was best – to cosset the child or make her go on as normal, when normal – no. Dorothy knew that the classroom was good when things were wrong at home. But then there was the jolt of the present moment, when you found yourself alone without distraction, unable to control your thoughts.

'How's Eve?' Tania asked.

'It went well. Longer in recovery than we expected.'

'Nathan's got five casseroles here. It's a bit on the much side. Shall I freeze them?'

'Thanks. Keep one out for yourself.'

'No it's all right. You'll need them.'

When she tried the number she had for Michael the line connected to a pre-recording, a bloodless approximation of a human voice that said sorry but this number was no longer available. 'Oh fuck you,' she said into the phone, and people in the contemplation garden outside the glass doors turned their heads. She raised a palm in apology.

Nathan was still out. The nurse who came in to check the catheter bag said Eve had been awake for a little minute and Dot felt cheated, sorry that her sister hadn't seen her there. She picked up the crossword she'd left on the side table.

'Hi.' Evelyn's eyes were open, tiny slits through the swelling, and Dorothy stood to see them, to gaze at this sign of life, the sheeny curve of eyeball so wet and the colour deep inside, a golden frog at the bottom of a well. The eyelids closed again, a gesture that felt mammoth in weight. Dorothy knelt on the grey lino beside the bed and reached a hand between the safety bars to stroke her sister's arm.

There was a denim jacket on the floor between the visitor's chair and the bed. Instinctively Dot glanced at the end of the cubicle to make sure Nathan wasn't there. This was not his jacket, not the tobacco pouch in the pocket, the thin paper strip of a bus ticket, the scuffed, faded cuffs and collar, the loose threads coming off the stitches around the metal buttons. The fabric still held the coldness of outside. She smelled it. She clutched it to her, buried her face in it, dark spots on the fabric where it touched her eyes. *Was* it Daniel's, or did she just want to believe it was Daniel's? Could that smell be what created, now, a blooming of leaves, shade, underneathness, the smallness of being a child? And everything, the green leaves, the stippled grass, Daniel cross-legged in their hiding place, all of it belonging to her and to time, time that went so slowly, marked by the long silence that came before the small clean cluck of the second hand on a stolen watch, and the silence that came after it. The cells of her body just the same as the cells of the air, the grass blades, the sunlight and the cells of Daniel's skin.

The nurse behind the desk knew nothing about the jacket or a random visitor. Blood thumped in Dorothy as she strode the corridor, circled the area by the lifts, the jacket over her arm. It was a fantasy. He was in another country, with someone. The last postcard long ago, *Met a girl. Clowning El Salvador.* Then nothing. She had got on with mothering children and being married and teaching, absorbed by the dense volume of things to do in her day, as though this was where her life belonged. Or that was an illusion. She had mistaken being busy for being involved. No, that wasn't fair. Where else could her attention go? She rounded a corner and came upon a woman sobbing against a wall. 'Sorry,' Dot said, before backing away.

She should have known if Daniel was back. Should have been told, but should also have just felt it, like knowing bodily where Eve was, that she was all right. Until this. Their connection had told her nothing about this.

Leaving the hospital into the chilly night, she thought she saw him in a wheelchair outside the main entrance, the wind tunnel where the smokers went, but when she went up and opened her mouth to speak it was another man. Dorothy hid the denim jacket in her bag and much later, when everything had happened, she took it home and hung it on a hook in the hallway, where after a time it was covered by a torn, child-sized anorak to be taken for repair, a yoga-mat carrier and a rope-handled beach bag, sand collected like a wiggly line of handwriting in the bottom of the white lining.

Dot sat with Lou, stroking the hair back from her forehead and humming a lullaby until she fell asleep. Her own kids were fine. She'd cried on the phone to Andrew, the sound of his voice. The folders on Eve's desktop computer were named Home, Lou, Finance. Blood in her ears pounded as Dorothy typed in a document search for *Daniel*. A subfolder appeared, and in that a word document contained text that looked to have been cut and pasted from emails. Fuck. She closed the file before she could read too much. So, there it was. Daniel and Eve. Of course.

She had fucking known it.

Nathan decided not to take Lou to the hospital while Eve looked like she did. In the morning Dot ran her a bubble bath, which she was still in when Tania came to the door with a Tupperware dish of pumpkin soup. The laundry was all done, the floors vacuumed and the windows cleaned. Dorothy held her at the threshold, a spray bottle of vinegar and a scrunched sheet of newspaper in her hands, and asked point blank if Eve had ever told her about Daniel.

'Is Nate home?'

'Of course not.'

Tania glanced back to her car, where her husband waited in the driver's seat. He passed a wave towards Dorothy, who nodded back. Quickly Tania walked through to the kitchen and placed the sloshy container of soup on the bench top. Dorothy marked her progress, breathing hard.

'Yes,' Tania said. 'It's over, but I think they're still in touch.'

'Does he know what happened?'

'I called him. He knows.'

'He's in town.'

'Yes.'

'OK. Thanks.'

'Do you want his number?'

'No.' She kicked the door shut with a foot, pulled the trigger on the cleaning bottle and squirted vinegar all over the wall.

Their parents flew in from the States accompanied by Ruth, who despite having left her twin girls at home was definitely a mom, in her pale-pink polar fleece and easy-wash layered hair. Dorothy waited at the airport barricade amongst uniformed men holding name boards, as matted backpackers, men and women in business suits, stunned families and countless senior citizens ambled through the electronic doors, their faces expectant, uncertain. Her family came near the end of a large tour group, her mother and father disguised as old people holding hands, Ruth just behind with the teetering trolley. Frank wore the sashed camel trench coat and round tortoiseshell glasses of an Anglophile American. Lee's pearl earrings looked real. Bless Ruth, she had a photo of her twins right there in her wallet, and Dorothy pored over it while her parents buckled themselves into the back seat, taking their time, older.

'Gorgeous girls,' she said, handing the photo back to Ruth.

'They are.' Ruth started to cry.

'It's OK,' said Dorothy, patting her hand. 'You'll feel better when you see her. Eve's going to be fine.'

As Dot drove them into town to shower and 'freshen up' at their hotel before the hospital, Lee murmured from the back seat in a fully American accent about the changes to the motorway, the new bridges, the buildings in the hazily approaching city that had never been there before. The rear-view mirror presented a slim rectangle of her swept-back ash-blonde hair, the sensitive indents at her temples more pronounced with age.

'Oh look,' she pointed at the new Sky Tower when they reached the city. 'It's like something from the future.'

Hospital quickly became ordinary, the place where their days happened. There was the institutionalised gravy smell, and the man with half a head and the kindness of every single person, even the friend who said 'Boxing on' each time they spoke, which made Dorothy want to punch her. The hierarchy in a corridor. People going to the shop in their pyjamas. 'Slippery slope,' Nathan finger-wagged, laughing at Dorothy when he saw what she had taken to wearing. 'It's a slippery slope once you start wandering the halls in your slippers. You're not even a patient.'

And the peeling paint over the plaster walls in the hospital corridors, psoriasis on an industrial scale. Scurf tide in the shower. The male orderly who all night was trying to kill Evelyn, sending a signal to his murderous colleagues by the clicking of his pen. The one time Eve lost it, crying at Nathan and Dot, 'Would you just go? Would you go, please, so that I can start waiting for you, so that I can start counting the fucking paint-drying hours until you come back?' Toast on a tray. Sleeping in the afternoons, her head shaved and stapled, a cannula plug sticking out of her hand. Taking the anti-fitting pills, the steroids that made her paranoid. The move to a general ward, the visitors and flowers and boxes of home baking, Evelyn's friends sitting on the end of the bed, women in their thirties cross-legged like schoolgirls still.

Across the café Dorothy saw her mother's back, the age in the hump of her upper spine. She was perched on the end of a table that another family occupied, big kids eating burgers and parents with chips and soda, the paper on the chip bag soggy, streaked red with ketchup. 'Hi, Mum,' Dorothy said, and Lee startled. She folded the newspaper into her handbag, put away the pen.

'How is she?'

'Sleeping. Shall we go and sit over there?'

They moved to an empty table by the floor-length windows. A bird had gotten in and hopped along the wainscot, pecking at crumbs. 'Where's Dad?'

Lee shook her head. 'Don't ask.'

'What does that mean? Where is he?'

A one-shouldered shrug. 'Out somewhere.'

'Do you not care?'

'Of course I care.' The words snapped out of her. She sighed, and regained control. 'I just do not know where he is.'

Now Dorothy looked away, exasperated. 'He should be here.

Or he can always visit my kids again if he doesn't like the hospital. Go and spend some time, get to know them a bit.'

'I know, darling. And we will,' Lee said, a bony hand patting her daughter's wrist. 'Of course we will, but we're thinking about Eve right now.'

'That's not what I meant.' This was infuriating, that Lee had become frail and tremulous in direct relation to Dorothy's growth in perspective, her strength. The rage of teenagehood swelled biliously inside her, but she could not let it out. She was afraid of this power she felt, that she might kill her mother.

One day Eve came home. She slept for a long time getting over the discomfort of the car journey, and when she woke, Lou and Dot sat on the bed and dealt her into a game of gin. Lou was being shy with her mother.

'Wow,' Eve said. 'I've got a great hand.' After a minute she shut her eyes. 'Sorry,' she murmured through a face that looked close to sleep again. 'Hurts to look at the cards.'

'Lee's managed to get hold of Michael,' Dot said. 'He sends his love. Can you believe it, of all of us she's the one he keeps in touch with?'

'Why is that strange?' asked Lou, and Dot said, 'Your grandmother is a strange woman.'

'I think she's nice.'

'Well, that's because you're nice.' She split the deck and arched the halves into a bridge and shuffled them together, like Daniel had taught her to do. 'Come on, we'll just sit here and play quietly while your mum has a rest.'

★   ★   ★

The Forrest seniors announced that now Eve was home they were going to leave. 'End of the week,' Frank said. It was Thursday. What were they racing back to, their golf handicaps, their lunches? But that was how it was with them. The thread count of Frank's shirts and the sheen of Lee's gold fob chain revised the past, as though the years they lived here and had children and were broke were their wilderness, an interlude. They'd reverted to type, and Ruth was the only child who'd had it in her to adapt. Dorothy stepped into the cold garden to take it out on the weeds.

'Dorothy.' Frank stood by the back door.

She rocked back on her haunches, balanced with her dirt-smeared hands on the trowel. 'Hi, Dad.' Breath briefly visible in the air.

'You might recall that trouble from the traffic fines. From ...'

'God, from like twenty years ago. Yeah.' A snail crawled up the trunk of a broccoli plant and she picked it off, tossed it into the hedge.

'Something I meant to deal with at the time, but ... It slipped my mind. Just to let you know, in case they call, looking for you.'

'The who, the Ministry of Justice?'

'Yes. I'm sure they've forgotten all about it.'

'But why me?'

'You were the driver. Weren't you? Anyway I'm sure they won't track you down.'

'But, Frank ...' He'd told her he would deal with it. Hadn't he? Had the fines been forgotten? Or was she some kind of unknowing fugitive? 'I can't worry about that shit now.' A small satisfaction, watching him flinch at the language. She dug the fork into a root system and raked it out.

The water, running warm in the kitchen sink, felt delicious over her hands. Dot squirted a perfect green jet of detergent onto her palms and rubbed them vigorously. Movement caught her eye; a neighbour's cat trotting through the vege garden, and she clapped her hands and hissed through the window. Its back twitched and it slunk quickly through a hole in the bushes. Ruth spoke from the fridge, her head inside it, reorganising. 'Did Dad tell you we're going home? I feel bad but I really miss my girls.'

'It's OK. Eve's going to be fine.'

'Even though they don't really need me.' Her delicate pink nails caught the light as she lifted a bowl to her nose, removed the cling film, sniffed it and put it back.

'Who, your girls? I'm sure that's not true.'

'You know. *Twins.*'

'Oh but they still need their mom.'

Ruth smiled, unconvinced.

'Ruth. They do.'

'They're very close.'

'Well. That's lovely. Anyway, I envy you.'

'What do you mean?'

'Living somewhere else. I hate being this age. I'd like to turn back on the past with a flame-thrower. One of those hoses that sprays fire. But I bet you don't even feel it, the weight, dragging around behind you. I mean you're American now, and your life – is it like our childhood was another planet?'

Ruth said, 'Isn't everyone's?'

A call came from upstairs. 'I'll go,' said Dot.

'Anyway,' said Ruth. 'Getting older is a lot better than the alternative.'

Later she borrowed Nathan's car to explore their old neighbourhood, look at the family house, a thing that Dorothy never did. 'Visiting Mars,' Dot said, and Ruth nodded, tucking a house key into the back pocket of her dark-blue jeans.

'Evelyn and Lou are coming. Change of scene. Are you sure you won't?'

'I'm good, thanks. Bring me a souvenir.'

The medication prohibited Eve from driving, so she sat in the back like a foreign dignitary, Lou beside her and Ruth the chauffeur. 'Six months,' Eve had said that morning, not griping but bewildered, the way she sounded about everything now. 'I can't drive for six whole months.' The street was fresh with the feel of coming rain. Dorothy gave Ruth a jaunty wave and said, 'Take 'em down memory lane, thanks, driver,' in a silly voice. Ruth fired her the finger as she shifted the car into gear, and Dorothy burst out laughing. They drove off, Evelyn's profile still and serious like a child's, Lou snuggled into her shoulder.

Dot spun right into her mother who had been standing behind her in silence. Lee took her glasses off and clung to them, twisting the stems. It was odd to see tears appear in her eyes. Her mouth jerked and she said, 'What if we'd lost her.'

'Oh Mum.' Dorothy leaned in and hugged her awkward, starchy body. 'We didn't,' Dorothy said, and stroked Lee's arm as she drew a shuddering breath. 'She's going to be fine. Come on. You ready to come inside?'

'I'd like to head back to the hotel. Start packing.'

'It's great you've been here,' Dorothy said. 'We needed you.'

'Really?' She was wiping her nose with a white handkerchief, her eyes searching Dot's face.

Dot hugged her again. 'Yes, Mum.'

Upstairs, the tray with crumbs, the soup bowl with its tidemarks were evidence of Evelyn's health. In the tangle of jewellery on the dresser were the earrings they'd both been given, all those years ago. Dorothy held them to her ears, looked in the mirror, her own pair lost to house moves, carelessness and time. Lee would be pleased to see those, if she remembered. There was a small crater in the pillow where Eve's head had lain. What did she think about up here? Kneeling on the floor beside the bed, Dot leaned her forehead on the blue sheets. The pillow smelled of her sister's perfume. Light came through the window and she was second base on the field at the commune, followed Michael's gaze from the batter's mound to see Eve and Daniel plough towards her through the long grass. Michael thwacked the bat into his palm. Gold lit the grasses. Daniel's steady stride, Eve behind him, a shadow. She woke up to the front door slamming shut, the sound of voices. Dot's knees cracked as she stood too quickly. Blood drained from her head, the corners of the room rocked.

'Who made this?' Evelyn was sitting at the table, eating dinner with Louisa. 'It's delicious.' There was deep peace in the repetitive motion of her hand as it glided between the plate and her patient mouth. Dorothy touched her sister's shoulder, settled the tray from her room on the bench, put the soup bowl in the sink and ran the tap on it. 'How's the old neighbourhood?' she asked.

'Smaller,' Ruth said. 'Eve got a bit antsy. Wanted to come home.' The smile that followed this was meant to be relaxed, but a current ran between Ruth and Louisa, the discomfort they must have felt in the confined space of the car while Evelyn's voice got louder.

Later Dorothy tucked Lou into bed and brought Evelyn a cup of camomile tea on the couch. She turned the music down and sat below her sister on the floor. 'Has it been good having them here?' she asked. 'Mum and Dad?'

Eve nodded. 'Mum's hair looks nice. Dad's older.'

'Of course it took you nearly dying to get them back.'

'Yeah,' Eve laughed. 'Should have done it sooner.' Rain started, pattered the window. 'Isn't that lovely.' She stroked Dorothy's hair. 'Did they come when Amy was sick?'

'No. It was all over fast, and she's so fine now.'

'Mmm,' Evelyn said. 'But still.' The rain came in earnest now, enveloping the house. 'Where's Nate?'

'Upstairs. I think he's on the phone.' She and Nathan were allies now; he told her things. 'You've got a good man there.'

Eve's hand stopped stroking. Dorothy felt it leave her hair. 'Has Daniel phoned?'

'I don't know.' Breathing seemed to require thought, volition. 'Not while I've been here.'

'I just wondered.' Eve's voice was dreamy. 'I thought someone might have told him, seeing as he's family.'

'Tania has spoken to him.'

'Tania?'

'Yes.'

Evelyn moved her arm. 'Oh, OK.'

'I don't know how to get hold of him,' Dorothy said. 'Ask Tania.'

Eve began stroking her hair again.

'You're my family.' Dot leaned her head back into the sofa seat and looked at Evelyn's upside-down face. 'I mean, thank god we've got each other. I love Ruth, but she's from outer space.'

'I feel like the one who's a Martian. Changed.'

Dorothy squeezed the hand that Evelyn had rested by her shoulder. 'We all are.'

That same night the fever came, vomiting and delirium. Eve mangled her words. Nate drove her back in to the hospital. The doctors couldn't tell them. Maybe an infection they couldn't locate. Scans revealed nothing, nobody knew why, meningitis from an infected bone, the blood/brain barrier, quarantine Louisa, visit in a surgical mask, we've only got room in the chemo ward, no high risk on the chemo ward and we've had some results, it might not be meningitis, let's get her into the chemo ward where beds come free regularly, where there's always a guy in trouble for smoking in his bed and how do you enforce that ban, how do you discipline a person who's got nothing to lose, could you roll over, darling, we've got to do another LP, let's get you on your side, can you hold her hand, Nathan, that's it dear just look into your husband's eyes, hold on, we're going to be gentle as we, yes, there it goes, yes, it's in, not long now, good girl. The syringe came back – still cloudy. They'd try the other kind of antibiotics. Wait.

Tania appeared in the doorway with Lou. 'Thank you,' said Dorothy, hugging this very good woman, holding the sides of her worried face and nodding. 'Thank you.' Nathan clutched the girl's shoulders and she walked over to her mum and stroked her arm, then ran into her father's arms.

Her parents were called at their hotel. A chest X-ray and a cranial scan revealed nothing. An MRI showed the abscess. Another drug was tried. They waited, again, but the infection had her in its grip. 'We're going to operate,' the surgeon said. Dorothy heard *drainage, shunt, bone flap*.

In the flurry of medical preparation, nurses adjusting drip bags and the catheter, the machines started telling a different story. 'Are we getting her into theatre or not?' said a nurse.

'Wait.'

'Right,' the nurse said. 'Time for theatre.'

But there, at the last minute, it all stopped.

'This looks like stroke. I'll get the specialist,' an orderly said. 'Wait.'

'Should we leave?' Lee gestured to the door.

Nate and Lou approached the bed. Lou climbed up and lay next to her mother. The nurses backed off.

'But she was fine,' their father said. 'She was fine.'

Dorothy nodded. OK. There was the click of relief that the worst was arrived at, the tension and fear floating away. For a second. Straight after that, she knew the fear had been the only thing that held her together.

Afterwards, she drove Nate and Lou home. Andrew and the kids would be there now; she'd rung them from the hospital. Her husband had said, disbelievingly, 'No.' She parked away from the lights of the house and the three of them sat there in the dark and clutched each other's hands across the handbrake. Louisa passed her dad the box of tissues from the pocket in the back of the passenger seat and said, 'Come on,' and they waited a minute longer until he was ready to face the house.

Near dawn Dorothy found him in the garden, looking at the council block behind the house, the high walls covered in scaffolding. Rusty metal rods rattled and the wooden platforms creaked. Blue tarpaulins sheeted in the wind.

'Looks like the whole thing's going to take off,' Nathan said.

'It might. Tania brought another lasagne.'

'People are amazing.'

The morning was cold. He blew on his hands to warm them and put them over his ears. Inside his head it would be stifled, there would be the seashell sound of his blood. This was what Dorothy was thinking about, so that it was a surprise when Nathan said with perfect clarity, 'Looks like the whole thing's going to take off and fly away.'

The music from the stereo inside flared across the garden; one of the kids must have gotten hold of the remote control.

11. LOOSE

HE WAS A young man in a beanie and a suit, carrying a plastic bag full of paper. Dorothy saw through the bubbled glass of the door his figure approaching, his clenched fist raising, getting closer. He knocked on the door as if he was a friend. A rhythmic, *it's show-time* knock. She was surprised, expecting a Mormon or Jehovah's Witness, the young evangelists in striped shirts and suit pants, black wraparound sunglasses, pineapple hair. This guy was slim, with prune-coloured smudges under his eyes. He'd come from a local mechanic's. Was on the hustle for new work. 'We already have a mechanic,' Dot whispered.

'I beg your pardon?'

She cleared her throat. 'The baby's sleeping. We already have a mechanic.'

'Thank you. I won't take up any more of your time.' He didn't move. The sky cracked and rain drummed on the trees in the street, shattering over the parked cars, pooling on the ground.

She stepped out from behind the door. 'Do you have an umbrella?'

'Sorry, goodbye.'

He was halfway up the path, his woollen hat already plastered, when Dorothy called after him, her voice raised over the roaring rain. 'Excuse me? Do you want to come in?' She held the door open – he smelled of wet suit cloth – and when he crossed the threshold she said, 'Oh my god, the washing.'

In the back garden she tipped the red laundry basket upside down to shake out the water and unpegged the washing, hands stiff and fumbling, casting pegs aside, bright pink and yellow legs fallen on the slushy grass. The man helped, throwing half-folded sheets, towels into the basket. Andrew's gym gear, his underwear, her nursing bras, Grace's shorts, Amy's rabbit, Donald's dinosaur pyjamas, Hannah's tiny striped T-shirt. The man followed her up the back steps into the house where she said, 'I'll put these in the dryer, please sit down.'

His eyes were bloodshot and he dabbed at them with the tissue Dorothy handed him once they were sitting opposite each other at the kitchen table. 'Feel free to take off your jacket.'

She passed him a towel. The front of his white shirt was soaked through, and droplets of water glimmered on the woollen ridges of his hat. A leaflet from his plastic shopping bag sat on the table in front of her, the cheap paper splodged with rain. He only made money on commission. Nobody wanted to change mechanic or to hear about his offer, his deal. The deal involved tyres but already Dot was waning, regretted inviting him into the house. She listened out for the rain to ease. Grace and Amy were at school and Donald at nursery and Hannah was sleeping. She was meant to rest now too, which was infuriating enough that it pleased her all over again to have this strange, sad man sitting at the kitchen table. 'Me?' he said. 'Two children.' Neither at school yet. She imagined the scene when he left his house each day, kissing his wife goodbye as she stood there with a baby in her arms. That morning, Dot had been in the shower when Andrew left. Donald, four, had stood to one edge of the shower curtain, just staring, boring a hole in her body. Before long Hannah would be old enough to pull herself up to standing and she would notice when Dot left the room and balance at the side of the bath holding onto the edge, crying while Dot washed herself, away from her. This was one of the stages that would happen, just as now she was at the stage of crawling confidently, briskly, towards cigarette butts whenever they were in the park. When she sat up it was a miracle of posture, her back beautifully erect, her big round head a weightless balloon.

That morning Dot had asked Andrew whether he was angry with her and he had been genuinely surprised. It was unclear whether he was walking around enraged but not knowing it, or whether she was projecting. Dot wished she didn't know the word *projecting*. *Latent. Trigger.* Someone in the house was angry, it must be so, even though the cake tins were full. Maybe it was both of them. Angry at the *out there*. Angry at the *chance*. 'Do your children go to playgroup?'

'Yes.' He named one Dot hadn't heard of, just as she hadn't heard of the mechanic's. While she stayed indoors the neighbourhood was rearranging itself.

'Does your wife work?'

'She's at the bank.'

'Right.'

He was sweating, water dots the size of ladybirds glistening on the sides of his nose. Perhaps there was a cultural reason he didn't remove his hat, or perhaps that was a racist assumption. Dorothy liked to keep the house hot. She liked not having to put on a jumper. It was wasteful but temperature was one of those things now like appetite, where what she wanted was what she wanted. The children had grown used to it. It was quite good being a fat mum. They liked her softness, the cuddles. She didn't spend hours walking or doing Pilates or running nowhere on a treadmill. They helped with the biscuits and the cakes. Fingers stroking the bars of the electric mixer, licking grainy raw dough.

She offered the young man at the kitchen table a slice of Madeira cake, which he declined. 'No thank you. I'm allergic to gluten.'

'An apple? Mandarin?' Dot pushed the fruit bowl towards him.

'What sort of car do you own?' he asked.

'A metallic salmon people mover.'

'Does it run well?'

'It's ugly,' she said. 'But I don't drive it. Everything I need to do is close by.' She didn't say, I don't leave the house without the aid of lorazepam, so not a lot of operating heavy machinery.

'That's nice.'

'Which street are you in?'

'Oh, I don't live around here.' He named a suburb she had vaguely heard of, which might have been one of the grotty old suburbs, rebranded by estate agents. Pylon Valley, Abattoir View.

'But you work for this mechanic?'

'It's freelance. We generate contracts for local businesses.' He laughed. 'I came here a few weeks ago to see if I could interest you in some tree pruning but there was nobody home.'

'Really? I wonder where we were.' Dot dug her thumbnail into a mandarin, the bubble-like pores popping, limonene spritzing invisibly over her hand. 'We have a plum tree that needs to be crowned.'

'Yes, I saw it from the road. But I don't work for the tree surgeon any more.'

The word *surgeon* sat on the table between them like a fish. He ate his mandarin, but the room was too quiet, and Dot was afraid she was going to hear him swallow, so she stood and said, 'I'm just going to check on my baby. She's sleeping.'

Internal motes floated across her field of vision as she walked out of the room, feeling the drop in blood pressure. She wasn't going back to therapy because there was only so much therapy she could handle. That was why Andrew was pissed off. The realisation made her smile, and then she felt regretful, and told herself she must make more of an effort. She should stitch that on a handkerchief. Pull your fucking socks up.

She leaned over the cot sides to lift the girl. With the first baby, Dorothy had been small enough to fit inside the cot too, to curl up and comfort Grace when she wouldn't stop crying, and then she got bigger and bigger and bigger until now so much of herself pressed against the cot sides while she leaned down that its bars creaked and scraped against the wall. A little rubbed line was appearing in the paint. When Hannah moved into a bed and they dismantled the cot for the last time and tried to sell it online they would have to paint over that rub mark. Or perhaps by then the cot would have had it and they would just leave it out for the inorganic rubbish collection, or take it to the tip. The baby was still asleep, undisturbed even by being lifted, and she was breathing. There was a timetable, a schedule, by which everything was meant to happen but now it seemed a good idea to lower her back onto the blankets and go and ask the salesman if he was ready to leave. In this room you couldn't hear the rain. As she slowly removed her hands from under the baby, Dot felt a creeping up her back. It was wrong to have this stranger in the house.

The man had taken off his hat. It sat on the table, a flat half-oval. Dorothy stared at his head, where the hair grew short and tufty out of a rectangular shaved patch. Staples held the seam of a surgery scar together.

He grabbed at the hat and went to pull it back on. 'It's OK,' she said. 'You don't have to. Sorry, I know it's very warm in here.' She reached the tin of chocolate chip cookies down from the top shelf, pausing to lean a wrist against the shelf, her head on her arm, tears hot in her eyes. 'Condensed milk and brown sugar,' she told the man, her voice wobbling and jolly, and sat back down.

'Thank you. But I won't have one.'

'Of course. The gluten thing.' She bit one and chewed.

'I should really be going.'

'My husband would know if we need to switch mechanics,' she said. 'It's his territory.' They both looked at their hands. 'Do you mind if I ask?' Dot pointed to her hairline, to the place on her head that corresponded to that place on his.

'No,' he said, 'just some surgery.'

'Were you a surgeon, back in India?'

He laughed for a long time. 'No.'

'Sorry.'

'Don't be. I'm flattered.'

'Do you mind if I ask how old you are?'

'I'm twenty-two.'

Dot thought about what she was doing at twenty-two. At twenty-two she had bumped into Daniel in town and gone back to his place where they had made love, a holiday from real life already, over a long afternoon. Later they'd gone to hear a band. She couldn't remember the flat she lived in then but she remembered the Uprising poster on the wall above Daniel's bed, the soft cotton of the paisley bedspread, the sweet, dusty smell of the carpet in his room. The way he said, 'I just want to check . . .' and did something and she responded involuntarily and he said, 'Gotcha.' She wondered what she would do if she bumped into him now. She hadn't seen him since the funeral, where Ruth had reported that he smelled of beer. 'When I was twenty-two,' she told the man, 'I didn't have two kids to support.'

'What did you do?'

'Well, I was a teacher. I'm still a teacher. Maternity leave.'

He nodded and looked down at the orange-and-white peel on his plate. 'Really?' he said. 'Very interesting. What subjects?'

'Art, English, but I really haven't taught for a while.'

'You're an artist.'

'No. I'm not an artist like you're not a surgeon.'

'Like I'm not a tree surgeon.'

Dot laughed. 'Yes. How long have you lived here?'

'Since school. My parents had family here, we came when I was seven.'

Same as her. 'Long time.' There was a simple sum to do but she wasn't capable of the maths.

'Fifteen years.'

Fifteen years ago she had been . . . she imagined a steamer docking. Crowds of people. Steerage. 'Did you come on a boat?'

'Don't be silly! Sorry,' he said.

'It's OK. Sorry. I don't go out a lot. Not that that's any excuse.'

'In a plane.'

'Have you been back?'

'Yes, every year.'

'Such a long way. With little ones.'

'But when we get there the family looks after us.'

The phone rang. Dorothy made a surprised face at the man, like, nobody ever calls this number, which was true. 'Hello?' She smiled at him while she listened, a bubble of hysteria rose in her throat and she felt hot, or hot for him, it wasn't clear. She mouthed 'The childminder'. He nodded, though he could not have understood.

Chloe was crying; sobbing, on the verge of hyperventilation. Dorothy walked the phone into the hallway. 'Slow down, it's all right. What's the matter?' The girl's cat had just been – she could hardly get the sentence out – the cat had been run over. She heard the brakes and ran out of the house and the car drove off and there was the – lying in the – just gone. 'Oh no,' Dot said. 'Oh, you poor thing.'

'I just don't think I can come in. I'm sorry. I know the children will be waiting. I have to go and bury . . .' Chloe's voice rose in a semi-wail and she said, 'Oh god, Dorothy, I'm sorry.'

'No you mustn't be, the kids will be fine, I'll call Kate, she can bring them home. You attend to your poor cat. Take care of your-self. I'll call you tomorrow.'

Her friend Kate's home phone and cell phone both rang until the recorded answering service picked up. It was very nearly time for the school bell to announce the end of lessons, and the chil-dren would stand there while the playground emptied, waiting. Grace haughty, head in a book. The frizzy-haired nursery teacher holding Donald's hand. Amy hanging off the monkey bars, fright-ened to jump down, no one to catch her. Dorothy thumped herself lightly on the breastbone with a fist. She was *there*. Never mind the constricted throat, the insects prickling her skin, the way she didn't exist from the ribs down. She poured a glass of water from the sink and drank it in two gulps. 'You know,' she said to the man, and wiped her mouth.

He rose to his feet. 'I should go.'

'Wait.' She put a hand on his arm. He looked down at it, and back at her, and she moved it away. 'Sorry. Would you like to come with me on the school run? The mums will all be there, you could bring your flyers.'

'Oh.' The man bit his thumbnail. 'We usually try to book people in to an appointment then and there. For the commission. But OK, sure. I'll come.'

'Great!' The burst of sound surprised them both. 'What's your name?'

'Sam.' Mandarin peel lay scattered on the table, cottony with pith.

'I'm Dorothy.' She looked in her bag for the keys but it was weeks since she had taken them out and the bag was full of rubbish, receipts and bus tickets and old tissues, soft as she sifted through them. She dumped the contents on the table and snatched a tampon and a crumby, lidless lip-balm out of sight. 'God, we're going to be late.'

Sam pointed to the copper tangle half hidden by a folded map for the family walk at the sculpture park, a walk they had abandoned early when the sky began to draw away from her and she needed to lie down and hug the earth. 'Keys?'

'Thank you. I'll just be a minute.' In the bathroom she locked the door, but the small orange prescription bottle was empty.

The air out on the wet path came as a shock. Thin trees shimmered against the sharp sky. Sweat covered Dorothy's body, under her bra, down the backs of her legs above the weatherproof boots that were stiff with lack of wear. She paused by the letterbox, one hand on the fence post, Hannah strapped froggily into her buggy, covered in the striped fleece blanket that was crusted in spots with old milk. It was possible Dot was going to be sick. The front door was still open but if she went to close it she'd slip back into the force field of the house. 'Can you shut the door?' she called to Sam, and turned away and sang to the baby a little.

'Did you stop teaching when you had children?' Sam asked, catching them up near the corner. Dot adjusted her step to match his. He walked slowly and time was running out to get to the school gates.

'We might be too late for the other mums,' she said. 'I think we need to step it up.'

They rounded the bend of the quiet street and got onto the main road. A car passed, close and fast, and Dorothy flinched. 'Do you mind if we —' she said to Sam, and dropped behind him to walk on the inside of the footpath. Other people walked in and out of shops and that woman with the pink hair was waiting at the pedestrian crossing with her ferret on a lead. Still there, still crazy. The colour lifted Dot's feet and carried her. 'What does your wife do at the bank?'

'She's a teller.'

'Does she like it?'

'Yes, actually. She does.'

'Do you have an iPod?'

'No.'

'I don't like how if you put the ear-buds in before you turn the music on you can hear the blood pulsing in your ears. Not so much hear it as feel it.' She made the noise, *doof doof*.

He looked at her and shook his head. 'Sorry, I don't get what you're saying.'

'I just need to talk.' She really needed to breathe, too, but if she thought about breathing it would become impossible, voluntary, and they couldn't have that. In a low voice she vocalised the words from all the text she read, advertising hoardings and car names, *Trail Blazer, Supa Deal, He Wants You, It's Back!!!*.

The neighbourhood gleamed under a slick layer of rain, and the air carried damp trees, traffic fumes, dry-cleaning chemicals. They passed the greengrocer with bright buckets of gerberas and lisianthus out the front, and the Turkish café and the fetish shop and the newsagent and the local councillor's office and turned another corner and the street was lined with parked cars and a long barred fence chained with bicycles, and reached the zebra crossing that led to the school gates. Adults milled in the schoolyard. 'You live close,' Sam said.

'Yes, we're lucky.'

Afternoons were apparently just the same as ever – scuddy clouds, leaves flipping, the community faces flushed and cheery, thick hair pitched in the wind, sturdy legs straddling linen shopping bags packed with crackers and fruit for the playground. At first the faces were strange, every one, and then the crowd began to split into individual blobs and features, animated mouths, eyes, Kate's horsy teeth, Fleur's freckles, people Dorothy knew. She steered Sam towards some women from the book club she had once belonged to.

'Wow!' said Fleur, arms wide. 'Oh Dottie, well done!'

Dorothy went sideways, stiffly, into the embrace. 'No big deal,' she said. The women looked questioningly at Sam. 'This is Sam. Fleur, Kate. He's from the mechanic's. A new mechanic?' she prompted him.

'No,' he said, 'but under new management.'

'He's got flyers.'

'Oh.' Fleur's gaze was stuck on the beanie. 'Thanks.' The women politely took them.

'Because you were having trouble with your brakes, weren't you?' Dorothy asked Kate.

'Oh – yes. They fixed it.' She shrugged and smiled at Sam. 'Not your mechanics, sorry. Rivals, I suppose! But we'll definitely come for a quote next time.'

'Thank you.' He nodded and wandered a little way off to pass leaflets to other people. The bell rang and the doors to the school building opened and suddenly children were everywhere, darting around the quadrangle, the thud of soccer balls against a wall, shrieks and giggling.

There was Grace, with her friends. Their pod circled the crowd, arms folded. Last time Dot had been here her daughter still ran around the netball court, playing games. 'What do they talk about?' she asked Kate.

'God only knows,' Kate said. 'I roll my eyes.'

The nursery kids were let out. Donald sprinted up and dumped his schoolbag at her feet and said, 'Where's Chloe?'

'She couldn't come today.'

'Mummy! Can I go to Ivan's house, please, can I,' and shook his hands in prayer and Ivan's mother from the other side of the playground raised an arm and nodded, and Dorothy called, 'Thank you,' and kissed her son's ducking head before he raced away.

'Are you going to that road-safety meeting?' Fleur asked.

'Can't,' Kate said. 'Ted's got shingles.'

'Oh no.'

'You should go.' This was to Dorothy, with significant eyes.

'I know.' The cautionary tale. Poster girl for speed limits, sober driving, pedestrian crossings, chicanes, judder bars, cycling helmets, slow down signs, check before you step notices, rigorous broken yellow line parking prosecution and not letting your life get out of control. 'Maybe it would be too much. I don't want to freak people out.'

'Dottie, you lost your sister. It happened. People are freaked out. It is a freak-out situation.'

'I don't want Eve to be some sort of exhibit.'

Kate nodded. 'Well. That's different.'

'How did Ted get shingles?'

'Kids. Chicken pox. Stress. Midlife crisis. Take your pick. At least it's keeping him where I can see him.'

The wind licked coldly at Dorothy's head. She had once had a beanie, like Sam. She shouldn't have thrown it on the fire.

Sam walked towards them, giving a half-wave. 'Thank you, Dorothy,' he said.

'Any takers?'

'A few. I'd better be going.' He smiled at Grace, who'd attached herself sinuously to her mother's body. 'Hello.'

'Mummy,' she said, nuzzling Dorothy's upper arm. 'You're here.'

Dorothy stroked her daughter's honeyish hair, wanted the hug to go on for ever. 'We're going to the playground,' she said to Sam over Grace's head. 'Would you like to come?' Amy doofed into the backs of her legs – 'Mama!' – and she nearly lost her balance. 'Don't do that,' Dot said loudly. 'Don't do that to me.'

'Don't do that to Mum you stupid idiot,' said Grace.

Amy looked at them. A decision was made and her face dropped and she hung her head. Dorothy lowered herself to the ground on one knee and pulled her into a hug. 'Sorry,' she said. 'Sorry for giving you a fright. I didn't mean to shout.'

'Who's he?' Amy's voice buried in her neck.

'This is Sam.' Getting up was going to be difficult. Dot put a hand forward to the wet asphalt, backside in the air, and pushed up all her weight through one knee. Fabric squeaked around the seams of her trousers and blood whumped in her ears. They were the last ones left in the schoolyard.

At the playground Amy chewed a blob of gum she had found under a bench. Dorothy opened a palm and the girl craned her head forward and spat out the gum, green and tooth-ridged. The bin was overstuffed with fast-food boxes, and Dot shook the gum off onto the streaky steel hub on the top. Sam was pushing Hannah on the smallest swing; the baby kicked her chubby legs and beamed.

'My brother owns a car dealership,' Sam said as the child swung back and forth in front of him. 'If your husband is ever interested in trading in the people mover.'

'Do you work for him as well?'

'Sometimes.'

'Older brother?'

'Yes.'

'Are you close?'

Sam smiled. He had dimples. 'It's very nice when siblings get on.'

'OK, not an answer.'

'Sorry?'

'Nothing.' Grace had joined up with some boys from the big school and was sitting on a skateboard at the top of the slide. 'Grace!' The girl ignored her. The skateboard tipped forward, front wheels in the air over the steep metal trough. 'Grace!' Dorothy ran to the slide, legs chafing, her voice low and betraying panic, as though her daughter was an unleashed Rottweiler. 'Get off there now. Get off!'

Grace scowled and pushed the skateboard down the slide. At the bottom it shot and skidded along the asphalt. She slid down after it, controlled, stately. 'Jesus, Mum, I wasn't going to do it.'

Raindrops spotted the playground as though shaken from the trees. The sky condensed. A large incongruous seabird lifted itself from the asphalt into flight, legs hanging heavy beneath it. More rain fell, and steadier, and mothers and children crowded to get out the safety gate. Sam brought the baby to the buggy and settled her in while Dot shook open the folded rain cover. She domed it over Hannah and the baby cried, as she always did, her little hands reaching for her mother from behind the clear plastic sheet, outraged that she had become removed by this layer, made blurry. Sam produced a broken umbrella from his plastic bag and held its stingray tatters over them all, pushing the buggy with his other hand as they made their way, centurions in turtle formation, through the security gate and along the street. Huddled beneath the waterproof fabric, Grace and Amy in front splashing water from the puddles, this kind man at her side, Dorothy's heart opened and she felt she could stay outside in all weathers, walk for miles. The rain, the clear plastic, the wet leaves – all were concrete, touchable, safe.

At the front door, Dot shooed the girls inside and rocked the buggy over the threshold, unclicking the domes on the plastic cover and pulling Hannah into her arms. Sam hesitated.

'Do you want to wait out the rain again?' she asked.

He doffed the umbrella. 'You did have an umbrella,' she said, as though naming the object for the first time. She reached out and softly pinched the rim, where a spoke bobbled through the nylon. 'Sam, thank you.'

'You're welcome.'

For a moment longer they stood grinning at each other.

'I'll talk to my husband about the car. You could come back and I'll sign the forms. Make an appointment for an engine check or whatever it is mechanics do.'

'Can we watch TV?' Grace in the small entranceway, tracking mud over the floor.

'Grace! Shoes off! Help your sister.'

Sam said, 'Yes, I'll come back. Thank you for the fruit.'

She was distracted, crouching down to put Amy's slippers on, and when she looked up he was running through the rain, his heels lifting behind him.

'Thank you,' she called, and he waved, the umbrella flapping above him, shattered raindrops spraying from it, every which way.

The next day while the baby was sleeping there was another knock on the door. Dorothy shut the oven door to keep the heat from escaping, and ran to answer it. A woman with a clipboard introduced herself, waving the photo ID on her lanyard as though it were a hypnotist's watch chain. 'I'm from the council. We're doing a survey about neighbourhood feeling, the sense you have of belonging in this area. Do you have twenty minutes now or should I come back?'

She ticked the 25–39 age box. Her last year in that bracket. The urgent need came over her to *make the most of it*. Yeah! She beamed at the council worker, wanted to throw a hand up for a high-five.

'Are you satisfied with this neighbourhood as a place to live?'

'What is your experience of road safety in this neighbourhood?'

'Do you have access to physical and mental health facilities in this neighbourhood?'

'Do you consider most of your friends to come from this neighbourhood?'

'Can you describe for me, demonstrating with boundaries on this map, your sense of where the neighbourhood begins and ends?'

There was a mechanic's on the back street behind the bank. And another on the edge of the playing fields by the adventure playground. Everywhere she walked now, Dot looked for those large roller doors, the open squares of darkness within, the dank air that smelled so headily of petrol, cubicle offices with glass windows like the graphed pages of Grace's maths book, men in overalls, turning pads, hydraulic lifts, oily floors.

12. TAKE IT TO THE NEXT LEVEL

DRIVING HOME FROM the campground Andrew said, 'I think I need glasses.' Their children and Lou were in the back seats and Dot looked over at him from the passenger's side and thought oh yes, that would be right. He was hunched over the steering wheel, frowning, and the skin of his face had lined and thickened, and the hair was maybe more dry or thinner or something but the head, the shape of the head was the same.

Suddenly the traffic in front of them stalled and he nearly drove into the back of another car. The bend in the road that they inched around finally revealed a lane closed, police cars, an ambulance, the puckered metal of a wreck.

'Don't look, darlings.'

Of course, they did. There was a medical sheet over a stretcher on the side of the road, but you couldn't tell if anyone was under it.

★ ★ ★

At the public baths, the sounds of shouting and water sloshing against the pool's sides ricocheted through the hangar-like space. Holding Hannah's little hand, Dot stepped down from the raked benches and through steamy air to the soft, faintly gelatinous water that puddled over the top metal step down into the cordoned-off recreational pool. Tepid at first, the water cooled as more of her body was immersed, and she floated her daughter through to a gap in the playing children and drew her in towards her, their skin touching under the water, slippery cold and warm at the same time. She held Hannah by the wrists and whooshed her in a semicircle back and forth, then supported her back while she kicked with shonky glee, her eyelashes spiky and wet.

'Evelyn!' The name came from the general mass of bodies in the water and might have been just a random shout if it hadn't happened again, more clearly, and a woman broke through a pair of dunking pubescent boys and space-walked towards Dot. 'Evelyn Forrest! Oh my god. Is this your little girl? She's so cute!'

'I'm Dorothy, Eve's sister. This is Hannah. Say hello, Hannah.'

'I can hold my breath. Watch this.' The girl puffed her cheeks out and plunged her face beneath the water.

'Oh you're Dorothy, of course you are. You're not twins, are you?'

Dot hitched up the straps of her swimsuit. 'How are you?' Hannah came up gasping. 'Well done, darling.'

'Really well.' The woman waved an arm towards the big pool. 'My boys are huge now, they're in squad practice, for my sins. Five a.m. every day! They love it but talk about nearly get a divorce. How old's your girl?'

'How old are you, Hannah?'

'I'm five. But I'm short for my age.'

'She's three.'

'Look at those eyes, she's so like you. Freaky. Have you got any others?' She craned her neck.

'At school. Seven, eleven and thirteen.'

'Four, wow. You don't look it.'

'I've been on a diet for about two years.'

'Well they *wreck* our bodies. I miss babies, I adore babies, but no more.' She made a scissoring gesture with her fingers. 'No. Way. O. Ver. Hey so the reunion! Did you get the email?'

'No, I . . .' Hannah pulled at the neck of Dorothy's swimsuit and Dorothy moved her hand away. 'No, darling.'

'I can see your boobies.'

'Stop it.'

The woman was still talking. '. . . can you believe we're so frigging old? You've got to come, I'll flick you the thing, we're all going.'

'Really?'

'God yes, if you don't go everyone knows it's because your life is shit.'

'How old are your boys?'

'She said the S word,' said Hannah.

'Thirteen and fourteen. Monsters. I mean, we were fourteen! Oh my god the laundry I have to do. The smells. The secretions. I look at them sometimes and think a girl is going to kiss you?' She throttled herself with one hand and leaned back until she had fully sunk then came up choking for real, spluttering, and Dorothy pounded her between the shoulder blades till she stopped. 'God knows what I just swallowed. Such an egg. Sorry.'

'Are you OK?'

'No more sight gags. So. Are you in the book? I'm going to stalk you. We need all the moral support we can get.'

She was either the Tollerton girl or Amanda Marshall. One of them went out with Peter Smythe and the other one went out with Paul Baxter. Peter could do one-arm push-ups for fifteen reps and Paul was the school beer pong king. The woman in the pool now looked like the woman who was either the Tollerton's or Amanda's mother, who had worked part-time as a guidance counsellor and who specialised in passing out sanitary pads the size of light aircraft. Mrs Tollerton. Mrs Marshall.

Hannah said, 'Mama, I want it,' and lunged towards a randomly floating orange flutter board, so that Dorothy had to follow or let go of her. At the dring of an electric bell the woman spun towards the pool's edge and marched through the water, arms extending and retracting as though pulling partners towards her in a square dance. She called something over her shoulder as she reached the metal steps. 'Tell Evelyn.'

Maya Kumar's house was in a new subdivision near the school. The taxi dropped Dot at the end of the road and she walked the wide clean path past half-built houses on bare sections, under street lights endowed with pretty curves and hexagonal glass bulb-protectors, as though they were flowers that had grown there since Victorian times. Light blazed orange from the open front door to Maya's house and several cars were parked on the street, cars that looked modest but more reliable than the rusting Beetles and shark-like Holdens of the school days. There was one black-tinted four-by-four.

Dorothy put a bottle of wine on the kitchen bench.

Maya kissed her. 'It's so great you're here. Mandy said you'd pike out. Also, I told her about Eve. She didn't know. We're all so sorry.'

Something about this environment, the pressing sense of a past with Evelyn in it, made the stock response impossible.

'Wait, I'll get you a drink. My husband has vanished for the night, wise move.' Maya had married one of their old teachers, which for a while had been a scandal. She'd quickly got him out of teaching and into computers. 'Can you believe he was younger then than we are now?'

In the large picture window beyond the kitchen, Amanda Marshall stood silhouetted, a man at her side. Dorothy caught her eye and waved and Amanda resumed animated chat with the man as though she hadn't seen. Through the window was a view of the school's top field. Maya slid a wine glass into Dot's hand. Her perfume smelled of jasmine and gardenias. It was time to brave the living room, where about twenty people in small groups stood dotted around, not all identifiable without staring. Many of the women had moved to the short, bran muffin hairstyle of the forty-plus.

An air of the Principal's office hung over the closest group as they stood in silence, casting around for what to do with olive pits and dirty paper plates. Someone said, 'We live at the end of the train line now, isn't that awful?' A conversation started about children. None of them were sending their kids to the school where they'd all met.

'Not even me,' said Maya, 'and I could probably hit the roof of the common room if I threw something from here.'

'You should try it,' Dorothy said. 'Maybe an egg.'

Maya glanced around and spoke as though to herself. 'I wonder if this is everyone.'

Later, when Dorothy was talking to Nicky something and Elaine Woods-now-Rogerson, she heard, 'Is Daniel coming?' and the women's words churned and bubbled over the floor, all the sound of the party underwater except Maya's response.

'Yes of course! He'd better be.'

Jason's group exchanged information about Philip Lloyd, who had become a dealer in Australia. 'Really?'

'A car dealer,' said Jason's wife, who had been a few years behind their group at school, 'not a drug dealer.'

Jason said Daniel was definitely out of jail and someone else said he'd never actually been in jail and a third person said apparently he'd found God since getting off the smack. 'The NA God, where everything's a pathology. You can't sneeze without wanting to make it with your mother.'

'I always wanted to make it with your mother,' said a man Dot knew but couldn't name.

Jason laughed. 'Yeah well we're about to move her into a unit at the bottom of our garden so come round any time.'

'Where's your dad?'

'He passed away last year.'

'God, sorry.'

The conversation shifted to choosing funeral directors and Dorothy drifted on. A man who didn't look familiar sat in the corner of a black leather sofa and a woman with great legs sat next to him and held a champagne glass to his lips. Down the hall in a room that might have been a study four or five people murmured and laughed over a wall display of photographs from their time at school. The outgoing cluster squeezed past Dot in the doorway. The room was empty now. The photos were on the walls. Evelyn would be there, and Daniel, and Michael, and Ruth. Her email to Michael about the reunion had bounced back. From the living room came the opening chords of a song that was number one for the summer she learned to drive. Someone shouted, 'Maya, we've got the whole night to get through, pace yourself!'

Dorothy stepped back from the photo room and into a girl of five or six. 'Hello,' she said. 'Can't you sleep?'

'The music's annoying me,' the girl said.

'Come on. I'll take you back to bed.'

The girl led the way up the stairs, along a hallway and into her bedroom, which was decorated with richly coloured taffetas and sparkling hanging mirrors that sent spangles floating over the walls. 'Wow,' Dorothy said. 'This is amazing.'

'It's like a princess,' the girl said. She hopped into bed and leaned over to turn on the slowly rotating nightlight.

Dot blocked one ear with a finger and listened. 'You can't really hear the music from here.'

'Yes but it was when I got a drink of water,' the girl said. 'From the bathroom.'

'I see. Do you think you're going to be able to sleep now?'

The girl plonked her head down on the pillow. 'Yes.' She clutched a plush toy puppy to her and closed her eyes. The lids trembled. Stars from the nightlight wandered over the bed, stretching and shrinking on the contours of her face.

'Goodnight,' said Dot. 'Do you want me to send Mummy up?'

The girl nodded, her eyes emphatically shut. 'Yes.'

The woman with the legs asked if Dorothy knew where the bathroom was.

'There's one upstairs. I think it's all right to go up.'

'Can you show me?' Her name was Monique and she was the second wife of a boy from school, the boy who had now become the man sitting on the black couch being fed champagne. Monique was a decorator. On the way up the smoothly carpeted stairs, no fuzz gathered in the angles of the risers, she speculated on the cost of the leadlight windows, the oak ceiling beams, the glass bricks in the kitchen, the marble bench tops and the under-floor heating in the bathroom, asking Dorothy to guess how much the house was worth.

'I know nothing about real estate, sorry. There are children sleeping,' Dorothy whispered.

Monique drew her into the bathroom by the elbow. The women smiled at each other in the mirror. Monique's smile was toothy, almost goofy, and her eyes glinted.

'Who's that guy you're with again?' Dorothy asked.

'Ian Abernethy.'

'I don't remember him.'

'He doesn't remember anyone. He's had an accident. Rock climbing. No helmet.'

'The guy on the sofa? That's him? Oh. I'm so sorry.'

'Yeah, but he wanted to come, he's doing pretty well apart from can't use his arms for some stuff or really walk. And he *talkth like thith.*' She was rootling in her silver leather shoulder bag and pulled out a small envelope and from the envelope took a pill, which she bit in half. She ran some water into a tooth mug and swallowed the half that was still in her mouth, waving her fingers in front of her lips and making a face. She offered the other half to Dorothy, who said, 'No thanks.'

Monique shrugged and popped the second half in her mouth, gulping some of the water that flowed from Maya's shiny bathroom mixer tap. She pulled at the ends of her hair and wet her fingers in the small ring of water collected around the plughole of Maya's basin. 'Design flaw,' she said, and brushed a finger over each eyebrow. Then suddenly she was at the toilet and lifting the lid and pulling her skirt up and her knickers down. Dorothy slipped out the door and stood on Maya's thick carpet and saw herself reflected in the full-length mirror on the landing opposite. From the bathroom there was the light scooshing sound of Monique's pee hitting the water in the bowl, followed by the whirlpooly flush.

They stood in the doorway to Maya's bedroom counting the pillows on the bed. 'It's like how many jellybeans are in the jar,' Dorothy whispered.

'Any more than four pillows is disgusting,' said Monique. 'What's next, soft toys? Let's get a drink.'

Master bedroom: one of the phrases Daniel used to use to make her squirm. They heard Maya coo, 'Goodnight,' in her daughter's doorway, and ducked into the bedroom and pulled the door shut. Dorothy flapped her hands to indicate that they should go out and front up, but Monique gripped her shoulders, holding her in place. A pulse thudded in Dot's ears, as though there was wine instead of blood in her veins. In breathing silence they listened for the sound of Maya going back downstairs but the carpet muffled any footsteps. Monique thrust her head forward and kissed Dorothy on the mouth, and she ducked away, Monique's lips smearing her chin, and shook her head. 'Don't.'

'OK.' Monique thumbed the lipstick off Dorothy's face.

After a few seconds Dot opened the door a crack and they darted down the empty hallway to the stairwell landing, where they paused for breath. 'I have soft toys on my bed,' she said. 'I used to.'

'Bullshit,' said Monique. She scowled in the landing mirror. 'You were the weird shit Blu-Tacked above the desk type.'

'Really? Can you tell?' Dorothy checked her reflection for lipstick remains.

'Oh sure. I've decorated your fifteen-year-old bedroom a million times over and I know all about it girl, I can tell you those stains never come off the wall, you've got to completely repaper.'

'You can look at me now and tell?'

'Come on, you love it. Your little symbols carved in the wardrobe door with a compass.'

Dot leaned over the banisters. People stood in the hallway below, talking. She waved to a girl from one of her classes. 'God, she's a cosmetic surgeon now. I've done nothing with my life but have children,' she said to Monique.

'You're one of those women, your husband only has to look at you, right? We're not going to have kids. Ian could, still, but oh dear, I won't say it! Let's get you a drink.'

Dot sat next to Ian Abernethy and introduced herself. He

nodded and smiled and said 'Yes' when she offered him a sip of her wine. She held the glass up to his lips and dabbed at the edges of his mouth with a paper napkin after he sipped. The song that came on made her heart beat faster. There was music that for years had been out of bounds because of its time-machine properties, its ability to land her in a place from before. That kitchen with the paint samples brushed on the walls, Donald in his bouncer on the table. Her parents' front room, lying behind the sofa with the thickly lined curtains pulled, the seared smell of cold ash. Driving through a landscape of low scrub, a bottle of Coke between her thighs, a pack of cigarettes on the passenger seat, the element-orange glow of the cigarette lighter after it popped from the control panel, the sky behind clouds in thin towers. In front of them some people were shouting and jigging, and others including Monique were properly dancing, and the music was too loud to talk. Ian said something and Dorothy pointed at her ear and shook her head. He pushed his head forward towards the dancing people. She leant over close to him and spoke into his ear. 'You think I should dance?'

'Yes.'

'Wow, Ian, you smell amazing,' she said. 'I could drown in that smell, I could just spend all night smelling you, what is that stuff?'

He smiled and shook his head. She sniffed his neck. 'That is incredible. OK. I'm going to dance.'

He took another sip of wine and she left the glass balanced around the corner of the sofa behind Ian's unmoving feet. Dorothy had just started dancing when the music stopped and Amanda Marshall clapped her hands and shouted, 'So are we going to this thing or what?'

'What,' shouted a boy who had become a man with a red face and a solid, protruding butt, roundly muscled in beige cotton trousers. He was wearing hard shoes and had once cried when he missed a penalty kick at the inter-school final.

'He dashed the tears from his face,' Dorothy said to Ian. She was sitting next to him again. The energy was gathering, and Daniel wasn't here. He had to come. He had to. Around them people were on the move, placing wine glasses on Maya's low, generous windowsills and between the vases of papery poppies on the table. Women bent and picked up handbags and someone inched into the room hidden behind a giant armful of coats, which the guests extracted one by one.

Maya was in the kitchen, holding plates streaked with hummus and baba ganoush under the running tap. The tap sprayed out softly as though there was a shower nozzle over it. Dorothy bent down to look. There was a shower nozzle, and the tap itself was on a bendy stainless-steel concertina-like tube so it could be moved around. Maya made the water swirl and bubble in a circle over the plates. Dot handed her another one off the dirty stack.

'Did you have some food?' Maya asked.

'No, I'm fine. I ate with the kids.' Feeling suddenly that there might still be cheese sauce on her top or a globby seed from the raspberry jam sticking to her hair she bent down to check herself in the side of the espresso machine. The unfaced marble of the sink bench was rough beneath her fingers. 'So is everyone going on to the school?'

'Yeah. We've got to show up otherwise it's that whole thing again, like last time.'

'What happened last time?'

'You were here.'

'No. Have you got any tea towels?' Dot pulled the handle of one of Maya's kitchen drawers, and it opened so glidingly that she staggered backwards and had to clutch Maya's arm for balance and Maya nearly fell on her. 'Sorry.'

'I'll just leave them to drain.'

The drawer sat open like a projected tongue. Dot bumped it shut with her hip.

'Whoa, Big Chill!' Mandy grabbed Dot's hands and swung their arms around in a kind of dance. 'Yeah, I'm the younger dark-haired one they all want to fuck.'

Dorothy extracted her hands under the guise of doing a cosmic sort of dance move then crossed the expanse of the kitchen to the water jug. The genteel doorbell chimed. She poured a glass and held it to her lips, lightly bit the rim.

'That might be him,' Maya said. 'Fucking late as ever.'

The party noise obscured any footsteps that might have sounded up the polished hall. Daniel would be wearing trainers anyway. Here came the figure appearing in the kitchen doorway and it was a middle-aged woman, no, *Dorothy* was a middle-aged woman, this was an *older* woman with short greyish-blonde hair and wearing a brightly coloured dream coat. There had been a production of that musical when they were at school and although, or because, their father disdained 'Lloyd Webber' the Forrest children all auditioned, but Ruth was the only one who got a part. Maya greeted the woman, who was here to mind the sleeping daughter, and clapped her hands and said, 'Doors are closing!'

'Is everyone here?' Dorothy asked. 'Who you invited?'

'Too late now,' Maya said. 'We're O for outta here. Time to kick this party to the kerb.' Horror struck her face and she said, 'Oh – sorry – I didn't mean,' and shook her head and shouted, anger in her voice now, 'Come on, you guys.'

Dorothy said, 'It's all right.'

'Did you see the photos?' Maya asked. 'I was going to do an In Memoriam but then I couldn't find a good picture, and I didn't know if I should, and . . .'

'Oh Maya,' Dorothy said. 'Thanks. It's fine.'

In the hallway by the stairs a small table housed a telephone and its charger. Dot stepped up onto the bottom stair to make room for Monique and Ian in his wheelchair. 'Coming through,' Monique sang out. 'Don't want to run you over.'

The night was warm, close, and the Victoriana lamplight was soft and tawny. The new houses rose like cardboard cut-outs from their blank sections. Apart from one carload of boys and their wives, crushed into the back sitting on knees, heads bent under the low ceiling of the Ford station wagon, everyone walked down the gently curving slope like a wedding procession. In the boot of the Ford a couple who were both married to other people did fake waggly-tongue kissing as the car drove away. People whooped at them. The car suddenly braked and the couple jerked forwards and everyone laughed. The man with hard shoes and Dorothy helped Monique lift Ian into her car and collapse the wheelchair and stow it in the boot. 'Actually, John,' Monique said, placing a slim hand on his arm, 'would you mind driving us?'

Dot waved them off and said, 'Just checking in with the kids.'

The car disappeared around the corner, leaving the smell of exhaust and the optical print of tail lights. At home, Andrew answered the phone, TV commercials playing loudly in the background. 'Sorry hang on.' He pressed the mute button on the remote, cursing as the low battery did nothing to the volume.

'They only sound louder,' Dot said. 'How's Donald's temperature? Should I come home?'

'You mean bottle out? No.'

'We're just leaving Maya's now.'

'No rush.'

'I don't want to go.'

'And yet there you are.'

'Ha.'

'Aha.'

She hung up the phone and checked that it was hung up, and checked that it was hung up again and put it back in her bag. Must have been about a year ago she'd left the phone with Daniel's number in it at the toy library, lost the SIM card, all her contacts. At the bulbous end of the cul-de-sac there was a turning circle like the bottom of a test tube, the place children would ride tricycles and sell lemonade to foot traffic made up of people their parents already knew. A path ran off the end of the cul-de-sac and the last light in the street cast a muzzy white triangle as far as the grassy wasteland beyond. From here she could see over to the floodlit top field and the school buildings and possibly the dark shapes of people walking along the road towards the school gates, before they were obscured by a lump in a hill.

The light petered out at the end of the path, where a wire fence blocked access to the undeveloped hills. A sign was planted in front of the fence and Dorothy stood on the edge of the light, on the point where it gave way to nature, and reached one hand out to touch the high tensile fence wire. An electric shock snapped up her arm and she yelped as the arm flung back, and shook it and staggered down the path a little bit, laughing soundlessly.

Time had passed since everyone else had arrived at the reunion. Blisters stung on her toes, pulpy and jammed into the ends of her shoes, from running down to the school in high heels. The registration people outside the hall had never heard of her. Through the double doors came music that they had danced to a hundred years earlier, at the graduation ball. Dorothy dropped Maya's name and Mandy's but the younger woman said, 'We've had to step up security since your day.'

'Yes,' she said, leaning forward on the desk, her face close to the woman's, 'I did have a day. A school day. I went here. My whole family went here. Why would I make that up? Do I look like a terrorist?'

The woman's gaze drifted over to something behind her and a voice said, 'Yes. I think so.'

It was Daniel. He was wearing a black suit, smiling, and his teeth were peggy and brown. Those dark eyes, oily like coffee beans, looked at her while he spoke to the woman. 'Someone put my name down,' he said. 'Daniel Hill?'

'Danny Hill. You scumbag.' The chemistry teacher clapped a hand on his shoulder.

'Hello, Mr Crosby.' He was still looking at Dorothy. His face made her want to pull her jacket up to hide her own. 'Hi, Dot.'

'They don't recognise me,' she said. 'I can't believe it.'

The suit was second-hand and smelled it, and the worn lapel felt rough against her face when they hugged. Some crying fell out of her. He held her shoulders. 'We don't have to go in if you don't want,' he said.

'No no we should. It's just – like the water closed over our heads, you know. We're just gone. Doesn't matter.'

The three of them walked through the doors into the school hall. Mr Crosby headed for the bar. There was a student band playing music that wasn't quite loud enough. Light splintered around the room from a disco ball. Faces, bodies loomed and receded. Someone said, 'Weren't there more of you, didn't you have a sister?' and Daniel hung back and when she began to explain about the accident a group of guys swallowed him. The woman's mouth flew open and she whispered, 'Oh no,' and Dorothy hugged her. 'It's OK.'

In the middle of the dance floor Monique was giving Ian a kind of lap dance in his wheelchair. 'Wow,' Dot said, and the woman pulled out of the hug and looked at her with a furrowed brow, performing confusion.

'Check it out.' Dorothy pointed to Monique. 'I can't work out if that's really amazing or a bit cruel.'

'Probably only so much Viagra can do,' the woman said. 'I'm so sorry about your sister.'

'Thanks. Me too.' She squeezed the woman's arm and said, 'I'm just going to the bar. Do you want anything?'

The barman filled the softish plastic tumbler to the brim with white wine. It dimpled under the pressure of Dot's thumb and fingers and she tried to hold it lightly with both hands, sipping wine and looking out over the edge. Danny was in a corner by the stage, flanked by three or four men whose past boy-faces floated somewhere beneath the surface of their current faces. He finished saying something then looked around the room. All the wine in her glass disappeared down Dorothy's throat and she swallowed a lurch of joy. Mandy Marshall and the now-Rogerson girl danced over and Mandy squeezed Dot's waist and shimmied up and down. To now-Rogerson she said, 'Remember Dorothy? Freak or unique?' She leaned right in. 'You were rocking that swimsuit at the pool!' Her breath was a mist of vodka. 'Have you had any work?'

'No.'

'I know someone. Comes to your living room.' She pulled at the skin of her temples so that her face went taut.

Now-Rogerson said, 'Really? Call me next time. John's given me the all-clear.'

'Just a minute,' Dorothy said. 'I've got to find the loo.'

As she left them, now-Rogerson said, 'Did she even go to our school? I don't remember her at all.'

'Remember the Forrest girls?'

'There were more than one?'

Danny was in the queue when she came out of the toilets. The lifeless smell of drains mingled with the mothball scent of the chemical blue plugs they used in the bottom of the urinals. 'So I saw you at the funeral,' he said.

'I know.' He had left straight after the pall-bearers slid Eve's coffin into the hearse that was to take her to the crematorium. The image that stayed in Dot's mind was of the back of the car, the brake light that glowed red on the rear windscreen when the engine started. Later she had scanned the mourners, an arm around Lou's shoulder, wanting to introduce her to Daniel, certain that this was important. But he wasn't there.

Dan was openly staring. 'You've got like, a billion kids.'

'Yeah.' Guilt twanged in her, but she didn't know if letting his flippancy pass was a betrayal of her children or a protection. 'You?'

He shook his head. 'Nope. How's Andrew?'

'He's good. Busy.'

'How's Nathan?'

'He's all right, he's OK, yeah. Doing well.' A muscle in Dot's upper arm started twitching and she held onto it, felt the jumping tic beneath her hand. 'Are you . . . with anyone?'

'I was fucked up that day. I shouldn't have left early. I should have talked to you, talked to your parents.'

'God, Daniel, I hated that we lost touch.' She took a deep breath. 'I mean, what happened?' Probably he was sober, this close to recovery, and the thought made her woozier, drunk.

'Dottie, I never properly made amends.'

She shook her head. 'For what?'

'Well, you know. All of it. My sort of vanishing. And then Eve.' He ducked his head to the left, to the right. 'Maybe we should talk about this somewhere else.'

'You don't have to tell me about that. I'd rather you didn't.' She had taken his denim jacket to a fundraising fair for the girls' hockey club, her stall with the clothes rack and boxes of old children's books and vinyl, and sold it to one of the hockey dads for next to nothing and watched him walk away with it on, and then seen him wear it at Saturday games for ages afterwards until she no longer thought hey, that's Daniel's jacket when they were talking. He'd bought it, and wore it so often, she guessed, because they had a thing going on between them, a flirtation, and him in Daniel's jacket was a part of that she could never explain. After a while, prolonged exposure, an embarrassed dance at the prize-giving, the strange sexual energy had evaporated and they were just people in the same community again, without the heat.

'I didn't want to hang around because. It was a time for her and Nathan. And family. You guys together.'

'You are our family,' Dot said.

'I know, but.' Daniel shrugged.

Don't shrug, she wanted to shout. *Shrugging is not an option.*

'Maybe it wasn't that,' he said. 'Maybe I was just too chicken.'

An awful sense suffused her that he hated himself. No. Please let him not be stuck in that loop. 'Listen, Daniel, you don't have to make amends.' It was easier if she looked at the wall behind him but there was his face, those dark, dark eyes, and the time on him, the years all over him, emanating like a heat mirage. 'If it's part of your programme or whatever. You don't owe me anything. We were just kids.'

He frowned. 'That's not true.'

'Hey look,' she said. 'You're still taller than me.'

'You must have stopped growing.' His hand reached up and held her arm – a soft, slow shock. Her whole body expanded. She would kiss him right here if he leaned down. 'Feel your arm,' he said, squeezing the jerking muscle. 'That is so weird.'

Feedback screeched from the hall. 'I love that sound,' Dorothy said. 'So.' She exhaled as though blowing out a candle. 'How long have you been back for?'

He let go of her. 'This last time, couple of years.'

'Do you see much of Maya?'

'Not really. I used to hook her up sometimes. In the bad old days.'

'Before.'

'Rehab.'

'Right.'

'But it's all good now.'

'All good?'

'Jesus, Dorothy, you're kind of drilling into me!'

'Sorry. I don't mean to. It's just that phrase.'

He levelled a look at her. 'So, you are a mum. You're like, *fecund*.'

Blood began to rise beneath her skin. 'You're a shunt.'

'Ointment,' he said.

'Diphthong.'

'Tumescent.'

'Gristle. Slack.'

'Do you feel old?'

The question surprised her. 'No,' she said. 'I never think of that. Do you?'

He tilted his head. 'I feel like I'm dying.'

They stared at each other. His grin faded. The urgent need to say something, to touch him, pressed on her, and she didn't have the words. She shifted her weight and stepped a foot to the inside of his, her leg almost between his, then the door to the bathrooms opened and someone said, 'Are you going in?'

He put a palm to the door. 'Yes.'

'I'll wait by the bar,' she told him, sliding her foot away, at the same time as he quickly said, 'Hey I'm going to head home. But maybe we could meet up?'

A billion kids was who she was to him, he would never know. Daniel didn't want the power any more, and she would just be giving it over in order to what, to break through the G-force of her family life, to jerry-build a rocket ship and climb into it and blast off. Some people took drugs. Some people went rock climbing.

'Do you work?' And yet here she was, punching her cell phone number into his phone.

Daniel nodded. 'I'm a drug counsellor.' He shut the door. At that moment the band started playing a song from when she was fifteen, a song her body heard before her brain did. The music was like lying on the runway as a jumbo jet took off just above you, scraping the air.

Her shoes lay emptied on the wooden floorboards and she thrash-danced up and down, everything around her streaking lines of movement and light. In a split second of self-consciousness she could feel her middle-aged face moving as she jumped so she thrashed her head back and forth to hide behind her hair, threw herself into the music even deeper to forget. The impact of a shove, and she went sprawling into Ian's wheelchair and saw the chair spin before she hit the ground and drink got spilled on her and some-one shouted, 'Piss off.' Dot scrambled to her knees to check on Ian, leaning over the arm of his chair, apologising. He shook his head. Monique intervened.

Dorothy's knee ached as she scooped up her shoes and walked straight for the exit, panting, bouncing her palm against the wall that was hung with display boards and enlarged photographs and posters advertising the decades-old Battle of the Bands and the school magazine. Five or six unfamiliar people were smoking cigarettes under the sheltered entranceway to the hall. A taxi swung into the school gates and pulled up outside the hall and Dorothy limped towards it, the shoes in her hand, and leaned in to the open passenger window.

'Rogerson?' the driver asked.

'Yes.'

★

In the children's bedroom the curtains were still drawn shut. Donald had a devil dress-up cape on and a torch in his hand and was repeating to Hannah in a sing-song voice, 'I'm going to eat you.'

'Come on darlings, breakfast time,' Dorothy said, picking up toys on the way to the windows. 'Feed the fish. And then you need to get ready for school.' Her body operated in space, not her. The tangibility of the mini stegosaurus and cloth doll, the need to remove them from the floor before someone turned an ankle or broke the wing off a kitset aeroplane, the silver light in her eyes after pulling the curtains, the lid of the fish-food jar to replace, the rumpled pillows and sheets to straighten, bedside books to pile, the papery skin of oatmeal that lined the saucepan as porridge thickened on the stove, the facts of rubbish day and buying a board for Amy's science project and letting gorgeous, leggy Grace cycle off without laying anxiety shit all over her independence and knowing already how much she was going to miss that girl and school bells and bus timetables and volunteer morning with crossing duty, these things saved her.

Hannah swivelled enthralled eyes to her mother. 'Go away.'

The bus driver tried to close the back doors before Dorothy could get the pushchair through. 'Wait,' she called out. The buggy rocked side-to-side as she stepped down onto the footpath and Hannah complained in her dream. Halfway across the road they had to pause as more traffic passed, a pulse in the base of Dorothy's throat knocking when the cars drove too close to the wheels of the stroller. At last she was walking to the other side.

Indoors wouldn't do; the café was empty and hushed, no music playing. On the pavement she moved one of the outside tables along, the heavy legs scraping the asphalt, so there was space next to it for the buggy. Hannah continued to sleep. Dorothy squeezed the wooden chair over, sat with the café's wall at her back and watched people pass by. A waitress came, a young woman in a tank top with a tropical bird tattooed on her shoulder. Dot ordered coffee. 'I'm so jittery, coffee's probably a mistake.'

'Go crazy,' said the waitress. 'Go wild.'

Dot twisted the ends of a sugar sachet, picked up another and shook it like a tiny maraca. A man carried a cardboard box down the street. A toddler and her mother crossed the road holding the handles of her toy pushchair between them. Hannah still loved to be swung between her and Andrew's hands whenever they walked through the park. No, Daniel could not be in her life. She was almost afraid of seeing him in daylight. In the far distance a heli-copter traversed the sky, a snub-tailed dragonfly. The coffee came. The presence of the waitress, her care in placing the cup on the table, turned the volume up on the world. 'This is the BirdMan café, isn't it?'

'Yes.'

'And there isn't another one, round here.'

'Another BirdMan café?'

'Never mind, sorry, I'm just confused.'

Dorothy drank her coffee and looked at the newspaper. She checked her phone but there were no further messages. Yes it was Wednesday. Yes it was the right date. Where was he? When Hannah woke she would have a sore neck and be thirsty. Every now and then someone came round the corner and Dorothy's solar plexus gripped although her fingers retained their placid immobility over the paper on the table. She was a body divided into parts.

The waitress cleared the cup, its lining of froth dregs like the scurfy foam left on the mudflats when the tide went out. It was time to collect Donald from school. She paid for the coffee with cash Andrew had given her that morning. The older woman at the bus stop helped her lift the awkward buggy up the steps. Hannah woke up when the bus rumbled out into the traffic and said, 'Are we there?'

Andrew ran water into the saucepan for pasta and Dorothy stood behind him, eating peanut butter on a rye cracker, her mouth glued up. He lifted a single long hair from the pyramid of grated cheese on the chopping board and let it float to the floor.

'Gross.'

'Sorry,' she tried to say.

He turned, smiling. 'What?'

She thunked her head into his chest. 'I can't talk.'

He wrapped his arms around her and they swayed for a few moments. Footsteps padded down the stairs and Donald appeared in the doorway in his pyjamas, scowling.

'What's up?' Dorothy smoothed the boy's hair back off his face.

'I'm scared.'

'Why?'

'I scared myself today with the devil.'

'It's just dress-ups,' Dorothy said. 'We don't believe in the devil in this house.'

'Why have we got that costume?' He stretched his arms wide and she leaned down into the tight embrace, slid her arm around her son's back and hugged him, speaking into his hair. 'For Halloween. I'll put it away until then.'

'Yes.' Donald nodded, his eyes shiny. 'Get it out of my room.'

Dorothy hoisted him into her arms and said, 'Come on, heavy boy. Say goodnight to Daddy.'

'Again,' said Andrew.

After kissing the little children one more time, closing the door on Amy in bed with her headphones and a book, removing Grace's plate of leftovers from the essay notes on her desk, Dorothy stood at the top of the stairs with the orangey-red devil cape folded over her arms. She put the hood part with its squishy black horns over her head but couldn't do up the Velcro at the collar because it was too small. The fabric rustled as she walked down the stairs. She stood in the kitchen waiting for Andrew to turn around from the sink.

'Are they all good?' he asked.

'Yeah.' The ringing of the telephone cracked the air. She headed towards the living room, the ongoing sound, was halfway to the door when he spoke again.

'That might be Louisa. She wants to come and stay.' He lifted his arm high to drain the pasta, and the kitchen filled with the starchy, salty smell of steam.

Dorothy walked slowly to the phone, the cape swishing.

'Is this Mrs Dorothy Forrest?'

'Yes. Ms.'

'Hello, ma'am, how are you this evening?'

'Fine.' She waited.

'Ma'am, this is Peter calling about your Internet provider at home there. Just a courtesy call wondering if you or anyone in the house is looking to upgrade their ISP at no cost at this present time?'

Inside the hood her head grew hot and she pushed the cape off, to the floor. Andrew called something from the kitchen. She said into the phone, 'No, sorry.' She hung up and then rang on again to check the dial tone. It was broken, stuttering to indicate that someone had left a message.

'Sorry,' Dot mouthed to Andrew as she sat at the table with the phone pressed to her ear. The message was from Donald's after-school karate teacher, a reminder about the upcoming exams.

★ ★ ★

The car park at the public baths was flooded and they waited in the Honda for the rain to ease up before making a dash for the indoor pools. Another song from years ago came on the radio. Dorothy turned it up and listened, the red digital minutes ticking closer to the swimming lesson's start time. Through the aching shone a shaft of pleasure: Hannah was a quick learner; by the third chorus she was singing along.

The song ended and Dot turned the engine off and stood by the door with rain soaking her back as the stuck little buckle wouldn't unclasp down by Hannah's hip. Once her daughter was free Dorothy lifted her under an arm and kicked the door shut and locked it and dropped the keys by the tyre and lowered, squatting under the weight of the child and the swim bag, and walked her fingers forward along the wet asphalt without letting go of the girl until she hooked up the key ring and pushed down into the ground with her feet in order to stand. Hannah was on a funny angle and Dot righted her with a hip then ran through the puddles, swerving to the left as a car backed out of a parking space towards them and jerked to a stop.

They arrived at the entrance desk. The swim-bag handle was crooked cuttingly into Dot's elbow, and water seeped all up the legs of her jeans. She placed Hannah upright on the floor and mopped at the girl's head, and shook droplets from her own hair like a dog. Hannah ran to the sweets dispenser, a transparent globe of red and yellow candy drops, and jiggled the coin return and asked for money. Dot took the membership card from between her teeth and slid it through the barcode scanner, then waddled through the automatic glass doors into the swampy air of the pool room, suddenly sniffing from the chlorine, nudging Hannah forward with her knees, steering her daughter now to the changing cubicles at the end of the Olympic-length pool, smudging wet cords of hair away from her eyes.

In the dim, bare changing rooms Hannah was asking for lollies but she couldn't have one now. Dorothy helped her out of her fleece-lined jacket and sweatshirt and T-shirt and pulled the elastic-topped trousers down and then up again so that she could see to get Hannah's shoes off, and lifted her to sit on the bench so the socks wouldn't get wet on the Petri dish floor. Dot unpeeled the socks from Hannah's hot muppety feet and bunched them into the shoes and pulled the trousers down again and there she was, standing, all prepared with her swimsuit on underneath, her lung-shaped ribcage, the swelling diaphragm. Dorothy planted a kiss on her shoulder. Through the door, at the end of the pool, the large racing clock and the clock next to it that displayed the time were visible, and they were late.

'Let's go,' Dot said, and jammed the girl's clothes on the top of the swim bag and held her hand past the giantesses getting changed, the slap of Lycra against their freckled skin, past a topless woman blow-drying her glossy black hair and through the other doors to the children's pool and the class. She stretched the thick rubber-goggles band over the back of Hannah's head without snagging her hair, and lowered the suctioned lenses softly over her blinking eyes. The instructor reached up, arms dripping, and took the girl by the torso and flew her above his head and slowly feet first into the water. Next to Dorothy a baby began to wail, his voice piercing the white noise of the swimming pool. The baby's mother comforted him, rubbing along the ridged gums where he was teething, while Hannah plunged face first into a starfish shape, her body slightly jack-knifed, her bottom sticking up and her feet kicking randomly, never breaking the surface of the resisting water. All around the air was thick with splashing, shouting and the smell of chlorine, and in another learners' lane a woman of about Dorothy's age free-styled her way up the length of the pool, her arms whaling at the skin of the water as though she was fighting it. Dorothy called to her daughter, 'That's great darling.'

13. SPELLS

COULD YOU BE in your forties and still hate your father? Did Dot really hate Frank or was this some kind of habit to keep her infantilised, a hotline to childhood? Dreams about Eve came on her unawares, the grief in them freshly ripped. Grace got a boyfriend, a sweet teenager with hair falling in his eyes and a fireworks obsession, Hannah made the transition to school, and Dot started getting more loaded than all of their friends at gatherings, so that people remarked on it, smirking as they issued invitations. 'Party's started!' they'd shout on opening the door to her and she envisaged a future where she took that on herself, started dressing in fun colours and wacky shoes, became the woman with a loud voice, bumping and grinding off the table of canapés. Out of party mode, the bossy parent in her emerged and she couldn't leave Donald or Hannah's teachers to do their work in peace. They were called in for a meeting with the principal and a Board member, boundaries gently but firmly set. On the way home Andrew shouted at her, *That was fucking humiliating. Sort yourself out.*

So she went to the BetterSelf Program and gave them a lot of her money, no, it was Andrew's money, which they couldn't strictly spare. That's right, Andrew was the one flecking spit from shouting, and she was the one going to a course on how to behave. His paintings had been through a black phase and now he worked on hyper-realist portraits of politicians, which surprisingly no one wanted hanging in their living rooms. By this time her father, the erstwhile hate object, was deaf over there in upstate New York, nothing more than a trench coat, a pair of spectacles, a thinned blond comb-over and a giant flesh-coloured hearing aid. 'Hearing-assistant device', her mother called it, her mother who could never have been the woman who'd dragged her kids to a commune in the night, that wild beast who had stood down the bottom of a deep hole in the earth in her rubber boots and kept digging. Lee's cells had turned over what, four and a half times since then, if regeneration was a seven-year cycle, if that could explain it. No, Dorothy could not phone her father to make amends or – no, hang on, that was the other thing – but she could not make the call to apologise or, what was she supposed to do?

Could she extend her hatred to men in general? The other day she heard people on the radio talk about masculinity studies. Sorry, what? What? There must have been something in her ear. Perhaps her husband's finger was in her ear.

The Program people had confiscated their cell phones. Red plastic-coated wire baskets at the door. They sent them out to pay phones in the street to make their life-changing calls. It was her second day in the Program and so far she hadn't been brought up on stage, hadn't been dismantled in front of everyone and told that her story, her life narrative, was nothing more than an illusion or a lie.

But Andrew was looking after the children for the long weekend, he had stayed home from a hunting trip so she could do this, his friends had probably called him whipped *to his face* and she was in deep. So instead of wimping out she waited her turn at a phone booth, smoking a cigarette because she was not yet broken down enough to not need a cigarette or a drink ever again. The tall woman ahead of her emerged, her face watery and joyous as though a mask had been removed and her skin was feeling air for the first time.

The telephone receiver was thick and green in Dot's hand. The booth smelled of cigarette smoke and so did she. She pulled out her address book, which was so old and out of date that there were people in it who were no longer alive, including Eve. Loose leaves of the address book fell out into her bag as she looked for the right page. The spine was broken. She'd used it to call her mother last night – two numbers always transposed in her mind and when she tried to ring her parents she could never remember which ones they were. Michael had finally been in touch with them and Lee had passed on his number, which was scrawled now next to her parents' in a green felt pen that had been the only thing to hand and the ink had nearly dried out, just lasting long enough to faintly record these digits, and afterwards there had been the intense satisfaction of throwing the pen and its lid in the rubbish bin without bothering to connect one with the other, there being nothing left to protect.

The old handwriting in the address book gave Dorothy pause, the receiver by her ear. Perhaps subconsciously she had known that this day would come, although that morning she had been told that there was no such thing as fate, and no stories in anybody's lives other than the ones they invented. Maybe she had invented herself into this place. The cord coming off the receiver was covered in a flexi kind of metal coil. The square buttons were silver. No dial, no black cubed pair of activators like the sort she and Evelyn used to be able to tap to make their prank phone calls for free. Everything was greasy. There he was. Michael. She sighed, nervously – she had been breathing hugely ever since the announcement that the time had come to make this call. Her hands felt sickly, needed a shake-out. She punched in the numbers. If he'd moved again or wasn't home, would that be a get-out clause, or would they make her *take it to the next level*? Part of her hoped they had some other level in mind and that this would be the skin-lifting experience of promise. Public ecstasy. But this was before she got into 5Rhythms.

The phone rang into her brother's flat. He picked up and her gut seized. Did she hear right what they were meant to do? Or was she the only person in the world of the Program laying herself on the line? 'Michael? It's me. Dorothy.'

'Dorothy.' There was a pause. 'Oh yeah.'

'Um, you probably get these calls a lot but I'm doing BetterSelf . . .'
'What?'

'The Program. It's a personal-growth thing.'

Another, longer pause, in which he might have been silently laughing. He finally said, 'So what are "these calls"?'

'Oh, we're meant to contact someone we've . . .' Could she describe their relationship as broken? Was it a rift? A falling out, or just the distance of time? 'How are you?'

'I'm OK.' His voice sounded really different. Not the renewed accent of her parents but weird, like he was talking through a neck brace.

'So, I got your number from Mum. Where are you?'

'Friend's place. The landlord sold my flat. I mean I was sleeping in the fucking warehouse. Until those guys screwed me and the fucking company tanked. You heard about that, right? Cos you didn't call me. "How are you getting on, Michael, are you OK, do you need any help?" '

Lee had told her he'd been importing Turkish carpets. She couldn't resist: 'I heard there was a hole in the rug business.'

'What do you want?'

'Could we maybe meet up?'

'What for?'

'Just to talk, to see each other. You're my brother.'

'Hang on.' She could hear him talking to someone else. He came back on the phone and said, 'Hang on, I'll just be a minute.' The other person's voice got louder. Michael got louder too – did he say 'You're a fucking thief'? The background went silent and it was hard to tell if she was hearing the sound of Michael breathing or the cars driving past. Lately one of her ears had felt a bit muffled.

'Michael?' Part of her brain tried to calculate how long she had been out here and how much longer she had to achieve the act of reconciliation. It was possible he had hung up.

'Yeah I'll meet up,' he said. 'Not here. There are *arseholes here*.' Her head jerked away from the blast of sound.

'Do you want to come to my place? You could see the kids. Grace is fourteen now. Or you could come during the day?' When Andrew would be at work. Yes. That routine.

He didn't want to come to her place, but named a pub on the other side of the city, gave some cursory directions. 'Tomorrow afternoon.'

'Oh, well we've got the rest of the – the course doesn't finish till tomorrow night – but – yes, definitely, tomorrow afternoon.'

'OK.'

The street outside the conference centre was empty and she ran up the stairs to the foyer two at a time in a panic that they would have started without her. In the morning a woman had come in late and she'd been brought up on stage and called out on her commitment issues shit in front of everyone until she cried. Dot was the last person through the doors. She slid into her white seat just as the Speaker approached the podium. A bruised feeling swelled and his words were lost and when once again tears wouldn't stop leaking down her face the woman in the next seat passed Dot a tissue and patted her knee and said, 'Never mind, things will change.'

★

Hare Krishna Hare Krishna
Krishna Krishna Hare Hare
Hare Rama Hare Rama
Rama Rama Hare Hare

She took the kids to eat at Gopal's. It was cheap! They pushed dhal around their plates, hating it. Amy caught her mother in conversation with a serene-faced woman in a pale-apricot sheet, a white bindi between her eyes, and said as she dragged her away, 'Don't you dare become one of those. How could you do that to me.'

★

Dot and Andrew met Nathan at a restaurant bar and the three of them perched on high wooden stools. He showed them photos of Louisa with his new girlfriend, an actress whose accounts he'd been doing for years, and who had become well known. 'You've probably seen Lou more recently than this. But here's Estelle.'

The pictures quickly replaced each other on the small screen as Andrew moved his thumb.

'Nice gear, dude,' said Andrew of the camera. They started talking about the tricks it could do.

There she was, her famous face shining right at the camera, her arm slung over Louisa's shoulders, and then she was gone, and there was a picture of Louisa in a T-shirt Dorothy had given her, joke-posing like a model. 'Go back?' Dot said.

'There.'

Estelle was tiny, one of those people with a miniature body and big facial features that seemed to be drawn to acting. 'She's gorgeous,' Dot said.

'Apparently so.'

Andrew's thumb kept swiping the photographs along, so that looking at them caused a kind of motion sickness.

Dorothy hugged Nathan. 'You know . . .' She wasn't sure if it was her right to say it. 'You know Eve would have been happy for you.'

He squeezed her hand. Tucked the camera back in his jacket pocket. Dot waited until the maître d' directed them to a table then mumbled an excuse and shut herself in a rest-room cubicle and cried. Footsteps clacked into the room. They paused. She bit down on the length of her index finger. A few more steps and the hingey sound of the door opening and closing again. By the basins, she dried her face on the roller of thick blue paper towels. She stood for some moments longer, listening, looking down at the running water.

Three hundred and fifty people came to Nathan and Estelle's wedding, including Dot and Andrew and their kids. After the al fresco dinner there was a display of belly dancing, and the guests were given tambourines to shake along while waiters cleared the plates. 'Three hundred and fifty tambourines,' said Donald, who played percussion in his school orchestra. 'This is going to be awesome.'

The new bride made a speech to Louisa. Dorothy clutched Grace's hand as Lou then stood before everyone in her vintage bridesmaid dress and glasses, a pink streak sprayed in her hair, and thanked Estelle for becoming her second mother. In turn, Estelle thanked Evelyn – the spirit of Evelyn, her arms out in an all-encompassing gesture, as though Eve hovered everywhere under the blazing white pontoon lights – for having given birth to Lou. She waved a balletic arm at Dorothy and Andrew, and the guests who couldn't see them through the thicket of other guests called for them to stand up, which they did, halfway, briefly, and Dorothy nodded her thanks to Estelle and sat down again wiping her eyes with one of the linen table napkins. The other people at their small round table smiled and one of the strangers patted Dorothy on the arm and said, 'It's so great you're here.'

'My lady and me, twenty-seven years. It's a thing,' their tablemate said while they stood to watch the fireworks whistling, fizzing gold, traffic-light red in the sky, 'being married to the same person, the same person for so long.'

'The problem isn't that they're the same,' Andrew said, 'it's that they change.' The night had become cool, and he put his suit jacket around Dorothy's shoulders for a cape. Their children had banded together with other kids and were leaping on the slope of grass, going crazy at the fireworks, even Grace and Lou exploding with squeals and applause, falling to their knees, rolling around getting juicy green stains on their brave teenage party dresses. One of the boys hit another one in the face by mistake and Dot inhaled, poised to run to the scene, but Grace was there, calming them, crouching down to hug a teary child and send him off to play again, not looking around for adult approval, just doing it. What had happened to that insecure toddler Eve had predicted such dark things for? Dorothy softened, watching her daughter. They were the lucky ones.

'Excuse me, guys,' one of the wait staff said, his hands gripping their plastic table and lifting one side off the ground, 'we're just setting up the limbo dancing here.'

'Any time you want to leave,' Andrew said to Dot.

'My wife is awesome at the limbo,' said the other guest, and he walked into the crowd of firework-lit faces to find her.

★

It had happened a couple of months after the school reunion, when she'd long stopped waiting for the call. One afternoon the phone had rung and it was actually Daniel. He was sorry for standing her up in the café, said a young man he sponsored ended up in hospital that day. He'd been thrown, had lost his bottle, wanting to see her was the old him, part of his disease. But he was going on tour now, to Sarajevo, and had something of Eve's to hand over.

'Post it,' she said. She walked the phone to the window and checked down the street.

'OK, that was an excuse. A Trojan horse. I want to see you.'

'Now what is this, some kind of honesty high?'

'Did you tell Andrew you were going to meet me at the café?'

Dorothy helped Hannah climb down from the table and wiped tomato sauce from her face with the paper towel. 'I didn't meet you at the café.'

'Did you tell him though?'

'No.'

'How are your kids?'

'Great. Amy's broken her arm.'

'Amy? She's the second one?'

'Yes. She came off a flying fox.'

'Please, Dottie.'

Hannah was staring into the distance, scratching her bottom. Worm pills. Dorothy squeezed her above the knee and the girl imploded with giggles. 'If we are going to meet I'm going to tell Andrew.'

'Good.'

Instead she backed out of the room when Hannah wasn't looking, hid in the bathroom and shut the door while they agreed a time and date for Daniel to come over, even though the only other human being in the house was three years old and not really listening. The phone disconnected. For a second Dorothy saw that the room she was in, and the bath, the cabinet, the towel rail, were made of cardboard. Through the window the bleached sky busted in. She ran to Hannah, slung her onto the sofa with an alphabet book and began to read it out loud. By the time the book was finished, home had solidified, become three-dimensional again, and when Andrew came back from polytech she had already given the children dinner and cleaned up, and it was six o'clock so the open bottle of wine was par for the course. Amy and Grace were breaking their brains over algebra and Donald knew all of his spelling words. She and Eve used to think their mother insane for making a cake each time she raised her voice to Frank. Now Dorothy opened the oven door and stuck a wooden skewer into the tin. Of course she wouldn't tell him. She dropped the skewer in the sink; it had come away gooey with warm, unset batter.

When Daniel called out hello and pushed the door open it was as though a character from a dream, an animated cartoon, had entered the waking world. But she was the one who'd told him to come now, while Andrew was at work and Hannah playing at a friend's, the one who'd felt alive – alive to the glimmering leaves, the light in the sky, the smoky colours in her children's hair, the smell of the daphne bush and lavender, the gliding closeness of birds, every-thing. Now here he was, real on the couch. Unasked, he'd removed his shoes in the hall. She hated it when people did that – *totally unnecessary* – but she'd disappeared into the kitchen as soon as he came in, so hadn't seen it happening, just the resulting socks. He didn't look around the house and this lack of interest miffed her but was also a relief. The fewer things he touched the better.

She put lunch on the table and thought she wasn't hungry but as soon as she tasted the bread realised that she was. Daniel draped his suit jacket over the arm of the couch and sat at the table in his shirtsleeves, ate and drank easily, relaxed in his body, and she searched his eyes for evidence of the past, of anything other than this innocuous moment – her mind flipping back and forward over what it meant. No, it meant nothing, had nothing to do with her life. Yes, it was a good thing to have him here with the dandruff on his shoulder and debunk the whole fantasy. She should get him round another time for dinner; they could all talk about the old days. Ask him to babysit the kids while she and Andrew went out. They could be movie friends, sneak off to daytime sessions when Hannah was at preschool and he was between saving needy addicts. Yes.

While they ate he told her about the clown school and afterwards, performing for kids in refugee camps, the travel, the drugs, rock bottom, coming home. She prompted him for stories. Daniel wouldn't say much about the harder things he'd seen, but there was still plenty to tell. He had sat in the YWCA in Nairobi, watching as a tall thin woman lowered sugar cubes into her cup of tea: one, two, three, four, five, six, seven. He'd dropped his wallet, passport, credit cards, everything, into a hole-in-the-ground toilet in Indonesia and had to lower himself in to fish them out. Cuban families had welcomed him into their peeling Havana apartments and fed him cured meats and rum. He had slept, or tried to sleep, on the deck of a ferry travelling to a remote Greek island, velvety water black beneath him, hard bright stars above, been abandoned by friends to card games in Marseilles when the luck was not going their way, got stranded on the wrong side of the river in St Petersburg as the bridges were pulled up for the night.

She wanted to know more about the low he hit, was greedy for disaster and humiliation, the appalling behaviour, smoking coals left in his wake. He mentioned a couple of women and she thought poor them, no wonder they hate you, and then she thought what a couple of crazy bitches and then she thought oh, I just want to be special and she cleared the table and said nothing.

'So what about you? You were practically a teenage mother,' he said.

'Not quite.'

'I wish I had kids.'

'You still could.'

'Yeah, no.'

She tried to imagine her life without its family life. Half-awake in her father's arms, being carried up the stairs to bed. Keeping lookout while Evelyn squatted for a wee in the long grass by the estuary at the commune. The living room at home full of Lee and her women friends, jigging on the spot, watching them swing their hips with their eyes shut, arms fronding the air. A baby's slow turn inside her, like an astronaut. Her son's hilarity at his own sense of humour. The mailman paused on his bicycle by their letterbox. Daniel lay on the sofa, clutching a cushion to his chest. 'You look as though you're at the shrink,' she said.

He put the cushion on the floor next to him and patted it. 'Come and sit with me.'

Maybe there was food in her teeth. Dorothy had a long drink of water and wished people still smoked. Hannah would be eating lunch at her friend's house, creamed corn or whatnot, and after that the play-date would come to an end and the mother would drop her back. At the thought of her sweet, shy three-year-old minding her table manners at someone else's house, a pang slowly shot through her.

'Did you bring the thing from Eve?'

'Come here.' He patted the cushion. 'Come here and I'll show you.'

She knelt on the cushion next to his head. No accident she was wearing a skirt. Close up he looked pretty rough, his skin leached of youth, his hair quite grey. She wanted to touch his hair, feel the skull beneath it. He smelled great. 'What is it?' she said, inches from his body, waiting for a message, or a trinket, or a piece of paper, not for him to open his hand and show her the scar on the pad below his thumb, a shiny purple whorl of cigarette burn and say, 'This.'

She held his hand. Bent back the fingers slightly. The burn scar was like a tiny eye. She wanted to kiss it. The cords of his wrist, the embossed veins ran up into his shirtsleeve. She pushed her fingers up beneath the cuff, felt the hair on his forearm, the twisting muscles. He leaned his head against hers.

'Nothing can happen here,' she said.

'I know.' Daniel lay back, shifted onto his side and pulled her up onto the couch towards him. 'Come here,' he said again. 'Come and lie on this lovely Chesterfield with me.'

'I think you mean davenport.'

'Lofabed.'

'Lofabed?' She laughed. 'I never heard that one.' They lay next to each other but there wasn't really room. 'There isn't really room. My body's changed.' She was worried she might cry. 'I'm older. I'm not the same.'

'Here. Come on, beautiful. This way.'

Later he asked if she remembered the commune, the gold chocolate coins, the rabbit. 'It's funny,' he said. 'How in real time we probably weren't there for very long. But I feel like part of me is still in that place. Alternative self still running around with those frogs and all that.'

'I remember the shotgun,' she said, propped up on her elbows beside him on the floor. She didn't remember the rabbit.

Daniel moved a hand down her back, up the side of her waist, cupping her breast. 'Oh my god,' he laughed, 'I can't believe I'm actually here.'

The kitchen clock ticked. By some act of grace, time played it slow. 'So, this is what I imagine,' Dorothy said. 'When we're old, and that stupid passport of yours is lost in a fire.' She saw it, the last ship he would ever be on, drifting charred and blackened up the coast, bumping the sand on a rain-soaked night, tumbling Daniel out, choking on seaweed and saltwater, onto the earth. 'Then you'll come back to me, all aged and useless, and nobody else will want to know, and I'll make you feel better.'

'Like this? Like it is now?'

'Yes. Except you'll be old and scrawny.'

'You'll be fat,' he said. 'A big fat babushka.'

'And you'll dine out on your famous northern lights and young women sashaying in cobbled town squares and swimming races in fucking Niue or whatever, and we'll all say oh that's just Uncle Daniel with his stories, and it won't matter that you have nothing left.'

'I'll have nothing left?'

She sat up, then stood up. Blood rushed from her head. 'Hannah's going to be back.'

He nodded. 'I know.'

She turned aside to clip up her bra and saw in her peripheral vision a blur of movement. Daniel had stood, and begun to juggle the contents of the fruit bowl. Fruit circled the air above his palms. An apple left his grasp, flew high in the air to smash against the ceiling and thudded along the scuffed floor. He kept juggling, his eyes locked on Dot's face. A mandarin followed with an orange splat. Now a banana, boomeranging off to the corner of the room – another waxy green apple – a whole bunch of comical grapes, rising, turning like a heart to fall and land squashily on the bumpy rag rug. She had a hand to her mouth, shaking her head. From his pocket Daniel tossed her an apple. It was mottled with bruises but she bit into it. He presented her with his empty hands, a clown mouth turned down at the corners, a shrug.

Minutes later, when he was leaving, he reached his hands up to hang onto the lintel and she put her face to his chest then stepped away, the gesture too much like the way she was with Andrew. She had the sudden sense that there was a mask over Daniel's face she'd never be able to pull back.

'Hey, Dottie,' he said. 'What if you're not here when I come back? When I'm all had it?'

She nudged him out the door. In the pathway he paused, made a show of examining his fingers, wiping them on his trousers. 'You need to dust that doorway,' he said. After he'd gone down the path and the coast was clear she took a quick shower and rearranged the living room. For a second she studied her face, which was *exactly the same*, and opened all the windows and the doors and waited for her youngest to be delivered home.

14. LEASH

HER BROTHER WAS waiting when they came home with the industrial cleaner, brick sealant, gloves and goggles. The dog trotted at her side and stopped by an unfamiliar car to sniff the tyres and Michael ambled over. 'Hi,' he said, not looking at Andrew.

Andrew said, 'Morning, Michael.'

'Hi, Andrew. How's the painting?' Michael sniffed. He said 'Andrew' and 'painting' the way nine-year-old Hannah said 'Duh-uh'.

They stood under the branches of the oak in the Boddys' front yard, and the air was steamy and the pavement still dark in patches from the night's rain.

'Where have you been?' Michael asked.

'Hardware store. Look.' Dot pointed at the clinker-brick fence outside their house, where hot pink spray-paint ran across the centre in a broken, wobbly line, ending in a coded symbol. 'We've been tagged again.'

Michael stepped back to study it. 'Jesus,' he said.

Andrew said, 'Let's do this later. I'll get the pressure thing. Hose thing.'

'Amy's going to the skate park after school. And Grace is coming for dinner.' She took the hardware-store bags from her husband, feeling judged by Michael's gaze, that he was noting the way she and Andrew didn't kiss goodbye.

'See you.' Andrew pressed the remote unlocking system on the car – a descending three-note twiddle the birds in their street had learned to reproduce – and she raised an arm and waved as he drove past and tooted, sluicing the windscreen free of rain spots and stuck leaves. She and Michael got covered in a fine spray of liquid disinfectant from the windscreen wipers, and the dog barked.

Michael's eyes followed the departing car. He was talking about the job Andrew had found him in the transport department at the polytechnic, what a worry it was, the supervision wasn't good enough, yesterday afternoon he had seen toast crumbs all over the office floor, a crusty wipe cloth on the kitchen bench.

'That's OK,' she said, 'that's normal. Too clean is a worry, OCD. Are the people nice? To work with?'

'You know, I'm calling human resources. I'm going to report them.'

'But Michael, for what?'

'And could you keep an eye out for those little bastards across the road, they've been in my rubbish.'

'Mike, Andy's only just got you this job. There are no jobs, do you know that? Don't make trouble for no reason.'

A neighbour walked past, holding her umbrella so that the

handle looked like a hook emerging from her sleeve in place of a hand. Dorothy smiled at her and nodded and reined in the straining, sniffing dog.

'Also, while I'm at work can you move my car? It sits there too long and some idiot reports it stolen.' Andrew described Michael's car as 'an eyesore'. Tangy floor mats, the flaming embrace of the petrol smell from the can he kept in the boot. 'I'll leave the car key in your letterbox.'

'No, I'm teaching later. Just leaving the car for a day is OK, come on.'

'Can you help me or can't you?' Getting louder now.

'Michael, don't shout at me. I haven't got time to move your car.'

'You always do this! How long does it take!'

'Stop it.'

Michael had jettisoned everyone else in his life: their parents, his ex-girlfriend, Daniel long ago. The slights and disagreements were clutched and nurtured, too complex to understand. You couldn't point out that he was the common denominator. He was demanding and rude and most of the time Dorothy thought he hated her, but having him live next door was a family duty she was glad to fulfil, especially now, in what everyone had taken to calling 'these times'. He needed her. In the winter he'd got stuck in the bath and it was only when she dropped some mending round, coming through the unlocked back door with a pair of folded jeans the size of a tablecloth, that she heard him yelling. Together she and Andrew unwedged him and for a while she'd made him go on a diet, bringing pots of low-GI casseroles, but nobody could make her brother do anything he didn't want. Dial-a-Pizza pulled up outside his place almost every night.

Now he came very close to her. 'They are watching, and waiting, and they are going through my rubbish.'

'Michael. You need to take your meds.' *Meds*: she hated that fake flak-jacket word, but it was her brother's language, a way to butch out the shitty passive business of being a patient, someone who needed help. 'I'm coming in with you.'

'No you're not.' He turned abruptly and galumphed the few metres to his house ahead of her, surprisingly fast given his bulk, and she stumbled over the dropped bags of cleaning product and into the hot muscular flank of the dog and raced to his door but he got in first and was too wide to overtake. The door slammed in her face.

'The police helicopter was out this morning.' She yelled it through the wood, held a finger in the air and spiralled it. 'Did you hear? Keep your doors locked.'

On the news they'd reported an escaped prisoner, a double murderer. How did they escape? That was what Dorothy wanted to know. Buddleia tumbled from the brick wall, purple flowers spilling into the air.

She shouldn't have mentioned the helicopters. It was the last time she saw Michael for a while.

Light gathered in the valley of the bank, hung pale brown in the long fronds of grass. On another hill the grass furred in the wind, pinkish gold. The path took Dorothy from her house to an unsealed track that tailed off, and along the bank to the fringed beginnings of the woods. A very few wild flowers dotted the slopes with red and purple, the sparse colours fleeting, as though they would disappear if looked at too long, and cabbage white butterflies butted the grass feathers with greenish wings. The person emerging from the thin leggy trees – birches, bark lined with cracking peel, the trees inside sloughing their skin – was a scarecrow of purple clothes beneath a mushroomed umbrella, a shock of grey hair. Dorothy's dog ran up to the figure, its black hide shimmering over the muscles that crossed beneath the skin. The figure made a half-beckoning hand gesture towards the dog, the umbrella buffeting in the wind.

The brushing grass against her calves whispered louder, its smoky scent intensifying as Dorothy walked towards the woman and the woman walked towards her without looking up, the world behind her head blocked by the umbrella, her stare somewhere on the ground. With a plunging certainty Dorothy recognised her. Rena. Her mother's friend from Hungry Creek. 'Hello,' Dorothy said loudly, passing. The woman stalled and smiled frowningly and said, 'Hello. You're . . .'

'Dorothy Forrest. You knew my mother. At the commune.'

Rena's face was wrinkled, blue in the glow from the umbrella. Her gaze sizzled, and the smell of recently fritzed marijuana clung to her. 'Dorothy. Look at you. My god.'

Each made a small, aborted movement towards the other, stopping short of a hug. Yes, Rena looked older, but not by that much – surely not by the same number of years as Dorothy had aged. It was forty-odd years ago. Rena must be seventy.

'I'm looking for your brother Michael,' she said. 'Do you know where he is?' She had the determined gaze of the embattled, and Dorothy got the dumb, shameful feeling that she was resisting knowledge, the salient detail. What did this woman want with

Michael? The dog had its nose in something under a tree, and Dot smelled or imagined the smell of a rotting animal, a poisoned squirrel or rabbit, and called to the dog in a deep, stern voice and it returned, breathing quickly through its open mouth, its lips squid-ink black and wet, the tongue a happy pink. 'Really? You're looking for Michael?'

'I need to talk to him about something.'

Dorothy gestured towards the street. 'Have you tried him at home?'

'We need him to sign something and,' Rena turned as though he might be coming up the path behind her, 'the phone's just ringing and he isn't at the work number Lee gave me, either.'

'He isn't at work?'

'No. His car's still there. I don't know.' She laughed wheezily. 'He might be stuck in the toilet again.'

'It was the bath. Did Lee tell you about that?' She hated the thought of her mother and Rena clucking over Michael. That awful, female power.

'Have you got a key? When did you last see him? Someone should probably break in and check he's not in trouble.'

'Ha ha. Well I'm just . . .' Dorothy patted the dog, who was whining. 'I'll be home later. The cedar house over there. If you need anything.' She continued down the path a bit and thought once upon a time that witch saved my mother's life, turned and called, 'I mean would you like to come for lunch?'

But Rena was walking on.

The trees thickened and lace-holes of light swayed on the damp forest floor. Dorothy trod on fallen nuts, small broken forks of twigs, acorns that rolled glossily away from her progressing feet, looking boiled and indestructible. God, she was sweating, under her arms – the anxiety sweat of menopausal hormones, or of instinct. The woods continued ahead, thick with the crackle of insects. She looked over her shoulder as though Rena might be coming after her. The dog was somewhere. A couple wearing red-and-orange jackets of stiff, waterproof fabric chafed past, pausing in their conversation to exchange hellos. Light pearled in the raindrops that hung on the underside of branches, like the bellies of glow-worms.

An old van stood parked outside Dorothy's house, not the same van that had taken them away all those thousands of nights ago, but close enough. Its windscreen framed a dream catcher and a couple of dead flies lay in the dust on the thin ledge of dash. The memories wouldn't hold, they were unlatched, she felt blurred by some other place and time she couldn't really see. If Evelyn were here, or Daniel, she could ask them what was wrong about Rena. Easier not to grasp at the evaporating past, easier to focus on what was in front of her now.

A trio of figures formed a tableau on her porch. Rena introduced Dorothy to her daughter Mei, and Mei's daughter Susan, a girl of about eight, dressed in a hand-knitted jumper and white cotton knickerbockers. Mei must have been one of the younger children at the commune, or perhaps back then she wasn't born yet. They all backed away from the dog when it loped up the steps and skittered to a stop right by them, claws audible on the wooden boards. The girl's hair was in braids that might have been slept on, gaps appearing between the woven strands, a sparkled hairclip perched over one ear. The dog lapped noisily at its water dish and Dorothy opened the house and welcomed the small group inside, the hallway giving onto the cedar-panelled kitchen, autumn sun warm through the windows, setting the glazed bowls on the table alight. The women smelled of wet wool and old citrus fruit, and Dorothy lit the scented candle on the shelf.

The girl, Susan, sat down and reached across the scrubbed wooden expanse, lying nearly flat on it to arrange the bowls, the largest in the centre, smaller ones in orbit. 'There are some books in Hannah's room,' Dorothy said. 'Do you want to see?'

Susan shook her head. 'No thanks.' Her voice was husky.

'She's a wee bit older than you, I think. My kids are at school. Well, my eldest's at university.' Dorothy looked at Rena, expecting some reaction to this evidence of the passing of time, but the woman was impassive, maybe blissed out.

'I'm eight. How old are you?' the little girl asked.

'I'm forty-nine.' She'd just had a birthday; it was the first time she'd said this new number out loud. On that birthday morning she had lain in bed, listening to the shower running over Andrew's body, the mattress rising to hold her like an open palm, feeling closest of all to Eve. Later she lit a candle for her sister. Yes, she wanted a postcard from Daniel that never came, just as she wanted the phone call out of the blue, the unexpected knock on the door. It was easier to admit these things than pretend the ache did not exist.

Susan smiled. Her two front teeth were new adult ones, rectangular, wavy-ended. 'It was my mum's birthday yesterday.'

'Really?'

'Yeah.' Mei shrugged. 'The big three-o.'

The kettle hissed and Dorothy shook the teapot upside down over the sink until the sodden teabag inside was spat out. She set the tea and four mugs on the table. 'Out of milk, sorry. But there's apple cake.' Dense earthy slabs, the smell carried on the steam from the mugs of tea.

'Is this your birthday cake?' asked Susan.

'Yeah, why not. I remember an amazing chocolate cake at the commune. Vinegar and eggs. Does it still exist, Hungry Creek?' Dot asked Rena. 'Are you living there?'

'Can we borrow a ladder?' said Rena, coming out of her trance with a static fizz. 'There are louvres in a downstairs window but it's too high to get them out.'

'Sorry?'

'To Mike's house. We need to get in.'

The sides of the tea mug were stinging hot. It wobbled slightly as Dot replaced it and liquid slopped onto the table. 'No. You can't break in.'

'Have you got a key?'

'No. But if he's not there he's not there.'

'I'm worried. What if something's happened?' Rena stared at Dorothy, direct. The bones in her face were still strong and beautiful. She looked capable of anything. 'Like when he got stuck? Like if he hasn't got his medication?'

'My mother shouldn't talk about things like that.'

The girl Susan placed her hands over her ears, closed her eyes and began to hum a song.

'What if he's lying there unable to move? Unable to reach the phone?' Rena said. 'It's the louvre window or we bust the front door.'

'Sorry, but I don't understand why it's so urgent.'

Rena jabbed at her own chest. 'I'm dying.' It was almost a shout, full of terror.

'Oh my god,' Dorothy said. 'Rena, I'm so sorry.' She reached across the table to place her palm over the woman's wide, veiny hand.

'I need to know if he wants my place at Hungry Creek. She doesn't.' A thumb jerked towards her daughter, who was examining the papers on the bench – school permission notices, children's swimming certificates, a gas bill.

'So men . . .'

'Yeah hell, we let men in years ago. If he wants it, there's an interview process. But I need to know now. We've got to get back there tonight. So if he's home and just not answering the phone or whatever, I want to know. Susan, you're small enough, your mum can give you a leg-up through the window.'

'I can tell him to call you.' Dorothy was still wearing her puffer jacket and another bolt of her own body heat surged through her. 'Well, I've got to go out again,' she lied. 'Rena, I'm so sorry.'

The flat battery on the smoke alarm beeped. Something else to do later.

Outside the house Dorothy waited for them to get into the van.

'Oh, we'll just hang around a bit to see if Michael shows up,' Rena said.

Dorothy stared at her. Was she really having a stand-off with a dying hippy? The dog waggled around the back door of Dot's car, ready to jump in. She imagined, if she drove off on her fake errand, anything to get away from Rena, the child being pushed through the gap between the bathroom louvres. Rena waiting while the girl walked through the dark house with her hands covering her ears, a house that was strange to her. Past Michael's closed doors and drawn curtains. Looking for the front door, or the back door, any door to open onto the world outside, hoping not to pass an arm on the floor flung out of a doorway. Michael's enormous body sprawling from the end of it.

'Aren't you worried he's in there,' Rena persisted, 'stuck again? I mean, do you look after him or what? You know he'd be crazy not to take Hungry Creek. The world's going to hell. I'm glad I won't be around to see it.'

Across the road, a leaf zigzagged the air at dream speed and settled on the roof of Michael's car, joining the yellowing layer that covered the bonnet too.

'All right. I'll do it. Come on,' Dorothy said to the dog, and clicked her tongue.

The louvre panes were heavy, their edges bumpy and rough, and she had to push down hard on each one to slide it out into the bathroom, gripping tight so as not to have it drop and smash on the floor or the toilet that sat just below, lid down. The glass was thick and possibly unbreakable but still Dorothy was careful as she slid a removed pane out between the remaining slats and lowered it into Rena's ready palms. Mei held either side of the ladder's ridged metal rails. The top of the ladder leaned into Michael's weather-board wall. Susan was a small distance away, at the street corner of the house, with the dog. If she was on lookout, nobody put the language on it.

'Michael,' Dorothy called through the widened gap in the window, a mouth missing some teeth. 'Hello? Michael?'

From the road came the swoosh of a car passing without slowing down. Far away someone was mowing a lawn. The man's legs would be catching blades of grass and bits of grit that would smear if touched, the way things did after the rain. She called again, and listened, and a weak response seemed to come from somewhere inside.

The top half of her body fitted through the gap and she could easily reach the cistern, which she balanced on while she tried to hoist her hips over the window ledge. The flush button was in the middle of the cistern lid and an edge of a finger pressed it and the water gushed loudly. She was doubled, half in and half out of the window. Her mind was on holding herself up with her arms and not collapsing like an enormous tracksuit-clad snake into the bathroom, and also on the bottom half of her body sticking out the window and the possibility that Rena, Mei or Susan would have a digital video camera or filming capabilities on a cell phone. She leaned down to flip shut the lid and seat of the toilet and tipped forward, one arm outstretched, and lunged, like an acrobat shinning down her partner's body, from balancing on the cistern lid to the closed toilet seat to the floor and now her whole self was balanced on her hands in the small bathroom, and something happened with her feet and her legs thudded to join her so that she was sideways half on the floor half on the toilet and now she stood upright, panting.

'I'm in,' she called. 'Michael? Are you home? I'm in the house.' No reply. 'I'll let you in the back,' she called to Rena. She pulled at the filmy white shower curtain that surrounded the bath. No Michael, just matching pink plastic bottles of shampoo and conditioner. Dorothy peeled the leg of her tracksuit away from her left calf and felt the white-flaked skin where she had scraped it on the window ledge, pinpricks of blood dotting through over the shin bone. The bathroom door was closed. Suddenly she needed to pee and she did, and flushed the toilet again although the slow cistern hadn't refilled. There was a toothbrush on the basin ledge. The empty space behind her reflection in the mirror made her shudder.

A bit of light pierced the shady hallway, and she walked towards the kitchen at the back of the house. She startled – a peculiar split second of announcing silence, the echo before the sound – and the telephone rang. It was intensely loud and she picked up and said, 'Michael's house.'

'May I speak with Lord Waldegrave?'

Dorothy laughed. 'No, sorry, I think you've got the wrong number.'

'Oh. My apologies.' The man hung up.

Mei's dark head and Rena's grey one passed the kitchen window. She put down the phone and a light tapping came at the back door and a woman's voice quietly called her name. She turned the lock but the handle wouldn't move. 'It's snibbed,' she said through the crack in the door, or where there would have been a crack if the door hadn't fitted tightly into its frame. 'The lock needs a key.'

There was a wooden block attached to the wall next to the door, a curlicued pokerwork line burned into it, just like the key holders they had made in woodwork at high school. With a rushing sound a wave of rain swept against the house and the women shouted at her to hurry. Two keys dangled from the block's nails, one small and flat like a key to a padlock and the other a slightly rusted cartoon key. Neither of them fitted the back door.

'He's not here,' she said into the door. The rain was sparser now, spattery. Mei looked through the window at Dot and pointed two fingers towards the front of the house.

Aside from the burned knife by the stovetop, the kitchen was clean, a bowl of soft local apples on the table. The fridge lurched into a hum. The milk inside was sour. She leafed through the letters next to the telephone. The same city council rates bill she had in her own house, the gas company bill, a flyer advertising gardening services, lawn mowing, tree surgery, *Turk of America*, *Kilim Monthly*. And among these, letters addressed to Sir Michael de Waldegrave Esq., Lord Forrest Waldegrave, Waldegrave House, Sir Van Der Waldegrave, The Manse. An A4 envelope with the sender recorded as Who's Who. Who's Who. The phrase owled around inside her head, talons out.

Dorothy leaned against the bench for a few seconds then reached down to pick up the envelopes that had fallen onto the floor. From here she could see a spray of sauce flecks on the skirting boards, a swept line of crumbs in the corner, a squashed kidney bean. She opened the cupboard and a meal moth flew out. The women were knocking hard on the front door, ringing the doorbell. She checked the empty living room, then the bedroom before opening the door; the bedding was rumpled, the bed half made, and a pillow lay on the carpet next to a roach-studded saucer. The house hung with the stale stench of pot. Outside, the dog barked.

'He's not here,' she said, and walked out the front door and shut it behind her. Rena pushed at the door but it had automatically locked; there was no handle.

'No,' Rena said. The dog was out of sight, still barking, after a cat perhaps. The four of them stood on Michael's doorstep and Rena said, nodding towards the side of the house, where the bubbled glass louvres would be stacked against the weatherboards, spotted with rain, and the bathroom window blackly open, 'Why'd you do that? We're going to have to go in again.'

'Why? He's not there. He's probably gone away.'

'He would have told you.'

'For god's sake. He isn't there. Leave it.' Dot stood by Michael's letterbox, facing away from the house across the road.

'Come on, Granny,' said Susan. 'I want to go.'

Over by Dorothy's house the sound of the dog barking was incessant.

'What do you want to do?' Mei asked her mother. She stroked a hand down the crimped slope of Rena's shaggy hair and pulled her into an embrace. Rena rubbed her eyes into Mei's shoulder, while Susan patted her grandmother's back with a small, childish touch. When the old woman lifted her head and rolled it on her neck and sighed, the edges of her eyes were red. 'If he doesn't care,' she said to Dorothy. 'I'm *dying*. I need to know from him before I finalise the will. If he doesn't care, it'll go somewhere else.'

'Mum,' Mei said gently, 'please don't keep saying that.'

'What, I'm dying? What's the matter, it's not enough that I'm dying, now I'm forbidden to say I'm dying? It's the lying that gives you cancer, Mei, I'll tell you that much.' They were all speaking loudly now, over the maddening relentless sound of the dog.

'OK.' Dorothy stepped back towards them. 'Does he know how to get hold of you? Why don't you give me your number, in case he's lost it. I'm sorry, I've got to see what's bothering the dog. She brings rodents in the house.'

'I've been leaving messages for a week.' Rena's voice was losing some of its resolve.

'Can you wait a bit longer?'

'OK.'

In the glove box of the van they found a piece of paper from a notepad with a real estate agent's face on the right-hand corner, and Susan had a pink glitter pen in the back seat. The girl buckled herself in and picked up a comic book. Rena wrote her number on the paper, and *Urgent* across the top. 'I need to see him,' she said quietly. 'Can you tell him that, Dorothy? Even if he doesn't want what I can give. I need to see him before I die. I have to make amends.'

'Oh, Rena.' Dorothy took the note. She didn't want to ask *for what*. 'Michael's had a hard life.' She hugged the older woman, her velvety purple jacket, inhaled her smell of citronella. Ribby Mei stepped forward to be held too. From the van's back window, through a rubbed hole in the condensation, Susan blinked.

'Happy birthday for the other day,' Mei said.

'Oh yeah. Thanks. Same to you.'

The dog arrived at Dorothy's side, half-jumping up at her. 'Down!' she said, but the dog kept barking as they drove off.

Halfway up the path to her house Dorothy smelled burning. The kitchen was on fire.

Late the next night, after Hannah was in bed, some kind of dreamy folk music emanating from Donald's room and Amy on the back steps locked in a phone call with a friend, arguing over her new veganism – 'Vegetables are nature's meat' – Andrew answered a short hard rapping on the door. Dot heard male voices. Sometimes she hid from unexpected visitors, as though her agoraphobic self had reappeared. She and the kids made it a game, soundlessly gleeful as one extended a smooth leg and nudged the door of the television room so that it swung slowly to a soft close. But now she emerged from the blackened, soaked, foul-smelling kitchen into the hall, apron on, dishcloth and grater in hand. It was Michael's bulk in the doorway, and Andrew said, 'Mike's back. He says his house has been broken into.'

Her brother was sweating, breathing hard, distress on his face.

'Where have you been?' she asked.

'Do you have to know everything? Fuck man, this neighbourhood is totally unsafe.'

'Tell me about it,' Andrew said. He was shattered from sitting up all night guarding the open back door while they aired the kitchen. Half sleeping with his head on a pillow on the table, a tennis racket propped up next to him where another person would have had a shotgun.

'Come in,' said Dot. 'We had a bit of an accident.' She wasn't sure how Michael was going to react. Her older brother sat on the living-room sofa with his elbows on his knees. A crane fly stroked the window with one of its fine, hairlike legs. In a blur it batted across the glass sideways and settled again, resuming its thin lines.

'They found that guy,' said Michael, 'the one that escaped from Mount Eden. I was helping look for him.'

Dorothy picked up Donald's homework book and held it to her chest.

'Michael,' she said, 'I've seen Rena.'

'Rena.' It was as though she'd slapped him. Before she could mention the woman's illness, or the commune, or the inheritance that waited there, her brother lowered his big head to his arms and wept.

15. VIEW

ONLY TWENTY-FOUR HOURS since they'd finally determined to go, Dorothy and Amy found themselves halfway around the world. A different time zone, everything awry, from the row with Andrew about leaving in the first place to the dream-long flight to LA. Ruth's husband Ben, a wealthy, pigeonish banker, met them at the airport, where they hired a rental and followed him through the haze and tangled freeway, humming with Amy's buzz at the vast spread of city, Dot's own ongoing meditation about *observing the loss*. A month ago her parents had moved across the country to California, to be nearer to Ruth. Two days ago, they had died. The car tipped head first into a shallow ravine; consensus was that Frank had suffered a heart attack while driving, Lee in the passenger seat beside him, neither of them belted in.

People Dot didn't recognise gathered outside St Mary's, the modest Episcopal church in her parents' adopted neighbourhood. She embraced Ruth, whose hair was professionally set. A few rushed introductions while Dot tugged at her formless aeroplane cardigan: Ruth directed them to Frank and Lee's friends and the second cousins, the other Forrests. 'But you'll come back to the house afterwards. There's an afternoon tea. I've had it catered.'

'Yes. We'll see you there. Wait, Ruth – where are your girls?'

But Ruth had gone to greet more people, perfect in low heels and tan stockings.

A tall skinny young man, one of the cousins, blatantly appraised Amy through his tortoiseshell specs, worn in the style of Frank Forrest. He was disappointed to learn that she and Dot were not staying on.

'The return flight leaves tonight,' Amy explained. 'We'll sleep on the plane.'

'Why not come for longer? I could show you round.'

'We've got to get back. We nearly didn't come. I didn't really know my grandparents.'

'Aha. Tell me more.'

Inside, caught in a patch of sunlight on the left of the aisle, Rena sat away from the other mourners, bolt upright in a special padded seat. 'You came all this way,' Dorothy said. 'My god. You're amazing.' Light limned the wiry shock of hair, her skin, hair and bone just held together by her electric will, her rage.

'Your mother was a dear friend,' Rena said. 'A dear, dear friend.' Her hands twisted.

'How's Michael?'

'He didn't want to come.'

'I know.' After Ruth's phone call Dot had rung him to break the news. He lived at the commune now, with Rena, 'Until it's her time', as he put it, having been transformed by the rural life into someone who spoke like a medieval pastor, a crowing rooster in the background. When she told him about the accident there had been a long, long pause. Wind rushing the wires.

There they were. Ruth's twins. In the doorway, a welcoming committee, teeth gnarly with metal braces but so poised, shiny brown hair and black dresses, shaking the hands of the elderly mourners, accepting condolences, giving them. Dot went to say hello and let them check her out, the weird auntie from that place they couldn't find on a map. They were polite, told her about school and horse riding and drama class.

'You must have been close to your grandparents?' she asked, and both girls said together, 'Oh, yes.'

She waved her daughter to come over from the speccy flirt, but before she reached them the minister took the podium, and the girls melted away, and Dot and Amy quickly ducked into a pew.

The service flowed with loving testimony from incredibly old people about Frank and Lee's capacity for friendship. White-frosted men and women sticklike inside pressed cotton pastels, clean shoes. Maybe it was the jetlag, making her sway in her seat, as though one of the California fault lines had opened and was torquing the earth slowly. It wasn't until the flirtatious cousin stood up to read a letter from Daniel, 'who couldn't be here in person', that Dorothy really accepted he wasn't going to come. No – even then a corner of her mind imagined him outside, smoking, ready to throw an arm out as she walked past. But this was a long way, no doubt, from wherever he now lived.

Overwhelmed by the gravity of the situation, the cousin lingered too long over Danny's simple lines, delivered them in a suspenseful boom.' "Lee and Frank gave me a home when I needed one most. They gave me a family".'

'He should do voice-overs for blockbuster ads. *This summer...*' Dorothy whispered to Amy in the movie-trailer voice. '*Two people...*'

Her daughter looked at her. 'Oh Mum,' she said. 'It's all right.'

The pew rocked. Her body felt the motion of the plane, still sleeping in the awkward chair, holding there the knowledge of her own safe bed at home. In Auckland it was midnight. Little by little her parents' car approached the bend in the road. Funerals go by so fast.

Later they sat outside Frank and Lee's house in the rented car and watched people stream through the gates for the catered afternoon tea, rich yellow light dripping over the afternoon. 'Come on,' Rena said from the back seat. 'Let's go in.'

Dorothy turned to Amy. 'I think this is what's called losing your nerve.'

'I'll come in,' said Amy. 'Moral support.' She kissed her mother's cheek. 'Follow when you're feeling up to it.' She helped Rena's crabbed body out of the car and across the road, hobbling.

The magnolia in the front yard was broad and luscious, the white plaster freshly painted. Inside, Amy walked a cup of tea through the Forrests' retirement bungalow, watching her aunt and uncle and an antique-dealer friend in conversation that threatened at times to reveal itself as negotiation, linger over this sideboard, that rug. Pieces she described later for Dorothy to visualise, furniture that had bobbed back and forth on the ocean and crossed this country by U-Haul.

When Amy appeared in the front doorway after about half an hour the tall cousin was with her, and Dot gripped the steering wheel and craned forward to see better. He kissed Amy on both cheeks and they made a false attempt at parting and smiled, her fingertips to his chest both deflection and touch. From the shadowed hall, Ruth joined them and embraced her niece. At that distance she looked just like their mother. When they were younger Ruth had most resembled Eve, but now she had long passed Eve in age, the little sister outgrowing the elder. Dot waited for Ruth to glance over, walk down the steps and cross the road, but she did not. After a moment Dorothy tooted and waved. Ruth, to her credit, just stood on the doorstep and looked evenly at the car, then was swallowed back into the house. Amy slid into the passenger seat and pulled a small framed square from the inside of her linen coat.

'What's this?'

'A memento. Do you want it?'

It was a needlework piece, a picture of a cottage garden, little blue and purple stitches for flowers and a yellow thatched pattern on the cottage roof.

'No thanks. But you should keep it.'

'Cool. I love it.'

'Did you talk to your cousins?'

'Yeah, they're nice. Pretty upset. They kept talking about how their dog died only last year.'

'No Rena?'

'Apparently she's staying a few days. I wouldn't be surprised if the trip kills her. She's absolutely crazy. She tried telling me he did it on purpose.'

'Who?'

'Your dad.'

Dorothy had a pleasing image of running Rena over in this car. *Crunch.* 'What, he drove off the road on purpose, or had a heart attack on purpose? Or both?'

'Exactly. I mean she's nuts. When I left she was having a sleep on their bed.'

'Frank and Lee's bed?'

'Yes.' The children had never been sure what to call them; Dorothy knew this was her fault.

'Did you have a nice talk to your aunt?'

'She's my aunt? I thought she was the real estate agent.'

'Are you being funny?' The car bunny hopped at the lights. She wasn't used to a manual. 'Sorry.'

'Yes. But she did have that price-sticker vibe.'

'Noting the value of things.'

'Maybe it was just the pearls.'

'I mean what things are worth. Not the value of things. That would be a different question.' Dorothy turned on the radio. 'How was it in there?'

Amy smiled. 'Pretty nice house they ended up in.'

'Oh, yeah.' It would likely be sold now, she supposed. Ben had made sure to mention that there were complications with the will, which was fine with her; she'd rather that was all broached when they were safely home again through the sky, clouds reforming in the aeroplane's wake, covering the trail. 'They were privileged.'

'Why didn't they ever some to see us?'

'Because they were cunts.'

'Jesus, Mum.' Amy leaned forward and turned off the radio.

'Sorry.'

'Oh, just let's not talk about it.' She put the radio on again.

'Well, money sort of – bookended their lives. They came from money and they ended with it.' Dorothy gestured around her. 'Look at this neighbourhood. Do you see any graffiti, any homeless people, any social problems? No, it's perfect, beautiful – see, people drinking cappuccino on the street, look at the little dogs, they don't even shit, those dogs, they're just little balls of fluff, it's paradise.' She leaned on the car horn. The people in the cafés and outside the boutiques looked over.

Amy yanked her mother's arm away from the horn. 'Stop it. Why did you even come? You're so crazy.'

'Sorry. I shouldn't have said that. It's a nervous reaction.' A small keening escaped from her, somewhere between a laugh and a cry.

'Oh, whatever.' Amy stared out the window as though she could melt it.

'Amy. You know I'm one of four children too.'

'What's that supposed to mean?'

'That I love you. Thank you for coming with me. Now let's just leave. Oh dear.' Tears came properly now, slipping hot. She dropped a hand from the steering wheel to brush them away, and the car wobbled over the centre line and a passing horn blared.

'OK crazy lady, pull in here. I'm going to drive.'

After a while cruising the balmy streets, taking in the high-end health-food shops and the bicycles and prams and pretty trees, the freeway loomed and Dorothy fell asleep, drifting off with her daughter at the wheel, clutching the framed tapestry in her hands.

With something like disbelief, Andrew and Dorothy looked back on their thirties as their financially comfortable years. Something had happened to money; not just theirs, other people's too, even those like them without investments. There was less of it. Andrew was made redundant and the teachers' union lost a pay dispute. The kids needed help with student loans. Petrol. Food. The cost of moving house. To take the pressure off they sold up the burn-scarred cedar place in Waterview and moved to a brick-and-tile rental in the hills thirty minutes from the city, a suburb with the outlier's sense of itself, peopled by young hippies and retirees who liked their stories told. Donald and Hannah were in the thick of social lives, Amy was studying, subsisting in a fungal student flat in town, and Grace had become a series of South American postcards and video calls. This was the awful, dawning joke of parenting: that the early shock of children, their need and clamour and inescapable attachment, just as quickly became their blithe withdrawal. And they took everything. They took their friends, their jokes, their daily fresh discoveries, the gorgeous, ungraspable newness of the world. Look sharp, the tide's gone out. There was room for Dot and Andrew to look at each other for the first time in ages, bewildered. She was no longer a young mother. She was not a hippy or a retiree.

Doggedly positive, Andrew approached unemployment in his

mid-fifties as a self-improvement project. T'ai chi at the community centre; a men's book club; canvas frames. 'Now's my chance
to really paint.' Their neighbour, Dennis, was a local noble, and
Dorothy supplemented her practically voluntary job teaching art at
the maternity home with work in his garden. A bit extra.

When he wasn't working on his paintings, Andrew spent most
of his time in the library, researching the area and reading books by
middle-aged men who had found a new meaning for life through
their dog, or their father's diaries, or their dying football coach.
In a few months he finished a series of local portraits in gouache.
No mainstream dealer was interested, but he soon met Jennifer
from the local art gallery, a community powerhouse in chunky
necklaces and a smoker's growl, a woman who moved and shook.
She turned him on to the neighbourhood giveaway guide and got
him sketching, unpaid, for that. 'Promise you, darling, if we get our
grant covered again next year and no counting chickens in these
times, I'll give you a show. Or you could hit up Dennis for some
sponsorship? God knows we all need a bit of philanthropy.' And she
winked at Dot from beneath her pale-pink beret.

A postcard from Ruth adorned the fridge door, next to Grace's
latest from Guatemala. Ruth was coming to stay in the brick house
behind the green hedge, the house flanked by dark cypresses like
thick green flames. Soon she would appear on their driveway,
suitcase in hand. The late summer holidays were perfect for a visit:
long afternoons and less likelihood of rain, the sculpture park still
open to the public.

Dot mowed the lawn and hassled Andrew to fix the stuck

window in their son's bedroom and thought about a range of books – Dennis's catalogues of pioneer watercolours, local poetry, a novel – to place on the wooden chair next to the bed. There was plenty of time, a day to go. But then, when she was making space inside the refrigerator for crocus and hyacinth bulbs, came a crunching sound from the drive and she ran to the door, feeling red-faced and oh, breathless and wild, and saw the car – not the airport shuttle which Ruth had insisted she would take, declining Dorothy's offer to collect her, but a taxi. A woman got out and a man followed and at first she thought it was the driver, that the driver had emerged to help Ruth with her luggage, but then the bags were on the path and the taxi pulled away and the man and the woman both remained.

As Dot walked down the steps towards the couple who frowned at the house, at the cypress trees, the camellia bushes and clay roof tiles, it became clear Ruth was ageing in reverse. At the funeral she had been strung-out, dry-handed, efficient and too thin, and she now looked younger, the layer of dewy plumpness in the skin of her face at odds with the cage-bones above her unlikely breasts. The man at her side – it wasn't Ben – could have been a younger version of Daniel, at least how Dan might have looked if he never took the drugs or hadn't fucked off overseas and acquired the terrifying agelessness of the constant traveller. All of this registered while Dorothy was being embraced by Ruth and this American, kissed once, twice, three times. There was a tussle over the suitcases, which Dorothy won.

'We weren't expecting you till tomorrow.' Andrew marched up the hallway towards them. He would think he was being welcoming but Dot cringed at his tone. He kissed Ruth and clasped hands with the man, whose name was repeated – *Hank* – what a relief because it had flown straight out of her mind the first time she heard it, down there by the garage, and she could just see herself getting the name wrong, or never saying it for the duration of his stay, falling mute when the time came to introduce him to anyone else, Hank, Hank, and now they were not in the hallway any more but in the kitchen where she was pouring glasses of water from the jug in the fridge, which needed refilling, so she and Andrew had their glasses warm, from the tap. Ruth picked up the brown-paper bags of bulbs from the kitchen table and peered inside. She'd been confused by the hemisphere change. She often messed up dates, Hank laughed, it was tiresome, most of their friends were used to making allowances.

'Just last week we arrived at a cocktail party, all,' he gestured elegantly down the front of his shirt as if to say *gussied up*, 'and the host and hostess are sitting there in T-shirts and jeans, super relaxed, feeding their two-year-old grandchild her dinner. Well, are we early, we ask? No. We're a day late. A whole day. Because she doesn't ever pay attention.'

Everyone laughed. Hank was nervous, Dorothy realised, and the tension in her chest relaxed a little. She showed them the shared bathroom and Donald's room, the small view across the vege garden. She had been going to put lavender in a vase. 'Are you happy sharing? There's Hannah's room but we're painting it, sorry, I thought we'd be finished by now. The fumes.' The house must be modest, compared to what they were used to.

'Do you have a stretcher bed?' Hank asked.

'Yes, of course.'

They dragged it out from under Hannah's bed, and wiped the metal bars free of dust and a few long blonde hairs. Eve's daughter, Louisa, had used it last, when she'd begun nursing college. Now she lived at the hostel. Getting in to classes from here every day cost too much in gas. 'I hope you'll be comfortable.'

'How many kids do you have?'

'Four, just the younger two live here and they're off camping with friends. We're on our own!'

'Practice run for the empty nest, hey?'

But it was too late, she had disappeared down the hall to rescue the bulbs and chill them.

She took a pot of cottage cheese from the fridge and misjudged the lid's grip and it fell to the floor, splattering white globs up the freezer door and over the orange tiles. Andrew would say good riddance to high cholesterol but the waste made her so frustrated. Her hand as she wiped it up looked like somebody else's, the skin cellophane-shiny in places and spotted, the fingers red and swollen at the knuckles, the nails beginning to ridge. The bench-top helped her heave upright. That cut in the crease of her right index finger had opened up again. She ran tap water over it, stingingly. Good.

They ate outside, as the light faded, and the clustered ox-eye daisies closed purple undersides to the day. Turned out Hank had a friend here, an American screenwriter who spent summers in the suburb across the valley, where house lights were gleaming through the dusk. Dot forced herself to meet Ruth's eye when either of them were talking but even then she quickly looked away, and everything existed flat at the front of her face: normality as a performance.

'Where's Andrew?' asked Ruth.

'Oh, he's about somewhere, sorry, he gets a bit brusque when he's on an illustration deadline.' That was how he called it, although the deadlines were self-imposed.

'He's still in IT?'

'No.' He was never in IT. She let it go. 'Last year he was made redundant. Fifty-six, you know? I mean it's happened to plenty of people we know but it's meant to stay in that category of things that happen to other people. Turns out we didn't have the magic password.'

'That's the thing with the unexpected knocks,' said Hank. 'They're unexpected.'

'Yes. Redundancy's pretty awful. That quiet exit.'

'Well.' Ruth slapped at a mosquito on her calf, and Dorothy passed her the repellent. 'I'm sure he has his hobbies, no?'

'He wouldn't call his painting a hobby! I mean, he will make money from it eventually . . . it's hard for everyone.' She felt a constriction of guilt. 'He has to lock himself away. Don't take it personally.'

'Of course not.'

'How are your girls?'

'Horsy. Twinsy.'

Over the hills the air was yellow, a floating yellow cloak. 'Have you got photos? I'd love to see.'

'Your kids?'

'Great.' Dorothy drank some more wine. 'The usual teen-age stuff. I spent last Saturday night driving round Hannah's friends' houses to find what party she was at, had to haul her out of a bedroom with some boy. You know what she says to me? "Romeo and Juliet were fourteen." '

'Smart kid,' said Hank.

'Not by any stretch.'

Ruth smiled. 'I remember Lee waiting up for you and Daniel to come home. She'd sit in the kitchen and run upstairs to bed when she heard the car pulling up.'

'Really?' Her body reacted before her mind caught up. God, the rush dizzied her. It felt fantastic.

'Oh yeah. Doing those fucking crosswords.' She mimed stab-scratching at a page with a pen.

'She knew that we went out in the car?'

'Yeah.'

'You knew?'

'I knew everything you did. I'm your kid sister, I was obsessed with you.'

'I didn't think anybody knew about that.'

'Well, doh.' Ruth scratched the inside of her ear. 'Lee worried about you guys all the time. You, Eve, Michael. She always thought the sky was going to fall in, you know? I think that's partly why she never came back here . . . Darling.'

Tears spilled from Dorothy's eyes. 'Sorry, Hank,' she said.

'Oh come on.'

'I think it was a kind of love,' said Ruth, clutching her hand across the table. 'That fear. And then when Eve died, oh you should've seen her. Almost like she'd been waiting for it. The worst. Like she knew all along.'

'I did see her. She was medicated.'

'Yes. Of course. Oh, fuck it.' The tip of Ruth's nose was red. 'Fuck.'

'What?' In an ideal world her nose wouldn't run in front of Hank, but it was too late, and now she was dabbing under her eyes with a paper napkin, checking for traces of mascara. 'Are you OK?'

Ruth gathered herself, breathed deeply. 'So, darling, I've got to tell you, you don't feature in the will, all right? Ben and I tried to find an earlier version, but.' A turn of the wrist, the wine tilting.

'Ruthie, it's fine.' Dot glanced at Hank, who had discreetly become invisible as he ground pepper onto his salad. 'I didn't expect anything. You did it all, you were there for them for years in a way Michael and I just weren't.'

Ruth's head shook like a little bell. 'It's all just a bit,' palms out, the brightness in her voice, a clear attempt to keep it together, 'just bullshit, isn't it. Bastards. Anyway I'm going to split my inheritance with you and Mike. It isn't much. But that's what I've decided.'

Smoke twisted from the table candle. Dorothy's eyes smarted. 'Oh. That's very sweet. That's very kind of you.' She didn't want the money, desperately didn't want it, but to say so would be to ruin this moment.

'OK. That's done.' Ruth's phone beeped and she drew it from the inside pocket of her linen tote bag and said, 'Oh, it's Ben.'

In the pause that followed, while she texted back, there were the sounds of Hank's cutlery tapping his plate, an air bubble glugging in the wine bottle as Dorothy refilled their glasses, and then Andrew's car starting, driving away from the house.

★ ★ ★

They'd all gone to bed by the time he came home. Dot lay listening to the shower in the bathroom down the hall, wishing the shimmery sound of falling water would go on for ever. Once he'd climbed in beside her she whispered, unsure whether Hank and Ruth had left their door open, 'She dyes her hair.'

'So do you.'

'And she's had face work.'

'You think?'

'Her skin is so smooth. Look at my crow's feet. She hasn't got any, she hasn't got any lines. There's a picture of her in an attic somewhere, crumbling.'

Andrew rolled over. 'Do you want me to find them a motel tomorrow?'

'No.' Dorothy wiped at her temple, where what she had started to think of as 'old lady tears' had slid from the corner of one eye. 'Where were you?'

'Sorry. Late night at the library.'

I don't believe you. The words clogged in her throat. She woke at three, full of adrenalin.

As always the morning was better, the replenishment of faith that came with sunlight, and now in music — not hers, not Andrew's or the kids' — some fusion thing of Ruth's that filled the house and bore her on a wave of sound in her nightie, through the open doors to the garden where there was enough air for all this drumming, the horns, the astonishing upbeatness of it like an announcement, music to accompany a spontaneous dance number on a promenade, umbrellas twirling, striped T-shirts, full skirts. Ruth contemplated the vegetable beds, a coffee bowl in her hands. 'So,' she said. 'This is a lovely place.'

'Thank you.' Dorothy slung a wicker basket over her elbow, pushed her other arm into the sparsely bristled leaves and weighed a tomato in her palm, twisted it off the dark-green stem. 'Do you still have your house in LA?'

'Of course, Ben's there now.'

'Oh, I just wasn't – sure – about you and Hank?'

Ruth nodded and blew at her coffee.

'Sorry,' Dorothy said. 'If it's private.'

'Oh, yes.' Ruth laughed. Her voice was moneyed and sounded like a lifetime of polished floors. 'No problem, darling. No problem.'

Dorothy didn't think Hank had been at the funeral. Perhaps that was another reason for Ruth's antsiness at the time, her stress. She resisted asking.

'Hey.' He arrived by the pepper plants wearing gym shorts, a tank top and a baseball cap. 'I'm going for a run. Then we'll hit the markets, et cetera?'

Dorothy loosened her nightie away from the middle of her body, where it slightly clung in the heat of the morning, and fanned her face with her hand. 'Be careful on the roads round here. There isn't much traffic so people drive like dicks.'

'You drive on the left, right?'

They watched him jog away.

'I have to go to work,' Dorothy said. 'Will you be OK here?'

Ruth smiled. 'Of course.'

'So is that your music?'

'Oh yeah, take it off if you don't like it.'

'Maybe just Andrew. The distraction.'

Dennis opened the door in his dressing gown, surprised to see her. 'It's Tuesday. I thought you were coming tomorrow.'

'Is it all right? We've got houseguests, I thought I'd give them some space.' She blushed at this self-serving lie. A whole day with Ruth would have killed her.

He took the bunch of sweet peas with wavering hands and kissed Dorothy on both cheeks. 'These smell divine.' He inhaled the flowers. A petal dropped, gone, to the cool slate floor.

'I'll go straight through to the back.'

Dennis frowned. 'The pool man's coming today as well.'

'Don't worry. I won't let any clippings fly in.'

Dorothy cut back the box hedges until her back and arms ached and the ridges of the secateurs' handles were imprinted in her hands. The garden was full of exotics; this was how Dennis liked it, the anachronism, wearing his coloniser heritage with pride. She deadheaded roses and picked the flower heads off the last of the zinnias and marigolds and put them in her basket to store. An attack of breathlessness hit. She sat for a while beneath the umbrella of the willow tree, looking through the overhanging leaves at the sunflowers on the other side of the garden, ungainly freaks leaning against the fence. She stared at the sunflowers for a long time. The seeds would be ready to shake out and dry. A white sheet spread out on the grass. Cracked feet. Her father's bewildered squint, Lee emerging from the bush, Ruth in Daniel's arms.

The pool guy vacuumed the bottom corners of the pool and

stroked the water's surface with his long unwieldy poles. Dorothy waited till he was in the pool house before she crawled out from under the willow branches, so as not to startle him, or look like some kind of creature. She spread chopped leaf mulch under the new shrubs and found a small brown lizard on one of the potted plants and flicked it into the bushes. Some of the plants needed to be shifted indoors to Dennis's conservatory. She checked the undersides of the leaves for bugs. The old terracotta pots were so crumbly it was hard to wipe dirt from their bases without gravel-sized pieces of orange clay coming away on the cloth.

'Are you free tonight?' she asked Dennis, who was sitting at his dining-room table eating a sandwich.

'Yes.' Dennis's head swung side to side as though he was saying no. He grasped for the linen napkin that sat in front of him on the table, his hand batting the table twice before his fingers curled and gripped it, brought it to his pursed, trembling mouth.

Dorothy rode her bike slowly home along the unmarked road, suede hills on her right, that twinge in her knee shooting sciatically up to her hip. A vanload of German tourists stood where the tourists always stood, taking the necessary photograph of the sea nestled between those hills across the valley, hot blue in the afternoon sun. When they first moved here Dennis had talked about putting in a swimming pool at their place but then he needed more medical care and the expense was too great. Sweat ran down the backs of Dot's knees.

She rested in the corner doorway of the closed butcher's shop, where the blinds were drawn. The triangular junction was free of traffic. Two rental cars sat parked outside the deli and aside from that evidence of human life an atomising bomb could be dropped and you would know no different. A tree with polymer-lace bark like camouflage, and knobbled, amputated branches, stood in front of a second-storey sash window, which was open, the slight breeze up there sucking the filmy curtain in and out, in and out. Geraniums, fluorescent splats of red paint, clustered in the window box. As in a puppet show, a pair of hands appeared on the window ledge, the room behind them darkness. She couldn't take her eyes off the gripping fingers, the zigzagged light on the raised glass, the bright flowers. What was that, a couple in the afternoon, fucking.

In the welcome shade of the house Dorothy made some calls then spread out on her bed by the open window and slept for most of the afternoon. Hank and Ruth were still sightseeing when she woke, and showered, and put the chickens on to roast and made the salad and rice. She was lighting candles on the outdoor table when Andrew came through the back door, arms raised above his head, cracking his shoulders.

Dorothy shook out the match between her fingers and walked slowly towards her husband. His bristled cheek felt unfamiliar to her lips. 'Will you be home for dinner?'

'What's going on?'

'I've invited half the neighbourhood. I don't know what I've done. Is it the last thing you feel like?'

'Go for it.' Andrew tugged at one end of the wrought-iron bench seat, which made a harsh scraping noise along the patio. 'What are you wearing?'

Dorothy smoothed her hands down the front of her dress. 'I found it in the back of the cupboard. Too young for me?'

Halfway through dinner she leaned back in her chair and felt as though a flower, a peony or hibiscus, was blossoming inside her. The wine maybe, or the toke on Andrew's cigarette that she leaned over for, feeling his fingers against her lips as she quickly sucked, the hot prickle of the smoke on her tongue. How amazing to see her sister in the glow from the tea lights, powerful in her way, purring into Jim Wang's neck. Music played from the speakers that Ruth had shifted to stand in the French doors. Down the other end of the table Hank and his screenwriter friend were deep in conversation. It amazed Dot that people had these lifestyles, that you could own a holiday house a twelve-hour flight away from home, but she supposed it shouldn't. Hank smoked like a demon – like an American photographer. The screenwriter's wife was pregnant, and had eaten none of the cheeses that Hank and Ruth brought back from the market, and Dorothy shook the bread basket at her. 'Everything's pasteurised. But I understand. No point taking chances. Have some bread, you must be starving.'

The girl thanked her and almost shoved the roll into her mouth, just as Dennis asked her a question, his illness making it look as though he really cared for each word and struggled to find it precisely, ideas brimming in him before the body would allow them out. Dorothy carved and plated chicken for Dennis, Ruth, Hank, Hank's friend, Hank's friend's wife, Terry from the bookshop, the Hansens, the Wangs, Mareta and her teenage daughter, Andrew and herself.

'If I wasn't here,' said Destiny, the teenager, 'you'd be thirteen at the table.'

'Do you think that's dangerous?' Ruth laughed.

'All teenagers believe in that BS,' said Mareta. 'I've had a houseful of Ouija boards and spirits and creepy little rune-y relic-y things all summer. I'm over it.'

'Don't say over it,' Destiny said.

'Whatever.'

Hank nodded his head towards his friend's wife. 'What about her? She's pregnant, does that count as another person?'

Pontoon lights hung in the trees behind the table. The golden-whiteness shining from them made the sky look darker than it really was, and the stars couldn't be seen. Night-blooming jasmine opened its perfume onto the courtyard. There was a pause in the music, between tracks. Andrew was telling Ruth an anecdote, a piece of history Dot had heard a gazillion times before, and Ruth was laughing. The scent of the flowers was so elusive, there one moment and then gone. Dorothy gestured to her husband, twiddling her fingers to ask for another rolled cigarette. The compromises and frustration and loss were worth it, she thought, her eyes meeting his – if they could only stay in *this*.

A new song started and Mareta pushed her chair back and held her hands out to Terry and he bowed his head, rose from his chair and they started dancing. 'Shame, Mum,' Destiny called, but as Dorothy crossed the courtyard to the kitchen, everyone was getting up to join them.

She poured more water into the large earthenware jug. Hank appeared in the kitchen with the glass one from the table. 'Great minds,' he said. Dorothy asked how he was getting on and he said fine and leaned against the sink bench, the water radiant in his hands through the blue glass, and, 'You?' And she said yes. Yes. Hank poured a glass of water and held it out to her and as she reached for it she looked through the open doors at Dennis being led around the courtyard by Ruth. Hank's fingertips brushed hers as they released the glass and she turned in surprise, jolted.

In the heat of the day Ruth stayed indoors to protect her face. 'The light here is unbelievable. For sure it's stronger than when we were kids. I mean like, what fucking ozone layer?' Hank wanted to record Dorothy and Andrew. He showed them examples of his work in a black-leather portfolio; in the glaring afternoon of the garden the photos seemed stagy and stiff, and the people in them looked as though that was probably not how they imagined themselves. Andrew said, 'Not for me. I'd crack the lens.'

'You're a good-looking couple,' Hank said. 'Something for the future grandkids? Get a record before your teeth fall out.'

Andrew barked a laugh and headed back into the house, calling over his shoulder, 'Long gone, buddy, long gone.' Not strictly true; his teeth were mostly bridge but they were still in his head, they didn't come out at night, thank God.

'Where in the States are you from?' Dorothy asked.

Hank shrugged, and turned the heavy pages of his portfolio to the very back. 'Connecticut. There's the house.' A wooden mansion, with numerous windows, that must have been enormous, but he'd taken the photograph from far away or with a clever lens so that it looked like a model, a trick of perspective enhanced by the child he had placed in the front of the frame, looming hugely, his hand out as though to pat the roof. On the facing page was a picture of the same boy, wearing a striped T-shirt, a woman with long blonde hair, a golden retriever, and a younger version of Hank.

'Wow,' said Dorothy. 'Your family.'

He nodded. 'Yep. Actually, my son's in London now, studying. I'm going to see him in the winter. He's a great kid. You've got girls, right?'

'And a boy, yes.' It had always amazed her when people spoke of their children in this detached way – *London, I'm going to see him* – but now she knew that was what happened as they got older, just as her children now were all adult-sized and the family had changed shape, become a model of six people on the same scale. In fact the children looked bigger than the adults even though they weren't, their features yet to settle, hair abundant, full of life. 'How did you and Ruth meet?'

'In a French dentist's, believe it or not. We were both on summer holidays and we got talking in the waiting room. So I'm in Paris and my wisdom teeth are giving me hell, so a friend gets me an appointment with her dentist, and I'm sitting there in the worst kind of pain, you know it feels like someone is fucking me in the ear, and then there's some changeover with the receptionist and the new one doesn't speak English, et cetera et cetera, and thank God this woman comes to my rescue.'

'Why was she there?'

'Teeth whitening.'

'No, in Paris.'

'Oh. I don't know. Antiquing? The twins are in school, right, boarding? Anyway, I was in there for hours, they only got one tooth, told me I was going to have to come back the next day and go to some kind of terrifying overnight dental hospital, have a general et cetera, so I head downstairs, there's a bar. It's Paris, right? I'm going to drown my sorrows, a little preliminary numbing, and there, also drinking, white wine naturally, is your sister. And you know this year we thought we may as well do it again, only head south.'

'Is photography your full-time job?'

'I'm always a sort of editor at large for some website or other. They keep me in train fares and cappuccinos.' It was a practised line.

Perhaps it wasn't so strange that he and Ruth had found each other, two people on holiday from their lives. She was burning to ask if Ben, the banker husband, was cool with funding the trip, but instead said, 'I've tried for a long time not to be vain and now my face is falling off and I've just given into it. I can't have my photo taken. Sorry.'

He shrugged. 'That's fine. I would have given you free copies, for having me to stay.'

'Oh, there's no need.' A crestfallen moment. She'd been fishing, she discovered, for a compliment.

'And you, Ruth said you're a teacher?'

'Yes. I was full-time in schools but the admin nearly broke me. The constant testing. Now I work at a home for pregnant teens, doing art classes. Sort of therapy.'

'OK, I'm going for a run. Can you take this back into the house?' He passed her the portfolio.

'Now?' They'd been drinking sparkling wine in the sun. The lawn smelled of the new high-nitrogen fertiliser. 'Don't go now.'

But already he was jamming his feet into his running shoes, screwing ear-buds into the side of his head, touching his toes a couple of times in the cursory way he said 'et cetera et cetera', and gone, taking the curve of the road like a piece of film running on double speed, swallowed by the corner. Dorothy pulled her knees up and tucked her skirt around her ankles to keep from being bitten, and thought about getting a cardigan from the house, and rubbed at the goosey flesh on her soft upper arms, and pushed her forehead into a knee to press the alcohol burn away, and looked at the pink cotton of her skirt in the dark shadow made by her head and the way it lost its colour and became grey. There was a touch to the nape of her neck, the line drawn by a single finger. She raised her head and looked around, but nobody was there. Shouting came from the house.

It had stopped by the time she got inside, then started again – a sound that she followed to the living room, where Ruth and Andrew sat in front of the set watching football. Dorothy recognised the All Whites, but not the other team.

'Come on!' Andrew yelled, his voice gravelly. Neither he nor Ruth looked up from the screen.

'My girls play soccer,' Ruth said. 'At college.'

'I'm just going to make dinner.'

Dorothy carried the portfolio through to Donald's room. She knocked on the door, although she knew that Hank was running and Ruth was watching TV. In the pause after her knock, a feeling of dread beset her. Someone absent, returned silently. A clotted shadow. Sitting on the bed. She turned the handle and opened the door fast. The room, postered with ancient Communist propaganda, was empty. The stretcher at the foot of the double bed was neatly made up, looking like no one ever slept in it, and the novel

she'd left out for Ruth splayed face downwards on the floor next to
a spread treasure of discs without cases, tiny silver coins. She crossed
the threshold to set the portfolio on the mattress; leaving it on the
stretcher seemed somehow pointed. A red-and-white plastic wallet
on the chest of drawers bore the words *Travel Documents*. The exit
strategy, a plan to move on. Dorothy sat on the bed and reopened
the portfolio. The dark-paper backing pages were thick between
her finger pads and thumb. Her parents, in black-and-white, stared
at the camera, airbrushed, their teeth neat, a page Hank had skipped
over out in the garden. She last saw them – it must have been
ten years, alive. After their accident, everyone agreed closed caskets
were for the best. This handsome old man had been her father,
with thinning white hair and Photoshop space where his wrinkles
would be. Her mother's high forehead.

With clumsy thumbs Dorothy turned the pages. Who were
these people who had their hair set especially? What kind of
project was this, portraits of the well-to-do? There were numbers
in silvery graphite on the top of the pages. They might have been
dates but her glasses were not strong enough to decipher them.
Out the window the hedges cast a deep-angled shadow half the
length of the garden. When she looked back at the folder there
was another photo that Hank hadn't shown her, and a fond, warm
feeling suffused her. It was Daniel. She glanced at the doorway
as if someone might come in, and carried the book closer to the
window to get more light on his face, there, touched a finger to
the digitally removed scar, his crooked inward smile, the huge
black irises. There he was. She peeled the corner tabs from the
page and lifted the photograph out leaving the page empty, dotted

with residual glue. Abruptly, the hallway went silent – the television switched off – and she put the portfolio down, tucked the stolen photograph into the folds of her skirt and quick-stepped from the room.

Rainclouds enveloped the hills, promising the lightning storms of deep summer evenings. Dot was bunching up sheets from the washing line when Hank stumbled into the garden, gasping, a hand glued to his side.

'You look like a stabbing victim about to utter your last words,' she said.

'I like your friend Dennis,' he said when he'd recovered his breath, sweat still budding from his skin. 'I dropped in on him. He's very grand.'

'I don't know if he'd describe us as friends. He's our landlord. I do his garden.'

'But he came here for dinner.'

'He's lonely.'

'So be his friend.' He cocked his head and smiled at her. 'You'd be welcome company, I'm sure.'

God, was she blushing? Hank reached for the corners of a king-size sheet and together they shook it out and folded it, coming together as though in an Elizabethan dance. *Dance lessons* – when was that? Early girlhood in America, prehistory – and she raised her heels stepping forward, sank her feet down slowly in their house slippers into the dewy grass and bent as far as her knees would allow into a curtsey. In the trees the birds were raucous.

'You know what I'd really like to do here?' Hank said. 'Go scuba diving.'

She twiddled through the wire basket for the warm wooden pegs. Like a box of dolls. 'Hank, has Ruth talked much about our family?'

He nodded. 'Oh sure, that whole thing about your father. Not for a while now.'

'What thing do you mean? The accident?'

'Ah . . . no. I feel weird I said anything. It's nothing.'

'OK.' Together they looked into the shrouded hills. 'You know I think I would like a photo taken. If that's all right?' She wondered whether he'd looked in his vandalised portfolio. If he would say anything. How she would respond.

'Hold still —' He turned to face her, removed something from her collarbone. 'Bit of grass. Let's see your hands?'

She looked away as he examined them, traced his fingers over the calluses and pragmatic fingernails, her heart banging. Nerves all over her body hummed. Hank took a step closer, eyes full of evening light, his body smelling sharply from the run, and it was ridiculous how much he reminded her of another time, and she said, 'I have to go inside.'

The dive centres up north had either closed for the season or were fully booked. Hank and Ruth announced a plan to head south for whale watching, 'while they still could'. They were going to drive and take the ferry, and even Andrew snorting and saying, 'Overrated,' couldn't dampen their enthusiasm. The screenwriter friend would join them, a last fling before the baby came. Dorothy promised to call in on his wife. 'It's gone so quickly,' she said, 'your visit.'

'We'll be back.' Her sister smiled. 'I've got to see your kids.'

On the day before the departure, Ruth and Dorothy dropped Hank at the screenwriter's house for a swim and drove on to the sculpture park. An elevated wooden path extended between rimu and kauri trees. They passed a set of human figures that stood in a large half-shell, like a giant conch. Away from the sun, the air was cool and moist.

In silence they walked slowly down the side of the hill, abstract red shapes and bronze beasts rising from the first layer of bush, resembling deer or giant birds, not so much modelled as gestured at. Dot thought of the sweat welling on Hank's skin, in the hollow of his throat. The unseasonal cold ached in her joints and she didn't mind that Ruth seemed to be passing through the experience too quickly, ignoring the atmosphere, consigning it to recollection, *doing the sculptures*.

'Incredible,' Ruth said when they were out in the sun again, crossing an immaculate lawn towards the road. 'So what, those are someone's private collection? Is there any information, is there a shop?'

'Over there,' said Dorothy, pointing to the building that housed a gift shop and café. She had wanted to – what, to *keep something* of her sister but now Ruth was leaving and she was once again glossy, so controlled, and since the mention of the will they hadn't had a meaningful conversation and she felt stupidly scared of sitting in a café with her, of ordering watery quiche and attempting to intro- duce the real things, the state of her marriage, the hole left by Eve, her fear that she lived her life on the inside, ruled by the fantasy that someone out there knew her, held her true self.

'Any good?' Ruth asked.

'Not really, just smaller versions of the sculptures, maquettes, models.'

Ruth was halfway to the shop. Dorothy tugged at her sleeve. 'No, don't, Andy's girlfriend might be there.'

'I'm sorry?'

'She's not really his girlfriend. I don't know. Just this local arty type, she's everywhere.'

'But not his girlfriend.'

'I don't know.'

'Can't you ask him?'

The door was locked; a sign read *Open After 12.*

'I heard him last night, having a rant to you about the art world. "Gate-keepers". You know,' Dorothy said, 'it's funny that all that time ago I thought Andrew was so different from our father. And now he's kind of becoming him. Ruth –' quickly before they reached the car, before the outing tapered to a close. 'Hank said something about Dad, and I just wondered. What he meant?'

Her sister frowned. 'What did he say?'

'Nothing, but – was there . . .' It was stupid to feel of all emotions embarrassed in this moment, that she should already know, was exposing her ignorance, but she did. 'Was there some *thing* about Dad?'

Ruth was very still, squinting in the late-morning light. 'You know he liked men, don't you.'

'Men?' Dorothy blinked. The word hopped the boundary of her known world. 'Dad was gay?'

'Yeah, I guess you could say that. I thought.' Ruth shrugged. 'I mean obviously he wasn't out, but Mom knew, and some of their friends, it was a kind of side thing, but, you know – why did you think he left New York?'

'I don't know. I thought. Money. But what about Mum?'

'Well, she loved him. And they had us, and you know, they wanted to stay married.'

'Jesus.' The morning really was extremely bright. Dazzled, she fished in her bag for her sunglasses, wiped them free of dust and put them on, the ordinary movements happening at a distance. 'How did you find out?'

'Mom told me.'

She felt made of raffia, like she might float away in the sun. 'Is that why they left here, as well?'

'I don't know – there was that inheritance, remember – but it wouldn't surprise me. If there was someone Mom wanted to get him away from. She kept a damn close eye on him when we were back here for Eve, despite her beautiful Valium haze.'

Dorothy had never imagined Ruth talking about their parents like this. She felt so grateful suddenly, that Ruth had been able to live alongside them, be a daughter. 'But what about in the States, all those years, I mean you don't just relocate to change who you are. Surely there's always going to be someone.'

'I never met anyone. I think there were a few times Mom got jealous. But it was mostly only sex. At least, that was their story.'

'God. It's like seeing him as a person.'

'Yeah, I thought you knew.'

How odd that Eve never would. Dot felt a tug inside, the need to share it with her older sister, hear her incredulous voice on the end of the phone. 'Poor Dad,' she said. 'Not able to just be himself.'

'Yeah.' Ruth looked away, into the wooded part of the garden, where the walkway stretched under the canopy they had just emerged from. 'But I kind of think it *was* him, to have the two lives. Or it became him. He wasn't unhappy.'

The sisters walked to the gravelled parking bay, Dorothy still weightless, two-dimensional, held in place by Ruth's arm around her waist. Hers was the only car. She came round to unlock the passenger door, and pushed the sunglasses up onto her forehead. Up close you could see the reassuring wrinkles in Ruth's face. 'What about Daniel?' she said. 'How is he, where did you see him?'

'Yeah, about a year ago. Barcelona? We had dinner. He seemed well. Had a nice girlfriend. Think she was an architect.'

'I stole his photo from Hank's portfolio.'

'Yeah. He told me.'

'Does he want it back? I should pay him for it.'

'Don't worry.'

As she passed the front bonnet towards the driver's door Dorothy said, 'Now you know all my secrets.'

'Oh, I'm sure that's not true.' Ruth slid into her car seat and jumped up again, stung by the hot vinyl.

The rental car was electric, completely quiet, Hank and the screenwriter waiting behind its milky windows for Ruth to get in. 'Sorry to miss Andrew,' Hank called, winding down the glass. 'International man of mystery. Tell him thanks.'

'Sure.' Her basket was laden with baby squash and rocket and she wanted to give Ruth something for the trip, a memento, but she couldn't take vegetables, no.

'OK.' Ruth unhooked the basket from Dorothy's elbow and placed the basket on the gravel at their feet. They hugged. Dorothy felt her sister's body against hers.

'Have a great time,' she said.

'Thank you,' said Ruth. 'I'll miss you.' She drew away.

Dot nodded. 'Miss you too.' Ruth folded herself into the back of the car and the screenwriter backed down the drive, drove out of sight. The edges of the silence filled with a tinselly buzz of cicadas. Dot's sandals crunched on the gravel as she took slow steps back round the side of the house, towards the garden.

The photograph that came a few weeks later, from the States, had caught both sisters unawares through a soft-focus crinkle of peach-tree leaves. Amy stood at Dot's side, studying the picture. 'You do look alike,' she said.

Donald walked through the kitchen, carrying paint-splattered dustsheets from the girls' room. He followed their gaze to the picture and said, 'Who's that?'

'Auntie Ruth. I've met her,' said Amy in the airy tone of sibling one-upmanship.

'Why haven't I?'

'Come on, Donald, you didn't want to leave the beach.' She should have insisted that the kids come back early from camping. It hadn't even entered her mind, which now seemed inexplicable. 'OK, give me a hand to clear the table, it's dinnertime.'

'Where's Dad?' said Donald. In her peripheral vision, Dorothy could tell that Amy was giving him a look. 'What?' he said. 'I just asked where he is. I need the key to the shed.'

'It's in the door, you fool.'

He humped the dustsheets out there, calling, 'Your face is the fool,' over his shoulder.

Out of habit Dot slid her hand into the card-backed envelope that Ruth had sent the photo in, to check it was empty before it hit the recycling pile. Her fingers met paper edges: she reached in and drew out a cheque. The skin up her back tingled as she made sense of the amount. It was a lot. She turned it over and read scrawled on the back, in her sister's handwriting: *Your share.*

After she'd washed up and everyone had gone to bed, in the creaking, darkened house, Dorothy sat in the pool of light cast by the kitchen-table lamp and wrote five cheques, one for each of her children and one for Lou. She finished and put the pen down, rubbed at the ink smudge on her index finger. On the table lay a disc Ruth had left behind, a little silver moon. She put it on the stereo and listened.

16. FIRE

IT SAID HE was in a relationship. He listed himself as 'retired', a joke, and 'spends most of his time travelling', which might also have been a joke except for the photographs from a recent trip to Rio, for the carnival. The same elfin-featured girl was in most of them, looking to be about twenty-one, long brown limbs draped over Daniel, her short blonde hair catching the light. That would be right. She'd have been the one to design this page. Although Daniel had known how to use the Internet to his advantage, it only operated for him as an old-fashioned Rolodex might. Follow Daniel on Twitter! Poke Daniel! Send Daniel a gift today!

Daniel's page showed a photo of a man who looked older, but not old.

Dot left the tablet on the bench and paced the room.

Across the dry garden, between the house and the road, wisps of dirt rose as if the earth was smouldering. There came a sudden rattle of rain. Hannah and Destiny ran towards the house from the cruddy old car, towels tenting their heads, shrieking. It was crazy at the beach, they said, the wave-tips ultraviolet through the storm light, the sky so dark it looked like an eclipse.

The kids went round the house shutting windows and putting lights on, and the wind noise picked up, and from her bedroom Dot watched distant cars driving with headlights on, grass flattened on the hills, trees trembling. Andrew lay on the bed watching rugby. A battle long lost, the screen on the chest of drawers, and the truth was she didn't mind, enjoyed late-night cop shows and documentaries, a replacement for sex or conversation. If she wanted to read there was the living-room couch and sometimes she woke in the small hours of the morning under the thin woollen throw, neck stiff, the gadget hot on her stomach.

'Going to be a storm,' she said. Andrew hummed acknowledgement. She patted his foot before she left the room, and he twitched away, a reflex.

In the hot living room, which smelled of pine needles and Christmas lilies, the girls had laid out a Ouija board. Dorothy let Hannah pull her down to sit with them on the carpet. Silver baubles knocked against each other when she brushed against the spiky Christmas tree. 'I thought you'd outgrown this.' The board had taken a thrashing during Hannah's occult phase, but since she became a surfer it languished in her bedroom cupboard.

Hannah shouted over her shoulder, 'Donald, come on!' To her mother, 'Destiny's grandma died ten years ago today. We're going to call her up.'

'Have you got any dry clothes? Go and change before you start wakening the spirits.' They wore their summer wetsuits, the tops peeled down, bikinis underneath, hair tangled and damp. 'You'll catch cold.'

Weather like this should bring Eve, this storm that licked up water and dirt and flung them around in muddy flames. A funnelled tower of cloud massed across the hills. Wind scalloped the puddles. She stared at that olive tree across the road. A bulge in the trunk would swell and burst. Her sister would shake out of the bark, make her way here through the rain. Dot remembered, as she did every Christmas, her mother's schoolfriend – the woman who gave away her son. Years later the grown stranger standing outside the house, hoping to be taken in.

If only she had made more mistakes. If only time would deliver her a young man waiting on the driveway, his hand extended to be shaken.

Grace stuck her head through the door. 'Mum, Louisa's here.' She looked at the Ouija set-up, the arc of letters and the stone planchette. 'Can you get rid of that? We're not going to do it any more.'

'Good thinking.' She folded it into the drawstring bag.

Lou hadn't changed out of her pink nurse's uniform. 'Ta-dah, the home movies,' she said, brandishing a USB stick from her pocket. 'Finally.'

'How was work?'

'Bit tough.' She was doing a long stint on the coma and neuro wards. 'No change for Tina. Baby's first Christmas.'

Tina was a teenage mum Dot had worked with at the maternity home. Nearly a year ago she had given birth, and hours later had a brain haemorrhage. She was still alive, in that way. 'That way', Dorothy explained to her children when they moaned about their unjust world, meant on a respirator, in a nappy, fed through tubes, drained by tubes, unable to see or hold her baby. The other mums, the girls whose babies came around the same time, had visited at first. Now hardly anyone came. Their lives had moved on.

Thunder and lightning broke, and the rain roared. The hall lights flashed out and on again. The family piled onto Dot and Andrew's bed and watched the Forrest home recording that Ruth had reformatted and sent to Lou. Stop-motion children jumped into and out of a cardboard box, appeared and disappeared behind tree trunks, and waved halves of themselves beside a long mirror. Someone had added a soundtrack, a sort of Laurel and Hardy tune that made the past seem even more remote.

'Is that you?' Grace asked of a cartwheeling figure.

'God, look at our haircuts. There I am.' Streaking across the shot, Daniel leggily after her, the camera not interested, trained on the cardboard box on the lawn, the box that rose and was cast aside to reveal Eve, now in close-up saying something unrecorded, dropping the box to the ground and walking back into the house, bending to pat the cat. In the dim bedroom, Louisa reached for Dorothy's hand.

The camera followed Evelyn up the steps and into the house. Blackness fell as it crossed the threshold indoors, then the world revealed itself again in adjusted light. Eve stood at the kitchen sink drinking a long glinting glass of water. She set the empty glass down and looked straight at the camera once before she started to perform, a hand behind her head in a parody of a swimsuit model, cat-walking the hallway. The camera followed her up and down, up and down, swinging past its own reflection in the hall mirror: flashes of their father, a young man. Behind Eve the front door opened. Daniel burst into the hall and star-jumped for the camera, tongue sticking out, skinny-ribbed, his knees big lumps on stick-like legs.

Dorothy snuck a look at Andrew. His eyes were closed, head back on the pillows, his breath loud and heavy. The image on the screen cut to an outdoor public swimming pool where light blazed on the surface of the water. A teenage Michael ploughed through with a powerful stroke. They watched, mesmerised, until a few seconds later the image fizzed out in a power cut. Another pop came when Donald drew the cork from a bottle of wine. 'May as well,' he said, 'seeing as charades is fucking inevitable.' Dorothy lit candles through the house. She recited the names. One for each wick as it caught alight.

Amy sat next to a mound of broad bean husks, and a dark, glossy pile of silverbeet and plump tomatoes from the garden. Dot looked in the pantry. Rice and chickpeas. Her daughter shook the pale-brown china bowl with broad beans in it as though prospecting for river gold. 'Never looks as much once you've shelled them.'

Dot pulled the tablet towards her to look at that recipe site. A cold wave broke through her as the resume bar progressed along the screen – Daniel's web page – she hadn't closed it down. Now the surf report was up and who knew where he had gone. The page wasn't there. Daniel free, at large in the world.

'Amy,' she said, 'is this you?' But when she looked over Amy had gone, a bowl of pale green beans, and Hannah leaned on the

kitchen table, reading her old witchcraft manual. ' "Widdershins," '
she sounded, ' "Widdershins." '

The house creaked and began to turn.

'What, darling?' Dorothy said.

Hannah looked at her. 'There's someone calling.'

Dorothy said, 'Stop!' And although Daniel said, quietly, from
Rio, *Come on, darling, that wasn't the word*, everything did.

★

After a fifth and final goodbye hug, Dot drove the rental car around
the corner, parked it outside a university building, held onto the steering wheel and sobbed for Hannah's small room there at the hostel,
a room that to her eyes still looked empty without shelves of books,
though there was the band poster she'd brought from home, the big
plastic eyes on the stuffed toy puppy Hannah had had since she was
a baby and her brave smile as she sat perched on the edge of the
single bed, back straight and knees together as though good posture
was the key to independence. Dorothy growled through clenched
teeth and shook the steering wheel. There was a loud knock on the
car window, and she startled. The boy was maybe twenty, with wild
hair and cheeks that were rosy all the way down to his chin. She
unwound the window and took her glasses off to wipe her eyes.

'You all right?'

Dorothy wiped a sleeve over her face. 'Yes, thanks. I just dropped
my youngest daughter off for her first semester. I'm fine.'

A guitar was slung across his back. He adjusted the strap. 'Yeah,
my folks lost their shit pretty bad too. Thought you might have
been robbed or something.'

Dorothy smiled. 'Thank you. I'm in therapy.'

The young man laughed as though she was joking, then lifted his head, a response to some whistle only he could hear, and in the rear-view mirror she watched him lope over the road to his gathered friends.

★

At the maternity home she set up the charcoals and the glitter dust, all the art therapy doodahs, while one of the teenagers painted Jo's fingernails and Carla gelled her hair. Jo drew a line inside her lower eyelid with kohl pencil and sighed, satisfied at what she saw in the pocket mirror. The gesture was reminiscent of a teenage Eve, only Jo was eight and a half months pregnant. Through the steel-framed windows came the kissing noises of insects in the courtyard, its gravelled surface already dried and laced with dust.

'It's hot today,' said Dot. A bead of sweat ran down the side of her ribs as she pinned Jo's 'portrait of a future self' to the wall next to the printing screens. The girl had drawn her whole body, no longer pregnant, holding hands with a child of about three. She'd detailed the Gothic font tattoos over her breastbone, and she was wearing her Dickies and wifebeater, and there was no man in the picture.

'See that?' Jo said, beaming. 'Pride of place.'

'Whoop-de-shit.' Sondra screwed her self-portrait into a fist and thrust it at Dorothy's face. Dot stumbled back into the guillotine table, and the girl jammed the picture into the ridged bin in the corner of the room, the black-plastic bin that smelled waxily of crayons and vegetable dye.

'Sondra, come on.' Dorothy retrieved the paper and smoothed its creases. The girl had drawn a fly scribbled on its back, zigzag legs doing all the work of rendering its fuckedness, and a squashed red oval alongside. 'What's that?' Dot asked.

'A bean.'

'A bean?'

Sondra shrugged.

'Is it a foetus?'

'No, it's a bean.'

Dorothy handed her a brown-paper bag that she'd saved from the grocery store. 'OK, so we're doing paper-bag portraits.'

'Oh man.'

You could feel the mood spread through the group. Some days it was like this, past hurts and grudges seeped up and the coming babies, their dreadful inevitability, were a muffled chorus of curses from inside. The fabric scraps and junk art materials were housed by the sink. Dorothy jiggled a box jammed between shelves, trying to winkle it free. Behind her, Jo cried out. Arms raised, Sondra turned in a slow circle, the winning boxer after a prize fight. The scissors were in one hand, sharp ends out. In the other, a dark length aloft: a hank of Jo's hair.

Dorothy slapped the box down hard on the guillotine table. 'Sondra,' she said, 'this hair fuckery was over. Damn it, you're going to see Carmen now. Put the scissors down.'

Sondra drew her arm back as if to throw them at Dot. Everyone flinched. But she tossed the hair at Jo's face. 'Have it, whore.' The scissors, dropped, clattered on the lino.

'Go back to your rapey old boyfriend –'

Dorothy pulled Sondra's strong, squidgy arm towards the door. The girl shook her off. 'Don't touch me.'

Her phone buzzed in her pocket. Dorothy shouted, 'Shut up,' although no one was talking.

It was Louisa. 'Aunty Dot?'

She never called during work hours. 'Are you all right?'

'I have news,' Lou said, her voice alight, brimming. Dorothy held a hand up and waited till the girls were silent. 'Tina's awake. She's woken up.'

'Tina's awake,' said Dorothy, staring at Jo. The girl raised her head. The room stilled. All of them knew Tina. Some had been friends from high school, her life before.

'You can come and see her.' Even Lou sounded as though she didn't quite believe it. 'Bring the girls tomorrow.'

A tiny jewelled lizard ran up the window frame, fast as poison.

Just as dusk dropped into night and the frogs were at their most riotous, a strange car pulled into the drive. Momentarily she thought it was the police, or the King Cobras – that was the sort of vehicle they used, thickset – and felt a wash of guilt run down her body. She didn't move from the window. If, say, Sondra's boyfriend and his gang ever did come looking for the girl, if they decided her running away was *unacceptable*, she would lose all power when the doors slammed, be numb while the sunglasses peered through the mosquito mesh of the door, and open-palmed, acquiescent, when they pushed that door open and filled her house with their bandanas and black jackets. But it was Andrew getting out of the sedan, alone. She felt a queer, impotent ellipsis when the other doors remained closed and no children piled out of the car after him. *This is a time for the rediscovery of you. A privilege. Many people I see don't get this chance.*

He leaned partway into her hug, gave her a shoulder pat, *physical contact is important; you are telling him he is cherished*, and stepped back to splash water on his face at the kitchen sink.

'Is that new?' she asked.

'Yeah,' he said. 'What do you reckon?'

'Was it very expensive?'

'Not really.'

'How much?'

'Not that much.'

She spoke to his back. 'Guess what. Tina's come out of the coma.'

'Huh?' *Not all your interests have to be the same.* 'Give me a hand.'

They lugged a heavy black speaker system into the house.

'Are these new too?'

'Yep.'

'Why?'

'Dorothy, the old speakers are shit. Have you noticed? The sound's tinny.' He liked the retro stuff. *It might be valuing the past. Not clinging on.*

Andrew connected the thick, taillike cords from the back of each machine into the bedroom power point. She brought a dish of salami and cheese crackers, and opened a couple of beers and they drank them. 'Where did you get that? The sound system?'

'There's a mall down the road, Dot.'

He'd had a show of his paintings at the local gallery, where

Jennifer had sold half of them. It didn't make him any nicer. *Adjust your expectations, bitch*. OK. That last part was her.

When she got up in the morning, wrapped in her printed sarong, Andrew was prone on his karate mat in the awning's shade, reading. She stepped into the shadows and put a foot in the centre of his back, over his bumpy spine.

'Is that foot clean?'

'Shall I stand on you?'

'Could I handle it?'

'I doubt it.' She stepped off and sat on the edge of the deck.

After coffee, he walked her down the hill to the maternity home, and traffic trundled past. *Appreciate the little things*. Green light from the palm leaves surrounded his head. 'So I hear there's another nuke ship out there,' he said, nodding in the direction of the invisible harbour. A bird purred from the bushes by the roadside.

'Yeah, apparently junk. It's circling while they find a place to process it. Debt cancellation.' She was repeating what stood in for news, what presented itself as news these days although nobody trusted the source. Maybe debt would be cancelled; maybe it wouldn't.

'I thought it was a Chinese deal.'

'Could be. Law firms, tax havens, whatever.' Knowledge had been replaced by phrases that induced a vague paranoia. Like everyone they knew, Dot and Andrew had stopped looking out into the frames of the world. They crossed the road to dodge a couple of beige dogs that were snarling and chewing at each other's necks.

'So. When are we going to talk about what we've got to talk about?'

Dorothy fanned herself with a piece of paper from her bag. It was going to be a scorcher. 'What do you want to talk about? Jennifer? I've got nothing to say about Jennifer. I'm running late.'

'You agreed we would talk.'

'Here on the road? Is this why you're here? I'm late for work.'

'OK, you've got your work. Sure.'

'Do some paintings. Or go and see Jennifer. I like Jennifer. Say hi from me.' *Lying is counterproductive.* Or *Fake it till you feel it.* Or *Speak your truth.* Or *Have high expectations.* Or *How about a reality check* or *Listen to yourself* or *Get out of your own way.*

' "Do some paintings"? That's a fucking emasculating thing to say.'

'Sorry.' A fly zipped past her ear. 'We'll talk when I get back. Later. If you're there.' Through the low shop-buildings a view cracked open of the city and the sky above it, clouds banked in deepening shades of grey against each other, piles of rocks in the sky.

As Dot crossed the courtyard, Sondra intercepted her with the news that Jo's waters had broken, the baby was coming early, maybe too early, and they'd taken her to hospital. 'It's my fault.'

Dorothy hugged her close. 'Don't be silly.'

'It's because I cut her. Now the baby's going to be deformed.' *Dee-formed*, that was how she said it.

'Listen, she'll be fine. Where's Carmen? Are we still going to see Tina?'

The central hospital was a van ride away. Carmen, the maternity home director, organised them, Dorothy and the girls, all except Jo who was doing the hard yards in the birthing unit on another side of town. Sondra was not allowed to go. Dorothy hated Carmen's kind of discipline. She left the girl lying on her bunk bed, reading. 'Do you want my iPod?' Sondra said nothing. Dot laid it on the blanket near her feet.

The van's air conditioner was broken. The mothers sat on the splitting vinyl seats with legs apart, fanning themselves.

'Has she seen her baby?' Dot asked.

'I think so.'

'Imagine it, having a newborn, then next thing you know you wake up and you've got a kid who's nearly one.'

'Sounds like normal life,' Carmen said. 'Boom.'

Dorothy shut her eyes; let her body be rocked by the vehicle's bad suspension.

'Hey, Dorothy,' one of the girls in the back called over the engine, 'what would you draw on the paper bag? Your self-portrait?'

She thought about it. 'Breathe into this?'

The girl squinted. 'What?'

At the hospital she would find a moment to call Andrew, suggest they go for a walk later or dinner. This was an adjustment period, without the kids. *A new way of being*. It was natural they had no clue how to handle it.

The smell of the hospital was just the same. Emerging from the lift into the neurology ward, Dot felt her mouth parch up. Almost expected to see the same nurses or that man with half a head, leering round a corner. But this was a happy time, she told herself, the girls' chatter filling the foyer. 'Tina!' someone yelled out, the vowels bouncing off the walls. A nurse approached. It was Lou.

'In here.' She grabbed Dorothy's hands and kissed her cheek. 'I know, I know.'

'It's a blessing,' said Carmen.

'It's a miracle.'

Tina's body was obscured by the crowd of girls. Dot made her way to the corner by the window, where there was breathing room.

'She's not talking yet,' said Lou.

'Tina,' Carmen said softly, almost singing. 'Tina, Tina, you woke up.' She leaned forward and Dot could see the smooth, relaxed arm. The girls crooned quiet hellos and patted the bed or the body tenderly. For a few moments the air in the room held this gentle wakening energy, more like a ward with newborn babies than here where people were submerged, semiconscious.

Lou stood with Dorothy at the window. In the car park a girl pushed a young boy around in a wheelchair, careening around cars and bollards, the boy's arms stretched above his head. With no warning, the girl jerked the wheelchair to a stop and the boy tumbled out. For a second both children froze. Then he got to his feet and walked straight up to the girl and whacked her arm. The car park dissolved into an asphalt blur, the children out of sight.

A gull-like cry came from the bed, and one of the girls called out, 'She's pulling her tubes.'

Lou cleared them back to the corridor and passing the bed Dorothy saw Tina, her arms and legs jerking, her plump, unlined teenager's face awake, her eyes open. A doctor pushed the door shut. 'Come on, out of here.'

'Let's go,' said one of the girls, her pointed finger on the button, holding the lift doors open.

★ ★ ★

It was lunchtime when they got back, and Dot and the girls set pots of chicken and rice out on the communal table beneath the vine-braided trellis. Their usual loud, rude talk warmed up again now they were sitting down, far from the hospital's constraints. She and Andrew hadn't even kissed in months. *Focus on the positive.* But maybe that was a positive. Confused! The table was dappled by shifting blobs of light that filtered through the vine, patches of whiteness in the paddle shapes of stegosaurus fins. As a child their son had been a dinosaur obsessive; before Donald could tell the difference between letters and numbers he knew a baryonyx from a coelophysis. Tendrils and crinkle-edged leaves curled above their heads. Beyond this shade, the courtyard light banged whitely up from ashy gravel. Heat pulsed. Sondra handed Dorothy her iPod. Free of make-up, her face looked peeled, huge as she leaned forward, awkwardly, and said thanks. Dorothy took her bowl to the kitchen with some others to scrape the dark-grey, splintered bones with squashed purplish ends into the rubbish bin.

Several hours later, Jo was still in labour.

'They induced her,' said Sondra, 'her water broke and nothing's happened so they gave her the shot.'

'Going to hurt like hell now,' said Carla, the youngest girl. 'And they get the forceps in there too.'

'That suction thing,' Sondra said, 'like the plumbers have.'

'The ventouse,' said Dot.

'Gives the baby the pointy head. My nephew got one of those, but he turned back to normal.'

'They'll probably have to cut her open,' Carla said. 'Caesarean time.' She ran a pointed fingernail down the middle of her belly. Pottery clay sat drying in half-squidged lumps on the art table, its surface taking on a webby bloom. The girls' talk whittled into silence. After a time, through the walls between them and the administrator's office, came the faint trilling of the telephone. They held still and then, a few long seconds later, they heard Carmen cheer.

Dorothy walked home as fast as she could, wheezing from asthma and all right *all right* age. Cries and thuds came from the neighbour's kids, playing stickball in the street – a balding tennis ball rolled by her feet and with a grunt she scooped it up and lobbed it back to the pitcher who caught it flawlessly, like it was coming home into his hand.

The house was warm and smelled of toast. There he lay on the bed watching a cycle of BBC World News. *Your husband.* Dorothy held the stitch that gripped her side. On the screen, weather maps swirled. 'Jo's had the baby,' she said, a hand on her chest from the urgent walk and from the burning knot of this news. 'She's fine. He's a boy.' She took a piece of toast from Andrew's plate and ate a corner.

'Hey. That's mine.'

'I'll make you some more. Have one of these.'

She'd picked up a packet of biscuits on the way home and now she tossed it next to Andrew on the bed. Keeping his eyes fixed to the news, he pulled and pulled at the cellophane wrapper and finally she took it off him and used her back teeth, feeling a dangerous tug on her gums as she wrenched the packet away from her mouth.

'Ruth called this morning,' he said.

'How is she?'

'Oh, she's in NA and SLAA and OA and a group for compulsive shoppers. Got a lot of language. Had a lot to say about intimacy. Rationalisation. Narcissism. Ownership. Addiction.'

'Jesus.' These were Ben's terms, it appeared, part of his ultimatum. There would be no more solo trips to Europe or New Zealand; there would be no more Hank. Poor Ruth. 'How was your day?'

His eyes searched the room as though the answer was written in the air. 'Night school hasn't opened yet.'

In the kitchen she slid bread into the toaster and pressed the lever down. It was broken and she had to push it again and again, metal rasping against metal, and finally hold it in place with a heavy chopping board. Propped by the bread bin was an internationally posted envelope with her name on it. The handwriting made the room tip. She tore it open while she took spreadable butter from the fridge and honey from the pantry, too many things in her hands, the paper resistant, thickly glued, she tore right through the return address. The bread began to toast. The crumb smell streaked the air like charcoal. Eve's gaze. Her appetite had vanished; if anything she wanted a drink. From the envelope she took a printed rectangle of card that bore a photo of Daniel and a woman who looked about thirty. Dark-haired. Not the Rio blonde. The pressed text was notification of their wedding, the date already passed. Daniel's note said *Dottie — I finally did it — you're right, it's the best thing ever*, and ended with kisses and *love, D.* 'You're right'? Her name was Maria. 'You're right'? When had she ever said 'It's the best'? WHEN HAD SHE EVER

SAID THAT? Dorothy crammed the card back into the envelope. The stamps were from Spain.

'Andy,' she said — the word just came out of her mouth. In the window behind him the image from the screen was reflected: another weather map. She stood in the bedroom doorway and decided to do it before there was time to think. 'Turn off the TV.' In the kitchen the toast popped. The dark, cooked smell made her feel a bit sick. Her husband raised a godlike arm towards the screen and it fell silent. Unconsciously — *really, Dorothy?* — she lifted the words from Daniel. 'Andy, you're right. It's for the best. We'll get a divorce.'

The invisible cage around him atomised. You could almost see it break up into particles and float away. 'Dottie.' He looked amazed. 'We're having the talk.'

The phone rang, and they looked at each other until she said, 'It's OK. Answer it.' While he was talking, she went out on the deck and sat on his karate mat, then stood again and tried to do downward dog, and felt blood rush to her face and straightened up and walked to the edge of the kwila boards, her head thudding, and made herself stop, not move. The yellow leaves prinkling that dark green tree. Look. Orange droplets of rust on the wind chimes.

17. HUNGRY CREEK

THE COMMENT THREAD was a comfort, largely because the older divorcees who posted there were much unhappier than her, and seemed to struggle with language. 'Life is so cool to be sad and depressed.' 'God loves your wrinkle and your failing hearing.' 'YOU OWN NO ONE NO ONE OWNS YOU.' But Dot knew she should wean herself off. Someone had written 'I haven't been lonely once.' She closed down the connection and returned to the world – Grace's small living room – the chaos of morning.

Her grandson was making goofy faces at the crockery cabinet's reflective glass doors. 'Frankie!' An echo of words hung in the room – his mother had spoken, given an instruction – the sense evaporated. He sprawled on the floor and commando-crawled towards the mound of clothes on the sofa. His wrists landed on the cushions as though pulling himself towards a desert oasis. Lightly he popped to his feet, plucked underpants from the pile and flung them high into the air, where they somersaulted before he caught them. He did it again. 'Hey, Dodo, look.'

She was already looking. How could she ever wrench her gaze from this perfect boy, her grandson, his shiny shiny eyes. Dot began to fold the washing. This time Frankie bobbed up beneath his pants like a soccer player heading the ball. His mother said the same thing as before, more loudly, and he spun towards the sound and the underpants fell to the floor. Dorothy cheered as the boy kicked them down the hall, swerving invisible oncomers. Grace gave her a look. 'Are you sure you want to come with us?'

'Yes. I can help with Meg. If you have to talk to them separately or something.'

'I won't have to talk to them separately.'

Meg was being auditioned for a commercial, if you could describe a baby screen test as an audition. The kids were good-looking. It helped pay the rent.

Frankie emerged from the bathroom wearing the underpants and tossed his pyjamas in the air so they fell in a small heap of primary colours beside the hallway runner. He put his legs through the sleeves of the pyjama top and hobbled towards Dorothy, eyes glowing. 'I'm a cheese boy.'

'Time to get dressed.'

'Dodo, did you know that ten is not the highest number?'

'What is?' She lifted him under the arms, swung him onto the sofa beside her, and tugged a T-shirt over his head, feeling the old momentary resistance as his skull crowned through the double-stitched collar.

'Eleven,' Frankie said. 'Or a hundred.'

'What about a hundred and one?'

He stared. 'What about a hundred and two?'

'That's how old Dodo is,' said the boy's father.

'Aha,' said Dorothy. 'Today, I feel it.'

'We should do something for your sixty-fifth.'

'Hmm, maybe.' She just had to keep putting Grace off until being sixty-five passed.

Amsi held the shorts out and Frankie succumbed to the inevitable. He balanced with a hand on his father's shoulder and held one thin, knobble-kneed leg raised and lingering, crooked in space over the open waistband of the shorts. 'Come on, you're going to be late for school.'

Finally dressed, the boy climbed from the sofa to a kitchen chair, balanced his way over three more chairs, their legs grating on the floorboards with his shifting weight, then leapt to the hall carpet in a drop-and-roll move. He sat up and picked at the double-knotted laces of his shoes. Amsi leaned against the wall, calm, the air-traffic controller on his morning off, and watched. 'Do you want a hand?' he asked his son.

'I can do it.'

Over the boy's head Amsi spoke to Dorothy. 'So how's the apartment-hunting?'

Grace walked Meg down the hall towards them, holding the baby's hands as she proceeded in small, jerky lurches.

One segment of footpath outside the house had been repaved and three paw-prints were caught in the concrete, claws out as though freshly made for all time. Dorothy sat in the back of the car because

Meg cried if she was not in the front. When the engine turned over, music shrieked from the speakers. Grace cut the sound. The baby burbled and clapped her hands, and a rubbish truck ground towards them on the other side of the road, and the car passed through the dull smell of its contents and on, around the corner, up the feeder ramp and right onto the motorway that roared past the house for hours each night.

The waiting area was full of girls with curly dark hair between twelve and twenty-four months, and their mothers, or maybe nannies. Dot had never seen so many curly-headed toddlers; there must have been fifteen. She'd brought a book, but the place was too noisy. One lone man sat with his daughter on his knee, and she twinkled her hands and sang a wordless nursery rhyme as he jigged. 'I wonder why they call everyone at the same time.' Dot leaned forward over the low reception table so he would know she was addressing him. 'It's like Oz in here.'

He gave a shrug that was more like a mime of a shrug, as though they were in a nightclub or the kind of place where talk was pointless.

'My granddaughter's in there now,' she said. 'Do you come to many of these?'

'Sorry?' He held his daughter's chest with one arm as he leaned forward and cupped an ear.

'Do you come to many auditions? Does your daughter do a lot of this?'

He nodded. Then he sat back against the white faux-leather couch. The room was very hot and the adults' voices were loud and artificial. She had done it herself, talking to Mister Unfriendly, soared into that upper register that denoted false cheer. Dorothy looked down at her shirt and saw that the buttons were uneven. Starting from the top button she fixed it, then examined the polish on her fingernails, chipped in the shapes of tiny treasure islands, the miniature repeating asterisks in the striated skin on the backs of her hands. Next to her sat a short woman, a Filipina nanny possibly, of indeterminate age. 'I suppose this sort of thing pays well,' Dorothy said. 'Being in a television ad.'

'Yes,' said the nanny. 'It's a sick world.'

Dot smiled. 'You can say that again.'

Grace came out of the casting room, the baby in her arms. Dot stood, reaching out to take her, and Grace said, 'For Christ's sake, Mum, your shirt.'

Oh, weird, the buttons were undone; her bra was awful, a flesh-coloured satiny thing that appeared capable of standing upright in doubled mountainous peaks if unhooked and cast to the floor. Then the roll of stomach below the bra, the protruding curve of oatmeal flesh that looked, to Dorothy, as though it belonged to somebody else. Halfway up, the curve was cut across by the transparent black waistband of her tights, with a thick raised seam wiggling indecently down the middle and disappearing into the waistband of her skirt. 'Oops,' Dorothy said, her voice raised for the benefit of the room.

There was no time between being a child, really bemused by bodies like this, and having one of your own, no time at all, and on the way to the car she would explain this to Grace, who looked good still, though she wore a lot of make-up and you could always see a pink elastic thong strap when she crouched down to help the kids with whatever. Not that she herself was even too decrepit; some women her age dated men of thirty, though she suspected those men were unknowingly gay. And Carmen from the maternity home had only just come out. Hope for everyone. Rather than alarmed she should be grateful. This was what she would say to Grace, that daily, in amongst all of the *yeah everything*, she tried to be consciously grateful. So what if she had learned it from the Internet? And she knew, she could tell, that Grace loved her kids, and her flinty, faintly desperate women friends, and her sexy old husband bringing those planes home safely day after day after day, even if she didn't love the motorway whine and the oil refinery and half of Amsi's colleagues sucking up the stress leave every year.

'When will you know?' she asked as they waited to cross the road to the car.

'Oh, we didn't get it.' Grace rooted in her massive pink bag with one hand, the baby balanced on her hip with the other. 'They cast the parents as white.'

'They might change their mind.' Of course they would. If it were down to her she would gobble Meg right up, her brother too.

'God damn it, where are they?' Grace stared at her mother, one arm half swallowed by the bag. 'Did you give the keys back to me?'

'Did I?'

'After you went back for the nappies.' Grace stood on her toes and peered down the street. 'Where's the car?'

'The car's down there.' Dorothy gestured, loosely, to the line of parked cars.

'Where? I can't see it.'

They walked forward along the noisy street, the air thick with midday summer heat, as though in a trance. Meg pulled the floppy cotton hat from her damp curls and waved it, then dropped it. Dorothy bent to pick it up. Flat pods of melted chewing gum blemished the footpath. Sunlight badoinged off storefronts' plated glass. She should have unpeeled her tights in the bathroom at the casting place, shoved them in the bin that was sickly sweet with other people's grandchildren's nappies.

They walked on and the spot where she had thought the car was parked moved ahead of them, like the moon used to when she was small, and they were driving at night, all of them, the dark back of her mother at the wheel, the bony pressure of a brother's or sister's head against her shoulder, black hills on the black night out the window. A plane slowly tore the sky overhead and Meg pointed upwards, crying, 'Daddy.' She thought he flew them.

Dorothy tried to remember putting the keys in her skirt pocket or in her bag, or locking the car or unlocking the car. She looked at the floral, plastic-coated nappy bag slung next to the bright pink bag over Grace's shoulder and envisaged it sitting in the well below the passenger seat, or on the bench seat in the back. Certainty was ungraspable.

When she had come back from the car Meg was next on the list to be called in, and there was hissed panic in the white-tiled, corporate bathroom as Grace fumbled the nappies out of the bag and balanced the baby half on a raised knee and half on the bench that housed the basins, and Dorothy handed her a perfumed plastic bag and wipes in the wrong order, a nurse in surgery fucking up her first day. Grace had lobbed the taped parcel of dirty nappy across the room and into the swing-top bin, and Dorothy applauded her daughter's aim, left standing in the bathroom with the baby-changing implements all around her feet, the door that Grace and Meg had bolted through already sliding shut.

'Are you sure we haven't gone past the car?' she said now. 'Are you sure we came out in the right direction?'

Grace growled between her teeth, a surprisingly underworld sound.

'Let me take her.' Dorothy hoisted Meg into her arms. The child's towelling playsuit was moist with sweat. They were all sweating. On Grace it looked like a sprayed sheen of lacquer. 'Poor little thing, what a big morning.'

The road took a slight bend, which seemed to speak to them as they approached, the curve of lined buildings leaning in confidingly, *You didn't come this far*, and they turned and walked back towards the casting agency, the distance shorter in reverse. On the other side of the road, a bus pulled out into the traffic and revealed the boxy profile of Grace's car. 'Thank God,' Grace said.

When the traffic stopped for the lights they picked their way between idling cars, Grace darting her head forward and leading, Dorothy raising one arm to wave thanks to the drivers for letting them cross. The baby was heavy, and soggy, and the skin of their arms glued together and made a very faint sucking noise like worn-out Velcro when it peeled apart. Dot dabbed at the creases in the girl's neck with a tissue from the floral bag. The keys were dangling from the lock on the driver's side. 'For fuck's sake,' said Grace.

'Oh dear,' said Dot. 'God, really?'

'It's not funny,' said Grace. She nudged past her mother with a hip in order to unlock the passenger door. From a gilt-curlicued boutique, a very tall young woman in tight jeans emerged, a man with corrugated grey hair behind her. They swung rectangular shopping bags from plush tassels and spoke together in a language that might have been Russian. As they passed Dot, and Grace, and the baby, the young woman said something sideways to the man and threw her head back merrily and laughed. Grace threw the car keys to the gutter. 'You used to laugh whenever I lost my temper. Laugh and laugh and laugh and laugh and laugh and laugh and laugh. I hate my life,' she cried. Tears broke from her.

'Don't be ridiculous. I take you seriously!' But Dot had a memory. Having to leave the dinner table when one of them – who? – pushed yet another plate away, knocking over yet another glass of water, and she was unable to control her erupting giggles at the sheer fucking hopelessness of it all, the child wailing louder, real tears now, betrayed. She had stood in the hallway, wheezing with laughter, waiting till *all this* didn't seem just completely ridiculous again.

Dot clicked Meg into the car seat and handed her a plastic bottle of water from the bracket in the door. The little girl drank then waved it around so that droplets sprayed everywhere, spotting Dorothy's shirt. 'Get in the back,' Dot said.

Grace was under the wheel, retrieving the keys, sniffing. 'But you're not allowed to drive. It hasn't been six months yet.'

Without seeing anything, Dorothy stared at Meg. There was an unspoken rule not to mention the loss of her licence and Grace had just broken it. Five months ago she'd been busted for speeding. In court she had been described as a recidivist and held in contempt for expostulating to the judge, 'Don't be so fucking stupid.' Turned out there was no statute of limitations on driving offences, and over the decades her unpaid fines had racked up a lot of interest. The lawyer, who promised to get her out of the charges and minimise the costs, proved to be overly optimistic. 'A danger to road safety' was the phrase heard. Could there be, Dorothy wondered, a statute of limitations on regret? A question to keep to herself.

'We need to get the fan on. Sit down and have some water.' Dorothy inched between the car in front and the dinged, flaky bonnet of Grace's car. She sat behind the steering wheel and started the engine, and switched the air conditioner to high. After a few moments frigid air blew around them. 'Bliss,' said Dot.

'This is bad for the planet,' said Grace.

'I know.'

Back at the house, Grace laid Meg down in the cot. The baby rolled onto her front and put her thumb in her mouth, exhausted. 'You're a good mother,' Dorothy said when her daughter was back in the kitchen.

'You can't stay here any more.' Grace's voice wobbled.

Dorothy opened the pantry door, took out a small cardboard packet of raisins and lifted the flap with her thumbnail, loosened a few of the sticky black blobs and put the box next to the container of lunch that waited for Meg to awake. 'You're always so well prepared,' she said.

'I wanted to last till you could drive again. Or found an apartment. But you're not even looking.' Grace tipped sideways and donked her head on the wooden bench. 'Sorry, I know you're not a project.'

'Darling,' said Dorothy. 'I'm sorry. Please don't feel bad. You've been so generous. All of you children, I know it's not easy having your divorced mother living with you.'

'Dad's dating again, did you know that? He joined some online group. Why don't you? It's perfectly acceptable now.' His relationship with Jennifer had not survived the divorce. Dorothy saw her once, walking her dog, also curly and golden, on the beach at Takapuna. That sickening moment as she approached, Dot waiting for the encounter to pass, afraid she might just *flip out* and throw herself writhing to the sand. Dot had said hello. Jennifer pretended not to hear. She'd yelled it to the woman's back, the arm that casually swung one of those plastic ball-throwers, a long thin scoop that made her think of a speculum. *Hello, Jennifer.* Tossed on the wind.

'Good for him.'

'That guy, what about him, that photo by your bed?'

'He lives in Spain. He's married. He's just an old friend.'

'We think you're frightened of being on your own. Us kids. That's what we think.'

'Right. I see.' She could tell Grace was waiting for her to say something more. The warm, dark smell of raisins wrinkled through the air.

The commune had expanded from the few prefabs and A-frames it consisted of over fifty years ago. Dorothy didn't remember the way it looked; nothing would be exactly the same except the stern rocks, covered in lichen. She longed to lie on the ground with Eve, looking at Daniel wand the baseball bat, practising his swing.

They found Michael in the vegetable patch at the top of a

dusty path, and the children squinted at his white ponytail, his missing-toothed smile, and solemnly accepted handfuls of soft, cloud-shaped raspberries fresh from the canes. Dorothy showed them the sunflowers while he walked Amsi and Grace around the beans and lettuces and thick-veined leaves of some other vegetable, perforated with snail holes. 'We really have to go,' Grace said, and the boy ran back down the hill, tumbling into gravity's embrace, the adults coming after. There were brief goodbyes – Frankie's fierce squeeze, his head thudding into her pillowy middle, the show hug of the little girl, reaching out from Grace's arms to pat her cheeks, then the young family shut their car doors and drove off, taking the cattle stop slowly, leaving Dorothy standing there, the poker-worked sign that announced the commune's presence swinging from its hooks. She began the walk back up through the fine dry earth and trees to Michael, and the luggage she had left with him.

In the empty cabin she was given her suitcase looked too flash, out of place, and her knapsack leaned like a person against the end of the wire-wove bed. 'Smells a bit musty,' Michael said, 'but no one's lived here since Rena died.'

Dorothy opened the stiff, small window opposite the bed. A bee drifted in. 'How did she die?'

'Happy. At peace. It's a long time ago now.' He stood in the middle of the double-bed-sized room, looking around with his overly healthy eyes, large still but solid, muscular in a flannel shirt, torn shorts, wrinkly knees, tanned skin encasing the natural man. Of course, she'd meant, 'Did she die in this room?'

'Michael,' she began, and he said, 'Mike. Mike will do.'

'Mike. Thank you for this. It's only till I get my driver's licence back. And my teaching registration lapsed while I was at the maternity home. As soon as I get a job I can find somewhere in town. Of course there's always the pension.' A joke. The older she got, the further away they moved the pension age.

'What happened to your house?'

'We sold it ages ago, to put the kids through school. We've been renting. I had those fines; it's slowed me up. But I don't want to take anything on until there's some cash flow.'

'I don't really understand what went on there.' That gap in his front teeth was disconcerting, made him look a bit simple. One must have been knocked out.

'I haven't got much money. There's no getting around it. I just have to start again.' The bee crawled up the lichened door frame. 'Mike,' she said, wanting to take his hands in hers, instead sitting on her own hands on the wire wove, feeling the mattress sink nearly to the floor, 'do you believe people can start again? Do you think it's possible, at my age?'

'Of course,' he said, clear eyes floating. 'That's what this place is all about.' With that he shut the door. The knapsack slowly keeled over onto its side, and the springs holding the wire hexagons of the bed-base to the rusting frame let out a violent creak as she reached to snatch the canvas bag upright. The small wooden cross above the bed slid onto a diagonal, like the needle of a compass.

It was Mike's night to cook so she helped him, and the mostly young people he lived with all welcomed her and thanked them both for the food. They explained that 'Dorothy' had the word *rot* in it, therefore here she would always be Dot. Their names were Thane, Jared, Karen and a couple that might have been adopted by deed poll – Hope and Faith. 'Do you remember Name?' she asked Mike. 'Was she here when you came back?'

He didn't remember her. Karen said she must have been long gone. The roll call of former commune dwellers remained unrecorded. Prayers were chanted. Dot shut her eyes as everyone did, feeling warm channels of breath running in and out through her nostrils, until she heard the small sounds of cutlery against enamel plates, a wooden bread board being pushed across the table, a serrated knife sawing crusts. She produced the bottle of red wine from her knapsack but it didn't stay on the table. Later she saw it on the storeroom floor, next to a big box of potatoes, their oval spheres dark and fragrant with earth. She was looking for the ginger to slice for a pot of tea, and groped around the rough wooden battens just inside the door for a light switch before remembering there was no power.

Back in the eating area Mike sat with his arm round Karen's waist – she had an animated, sparkly face, was probably in her forties, with dark hair in a low ponytail, the ponytail Mike had now between his loosely curled fingers, thin ribbons between his paler brown hands. The ginger root was fibrous, the knife slicing through first the ridged skin and then the hard inner flesh, ringed like a felled tree stump, and the fine tough hairs in the centre. When she poured water from the whistling steam kettle into the teapot the slices lifted and bobbed near the surface, and the warm, bracing scent released into the air and mingled with the herby smell of Thane's joint.

Michael caught Dorothy looking at him, worried. 'It's OK,' he said. 'I don't do that any more.'

Karen snuggled in and kissed his cheek.

In the morning, when it was just light, Dot placed eggs one by one in the recycled ice-cream container, minute pore-like squirkles in the beige shells, some of them streaked with droppings or dried gunge. The eggs were fragile and weighted at the same time, the curved shells touching lightly against their neighbours in the plastic tub, each one thick with its own liquid contents. The coop smelled of straw, which smelled of feathers, which smelled of bird-shit, which smelled of sticks. There were seven eggs in total and the next day there would be a similar number, and the day after that and the day after that. You would not ever be alone at the commune.

The eggs rolled and knocked slightly against the smooth walls of the plastic tub, blueness glowing onto them around the edges, light shifting over her as she carried the container across the yard to the kitchen, dewy grass cold and ticklish on her bare ankles where the path ran out.

For a while the commune had financed itself from the orchard, Faith told her, but that income ran down over the past few years, with industrial greenhouses reaching tentacles across the country-side and the new supermarket a closer drive for most people in the town, and stocking organic produce anyway. A homeopathic-remedies venture was not cost-effective. She had seen the dark-blue glass bottles on windowsills and lined up along skirting boards, sprouting lumpy beeswax candles or pale at the shoulders with thick dust. Michael went into cider and exploded the storage shed.

It was agreed that the commune would no longer try to make money, but grow only the means of their own survival. No extra cash meant relying on their own skills for everything. 'All right if you're bunging a diff in a car,' said Mike, who was washing the breakfast dishes, scrubbing hard at the encrusted rings where fruit from a batch of muesli had burned to the oven tray. 'Not so hot if you need a crown replaced.' That explained the missing tooth.

Thane's partner had objected, and she moved out and started up a craft market in the city, the success of which mystified the remaining commune dwellers, given that it sold ironic macramé and peg dolls, nothing that would actually be any use. 'What's it *for*?' Faith asked the air, scattering sunflower seeds over her plate of stewed rhubarb. 'What's a block of wood that looks like a piece of soap *for*?' The rhubarb lay in coiled wet ropes in her earthenware bowl like someone's hair.

'What about Daniel?' Mike asked. 'You in touch?'

Flickered with adrenalin, caught out as always at the mention of his name, she told Mike that last she heard he'd gotten married. Adulthood was like this – your voice calm, your face normal, while inside, turmoil, your heart still seven, or twelve, or fifteen.

'So, not since I wrote to congratulate them.' Daniel's reply had intimated a possible move back home, *nostalgic in my old age . . . but María's family are here*. It hadn't been the time to mention her divorce. Since then, whenever the urge to contact Daniel came over her, she resisted. He had a different life. A vine had grown over the kitchen window and been cut back, leaving a tattoo of broken black swirls. Dorothy picked at the insistent tendril that crawled under the windowpane, its bright greenness probing the room, pale

green shoots emerging like arrowheads, or the tops of the spades
suit in a deck of playing cards.

There'd been some serious upgrades to the ablutions block since
their childhood, with pump bottles of lavender soap and warm
indoor showers. The water gleaming on Rena's young body in the
sun. Cobwebs clung stickily in Dot's hair. She pulled at them in the
tin-plate mirror but something that her fingers transferred, oils or
heat or dirt, made them glue up and harden. When she flossed her
teeth the taste of blood came into her mouth. It was normal, when
first among new people, to feel more alone; of this she was sure. Just
a little bit longer: first to feel at home here, then to leave. Her hiber-
nation from the world could not be permanent. She didn't have the
capacity of a Michael or a Thane.

Dimly she noticed shouting from outside and dropped her toilet
bag to the floor. Waves of panic crashed through the sheet iron and
the non-tanalised wood although the words were unclear; sounds
ran together the way dogs sometimes barked, unbroken.

She saw the car before she saw Mike. He lay on the ground
beneath it, under the front wheel, his leg pinned, and Thane stood
over him by the open driver's door, one arm reached into the car,
hand on the steering wheel. Mike's face was bright red – burning red. People stood around, someone clutching her own head,
someone with his palms raised. Mike roared, and his body twisted
as he pulled away from the leg. Dust eddied around him. Hope, or
was it Faith, had a length of wood, was holding it like a batter at
the plate, shouting at Thane. All this was processed as Dot ran to
Michael, spoke to Thane, and tried to lift the car. Squatting at the

knee she heard her jeans rip, the arse of her jeans, something went pop in her pelvic floor or near it, and she wasn't able to budge the tyre. Her heart wrenching. Now Thane lifted too, helping, inches of searing air between the rubber tread and the leg and Mike dragged himself out from its shadow. The leg was fucked, and he retched into the dust. A two-legged metal jack lay next to him on its side.

Blood streaked his jeans but there was no severed artery. The problem, Karen said when Mike was lying across the back seat and Thane was trying to start the car, was the distal tibia, which was splintered and crushed. She cupped the side of Mike's face with her palm. 'Listen to me,' she said. 'Something has happened to your lateral condyle. It might be split or it might be pulped. We don't know. They'll give you an anaesthetic and find out. Maybe the neck of the fibula is broken. These things sound worse than they are. They might put a pin in your lower tibia. Or you might go into traction, depending on the knee, but the knee looks OK. They're going to bolt you together,' she said. 'You'll be the bionic man. Screws and rods, the works.'

Dorothy asked her to come to the hospital with them but Karen said no, put a kiss on her palm and pressed it to Mike's good leg. 'I can't go into the city. Sorry. I'll be here waiting.' That *I know my boundaries* tone of the recovered person, the once damaged. It was a truth about life for those people that love had its limit. Survival came first. At last Thane had the car in gear and shouted at Dorothy to get in.

She sat in the back with her brother, holding the tourniquet she'd made out of her shirt as tight as she could above his knee, her knuckles and the pads of her fists green-white. She was hunkered down in the space behind the passenger seat to do it, hold him steady. He looked old.

'He going to lose the leg?' Thane said it stridently, as though she couldn't hear him although he was just there, driving, inches away. Where was Thane from? Who was Thane?

'No,' she said.

The car slowed, and she raised up on her knees to get blood back into her legs, and the world floated through the window – white roadside flowers, the bank dotted with purple and pink wild flowers, the raffia-petals of cornflowers or anemones, the road dust yellow and the faint sweet smell of cows. 'We need to get there fast,' she said, and then there was a bump and Michael moaned and the car slowly, carefully, tilted and lowered over the cattle grid, her brother breathing in pain with every rise and fall. Dot released one stiff hand from the knotted shirt. She held his enormous open hand that was like a catcher's mitt. Michael closed his eyes slowly and mouthed something.

'It's better than it looks,' she said, a tiny portion of her mind surprised that she could lie. They drove past a brindled cow, conch-shaped eyes either side of its head. Straggly agapanthus.

'There was a leak,' said Thane. 'Up the front here, antifreeze or something.'

'What colour?'

'Green, dark green kind of.'

'Not the oil?'

'Don't know, skid plates, makes it hard to see where the leak comes from. That's how come he was under the car. We've lent our

jack stand to the farmer down the road, there was just a scissor jack.'
Thane's voice was unmoored. He was losing it.

'It looked like you were running him over.'

'No.'

'What about what's-her-name, with the baseball bat?'

'Yeah, she tried to lever the car but it didn't work.'

'Are you worried about the leak? Will we make it?'

The engine groaned as the car climbed a hill, a stock truck
crawling in front of them, the hot smell of wool and live animals
jammed together in the dark. Mike's eyes were closed and his lips
slightly parted over his harlequin teeth. He wasn't wearing shoes. She
couldn't look at the foot that she had twisted back into place when
he briefly passed out. The other foot, the good foot, was brown and
cracked and the toenails had aged, coarse and square and yellowed.
Dark hair sprang along the ridge of the foot-bone and on the lower
knuckles of the toes. Michael's face was clammy beneath her hand.
She moved her hand away a bit and he grunted and rolled his head
towards it. Stubble bristled her palm. 'Fuck, Thane, can you go any
faster, how useless is this car?'

'I'm going to be sick,' said Thane. 'It's the adrenalin, it's draining
from me. I feel faint.'

'You fucking hippy. It's no better back here.'

'No, you have to drive.'

'Get out then.' She shouted it.

He stopped right there in the road and in a slamming of doors they
swapped places. 'I'm not licensed,' she said into the rear-view mirror.

'Just drive fast,' he said. 'Drive as fast as the car can go.'

And the road spooled into them like a retracting tape measure.

★

Michael and his foot survived, and Ruth fell back into line with her marriage to Ben. Andrew married again: Beth, the widow of a man he used to work with at the polytech. He'd gone to the man's funeral, he told Dorothy, and Beth had wept into his lapel and said, 'Thank god you're here. You're the only one he liked in that whole place.' 'Can you believe it?'

There would never be mutual visits, holidays together, but in the evenings, when she'd closed up the art room at the hospice and gone back to her quiet apartment, Dot and Andrew often spoke on the phone about their children and grandkids: about Amy's struggle through the ranks of retail management and Donald's coming out which had been no surprise, and what to do with crazy Hannah ditching an engineering internship for the ludicrous short-term goal of touring with a band, and how in hell any of them were ever going to afford their own home, and wasn't it good that Grace was back at work now Meg and Frankie were both in school. Together they thanked god for the barely surviving public education system and the fact that Hannah seemed to quite like slumming it and Donald was the one with the business mind, his software-development business in profit. Sometimes Andrew even bitched to Dot about Beth's sullen sons, who were taking their own sweet time to accept the marriage. 'They're still grieving their dad,' Dorothy said, and Andrew said, 'I know that. Jesus, I don't need you to analyse the world for me, Dorothy, just listen. Be a friend.'

But it wasn't Andrew she turned to when the eggs began to burn or her glasses disappeared. They should come with a sonar locator, she thought, there would be money in that, just as you could ring a cell phone to find it you should be able to do the same with house keys, remote controls, wallets. What was it Donald said, the Internet of Things? She lived alone. Only Diego, the caretaker who'd become a friend, saw the lists, but then the lists would appear in odd places, not on the fridge but tucked in the back of the bathroom cabinet, not taped to the front door but rolled into a wine glass. Lists were only useful if you could find them, and then only if you could read them, and reading was no problem apart from the giant hole torn in one afternoon when the recipe for spinach soup escaped her and she went blank, the bench spread with potato peelings. Spinach stalks. Onion peel. What to do with these? The cookbook was useless, the instructions made absolutely no sense, may as well have been in Mandarin. She slammed the book shut and wanted to weep. It was much later that night, tossing some apple skins into the compost bucket, that she discovered the white cubes of peeled and diced potato, the fresh green leaves nestled there in the dark.

18. DANIEL

IT WAS A new grocery store; new for Dorothy. She had taken a bus, also new, one of the yellow double-ended ones with a concertina segment in the middle that held two carriages together. Those buses belonged somewhere with wide roads and manicured roundabouts, not here with the narrow bricolaged streets and everyone parking arsy-versy where they pleased. All they did here was jam the traffic, but the council before the current council had ordered them and everyone was stuck with the decision, it would have been 'bad management' to reverse it, buy their way out, and this was all any ruling body seemed to do these days, live under sufferance with the choices of the previous administration, or at least make it sound that way. Dorothy sat in the back half of the bus, so when it turned she would feel a momentum swing, a surge of uncontrol. The window by her head was streaked with a whitish substance, as if an egg had been thrown at it and the glair dried in the sun. Out of the narrow streets, outside suburban stand-alone houses, trees flared with spring blossoms and magnolia, rhododendrons, daphne. Through the sliver of open window the scent of the daphne passed faintly, like something imagined. A tree stood bare-branched, surrounded by its fallen scarlet petals as though it had given an enormous sigh and shed everything. Dot scrolled the pages of her book, another book she couldn't read without her glasses and magnifying glass; all very well enlarging the font but not when it ended up three words per line. How did women go about the world on their own without books? You saw it, but she would never understand.

The grocery store was identical to the one on her corner, down to the point-of-sale promotions and the black-wheel streaks on the linoleum by the refrigerators. Dorothy had not eaten breakfast in the hope of generating some kind of hunger, but now the grabby feeling in her stomach wouldn't focus itself on anything. It was just before noon. The women shopping looked identical to the women in her neighbourhood. Their shoes were thrashed but clean. So sad. The phrase came into Dot's mind while she sniffed leathery oranges from the fruit bins, a two-note descending sing-song like the poor fucker caged bird in the downstairs apartment. So sad. So sad. Who had said that lately? Of what? Perhaps the women behind her on the bus. Women, it had to be noted, were every-where. There in the reflection of the fridge doors was a woman not unlike Dot, same height, same age, who looked as if she didn't care about food any more either, though she was wearing a thick blue sweatshirt and tracksuit pants, so where her body began was obscured. Yes, definitely a double reflection, not a trick of the light, nor Dot's usual surprise that the old woman caught ghostily in a shop window as she passed it was, in fact, herself.

Their reflections smiled at each other and the mirror woman's face became a walnut, deep creases from her mouth running all the way up to her temples. Dot leaned forward and pulled the heavy door open, its suction straps unpeeling like black liquorice, and the other woman's reflection swung closer as the door moved. The refrigerator puffed hot air around Dot's ankles and her fingers grew cold. She turned cheeses over looking for the ones that had further until their expiry date, the ones they always kept in the back. Cheese was a guaranteed pleasure. One of these days she would wake up and discover herself to be a giant mouse.

In one corner of the grocery store the fluorescent overhead lights were out. Dot had the feeling this had happened in the exact same corner in her local store – or perhaps it was the synaptic shudder of déjà vu. Diego made her take aspirin every day now, and that shit must be doing something. Here everything looked soft, grey, old. The edges of the cardboard cake-mix boxes were matt and worn, as though overly handled. A cloying smell rose from a tray of thin green aubergines that lay limply on pulpy-looking ridged blue cardboard. The baking soda she was looking for was not there. Her local store was also out. Why must this be? If they had to deal with the pigeons she had to deal with, they would ensure constant supplies of baking soda. In her neighbourhood people bought it because it was cheaper than toothpaste; here perhaps it was being used to bake cakes. Dot circumnavigated the store again, to check that there wasn't a shelving anomaly, and she should have registered as odd that the other woman was keeping pace with her at a distance of a couple of yards, but these places were full of weirdos. By the mysterious locked door in the back wall of the shop, a door to the staff toilet or stack room or an asphalt, oily car park, a teenage boy with acne practised impressive dance moves with his arms. At the pick-and-mix candy bins two blonde women with ponytails tonged hearts into a plastic bag, one by one. A pale tabby cat slunk a figure eight through Dot's ankles. The baking soda was nowhere to be seen. A young man in a blue store jacket passed her carrying a box of long-life milk cartons, and Dot followed him to the shelf where he was stacking them. He wore a nametag but the lettering was too small for Dot to read. She asked him where she might find the baking soda but he seemed unable to understand, or perhaps to hear her. There was nothing in his ears. She patted his arm and he turned to face her, and she asked him again, and he leaned in, but she may as well have been speaking Martian. She mimed measuring baking soda into a teaspoon and stirring a cake, then cleaning her teeth, then sprinkling baking soda on the windowsill to keep the pigeons away. She mimed being a pigeon, pecking at the baking soda and hopping back in fright. The man was apparently an imbecile. Disgusted, Dot walked away and over to the biscuit aisle where she threw the packet of digestives into her bag. She didn't even like them, the way they fell apart into the bottom of a cup of tea, but her teeth couldn't handle the old crackers any more.

The mistake was in stopping at the checkout to pay for a magazine that specialised in arts and crafts, which she wanted to use for work, and staring the checkout girl down when she glanced at the biscuits glowing radioactively on top of the book and spare jumper in Dot's bag. Dorothy got cold easily in springtime. *Feeling the cold* was what you called it once you were her age, oh yes, I feel the cold. But the sun was lighting up the street outside with its whiteness, and she walked out the door and towards that light, and was a few paces out of the store when there was a hand on her upper arm and some-one said, 'Excuse me.' It was the lady from the shop with the blue sweatshirt and the wrinkles.

'Yes?' Dot thought perhaps she was going to ask for directions. She had one of those faces. I'm not from around here – I just have one of those faces, she prepared to say.

'Did you pay for those biscuits?'

'What biscuits?' Pure coldness thumped through her body.

'Those.' The woman pointed a coral-nailed finger towards the bag.

Dot faked a double take. 'Oh my god. Where did they come from?'

'You put them in your bag in there.' She gestured towards the store. 'Could you come with me, please?'

'Well, I could. But truly, this was a mistake, I must have put them there by accident. Are you sure I wasn't charged for them?' Dot made a show of fumbling in her jacket pocket for the receipt. It was Diego's jacket, cut like a suit jacket, but made of denim, with deep pockets. He left it at the apartment last time he came to fix the microwave, and Dorothy wore it everywhere now. There were black grease stains down the sides and it smelled of a man's sweat, which was quite frankly a tonic. They should bottle that stuff. Dot pulled out some gum and her bus pass, but seemed to have done something else with the receipt.

'Please, madam. Come with me.'

And just like that they were back inside the shop. The blonde ponytails stood and stared as the woman put her gnarled hand on Dorothy's shoulder and marched her towards the mysterious door in the back of the store, and Dot kept her chin in the air. The dancing boy was gone. A small key from a plastic chain that was connected to the woman's sweatshirt pocket opened the door. Through the door was a short corridor, with a fire door at its end, a horizontal metal safety bar across it. On the left-hand side of the corridor was an open cleaning cupboard, and the smell of bleach burned the air. There was another door to the right, and the blue sweatshirt knocked on it.

A man sat behind a desk. Much younger guy. His hair was cut short, neat, and he had a sort of pubic beard that was trimmed thinly around his jaw line and up towards the corners of his mouth. The shaved skin in the middle was blue with stubble. Repellent as it was, the beard made Dot think about whoever had to kiss this man, or whether anyone did. He smelled keenly of a blue, minty aftershave. She wanted to grab him and shake his shoulders and tell him, 'You're human! Don't fight it!' But now was not the time.

'This lady has shoplifted a packet of biscuits.'

'Inadvertently,' Dot said.

'I saw you. It was quite deliberate.'

'No really. It was a mistake.' She rolled out a phrase of Diego's that she'd always hated: 'A senior moment.'

The man with the beard chuckled. 'Really? Oh dear.'

'I'm mortified,' Dot said. 'I would of course like to pay for the biscuits. But I assure you, I am not a criminal.'

'May I see some identification?'

She handed him her bus pass. He opened a drawer and took out a ring-binder folder. In it were pages and pages of photocopied returned cheques, photo IDs, student cards, sample signatures with the word *FORGED* stamped over the top, and even mug shots. If they had a reference here to the photocopy of her bus pass ID – the one pinned to the corkboard of villains and recidivists by the checkout tills of her local grocery store – Dorothy was cooked. He held the bus pass in one hand and flicked through the pages with the other.

'Doesn't much look like you,' he said. 'Doesn't do you justice.'

Dot blinked, slowly. 'Thank you.' Not that photo, but another one, years – decades – ago, there had been a day when she had gotten a new staff ID shot taken for the school where she was working. There she was smiling for the camera, dressed ironically like a 'lady teacher', but in the photograph when it was printed she just looked like a lady teacher. That was a day, yes, she remembered that day.

Sex with Diego would be epic. Dorothy knew this because he told her once, when he was having a beer at her place after he fixed the balcony rail. 'Sex with me, darling, it's epic,' he said, his legs stretched out before him, the bottle balanced on his solid, convex stomach.

'Good for you,' she said. She had the old photo albums out and was selecting, binning and gluing photos without being able to study them too closely. His presence was a buffer against falling into the pictures and the long crawling out again. 'Good for your ladies.'

'You want to ask me to scan those for you. I'd do it as a favour.' He swivelled right and left in the squidgy chair and thrust a look at her.

'Diego,' Dot laughed. 'I'm ancient.'

'Don't knock it till you've tried it,' he said.

'No knocking will occur. But thanks. I don't get many offers these days.'

'Your loss, darling,' he grinned.

'I'm sure.' Wind came through the open window and shifted the photos around. On the balcony the ladder rattled against the eaves.

Epic sex. Jesus. She would have liked to see him naked, but that was as far as it went. On the whole being unleashed from sex was a tremendous relief. But this was something, standing in front of the store manager's desk while he looked for evidence of criminality, and her heart quickened.

In the apartment Dorothy put some music on and knocked on the window glass to shoo the pigeons off the sill. With summer coming, and open windows, her great fear was that a bird would fly into the room, panicking and crapping everywhere. The happiness she felt on the bus home leaked away with the passing afternoon and now Dot was cross for having given in to the cheap thrill. She pretended her children were too far-flung to be ashamed, but Diego would mind, and he would be the one to come and get her if she ever had to make the call from the police cells. His face clouded with disapproval. Another crazy lady. Dot couldn't afford to lose him. She took out her magnifying glass to read the craft magazine.

Later she worked on a funding application to buy new sand trays for the hospice, reading patient testimonies – 'sacred multidimensional depths of psychic consciousness ... self-witnessing ... silent reflection ... I grew so much personally ... I am at home ...' until it was dark. She got up to put on the lamp and saw a strange man in the doorway of the locksmith's looking up at her apartment building. Just a couple of glances, but the feeling flew up from the street like a sparrow – he was looking at her.

The man was young, in his twenties, and though it was hard to tell from this third-storey window, he seemed to be tall. In the brief seconds of his presence she noticed his shoulders braced, how he stood on the balls of his feet, hopping slightly. Yes, he reminded her of Donald, her son, as though he'd stepped through the computer screen of their last conversation and into the neighbourhood. His hair was long around his face. He wore a suit jacket, sneakers and jeans. Maybe he was there to score, or to meet a person who never showed up. Maybe he was just getting some keys cut. They watched each other. He wasn't Donald but he was somebody's son – an adopted-out child. Then he was lost to the mass of children playing football down the middle of the road. Gaps in their calling and kicking let in the sound of old men nattering outside the newsagent's. She liked the old men's voices. The way they went on. Go for it, she thought, standing by the minimal breeze and listening to their gorgeous unwinding gossip. Don't stop. Go for gold.

The cloud of footballers passed and the new locksmith, a middle-aged woman, was there in place of the man, staring up. Dot ducked too fast and her knee went. Slowly she lowered herself fully to the ground, trying not to curse aloud. The music had long stopped and the floor felt cold through her jumper. The knee pulsed a sweet, nauseous pain up her thigh into her hip. 'Bastard,' she said, 'bastard, bastard.' Dot crawled to the kitchen, dragging the lame leg behind her. Rum first, then the liniment cream, then, when she had manoeuvred herself through to the bedroom to lie down, curled, giving in to the ache, a pill.

In the morning the knee felt a lot better. Diego came to drop off some magazines from the Laundromat downstairs, old ones with the covers ripped off, for Dot to take to work. When he saw that her knee was strapped he insisted on accompanying her the two blocks to the hospice. The spring air was perfumed, inhalable. Diego carried the magazines in a plastic bag and the fabric off-cuts for quilting in a giant checked carrier bag over his shoulder, and Dot told him about the mandala paintings the patients were doing and the woman who had decided her life essence should be expressed by pictures of Princess Diana.

He shook his head. 'Such a sad day when that lady died. There will never be another like her.'

'What would be in your mandala painting, Diego?'

'In mine?' He laughed. 'You trying to put me in my grave? Heaven hopes it is a long time before they wheel me in to sign the entry papers to that place.'

Dot looked at his profile against the moving colours of the mosaic wall outside the school buildings. 'No, Diego, I don't think you're ever going to die.'

He shrugged. 'Well, some day.'

They reached the hospice and the smoked automatic reception doors parted, waiting for Dot to enter. Diego placed the bags just inside the lobby and nodded at the young receptionist. 'Morning, darling.'

Dot touched his arm, suddenly longing for him to stay. 'Will you come in today? You know they love it when you do.'

'Ah, no, today I've got a lot of people to see.'

'OK. Lucky ladies.'

'Oh yes,' he smiled, 'and lucky me.'

After work she made some packet soup and ate a digestive biscuit, then went down to the locksmith's. The new owner looked curiously at Dot. 'I'm just about to close up.'

'Oh, sure. How are you finding the neighbourhood?'

The owner nodded. 'Pretty good. People always need keys.'

There was a moment while she waited for Dorothy to get the message that her day was over. Dot backed out again into the street. The Turkish men stood in the brightly lit empty shop they used as FC headquarters and talked, and teenagers leaned against the round doors of the industrial-sized washing machines in the Laundromat chatting into cell phones and flirting with each other. There was a sound like thunder but it was just the roller doors coming down on the greengrocer's and the mechanic's. The neighbours were cooking curry and a seductive smoky smell came from the kebab shop. A woman in a summer dress walked a giant dog, an exquisite thing, grey and huge and thinly wolfish, the length of the street, its gait casual, disdainful. It seemed that everyone on the block stopped to watch its hollow haunches pass by. Pigeons cooed, roosting in the plane trees. The evening fuzzed, as though molecules of air had thickened to hold the last of the light. Over to the west, laky streaks lined the sky, and the hills in the distance were the colour of morello cherries.

'There was a man here yesterday. I wondered if I might know him. He was standing where you are just now, and looking – up there.' Saying 'at my apartment' seemed impossible, would seal the impression that she was delusional, or paranoid.

The locksmith shrugged. 'Yeah? I don't remember.'

'Yeah. I thought – maybe – never mind.'

'I can't give out the names of clients.'

'No, of course.'

Back in the apartment, she ate another biscuit and thought about the young man who looked like Donald. That story of her mother's – the lost son in the driveway. He was her sign. Her young man, appearing through the window. Her message, her past mistake. She sat for a long time while the light melted from the room. One phone call. Not to interrupt his life or ask for anything. One phone call, just to hear his voice.

From the kitchen drawer, Dorothy took the softened, split-cornered card that carried the last phone number she'd had for Daniel. It was morning in Spain. She switched on the overhead lamp. With the phone pressed hard against her ear she leaned forward, head on her forearms and elbows on the bench, in the posture of someone waiting for seasickness to pass. The dial tone was a single metallic note that could have been a fault. She didn't know whether or not to hang up but then a woman answered. Dorothy was embarrassed by her lack of the language. She had to blurt straight into English. 'Excuse me ...'

The woman said something in Spanish.

'Do you speak English ... is this still the right number for ...'

'Hello,' the woman said, with a heavy accent. 'How may I help you?'

'I'm looking for an old friend ...'

'Daniel doesn't live here now.'

'Oh. I'm so sorry to bother you.'

'He is back in New Zealand.' And the woman, who might have been his wife, gave her Daniel's number.

They agreed to meet in the park, and to rearrange on the day if there was rain, and now it was showery in bursts, and Dorothy wasn't sure whether or not this counted. She could manage a raincoat, carry an umbrella, but the shoes were a problem, she had never in her whole life solved the question of what shoes to wear in the rain. Anything nice would be ruined, and nowadays if her feet got wet she invariably came down with flu, ached all over, oh my knee etc, but the shiny and water-resistant trainers the kids had given her last Christmas to encourage her fitness, love it or lose it, Donald had mumbled, were criss-crossed with hideous pink and silver stripes and lay unworn in the bottom of the closet. Not that she wasn't grateful. Perhaps she had never been nice enough about receiving presents, feeling too often that the object was hard evidence of how little the giver really knew her. Getting older had made Dorothy more mindful of her flaws, and that there were many more than she would ever know. Self-improvement had its limits. She took knee-length rubber boots from her sack of redundant gardening kit, scrubbed the dried clumps of dirt off them with a steel brush and pulled them on.

Over the phone she'd told Daniel about the end of her marriage. After a long pause, during which she walked from the living room to the bedroom and back again, he asked, 'Why didn't you say anything?'

'You'd only just got married,' she said. 'I didn't want to be a downer.'

'A downer? For fuck's sake, Dottie. A downer?'

She couldn't help but laugh. 'Bad timing, it was bad timing. And then once I was on my own – I don't know. It seemed important, to be on my own.' The words came unanticipated, but she realised they were true. 'It took me a while. But I like it.'

On the way to the park she noticed moss growing between cracks in the pavement, and the plane-tree branches budding with pale leaves. The light was indecisive, shifting between bright and low, and it disoriented her, made her hurry in case of being late, so that when she reached the floral clock, tightly coiled in this early spring but still marking time between the green minutes, the Roman hours, it took Dorothy a moment to be able to read that she was early. Raindrops scattered the bench like melting glass beads, and she was glad of the waterproof coat. Young people, black-jacketed students, passed in pairs, and cyclists wheeled sedately by. It was silly to sit in the cold this long but she fell into a kind of meditation or prayer, the wind against her cheek, gloved hands clasped, there beneath the shaking branches of a Moreton Bay Fig.

Through this middle-distance gaze an elderly man and a teen-age boy walked slowly along the path. Daniel, old. Everything in her body went hot. Not the cold pulse rush of outside the grocery store – hot thuds. A squall came and the man and boy ducked under the band rotunda and Dot fanned her face with her hand, another old lady having an episode out in the rain. It was crucial to stay calm, looking at the wet sheet of a band flyer plastered against the rubbish bin and to think of spreading protective paper over tables, on the floor, of her day tomorrow asking people who knew they were dying whether they wanted to make something with clay or with fabric.

Daniel and the boy looked out through the subsiding drizzle, not seeing her.

'Daniel,' she called. Then louder, 'Daniel.'

Across the bending path she watched him make sense of her – of what he was seeing. 'Dottie?' And he took in the full impact of the years, the decades. She rose, shedding raindrops. He stepped down from the shelter, using his umbrella to stabilise the descent, and slowly, awkwardly came closer until he was standing right here. Behind the lenses of his specs his eyes were dark and bright. His breath rose and fell. When he stooped to kiss her cheek the sides of their glasses knocked together.

'I wear these orthotics but it's too many gymnastics,' he said, 'my feet are no good. You should see some of those old clowns, really crippled, popped shoulders, dodgy hips – it's not natural.'

'We're all old clowns now.' She had touched him. He was there. 'Daniel. It's good to see you. Who's the boy?' she asked, nodding towards the band rotunda where the teenager was sluicing water from the railing with a finger, headphones on.

'That's Oscar. He's my son.'

Oscar was fourteen, in school and living with Daniel. 'His mother's had some troubles,' Dan said. They were walking now, the boy, who'd responded to the introductions with a grunt, alongside.

'This is – María?'

'No. María's in Spain.' He waited till Oscar was ahead a few paces and explained that a year ago he'd got the call. It was the first he'd known that he had a child. The boy's mother – 'We were never really together' – was in a bad way. 'Christ, it was my parents all over again but worse, meth, and so. She was a lot younger than me. Stupid. I mean me.' He'd wanted to bring Oscar to Spain, wasn't ready to live in Auckland again, the rain and isolation, but legally it was too complicated. 'I pursued it for a long time, but just as we were getting close María said she really didn't want to go through with it.' They'd been trying for a baby for years. He tried to persuade her to see this as their blessing, a child they could care for, raise together. But she couldn't. 'It wasn't what she had planned. I couldn't give her what she wanted. Too old, everything.' Daniel looked as sad as she'd ever seen him. He wore the hair he had left cropped close, white flecked with grey. The bones of his face were prominent, exposed; spoke of the cost of living.

'How's Oscar?'

Daniel shook his head. 'I can't believe him. You know?' They stopped there on the path, the thick arms of the *Magnolia grandiflora* bearing succulent flowers, the lemony white startling. 'We've only got a few years before he leaves home, but – to have this. It's pure chance. How life can change if you're lucky to be around for it.' Daniel called to his son. 'Slow down, we're senior citizens here.' When the boy reached them he said, 'Tell her, Oscar, we do all right?'

'Yep.'

'Some people think I'm your grandfather.'

'That is pretty awkward.'

'We go to soccer, he plays, I shout, we have our little things we like. I'm teaching him to cook.' He nodded in Dorothy's direction. 'I learned to cook from her sister. She would have nailed that octopus.'

Oscar smiled. 'It was kind of chewy. Daniel likes Spanish food. Do you like octopus?'

'Depends how it's done. Sometimes.'

'You can try mine. When I've improved.'

Dorothy smiled at the boy. 'You look so like your dad,' she said, taking her time over it, loving the sentence. 'Like he used to look.'

Above them a bird made a sound and Daniel mimicked it, up–down, up–down.

'I had this bird once,' Oscar said. 'It was a blue bird, with a green tail, I think it was a parrot. I used to bring it insects.'

Daniel raised his eyebrows. 'Really,' he said. 'A parrot.'

'Are you going to stay in Auckland?' she asked him.

'Oh yes.' Daniel cocked his head, smiled at her. 'You?'

She laughed. 'Yes. My kids are all here.'

They had reached the edge of the park, where it met the road. 'Right,' he said. 'So –' He stepped back as a helmeted cyclist whizzed past, spraying water. 'Hey,' he called after the muscled figure. 'Do you mind?' The cyclist stood on his pedals and turned, a feat of balance, and threw them the finger. 'Fucking arsehole,' Daniel said. 'Sorry, Oscar.'

'Dad.'

Daniel took Dorothy's forearm, holding her back while Oscar walked on. His voice was light with surprise. 'Stop a second.' He whispered in her ear. 'He doesn't usually call me Dad.' They paused for a moment, and her eyes drifted shut at the feel of Daniel's mouth up against her face, the warmth of his breath. 'What were we talking about?' he murmured. 'Oh. Yeah.'

She couldn't move away. 'We were talking about . . .'

'You live here. And I live here.'

'Yes.'

'So,' he said, pulling away to look at her. 'So,' and he began to shake a bit with laughter, water leaking from the corners of his eyes. 'We've got all the time in the world.'

A big dark-windowed car bounced down the street with music booming out of it and Oscar and Daniel and Dot all looked at its headlights flashing in time with the bouncing.

'That's so cool,' said the boy.

19. THE FORRESTS

THEY TOOK DONALD by surprise, the cards and emails, the number of people his mother kept in touch with. The traffic of words had slowed lately, but there was still the occasional former student writing of a success, an ex-hospice colleague having a party, a young woman visiting with her child who wondered whether she could come and stay. Donald asked Matt what he thought. 'Sure, write back, she can stay with us. Be good practice, having a baby in the house.'

'The girl is like ten. I think her mother was from the house of fallen women.'

'Ours will be ten one day. Bring it on.'

'Don't.'

There was one more box to take to the home. Residents weren't meant to have much, or to need things any more, but, 'There's got to be room for a few photo albums and a ceramic-frog collection,' Donald said to the manager. He could always sic Ruth onto them; his aunt was world class at demanding bang for her buck.

If every mother was secretive, walked around outrageously *in her own mind*, never really known, he wondered whether it was a female condition or true of all parents, and what this would mean for his own child. Dorothy shuffled into the living room. 'Hello, darling,' she said.

'How are the legs?'

'Restless. So strange, like I want to do a jog. Go for a jog. I've never jogged.'

'Here's the rest of the stuff we're taking. This is the last of it.'

She didn't look into the box. 'We have to phone Grace for her birthday.'

'You already spoke to her. Amsi made her a cake and then the cat ate it. Remember?'

'Why have they got a cat?'

'Why not?'

'Pets are quite dirty.'

'The kids love it.'

'Cake eaters.' Dorothy leaned forward and picked something up off the ground that wasn't there. 'Oh damn,' she said. 'I'm doing it, aren't I?' She shook her head at Donald. 'Do we want to know, or not want to know,' she said to the room at large. 'On the whole, not. But we do know. We do know, and that's why you, Donald, are so incredibly beautiful. Your energy, your kind heart. That's why those lilies smell so fucking spectacular. The prayer flags moving in the wind like that, the invisible force of the wind. Those grapefruit in the green bowl. That's a very nice touch. Thank you for that.'

She stopped looking around the room and nodded. 'Eve didn't know,' she said. 'Eve didn't know. I'm the lucky one.' Dorothy smiled at him, her hand to her mouth as always, until something changed. The hand moved away and of course she – his mother – was still there.

20. THE HOME

HER SISTER HAD come. She'd brought the paper and she shook it open, spread it over the bed with her purple hands, their freckles like tea leaves, the fingers that seemed to have grown out of the gold and ruby rings jammed down by the knuckles, and read to Dot. A resident at a care home was found with her mouth duct taped shut. Strange – when she held the paper up and showed Dorothy the photograph those words weren't there. Then the paper wasn't there. Nothing but the ceiling, the partial view of wall, the corkboard with photos Dot couldn't focus on, soft rectangles floating in space. The headline unravelled bluely in front of the corkboard almost like a real sentence, wider than it was long. Dot felt the words in her mouth, the sense memory of making sound with the musculature of tongue and palate and teeth. Being able to say the word *musculature*. An investigation was being held into the care home and a care worker had been suspended. Dot's sister patted her leg. She jiggled some irises in a vase and sighed ridiculously, given that Dot was the one in the damn bed with the phantom tongue.

The young man on community service popped in. People often 'popped in'. They 'just put their head in the door'. They said 'only me' and 'cheerio' and 'won't stay long'. Michael had lain on the bed in the hospital, before they'd saved his foot, saying, 'How long do you think I've got?' Time being measurable now. Suitcases on the landing and boxes in the hallway. The corkboard was pinned with copies of ancestral portraits, black-and-white men and women in high collars and middle partings, the joke gallery. 'Prop me up so I can see it, darling,' that was right.

The sister read to Dorothy about a petition to stop topless women riding motorbikes and another on the cost of a new airport. Her gentle voice recited the latest findings, and what was in their food, and the seven secrets of happiness. She read about the King Cobras and the Dead Rabbits. Sorry, she said, there used to be a photo there, the one she cut out for her son, a newly discovered species of frog. A dog went missing for three months and returned to its owners to raise the alarm on the night of a house fire, and Dot's sister read about that too. She read about people living in caravans and spotlighting in the woods.

Dorothy did manage a word while she sat there: *Sister*. And she denied it! She told Dot she was not her older sister, not Eve! This was the same sister that perched with Dot on their window-sill, peering down to the street a storey below, waiting for Ruth's boyfriend to walk up the path, giggling, ready with the bowl of water to douse him as he raised his fist to knock on the door. The skin of the water sliding, tipping in the bowl with their laughter.

Her bony spine like Dot's knobbled into the window frame, their heads ducked beneath the sash window. Always that tingle when she stuck her head out one of those windows – that the cords that held the glass above her might suddenly break, the pane slip, whoops. They sat in the window, Eve and her, and when Dot saw them in her mind's eye, from where she was standing unbodily just in from the bedroom doorway, they were in silhouette against the spring morning and the light-struck space between their bodies was symmetrical, one of those optical illusions, a vase. Standing in the doorway Dot very nearly remembered the sensation of floor beneath her feet, but not quite.

Outside the window rising up from the street was a tree they could climb into, when they were brave enough and before their father had it pollarded for their own good. The fuzzy yellow pollen made Michael sick; the poor boy spent spring days in his bed at the back of the house, the window down and the curtains drawn, their mother bringing him jugs of water and fresh pillowcases.

He lay in traction in the hospital and Dorothy sat by and listened to the stories of his active years, decades importing Turkish rugs and worrying about storm damage to the cabin at the commune, that rectangular box made of Fibrolite, with a tap, one living space and two bedrooms. The bathroom was an add-on out the back door. Although there were laddered wooden steps up from the beach path and a plastic bucket in which to dunk dirty feet, the cork floor inside was always gritty with sand. The inside walls were unclad, and shells, white coils of no particular beauty, sat on the raw battens alongside paperbacks with flaky spines and crazed brown mugs from a local potter. They were grown-up. Still there was the nodding white beach grass, the straggled leaves of the sunflowers against the grey Fibrolite wall, the trumpeting sky.

They sat in the stuffy cabin with Ruth, Evelyn, Michael and Lee, and it was raining, the world outside dripping, and inside everything was sticky and they played cards till their fingertips were blue and nobody spoke for at least an hour before Evelyn looked out the door and saw that the rain had stopped, and called to everyone to come out and down to the water. The room emptied until it was just Dorothy and Daniel, and the Formica table the colour of tomato flesh, flecked with yellow, like seeds, and the peeling wooden kitchen chairs and the rag rug on the floor and the large pages of newspaper streaked with mud and scrunched by the door where people had wiped their feet on the way in, and the stubs of candles puddled on saucers, their wizened black wicks cold to look at, and finally Dot stopped her looking all over the room and swung her gaze back round to him. He was counting cards. He patted the pack together and shuffled it deftly and split it and bridged the two halves and let all the cards flick together and arch, all the time looking at the cards, but with a small smile on his face that he couldn't quite get rid of. Dorothy said that she didn't want to play any more cards. She walked past him to the sink and poured a spluttery cup of water from the big creaky tap and drank it very quickly because her mouth was dry, her lips as dry as on a winter's morning. He was wearing his striped T-shirt and a pair of jeans and he'd kicked off his sandshoes by the door and his feet were so bare. He asked her to pour him a drink. When she put the cup on the table in front of him it shook. He reached to pick up the cup and his hand brushed against her wrist. He shifted over on the cracked vinyl bench seat and made space for her. Dorothy sat; her legs were shaking too. Daniel started to spread out cards as if they were going to play a game and he was still looking intently at the little collections of blue-and-white patterns, secret pictures decipherable in their geometry, when he said, 'How long do you think we've got?' He pulled at the neck of his T-shirt as though there was something inside it.

The sister was talking with the young criminal while he pulled at the closed-over plastic liner in Dot's wastepaper basket and shook the rubbish into his green sack. Tattoos peeked from the sleeves of his blue uniform jacket, which was slightly too short in the arms. They gave Dorothy a haircut and held up a hand mirror to show her what she looked like. Where was the duct tape of mercy then, she wondered, because there was nothing to stop the words coming out while she said, 'That's not me, that bouncy hair is not mine, those wavering eyebrows, those eyelids, the sunken cheeks, the neck you don't understand that cannot be my neck, my brittle shoulders, my pink cardigan.' They wheeled her back into her room while she was still talking. 'Why is there a teddy bear on my bed? Why does a doll sit with splayed legs in the armchair? Whose are these toys? Did I steal them? Do children visit me who want to play with them? Do they smell? There's something on my head. Did someone Sellotape a bow on my hair? Did that happen while I was looking at that collapsed face in the mirror? Do I smell? Have I soiled myself? When you lift me like that it hurts. Do I have a sore on my spine? Thank you for the medicine. Thank you for the clean sheets. Thank you for drawing the curtains back so light comes through the gauzy lining.'

The sister talked to Dot about when they were children and picking snails out of the letterbox and racing them along the painted concrete fence. She laid a hand on the blanket above Dot's scaly shins, purple yellow with bruises and veins and stuck with white medical tape where she barked them on the tea tray and the blood didn't clot well, and she patted and squeezed Dorothy's feet. Her sweater was the colour called jade and her hair bobbed above it soft and blonde. She removed one of Dot's feet from beneath the blankets and from the ticklish pressure and clicking sounds she must have been cutting the toenails. She was slow with the clippers and Dot squeezed her fingers together in sympathy but nothing moved.

'What are you doing community service for? If I may ask?'

The boy in the blue jacket stopped wiping the windowsill and looked towards Dot but he didn't answer. In the hospital with her baby the orderlies wore blue jackets. Amy lay flat on her back on a bed with sides, her face swollen from one of the things they were putting into her, the morphine or the ventilator. Lines into her legs, her neck. Her eyes swollen shut while the machine breathed for her. Windows at one end of the room, the other end, past more beds, each the centre of its own pod of drips and monitors and LED displays and sensors attached to little finger pads with band-aids, reading heart rates, oxygen percentages, sending the information in a flashing line, a series of rising and falling numbers, to a screen. Thank you. In the family room a woman prayed in the direction of Mecca. It was Ramadan and she was going the day without food. Dorothy pumped milk into a bottle and stored it in the fridge for the nurse to attach to the drip that would feed it into Amy's stomach. Thank you. A woman leaned her elbows on the table in front of her and held her face with fingers on her eyebrows and thumbs on her cheeks and sighed in and out before she cried silently, her stomach shuddering. Crying here was bad news. Two girls had been struck by lightning. Dorothy's friend visited and looked at the baby and walked straight back out into the corridor. A minute later she returned, her eyes bloodshot, and she sat beside Dot until it was time to express milk again. Thank you. In the family room some new people played cards, the blue rectangles glowing like lapis lazuli on the green table. A doctor changed one of the artery lines and the baby's leg went whitish grey, and a vascular surgeon with a moustache explained that Amy's body was too small for the bypass operation that was required, that the ratio was beyond the capability of the human hand. There was a meeting in the consultant's office and papers appeared and Dot and Andrew were asked to sign them and they did, and a portable X-ray machine was wheeled in and an image was captured and everyone waited for someone to say something, and they didn't know who it was that they were waiting for. It was a game where nobody wanted to be the one to say. Thumbs to the forehead, bags not. And then while everyone was standing around the bed, looking, the leg changed colour again, becoming rosy, so slowly that it might just have been something wished for. The sweating surgeon disappeared. The promises they signed to were not invoked. Amy was miraculously small and growing, she was inside Dot only days ago, and she cured herself. Thank you. Days later they returned home and the envelopes in the letterbox were lacy where snails had eaten them.

It was dark and her sister wasn't there. In the light that crept from under the door the outline of the corkboard appeared to float just in front of the wall. The pillowslip felt fresh and soft beneath Dot's head and the mohair blanket the sister brought her was warm and light. The spiky irises had gone; daphne smelled thickly, spriggily sweet. There was a vague pressure on her hand and when Dot try to raise her arm it increased, and panic pierced her – 'Don't strap me down,' but when she turned her head she saw in the half-light the liquid glow of a drip standing over her like a benevolent sentinel.

'Those morphine dreams are fruity, man,' the boy in the blue coat said, his tattoos falling to the floor like vines.

'You're proving your point,' Dot said. 'I'm so sick of gargling,' she said. 'Morphine doesn't mean the end. This is not over. I know what your game is.'

'You know it,' he said. 'You know.'

Her sister and the boy in the blue jacket played cards on a tea tray, both either side of Dorothy's bed. Dot had shrunk because they were playing over her legs but her legs weren't there, they were too short now to reach the end of the bed. The window was open slightly onto the rock garden and the little white flowers growing there sent a citronella perfume into the room. Koi carp were splashing in the pond. Those carp gleamed fatly and orangely like juice spilt into water on the day she was brought here. She poured orange juice into her daughter's water when she would not drink it, and together they watched the parabola of thick liquid plunge into the clear glass. Grace lay next to Dot in her floral pyjamas and jiggled her cheeks with her little hand, and her brother came in to snuggle under the blankets too and

The young criminal sat on the end of the bed. He had changed out of his blue coat; he wore a grey sweatshirt with an image on the front that Dorothy couldn't make out. 'Are you in a gang?' she asked him. 'The Dead Rabbits? Did you get done for tagging? Did a businessman push you up against the sprayed concrete wall of your old school, his arm across your windpipe? Did a cop car pull over? Did your friend run off?'

He dipped the foam cube on a stick in water and ran it around the inside of her mouth. The first time she did that for Eve her hand shook with nerves. She closed her eyelids in silent acknowledgement. There was a terminal narrative. It was a story until it stopped being a story and until then they kept wanting to know. Give up, the doctor told Donald, kindly. Surrender your need for the detail; there is only one way this is going to end.

Her sister talked about being a child and eating honeysuckle, picking off the flowers and sucking at the backs of their petals to inhale the flavour, which was like honey

The sound was like a box being pushed around on the floor in a downstairs room. It was like a dog clearing its throat. It was like a car with engine failure being pushed over gravel. The white barred sides of the bed were up and someone explained to someone that if Miss Forrest tried to get out of bed in the night she would hit the ground. The space between the bars was dusky, shadowed. She lay in the cot with baby Grace, just to be another body breathing with her, helping her fall asleep. This was the blanket, hairy beneath her fingers, and the smooth sheet under her cheek. Her sister was reading poetry out loud. Dorothy thought about telling her that thing she had been meaning to say but the effort of making sounds was

Her sister's voice, and she said, 'I've got to go, Mum. I'll be back tomorrow.'

'Time for some fresh air,' the criminal said, and he wheeled her out into the remembrance garden, past the living room where an old man saw squirrels on the curtain rails and heard his own bedroom slippers walk around at night without him. His wife visited him every day, while he, poor man, was rubber-banded into an armchair and spent his hours leaning forward to stand and being pulled back into the cushions by the band's resistant force. Up, down.

One of her favourite things to see was a freighter on the horizon. Or cargo barges lying like waiting crickets in a still harbour.

Women in blue jackets unloaded boxes of food from a van into the hospice kitchen. She wondered for maybe the hundredth time in her life why cartoon chickens advertised their own edibility by doing the thumbs-up with their wings. Her son came, a tall man in a suit, and brought her a baby. The baby was in her arms – someone else was holding him as well, there were cautious adult hands attached to that body, not just her twiggy wrists – the baby's face was clear, wide, his gaze roving the air, his body light as though hovering in space, just touching her lap. Donald lifted the baby and she kissed the top of his downy head. Caramel.

The growth on the rocks in the fishpond was like those canned Halloween cobwebs she sprayed on the windows for the children each October.

Rain fell straight into the pluming water fountain. The drops of fountain water slowed as they reached their peak and turned and fell, and turned and fell. Across the pond stellata flowers shone yellow-white against the pearly sky, the branches black in the rain. A marmalade cat pawed the dirt under the tree, turned and settled, and rested, its face content.

The young criminal smiled at her and walked over the miniature horseshoe bridge, towards the cat. The cat was enormous, the world a willow pattern on a flat plane. Slowly the cat blinked, rose and walked away, glancing back once, shaking itself before disappearing indoors. The young man smiled at Dorothy.

She leaned forwards in the chair and paddled her feet on the ground, inching out from under the awning so that the rain fell first on her bathmat-like slippers, now on her knees, on her hands, her lap, her hair. Rain hit the permanent wave they'd given her and some of the drops found their way through the jolly grey curls and down to the skin of her scalp. It was a balm.

Daniel stood in the smoked-glass doorway off the living room, where dances were sometimes held. His tallness was stooped with age, and he said to Dorothy, 'Something something.' She turned her head and Daniel shifted his weight, he had a stick, and like a tall three-legged creature he stepped closer, shuffle tap, shuffle tap, step ball change

His hand was large and worn, and his eyes were topped by peppery brows, the hairs ticking upwards as though surprised, and past the marks and wrinkles, deep behind all that those eyes were there and they were so warm and dark, and they really did flicker, and he sat back slowly in the rain with her

The tide was a long way out and they stepped down over the rocks carpeted with tiny blue-black mussel shells onto the mudflats, the sky high and ashen above. For a while they were walking close to the cliffs, beneath trees that captured light and held it clustered between their leaves, then braver they ventured out towards the moored boats that sat nakedly on the gunmetal-grey mud, near each other but not so close that they could swing and collide in a storm when the water was deep. The mud smelled rich and salty, and green algae lay streaked across it like handwriting. Some of the surface was ruffled and this was where the mud was softest and it sucked at their sneakers so that they took big quick steps like slap-stick astronauts, and Daniel talked about things that he pretended to find amusing but secretly loved. He laughed away his view of the world as a way of holding onto it. She would remember to tell him that, later.

They rounded a large yellow sailboat, its belly traced with mould, and a creek opened up in the mudflats, light reflected on its silvery water. The sandy banks of the creek were cut by the water into perfect angles. On the other side, shoots of some kind of estuary plant stood straight up towards the sky. Their feet were under the mud, they were sinking and doubled over with laughter, reaching down into the cold gritty mud to pull their feet out, to push at the heels of their mud-soaked sneakers, get the things off, now, feet and ankles caught, the mud spotted with wormholes and bubbles, and they both tipped over on their knees just as the rain started. The wind blew in a great thickening rush. A dandelion clock tumbled past mid-air, thin black-tipped wisps floating from the pored seed-head that rose, released, like the microphone thrown by the singer from the band they heard that time, and she remembered the fierce, elated way he flung it high into the air to turn and fall, an invita-tion, towards the upturned faces of the crowd.

ACKNOWLEDGEMENTS

THANKS TO MY friends and family, and to those who read early drafts, including Lisa Samuels, Travis Gasper and Damien Wilkins, Chris Morgan Jones and Suzy Lucas, and Gillian Stern, Georgia Garrett and Alexandra Pringle, for their generous advice. Thanks to Brita McVeigh and Fergus Barrowman for the serendipitous reading suggestions that also shaped this book.

Versions of two chapters have appeared as extracts in the *NZ Listener* and *Metro* magazine. A version of Daniel and Dorothy's conversation in 'Spells' appeared as part of a story 'Jack, Internationally' broadcast on BBC Radio 4.